WRITTEN IN STARLIGHT

WRITTEN IN STARLIGHT

A NOVEL

SLOANE BROOKS

ATRIA PAPERBACK

New York Amsterdam/Antwerp London
Toronto Sydney/Melbourne New Delhi

ATRIA
PAPERBACK

An Imprint of Simon & Schuster, LLC
1230 Avenue of the Americas
New York, NY 10020

This Atria Paperback edition October 2026

ATRIA PAPERBACK and colophon are registered trademarks of Simon & Schuster, LLC

Interior design by Davina Mock-Maniscalco

Manufactured in the United States of America

1 3 5 7 9 10 8 6 4 2

ISBN 978-1-6680-8131-0 (pbk)
ISBN 978-1-6680-8132-7 (ebook)

For Shawn,
because my story
didn't feel like home until you were in it.
You put the stars back into my eyes.

PART I

OUTSIDE OF TIME AND SPACE, there existed an infinite library. There was no door in or out, only rooms upon rooms of books. Librarians worked within, though no one remembered where they came from, only that for as long as there had been a library, there had been librarians.

Although the librarians were cursed to watch over others' stories, never to belong in books of their own, they were quite content. In return for their services, the library cared for them, shifting like a living labyrinth to create grassy courtyards so the librarians might build their homes under serene skies. And so, for an eternity, maybe two, the library existed, generations upon generations of librarians peacefully overseeing the books it held.

Until the graduation of a certain spunky apprentice book-keeper.

Librarian youths grew up following one simple rule: Never read the books. Reading was too dangerous an activity for ad-olescents. They might get *ideas*. Yet this particular apprentice prided herself on being a horrendous scholar, proficient flirt, and, most importantly, a devout breaker-of-rules.

So it was, on the day of her graduation, when she would

officially be recognized as a librarian in her own right, and would therefore at last be permitted to read the books, she had to pretend as though she hadn't been doing that very thing for over twenty years.

Unaware of her free spirit, the library elders assigned her to the most dreaded genre in the library with nothing more than a stern warning: *Beware the books, lest they make you feel something.* If only they'd known that she'd been willfully letting words manipulate her spirit for years—crying, laughing, and falling in love over the "borrowed" tales she read in secret under the midnight blanket-tent in her bedroom—they never would have placed a romantic like her in charge of the tragedy department. Such a thing could only lead to certain ruin.

For a while, she coped with the terrible tales she was forced to read by writing stories of her own when she returned home in the evenings. Whimsical fairy tales that started with a *Once Upon a Time* and always ended with a *Happily Ever After.*

And then one day, she started dreaming up alternate versions of the books she watched over, imagining different fates for the poor souls within.

Eventually, *inevitably*, she wondered what would happen if she swapped the ending of a library book with one of her own.

CHAPTER 1

Once upon a time . . .

Della Farley often reflected that her life resembled the unfortunate half of a fairy tale. As a penniless maid who secretly dreamed of adventure and love, she had much in common with the heroines from the stories her mother used to read to her as a child. Unfortunately, however, Della's tale never progressed to the bits containing princes, castles, and magic. It was as though someone had torn out the latter half of her story, for a happily ever after was nowhere in sight.

"Surely you don't mean to dash off to the city the moment I give you your wages, my dear," a saccharine voice called.

At her employer's deceptively light tone, Della paused in the foyer where she'd been tugging on her hat and wrapping a shawl around her shoulders.

The lady of the house was a widow named Mrs. Loughty, an aspiring aristocrat who strove to convince the high-class women she admired that she was one of them. She went about proving her supposed wealth by frivolously spending what coins she had. To signify her station in life, she employed servants to tend to her household. Well, *servant*, due to budget restrictions. Of course, Mrs. Loughty bragged to her friends that she simply had no need to employ a cook, lady's maid, and butler, for Della could accomplish the work of a full staff. Which sounded like a compliment but really wasn't.

"I'm going to the market," Della said now, hiding the envelope she carried under her arm. It wasn't a total lie. She would pass *by* the market.

Mrs. Loughty hummed. "Well. Be sure you're home in time for tea." *Be sure you're home in time to* serve *tea* was what she really meant. "And take care so you don't catch ill in the cold."

The warning sounded kind enough—most of what Mrs. Loughty said *sounded* kind. She had a knack for saying two things at once, and the thing she meant under all her pretty words was like a burnt pie crust hidden beneath sugary filling, unnoticeable until a person bit into it.

"I'll be careful," Della promised.

As she hurried out the front door into the street, she considered shedding her shawl and catching a grave illness out of spite. *That* would show Mrs. Loughty.

Della thought back to when she was sixteen, when her mother's heart had weakened until she could no longer work. To afford her mother's medicine, Della had responded to Mrs. Loughty's ad in the paper and moved to Poling to be her maid. Shortly after, Della had caught a deadly fever. When she finally woke, weeks had passed, and entire chunks of her childhood had faded. Doctors said her memories might never fully return, but Mrs. Loughty's only concern was when her new maid might return to work, because the house was in a terrible state of disrepair.

Eight years later, Della's memories were still fuzzy. She hadn't been able to afford the passage home to Reftshire to visit in all that time. When she corresponded with her mother via the post, Della could hardly remember her voice.

Della clutched her letter tighter. Mud squelched around her shoes with each hurried step, and grit clung to her hem, chafing her skin as her wet woolen skirt whipped around her ankles.

The city of Poling resembled the bottom of a puddle. It stank of stale algae and horse manure. Stone buildings pointed like peaks of silt into a watery gray sky. People bustled about like larvae, intent on feeding and breeding and dying, never once looking up from their little pool to realize that somewhere, oceans existed. Della desperately wanted to see an ocean.

Della drew a breath of damp, cold air and pretended it was warm and tinged with the scent of salt and sand baking in the sun, as described in books. Mrs. Loughty always said dreaming only led to disappointment, but dreaming was rarely to blame for heartache. It was only when dreaming ended that disappointment came. Any sorrow experienced was all reality's fault.

As she walked, Della tilted her chin to the sky. In her imagination, the city morphed from one exotic landscape into another. Buildings burst toward the heavens, their roofs elongating into snow-capped mountaintops, then doming over into windswept sand dunes. The sky brightened and brightened into a blinding blue, blue, blue.

Sometimes, Della wondered if the rest of the world truly existed, if you could actually travel to places with deserts and mountains and grottoes, or if they were as made up as fairies and dragons, written into books to provide an escape from a gray world that stretched on to eternity.

A passerby bumped into her, disrupting her daydream.

Ah, well, perhaps it was better that she remained focused. *Post office, mail wages to mother, home in time for tea. No distractions, Della. Ignore those puddles that seem desperate for someone to jump in them.*

Behaving as a proper adult meant you had to appear totally disenchanted with the world around you. You could not put puddles to their proper use. Smiling too easily made you a fool, and believing in magic made you a child.

Yet Della searched for magic the way others might search for a four-leaf clover—with the certainty that if she only looked long enough and hard enough, she would find it. For surely all stories must come from truths, and there couldn't be so many tales of extraordinary impossibilities if such things did not exist.

Before she could continue on her way, a small parcel lying in the street caught Della's attention. It was rectangular, wrapped in brown paper, and tied with a jute cord. Whoever bumped into her must have dropped it. She scanned the streets, her eyes first landing on the retreating back of a farmer, then on the page boy scampering past his elbow.

She tried to call for the boy, figuring he'd probably dropped the package, but he disappeared from view. She sighed. Part of her wanted to continue on her way, but perhaps if she delivered it herself, she could spare the boy an ear boxing. Mrs. Loughty would be furious if Della served tea late, though, so she would have to hurry.

Post office, mail wages, deliver the package, home in time for tea.

As Della crouched to retrieve the parcel from where it sat, precariously close to a large puddle, a rumbling reached her ears. She looked up, alarmed to find a carriage whooshing toward her. The coachman snapped his whip over a pair of horses lathered with sweat, their nostrils flared and billowing steam.

Snatching up the package and clutching it to her chest, Della scrambled back just as the carriage bounced into the pothole, spraying a cascade of gray water in its wake. The frigid water struck her sharply, and her letter slipped from her fingers. She grabbed for it, but the brisk wind snatched it away, carrying it end over end down the street.

Before she could chase after it, a grubby little girl darted into the road, plucked up her letter, and stuck out her tongue before scampering into an alley.

There was little hope of catching the thief in the network of alleyways where she probably had countless hidey-holes. Despair tightened around Della's lungs. Without money, her mother wouldn't be able to purchase the medicine she needed for her weakening heart. Perhaps Della could beg Mrs. Loughty for her next paycheck in advance. But it was likely that even if Mrs. Loughty pretended to agree, she'd conveniently forget to give Della her wages for the next four weeks anyway.

Icy water trickled down the back of Della's simple blue dress and into her shoes. Tucking the parcel that had caused all the trouble under her arm, she tried to wring her skirts out, but it was fruitless. Mud stained her white stockings up to her calves. Grime speckled her apron and splattered her face. While she may have been entertaining a daydream about puddle jumping, it was disconcerting and rather unpleasant to have a puddle thrust upon oneself unexpectedly.

Someone coughed behind her, and she froze.

"I do apologize, madam," a smooth male voice said. "My driver wasn't watching where he was going."

Heat rose in Della's cheeks as she turned to face the speaker. As soon as she caught sight of him, she fumbled her way into a curtsy, her feet making a ghastly sucking noise in the mud as her weight shifted. "Your Grace."

For he was Laurence Moreland, the Duke of Eshford, utterly handsome and unmistakable. She'd heard he was staying in Poling to visit family but never expected to lay eyes on him. He was so out of place here with his sharp, tailored suit, trimmed mustache, and top hat.

"Is there any way I can make up for the misfortune I cast upon you?" A practiced smile played about his lips as he awaited her response.

Della tried to straighten, but the muck suctioned around her foot, and she flailed to maintain her balance. The parcel slipped from her grip and plopped directly into the sludge between her feet.

Della did not consider herself to be a particularly daft or clumsy person, but speaking to people—especially powerful people—made her out of sorts. Powerful men in particular were just little rich schoolboys who never had to grow up. They always had that cruel playground look about them, like as soon as she turned her back, they would laugh at her. Even now, taunts echoed in her memories, from a time long ago when her mother could afford to send her to school. *You don't belong here. You will never be one of us.*

"Madam?" the Duke questioned as her silence lengthened.

Della opened her mouth, but no words came. She dreaded speaking. The things she wanted to say tended to come out crooked and jumbled, and she second-guessed them the moment they slipped out. She could never cram those wobbly words into the same neat patterns everyone else seemed to understand. Her patterns were always lopsided like poor embroidery, stitching pictures she hadn't intended and causing more harm than good. She preferred silence. She could not be considered foolish for words left unspoken.

"It is quite all right, Your Grace," she finally managed, because social grace dictated that it was better to lie to your fellow interlocutor than inform them things weren't all right at all. Dipping into another horrid, wet curtsy, she snatched up the package. "Good day to you."

"Right then. Good day." He tipped his hat. "And apologies again."

It did not escape Della that if she were in a story, her encounter with the Duke could have been the very point when her life turned for the better. If she were as brazen as the heroines she'd read about as a child, she would have snapped at him for splashing her, and he would have been charmed, so unused to anyone speaking back at him, given his title and wealth. Or, maybe she would have been sweet, lovely, and forgiving, and he would have fallen for her kindness and swept her away. But, if the Duke of Eshford had brought with him the lost pages of her fairy tale, Della was not clever enough to catch hold of them as they fluttered past.

Unable to be either witty or irate, she simply watched him go, feeling small and foolish as the tattered shreds of her future slipped between her fingers. An utterly unremarkable person like herself should only hope for an ordinary life. Perhaps one day she'd catch the eye of some kind shopkeeper, and he'd want her to have his children.

How dreadful.

She didn't want a simple life. She wanted a grand adventure, a grand romance, a grand life. Yet, with nary a godmother in sight, it seemed she was condemned to this life of servitude and filth.

Trembling with cold, Della slipped into the nearest alleyway and sank against the wall. *Stupid, stupid, stupid.* Why was she always making an oaf of herself?

And her poor mother. At the very least, Della should have requested monetary compensation when the Duke asked if there was anything he could do to apologize. Then she'd have something to send home. What if her mother couldn't survive another month?

All Della had left of her were fragmented memories. Her mother holding her pudgy hand as it grasped a pencil, teaching her to write one painstaking letter after the next, or making funny voices as they read bedtime stories at night.

Imagining a world without her mother in it was heartbreakingly easy because she'd nearly become as far-off a notion as deserts and mountains and grottos—a blurry idea Della wasn't certain existed. The rain on Della's tongue turned salty, but she couldn't even muster up a daydream this time and pretend the taste came from a spray of sea foam.

Wiping her stinging eyes, she looked at the ruined package in her lap. It bore no address that she could discern. The only way to save what was inside was to open it, so she unwrapped the wet paper. Disintegrating brown parchment fell away to reveal a small leather-bound book. On the spine, the title read

Ansel Tulzok, Vol. 5. Gently, Della opened its pages, which were only slightly stuck together. Though dirty moisture stained the paper, the ink was still quite legible.

She might be able to sell it, though most people in Poling were uninterested in literature. As she ran her hand over the book, she resisted the urge to press it to her face and smell the comforting scent of ink and parchment.

Long ago, when Della was a child and still lived in Reftshire, her mother worked as a housekeeper and sometimes sneaked home books from her employers' libraries—fantastic stories of distant lands and impossible adventures, tales of knights, mysteries, and romance.

"*To you, my love, I'd give the world,*" her mother would say with a dramatic bow each time she gave Della another book—another *world*—to escape into.

Della ran her hand over the books pages, remembering how she'd lose herself in those tales, growing so enamored with the stories that when she closed her eyes, she felt as though she were there herself, in a place where she was no longer shy and awkward, and no one could hurt her. Perhaps she did not lose herself in those tales after all. Perhaps she found herself in them.

Before Della tried to sell the book, maybe she could read a few pages. Her eyes were starving to see the world, but words could assuage her hunger. With the pressure of her life constricting around her, she yearned to escape. Only for a few minutes. Just long enough so that when she had to face reality again, she could bear it.

Read one chapter, sell the book, go to the post office, send money to Mother, home in time for tea.

The checklist had grown much too long now for the time she had left, but Della turned to the first page anyway, and she read.

CHAPTER 2

Ansel Tulzok scowled at the aquaplanet looming outside his spaceship's towering windows. The blue orb was only broken up by a few wisps of clouds and some fuzzy green splotches of algal blooms. No land in sight.

Ansel wasn't fond of water, but after four years rotting in prison and another four on the run after he escaped, all that stood between him and clearing his name was a little blue alien named Neegu. And Neegu was hiding down in all that water. So he'd brave it.

Not that absolving Ansel's name of one crime would make it totally clean. *Clean* was a relative term that meant the same thing it did when Ansel used it to describe his ship: the black bits scrubbed away, but still a little scummy around the edges.

Ansel sighed. They'd requested permission to enter the ocean planet's stratosphere at least twenty minutes ago and had been promptly put on hold by Atmosphere Control. The delay was infuriatingly unnecessary; judging by the vacant airspace around them, no one else was eager to visit the uninviting planet either.

Staticky hold music played through the ship's communication system on maddening repeat, setting Ansel's teeth on edge. He despised the trumpeting of icoths. Really, just because they were born with a hollow head crest, it didn't mean they were born to sing. That would be like saying that just because

Ansel was born with a heart, he was born to love. He'd long ago realized his talents were better applied elsewhere. His (far more valuable) skills included shirking responsibilities, brawling, and generally being a charming good-for-nothing bastard.

He leaned back in his chair and threw his feet onto the control panel. Closing one eye, he tilted the toe of his boot just so, blocking out his view of the planet in his windshield, as if he could grind this latest problem under his heel.

"You've kicked a rather important button there, Captain." His first mate's voice was dry and slightly distorted through her mask's speakers.

"Wonderful news, Xaks," Ansel said cheerily. "With any luck, we'll be ejected into space and put out of our miseries."

Xaks snorted. Bubbles danced in the water behind the crystal helmet that molded to the contours of her angular face. The pump that circulated the briny water through her space suit and allowed her to exist outside of her native planet's biome whirred gently. The sound was at odds with her less-than-serene expression. Her slitted nostrils were flared, round ears pinned back, tightening the rubbery skin over her bald grayish-purple head.

"Don't look at me that way," he said. "Why can't our prey ever have the decency to flee in terror for their lives to a warm, tropical planet? When's the last time I've gone on holiday? Don't I deserve some sunshine? Did you know, I was reading an intergalactic travel brochure the other day—"

"You read*?*" Xaks asked with mild awe. The gills on her neck flexed as she blinked her milky blue eyes.

Ansel ignored her mockery. "There was an ad in there for Creqreon's grand opening. Why couldn't Neegu be hiding out on *Creqreon*?" He said the name with dramatic effect, spreading his hands before him as though framing a picture between his fingers. "Home of the largest casino in the galaxy. A whole moon, dedicated to debauchery." Ansel gazed wistfully into the stars. "Imagine."

"Are you crying, Captain?" Xaks asked.

"Yes, Xaks. I'm overcome."

"You are a pathetic man." Xaks had gotten better over the years at understanding the intricacies of human banter, but at times "accidentally" slipped back into the blunt insults she'd used when she first entered Ansel's employment, when she was still learning the delicate balance between a loving insult and a hurtful one.

"Mind my tender heart." Ansel pretended to be offended, swinging his feet to the floor. "The point is, I would rather be shoved naked up the asshole of a Sichetian swamp beast than dive under the surface of this algae-infested slimeball."

"Everyone's allowed their sexual fantasies, Captain," Xaks said.

They lapsed into silence.

Silence, Ansel realized, was bad. Because that meant the hold music was no longer playing—and, now that he thought about it, it hadn't been playing for quite some time. Not since he'd kicked the control panel.

He scrambled forward, grimacing at the blinking green light on the dash. *Blast.* The button he hit must've unmuted his mic and sent his less-than-glowing opinion of the very planet they were trying to enter right down to the locals.

Sure enough, a clipped voice came through the speaker a second later. "Your request to land has been denied. Deepest apologies."

"Is it just me, or did he not sound apologetic?" Ansel asked.

"Your insight is astounding," said Xaks, who didn't sound astounded.

"I'll simply have to insist they reconsider." Ansel pressed a button that activated the ship's intercom so that the rest of his crew, Eryl and Yaggrel, would hear him. "Hang tight, everyone."

Gripping the joystick, Ansel shoved it forward, pitching the ship downward. G-forces sent his stomach lurching into his chest. Beside him, Xaks cursed, clutching the edge of the control panel.

Ansel's teeth rattled as his ship nosedived toward the aforementioned algae-infested slimeball. Warning alarms blared and lights flashed, casting the ship's bridge in varying shades of red, yellow, and orange.

The planet's surface rushed up to meet them as the ship devoured the sky. In a valiant display of optimism, Ansel decided to trust that the ship would hold together through the watery impact.

The bow of the ship plunged into the water's surface. A mighty wave of sludge smacked the bridge's semicircular windshield, and then the ocean swallowed them whole. Beneath the waves, their ride smoothed somewhat, dampened by the water. Aside from some creaking and groaning, the ship had miraculously survived.

"Does 'your request to land was denied' mean something different to your species?" Xaks snapped.

"No, 'denied' translates identically for both humans and judrax," a computerized female voice provided helpfully. Ansel's android mechanic Eryl stepped onto the bridge, her gangly form casting a long shadow across the control board. "Missile incoming," she added pleasantly. Synced with the ship's systems, Eryl provided an invaluable, if occasionally annoying, personification of the vessel, able to communicate its every complaint and update.

"Nobody panic," Ansel said while his brain said, *fuck, fuck, fuck.*

"Actually, many missiles are incoming." Eryl's abnormally long fingers came to rest on Ansel's shoulder.

He shook her off, grappling with the controls as the ship plunged deep into the water. A missile clipped them with a loud crack, sending the ship careening sideways, barreling through a school of pale fish the size of Ansel's leg.

"Shields up," Ansel ordered.

"We don't have shields," Eryl said amiably. "Don't you remember? I told you the conductor was faulty, but you said we'd just outrun any missiles fired our way."

Xaks regarded Ansel as though he was the least intelligent life-form she'd ever encountered.

"I didn't say that."

Eryl tilted her head. "My hard drive is in perfect condition, my memory uncorrupted." She played back a recording, complete with a date and time stamp, of Ansel's own voice saying: *"Shields? We don't need shields. We'll just outrun the missiles."*

"Are you suffering from memory loss, Captain?" Eryl asked after the recording switched off. "It could be a sign of early onset dementia, concussion, stress, a tumor, anxiety, depression, decapitation . . ."

As they plummeted toward the ocean floor, Ansel decided to revisit the idea of selling Eryl for parts. "Why are you here, anyway? Shouldn't you be down with Yaggrel on the gun deck?"

Eryl's yellow eyes flared a little brighter. Beneath her transparent humanoid hull, her golden circuitry flickered. "I came up to remind you we don't have shields."

Ansel smiled easily, concealing his unease. "Remind me, Eryl, how is the price of scrap these days?"

Oblivious, Eryl rattled off a number while Xaks shot him a disapproving look.

The truth was, Ansel couldn't afford to fix the shields. Funds at the moment were a bit . . . tight. They'd spent everything they had on a new Megacannon, as firepower felt like a more pressing need than armor. Maybe that was unwise.

"Okay, fine, I admit I wasn't worried about the shields because I wrongly assumed this planet had primitive defenses," Ansel said.

"As do you, currently," Xaks said. "Since you didn't fix the—"

"The shields, I know." That panic clenching his gut grew a bit more . . . panicky. Everyone always looked to him to be their good ol' unshakable Captain. Meanwhile, he perpetually felt like he had an earthquake inside him, threatening to rattle his composure apart.

Helplessness was not a feeling he tolerated well, and he was feeling it now, floundering in this mucky ocean teeming with rockets where he'd rashly dragged his crew, too blinded by the thought of sweet justice. Cold sweat broke out across his skin.

He shivered, and that was when the idea hit him.

The panic receded—a great beast flinching from a waved twig. It would be back, but for now, Ansel had triumphed.

Ansel began flipping switches and pulling levers. Light after light went out, the descending electrical sounds of systems powering off joining the racket of missile fire and shuddering metal. "Tell Yaggrel to hold his fire," he said. Xaks started to protest, but Ansel snapped, "Don't question it. Just do it."

She complied, using her commlink to send the order.

Ansel stood and stretched over Xaks's controls, pressing a few final buttons. The ship's headlights were the last to go, sending them into complete, inky darkness.

"What are you doing?" Xaks demanded.

"Cloaking," said Ansel.

"We don't have a cloaking device," Eryl said. "You can't afford one. Your current credit balance is—"

"Tragic. I'm well aware." Ansel settled back into his seat. "But if we can cool the hull, we might be able to slip past their infrared sensors. That means no engines, no lights, no laser cannons."

"No hotheads?" Xaks asked, eyeing him and then the airlock with a look he didn't love.

"This hothead's saving your ass." Ansel flipped a switch on the control column, and the ship's engines went silent, leaving them sinking, in utter darkness, into the seemingly bottomless ocean pit.

Everyone hushed, awaiting more missile fire to shake the ship, but none came. A few distant rumbles indicated shots had been launched but missed.

Ansel let out a long breath. "There now. I told you I had everything under control. We're pointed vaguely toward the coordinates of Neegu's last known location. All we have to do is find the little bastard and rocket out of here before anyone finds *us.*"

"*Vaguely toward his coordinates,*" Xaks repeated. "That sounds promising."

"According to my calculations," Eryl said, "it will take us around five hours to sink to the ocean floor. At temperatures below freezing down there, and without running our engines, once we reach the bottom, our fuel will gel up from the cold in roughly twenty-four hours."

"So only stop for one drink; got it," Ansel said.

Ansel made a quick, feeble excuse to get off the bridge before he lost his composure and his crew realized how panicked he'd been.

He sat, hunched, on the edge of his bed, clutching his head in his hands. Twenty-four hours. He'd have twenty-four hours to collect Neegu and get the hell out of there or else condemn himself and his crew to a cold, watery grave.

Perhaps they could seek shelter in an underwater city, but every bounty hunter within ten light years would be plopping their ships into this slime pit once they learned Ansel was stranded there.

He'd promised his crew fame and fortune as soon as they cleared his name and collected the bounty of the real perp responsible for the thievery of the Shield Stone. Instead, if they got caught before they could prove Ansel's innocence, they'd all be imprisoned for aiding and abetting.

The real perp responsible. Ansel mocked his own thoughts. It shouldn't be so difficult to think his name.

Balor. Ansel's once-accomplice turned enemy. Once-*friend* turned enemy.

Ansel squeezed his eyes shut past the mental image of himself and Balor when they were boys, fending for themselves in the slums of Lumeria. They'd been partners in crime, petty thieves who stole because they were hungry, not out of ill intent.

In his late teens, Ansel vowed to turn things around. He left his life of crime, earning an apprenticeship at a tech shop. But then Balor came up with his grand plan—a get-rich-quick scheme that would enable them to escape the planet and their modest existence for good: steal and sell Lumeria's priceless Shield Stone—the superconductor that suspended a force field over the entire city, shielding its inhabitants under its dome. Superconductors that powerful were rare, worth millions.

Though the planet hadn't necessarily been kind to him, Lumeria was peaceful, its inhabitants considered the healers of the galaxy. Leaving them open to attack from those who might want to use their herbs and medicines for less than noble purposes was an irredeemable crime.

Despite Ansel's protests, Balor went through with the theft. Furious over his friend's refusal to aid him, Balor planted the hacking device he'd used to unlock the superconductor's vault in Ansel's backpack before abandoning him for the Cooperation to find, framing him for the crime. The betrayal still smarted, which was annoying. Ansel should be too angry to hurt.

After Balor stole the Stone, he arranged to have it sold. Then he promptly turned on the buyer, slaughtering him and his whole crew so he could steal the buyer's fortune and keep the Shield Stone for his own protection. Not many knew the truth, but Ansel figured out that Balor had kept the Shield Stone when he nearly caught him several years ago. Balor had concentrated the Stone's power to create an impenetrable shield around his ship, allowing him to slip away without a scratch.

Well, nearly impenetrable. Thanks to their newly purchased Megacannon, the SPM-500, Ansel finally had the firepower to penetrate it. All he needed was to locate Balor.

That was where Neegu came in. Neegu was one of Balor's minions, some black-market dealer wannabe that Balor forced to do all his scut work. Usually, Balor's lackeys were hard to pin down. But thanks to a drunken photo with a blurry bar sign in the background that had been posted on Neegu's mating profile last night, Neegu was theirs. Hopefully, with some persuasion, he'd reveal Balor's next stop.

A simple ambush later, and Ansel would be returning Balor and the Shield Stone to Lumeria for justice. Then all of this could finally be over.

Ansel stood. Arched windows took up the far wall of his cabin, displaying a stunning view of the stars . . . when he wasn't comets-only-knew-how-deep underwater. The rusty, dilapidating panels of the room revealed ropes of wires twining across the ceiling and walls like the veins of some large beast.

Without starlight, Ansel had to rely on his dilated eyes to make out shapes illuminated by the faintly pulsing electronics, glowing weaker and weaker as they finished powering down. He crossed the room to his desk. Once, the decor of the room was supposed to give the illusion of warmth, but the rich wood was scratched now, the plush velvet threadbare. Shivering, he settled into the oversized chair. Ansel was always cold, and the dropping temperatures weren't helping. He even sweated cold. Cold space, cold ocean, cold heart.

"You're less of a scoundrel than you'd like people to believe." The sweet, teasing voice rang so clearly in his head, he startled a bit.

Ansel rubbed his chest as though he could iron his heart back into its proper place where it didn't feel wrinkled up and uncomfortable. His memories were too loud, never letting him forget the girl whose goodness was so bright, she outshone the darkness shadowing his heart until he believed he could love. But darkness was never truly gone. When you snapped a light on, shadows darted under your bed, behind your dresser, into the cracks of floorboards, but they were always there, ready to pour back out and consume you.

Ansel's gaze caught on a canvas rucksack sitting on his desk, half buried under a stack of papers. His breath froze in his lungs.

That shouldn't be here.

The last time he'd seen it was the day he escaped prison. He'd grabbed his pack of personal effects on his way out and tossed it in the cargo hold of the ship he'd stolen. As far as he knew, the bag had remained there ever since. It was better that way.

Ansel forced himself to breathe. There was a reasonable explanation for this. The cleaning bot had probably found the pack and dropped it off. (The fact that it had taken the bot four years to find it was a testament to how terrible the bot was at its job.)

Ansel lifted the rucksack, intending to take it back down

to the cargo hold, but it was heavier than he remembered. When he dipped his hand inside, a cool amber pendant was the first thing his touch encountered. He shoved the necklace aside before he could think of *her* again.

Then he found the heavy object at the bottom of the sack and pulled it out. It was a book. He knew what a physical book looked like only because he'd once visited a planet so far out of reach of the nearest communications wormhole, they had to store data in thick tomes. This book was much smaller than those had been, no bigger than his hand. He didn't remember stealing any *books* in his youth, so how'd this end up with the rest of his possessions from Lumeria?

Ansel flipped the book open, expecting to find some dry information on crop rotation or medical bacterium or some other boring nonsense he didn't care about.

Before he knew it, he blinked and realized he'd read five whole pages. It wasn't data. It was just . . . a story. A story about a woman doing *things* and thinking *stuff.*

Ansel had never considered reading for pleasure, even though Eryl frequently hinted that reading more would fuel his cognitive reserve. During the rare opportunities Ansel had free time and extra credits, he usually just went to a simulation theater.

The book called itself a fairy tale. Ansel wasn't sure what a fairy tale was, but it sounded a lot like a bedtime story. He knew what those were, even if he'd never been told one—fantastical fables parents told children where justice was always served, and kind people found good fortune in the end.

Ansel bit back a bitter laugh. In real life, things didn't just *work out.* Fate didn't play fair.

He skimmed over the next few lines but couldn't stop thinking about one: *A happily ever after was nowhere in sight.*

The smile faded from his lips. It was one thing for an

escaped convict to think the universe was a miserable place. It was a tragedy for a young woman who found joy in jumping in puddles to think it. He wished he could tell her to keep on dreaming and leave the nightmares for people like him.

Needing assurance the world-wearied dreamer would find her happily ever after—and needing a distraction for a few hours—Ansel read on, smiling over the line: *Della searched for magic the way others might search for a four-leaf clover.*

CHAPTER 3

Della gasped, falling back against the damp cobblestone alley wall, her mud-caked skirts fanning out around her. How could a fictional man have found a story about *her*? About something that had happened to her only minutes ago?

Her heart pounded. Maybe she'd discovered something magical, something really magical. It had to be, didn't it?

But it was impossible. None of it could be real. Eryl was something called an *android*, which was seemingly a woman made from steel, and Xaks apparently breathed water and had the features of an ocean-dwelling creature, yet spoke like a human. And what even was a spaceship?

She turned the word over in her mind. Spaceship. She supposed it was fairly self-explanatory, even though it made no sense. A man in a book with a vessel that could sail across the heavens to visit planets? She sometimes gazed upon the planets high in the sky, but even she couldn't imagine them inhabited by all manner of breathing, speaking creatures. The book was a fantastical story. Pure fiction.

Perhaps the book was spelled to fool the reader into *thinking* the characters within were real. It would be like something found in the stories her mother used to read to her, those tales full of whimsy and wonder. Maybe the book was cursed, designed to consume its owner's body and soul. If so, it was already working, for all she wanted to do was ignore everything else in her life and keep reading.

Della debated shutting the book . . . then shrugged. Being cursed might not be so bad. She'd always been more at home in books than reality anyway, so she read the next few lines.

Ansel read about the girl flubbing her way through what could have been a romantic meeting with a duke. Ansel had heard of dukes. They were part of an ancient political institution used by some planets before the Cooperation formed.

Della's breaths grew shallow as a new possibility came to her. Maybe Ansel was real, and she wasn't. Hadn't she often thought she felt like she was in a story? A fairy tale?

But she felt real, so she must exist in some capacity. Yet if she was real, then was the man in the book also real? And if so, did that mean every book in existence represented a real person in a real world? Della's head throbbed to think about it.

She read more.

When the Duke went on his way, leaving Della in the muck, Ansel felt a pang of empathy for her. She remained silent to hide her thoughts, and Ansel's mouth ran rampant to hide his, but in the end, they both wound up saying nothing.

Della shook her head in wonder. He'd read about things that had happened to her mere moments ago. Did that mean she was reading about things that were happening to him nearly *as they happened*? Somewhere, right now, was there a star captain with a smile full of bravado and a heart aching with emptiness, reading a book about her as he sank toward a foreign planet's ocean floor?

What a terribly dull way to spend one's final moments.

Della skimmed down the page. There was a brief summary of him reading about her slipping into the alleyway with the ruined package, and then—

Nothing. Della turned the page, revealing empty paper. She flipped through the rest. All the pages, save for the first handful, were blank. Peculiar. No, *peculiar* was too tame a word. Preposterous. Extraordinary. Utterly mad.

A fat raindrop plopped onto an exposed page, and Della quickly shut the book, tucking it under her arm to protect it. She got to her feet, turning one way and then another, torn with indecision. *What to do?* She'd meant to sell the book, but she couldn't do that now, could she? Yet her mother was relying on Della's wages. Della couldn't fail her.

Despite the fact that they'd had nothing, her mother used to make every day feel magical. Her optimism enhanced the small wonders of the ordinary until whimsy outshone misery.

"Perhaps our home is a bit cold tonight, but have you considered that's the wind's way of telling us it's high time we had a sleepover next to the fire?"

"Rainstorms are when the world turns itself into a ballroom made for dancing."

"It's not that we cannot afford a new coat; it's only that, just as this coat is your favorite coat, you're the coat's favorite person. So we'd best patch it along another year."

She was the most alive person Della had ever known, and the knowledge of her fading spirit broke Della's heart.

But her mother was too curious herself to forgive Della if she tossed away a chance at adventure before she had a good story to tell from it.

Still, Della wouldn't keep the book for much longer. Only until she understood what was happening. Then she could sell it and send her mother the money.

Decided, Della shoved the book into the pocket tied around her waist beneath her skirt.

Home, serve tea, complete chores, and then . . . discover the secrets within the magical book.

After stashing the book under the mattress in her tiny quarters in the corner of the kitchen, Della set about preparing tea. She practically floated through her tasks, no longer feeling the fatigue in her shoulders and the ache in her knees that came from long hours of labor. As she kneaded and baked and cooked, all she could think of was the book beneath her bed and, more interestingly, the man in the book.

If the man were real, he'd seen her speak with the Duke . . . and read her thoughts. That last part made her most uncomfortable. Usually, there was safety in silence, but silence was ineffective if your thoughts were on display. The things he'd mock her for if he could!

But there had also been a softness to him. The girl he'd thought of, the panic he felt, the hurt of his friend's betrayal.

"You're late," Mrs. Loughty said when Della brought in tea, quickly adding an overly sweet, "I hope you didn't run into trouble at the market."

Della mumbled an apology but really was thinking of how unfortunate it was that now Mrs. Loughty would make an appearance in her book, and Ansel would have to read about her—a fate Della wouldn't wish on anyone. So she tuned out Mrs. Loughty's voice as she gossiped with her daughters, hoping to spare Ansel the boredom of having to slog through it all.

While the family enjoyed tea, Della retreated to the kitchen and retrieved the book. With a racing pulse, she skimmed over everything she'd read earlier, confirming it was all as she remembered and not an instance of her mind conjuring a daydream so vivid that it felt real. It wouldn't have been the first time that had happened.

All the words were the same, impossible though they seemed. Letting out a sigh, Della lifted the last page, then released her fingers, letting the paper flutter over to reveal the empty pages beyond.

Only, this time, those empty pages weren't empty. Where earlier today the paper had been blank, lines and lines of new text had appeared.

Goose bumps rose in prickly sheets over Della's skin. Her eyes greedily devoured the new words.

Ansel believed things that appeared to be magic were just science that had yet to be explained. Which was why, after he read about Della unwrapping the book and finding his own name in its pages, he did not immediately assume a mystical force had connected them across the cosmos to fulfill some divine, predestined purpose.

He just figured someone was trying to kill him.

It was a conclusion he jumped to with disturbing regularity. Even more disturbing, it was a conclusion that frequently proved itself to be correct.

Ansel snapped the book closed, fully intending to toss it out the nearest airlock. Clearly, the book wasn't a book, but some kind of messaging device. Someone—probably a bounty hunter plotting his demise—had planted the device on his ship to spy on him.

But how had even his *thoughts* wound up in that book? As far as Ansel knew, reading minds was impossible, but maybe there was some new tech out there. Someone could have injected something into his brain when they stopped at that space station for fuel last week.

Ansel shivered, which he told himself had everything to do with the dropping temperatures inside the ship and nothing to do with the fact that he was scared shitless.

At once, Ansel's book became too heavy for Della's trembling fingers, and it tumbled into her lap.

She had no idea what a *messaging device* was, or what he meant by *tech*, but it didn't matter. The additional pages must mean her earlier hypothesis was correct. The book was transcribing their actions as they happened. Somewhere, within the last few hours, Ansel had been sitting at his desk, reading a book about her.

Obviously, their *every* thought and action wasn't being transcribed. Any book worth its salt would know doing such a thing would create far too long and uninteresting of a story. The book must choose only the parts it deemed pertinent.

Della wondered what type of story hers was. A love story? A mystery? Her thoughts darkened. Or maybe a more sinister tale, the kind filled with monsters that kept a person up at night. At once, her simple life felt anything but boring. She felt she must be on the cusp of exciting things, for no good story stayed ordinary for long.

She kept reading.

Deciding to let Eryl check the book for spyware, Ansel made his way to the bridge. Maybe Eryl could trace the origin of the messages appearing in the book to identify the sender.

Was the devious bounty hunter Della herself? She probably thought herself clever. She certainly had a flair for the dramatic, writing herself into a story as a hopeless dreamer to tug at his frayed heartstrings right before she took advantage of his momentary weakness. It was likely all one big distraction so he wouldn't see an ambush coming. Admittedly, the scheme felt overly elaborate. But it wouldn't be the first time a hunter had tried to seduce him into handcuffs, and not in the fun way.

Della's face flushed hot. This man truly thought she was a dangerous seductress? A *bounty hunter*? She wished she could speak to him so he would know she meant no harm.

If he happened to open her book before tossing it away, would he see that wish of hers? More than that, could he *respond*? If he spoke to her, would his words be sent through the pages?

At that notion, a zing of excitement tingled all the way to her fingertips. Ansel could absolutely not throw her book away before they tried to talk to one another. Her eyes flew across the pages. She needed to know he hadn't tossed out their chance at—at what? What could they ever do for each other when they were separated by ink and pages?

Ansel marched onto the bridge and slapped the book down in front of Eryl, who was scrambling all seven feet of herself out of *his* chair and fruitlessly trying her best to look like she hadn't been in it at all.

"I need you to look at this book and tell me what kind of technology it is."

Xaks got up, came over, and began flipping through the pages. "You've graduated from brochures to full-length novels? Look at our boy, all grown up."

Ansel could practically feel her eyes sliding over Della's thoughts, and for some reason, he didn't like that. He snatched the book away. "Don't read it. Just examine it."

"Examine the book without reading it?" Xaks repeated. "What's in there? Where did you get it?"

"Perhaps it's his diary," Eryl said matter-of-factly.

Xaks's orb-like eyes widened with delight.

"It's not my diary." Ansel sounded petulant, even to his own ears. "It's an extremely high-tech distracting device."

"A distracting device," Xaks repeated.

"Yes. A device designed to distract people." At Xaks's unimpressed look, he threw up his hands. "Fine. Maybe not that. But I wouldn't be surprised if it's some kind of bomb. So if you don't mind, look it over. And while you're at it, scan me for tracking devices, especially my brain. I think someone's reading my mind."

"I'll send them a condolence hologram immediately," Xaks said.

Meanwhile, Eryl did as he asked, her eyes flaring brightly as she scanned him. "Nothing is in your brain, Captain," she reassured him.

Xaks's amusement was palpable.

Ansel shot her a glare before she could provide more unhelpful commentary. "And the book?"

Eryl took the book and turned it over in her giant hands. Her eyes lit up again, casting a yellow line of light across the book as she scanned it. "I don't recognize the language it's written in."

Ansel's trepidation spiked. He, like most of the galaxy, had a translator implanted in his brain at a young age that allowed him to understand any spoken or written language. It had apparently done its job decoding the book—likely through process of elimination, context clues, and comparing the script to similar known dialects and common phonetic patterns—but the fact that the book wasn't written in a language recognized by any of Eryl's databases unsettled him further.

"It's made entirely of organic materials," Eryl went on, "and it's not emitting any electromagnetic currents."

"So it's technology we haven't seen before," Ansel breathed.

Xaks gasped and swiped the book from Eryl. "You're right, Captain! This is revolutionary."

Ansel nodded. "I knew it. The creature who made it must be very advanced. If we can figure out what sorts of materials it's made of, perhaps we can pinpoint its planet of origin."

"Trees," Xaks said flatly, slapping the book against his chest and walking away. "It's made of *trees*, Captain. Shockingly enough, not everything in the universe is obsessed with killing you. Fret not. You can safely enjoy your smutty novel without worrying if it will murder you."

Ansel hugged the book to his chest, feeling utterly stupid. "It's not a smutty novel!" He could practically feel his comeback bringing down the average IQ of the entire galaxy.

Ansel peeked into the pages. He didn't *think* it was a smutty novel, but that would be an intriguing surprise.

When he looked up, Eryl still stood there motionless, watching him with unfaltering yet somehow judgmental glowing eyes.

"What are you looking at?" he snarled, snapping the book closed.

"A moron," Xaks called across the bridge, answering for her.

And that was it, the last of the words. They stopped only a few lines from the top of a page.

Considering her book was written in a different language than Ansel spoke, Della was uncertain why his book was written in a tongue she could read perfectly fine, even though she didn't have a—what was it? *Translation device?* Perhaps it was the magic—the book translating his words for her, knowing she didn't have one of those devices.

Of course, it wasn't as if Della *entirely* understood his story. There were too many unfamiliar concepts: circuitry, electronics, databases—but she was fascinated all the same.

Leaning forward until her nose nearly brushed the paper, Della watched the empty space below the last sentence, waiting to see if she could catch the words appearing as Ansel did or thought something new the book found noteworthy.

Apparently, the Captain was not having any significant thoughts—poor lamb—because no new words appeared before Della's eyes.

Looking up from the book, Della gazed out the window as though she could see through the fog to the heavens beyond. She wondered if Ansel was out there somewhere, or if they were in different realities altogether—a scientific concept she'd once read about even though it hurt her brain a little.

If Ansel existed here, somewhere in her reality, maybe he could be persuaded to find her. She would beg if she had to, beg him to fly his ship across the stars and take her and her mother away from this wretched place.

Della glanced at the clock on the wall. If time were passing the same for Ansel, in only a few hours, he'd be nearing the ocean floor. If she wanted to try to talk to him, now was her chance.

She could simply *think* of what she wanted to say to him and hope the book showed him her thoughts, but that was sure to be a jumbled mess. Speaking would lead to only moderately better results. Her fumbling words would be incoherent.

Instead, she decided to write a letter, hoping the book would deem her words important enough to record them for Ansel to see. She was always better at assembling her thoughts in an orderly manner when she was holding a pen.

With sounds of the family rustling safely in the parlor, Della sneaked down the hall into the library—a space frequented more often by the family's despondent accountant than by any member of the household. She found a scrap of parchment, a quill, and ink easily enough and settled herself behind the big wooden desk.

Giddy apprehension buzzed in her head so loudly, she feared she wouldn't hear the creak of the floor indicating the approach of someone who might catch her. She shuddered to think of the trouble she'd be in if she were found like this, touching what didn't belong to her. She'd be let go without references, and her mother—

She couldn't think of that. She had to make haste and write something to give Ansel a chance of seeing it before his ship landed. The ticking from the clock in the hall served as a reminder that the minutes were slipping away.

"*Words have power, Della,*" her mother's fading voice rang in her head. A memory surfaced: Della crying in her mother's lap after her schoolmate had been particularly cruel in his speculations about her unknown father's character. Her mother understood the hurt of being scorned and outcast. Yet she had the ability to turn misfortunes into adventures. "*Words can conjure either good or evil,*" she'd said. "*What that little boy said was horrid, and just look at the curse he cast on your spirits. But if I said, 'Why don't we skip dinner, get ice cream, and set off fire-crackers under his window?' Ah, there it is. Presto. A smile."*

Della was tired of being wordless. Powerless. She would pour out her heart and hope it would be enough to . . . to what? To redirect her tale toward greater things?

Whatever happened, at least she would know that she'd tried. She wouldn't make the same mistake she had with the Duke. She would seize hold of opportunity before it passed her by.

Her heart pounded so hard her skin throbbed as she pressed her quill to the paper.

Dear Mr. Tulzok,

Rest assured that I do not wish to murder you.

I know you don't believe in magic. Earlier today, I didn't believe ships could sail across the stars. You say magic is unexplained science. I suppose life is less disappointing that way. But I say it is better to wish for magical things and be disappointed than never experience the joy of dreaming at all.

I've read many stories with words that felt like they were being spoken directly into my heart. I never considered that my story could speak too, that I had the power to touch someone's soul. I never felt significant enough, until today.

I think we are destined to meet. You may wonder why fate would throw together a dashing star captain and a quiet maid. I think the adventure lies in trying to figure that out.

While it's disconcerting and a little embarrassing for someone to have access to my thoughts, I think, in time, I could learn to cherish such an extraordinary connection.

You have companions of course, but do any of them know the hopes and worries that cross your mind when you lie in bed late at night? It's a funny thing, how we are different people in the eyes of everyone who knows us. Mrs. Loughty, the stable boy who was my lover, the hawker selling his wares at the market who caught my eye for a fraction of a second—each holds a different version of me in their mind. Everyone you meet creates a perception of you based on the fragment of your person that they witness. Even your closest friends don't know every piece of your soul. No person is one person, but a thousand false persons. The only real you exists, trapped inside, for no one to know but yourself.

Because how could anyone know the real you? The you that exists in blurry memories, secret thoughts, and shelved dreams? Who could possibly know of the nostalgic indescribable smell that reminds you of your childhood home, the longing you feel when you hear a love song, the fog of sadness hovering inside you late at night when you feel low for no reason at all, missing someone or something you've never known? There are parts of us we cannot even express in words or actions. They rest closest to our hearts, so crucial to our identities, yet they can never be shared.

I could know you, Ansel Tulzok, and you could know me. Cast my book into the ocean, if you want, but I can't let go of yours, not yet. What do you say?

Will you dream with me, or would you rather wake up?

—Della Farley.

CHAPTER 4

After she penned her letter, Della hurried back to the kitchen, where she could watch the book without fear of being caught.

Heart racing, she opened the pages—and nearly dropped the book. New words had already started to appear.

Ansel returned to his cabin, grumpily stacked a few pillows against his headboard, and settled onto his bed. "It's made of trees," he muttered, mimicking Xaks as he cracked the book open.

Using a small flashlight on its dimmest setting, he found where he'd left off. As he read about Della discovering new paragraphs in his book that had appeared throughout the day, a feeling of chilling vulnerability washed over him. She could probably see as many of his thoughts as he could see of hers. He pulled the bedsheets over his legs like a child hiding from the unknown lurking in his closet. The last person he'd shared his thoughts with had broken his heart when he needed her most.

As he scanned ahead, his gaze caught on his own name.

Dear Mr. Tulzok . . .

. . . You may wonder why fate would throw together a dashing star captain and a quiet maid. I think the adventure lies in trying to figure that out . . .

Will you dream with me?

After Della's letter, the rest of the page was blank. He'd noticed that the book didn't transcribe insignificant events. If it did, all the pages would probably fill with menial everyday actions and fragmented nonsensical thoughts in a matter of hours. No, it evidently recorded only the important parts of their lives. And it deemed Della's letter very important. She must now be awaiting his response.

Ansel read the letter again. His instinct was to respond with a joke, maybe comment on the fact that she called him dashing or tease her about the stable boy. But such a heartfelt letter did not deserve his heartless reply.

Strangely, he believed her when she said she didn't wish to murder him, even though that was exactly the type of thing a murderer might say. She'd found the book on the ground and seemed as surprised as he was to find a living person inside.

I could know you, Ansel Tulzok.

He didn't want to be known. He'd rather fade into peaceful oblivion. He wanted his name erased from every wanted poster, criminal record, and database in existence. Meanwhile, Della was a dreamer who desperately wanted everything *he* wanted to leave behind—adventure, romance, and for her name to leave an impression on the universe. He couldn't give her that.

He was an outlaw on a spaceship, not some hero who'd sweep her away from her unhappy life. She should find her duke and try again. Maybe he'd be able to appreciate a pretty letter better than Ansel could.

"Wait." The word darkened the empty page below Della's letter.

Della had hardly known she'd spoken the word until she saw it appear in the book in her hands as Ansel read it. She went a little dizzy as more text rose through the page like spilled ink seeping through the paper. The words formed, faint and blotchy at first, then complete.

"Can you . . . Can you hear me?" Ansel asked softly into the room, feeling foolish but hoping, despite his better judgment, that the words would appear in the book for Della to read.

Leaning in, Della read Ansel's question as it wrote itself onto the book in her lap. Black lines swirled into letters, then words, punctuation popping around sentences with a flourish. His thoughts appeared soon after, surrounding his dialogue, just as a character's inner thoughts might appear in any other book.

Della could hardly believe the incredible magic happening before her. For the first time in her life, she felt significant. Chosen. Worthy of adventure.

Before she could figure out what to say, more words flowed onto the page as he spoke again.

"You stole the book, remember?" Ansel said. "I hardly think you can claim you were chosen when you accidentally stumbled upon it."

Della gasped. His book hadn't explicitly shown him reading her mind, but he had to be able to see her thoughts the way she could see his, for he responded to her as though she'd spoken them.

Her fingers trembled. A strange man was reading her thoughts, the ones she never let out. And he was making fun of her. Of course he was. She knew he would, even if some part of her hoped he wouldn't be mean and spoil everything.

More words scrawled themselves into the book.

Mean. Ansel had been called countless worse things, but that simple descriptor made him feel like the biggest bully in the galaxy. *Shit,* Ansel thought. He was only trying to tease her, but it hadn't translated well as written word. Blast, could she see him thinking all this? Damn it, he should stop cursing. *Fuck, stop thinking, Ansel.*

Della believed he would be able to accomplish his goal quite easily.

"You're not as sweet as you'd like people to believe, are you?" Ansel asked in surprise.

Della's cheeks flamed as she read his question. As was typical, she was already making a muck of things. She would have to start keeping her more cutting thoughts suppressed.

"Don't on my account." Ansel chuckled. "Some of us like sharp things thrown our way on occasion. Keeps life exciting."

Hardly able to breathe, Della stared at the new words. His book did not show exactly which of her thoughts and actions were transcribed for him to read, only his reactions to them, which she supposed made sense. Otherwise, they'd be stuck in an endless loop of reading about each other reading about each other. Goodness. Her mind reeled to think of it.

"Stars, my head hurts." Ansel glanced out the window where the water grew darker by the second as they continued to sink. "Let's try this again. Hey, I'm Ansel."

Della knew she ought to say something clever quickly before he thought her a complete dolt. Words lodged in her throat as her mind raced, trying to determine the correct combination of consonants and vowels that would make her appear normal and proper and like someone who most certainly understood social conventions. On the best of days, Della barely understood decorum. Factor in mind-reading, and she was at a complete loss for what type of greeting the situation required.

"A simple 'hello' will do," Ansel said with bemusement. "We can save solving intergalactic peace for our second conversation."

Della's face burned hotter. Biting her thumbnail, she stood and began pacing the floor but remained close to the window so she could still see the pages.

"It's okay," said Ansel. "I know you're shy."

Shy. She despised the word. The term was far too trite, as though the debilitating helplessness caused by the betrayal of her mind and mouth were an endearing trait.

"Sorry." The apology surprised Ansel himself. He didn't often feel compelled to speak apologies out into a universe that had been nothing but unjust, but he understood the hurt of betrayal inside and out and could only imagine how awful it must feel for it to come from within one's own self.

Della drew up short. For the first time in her life, someone understood her, just a little, and she wanted to weep from both embarrassment and aching relief.

Ansel took a quick peek at the timepiece in his pocket. In a few hours, they'd be touching down on the ocean floor. "Listen, you need to get rid of the book. Whoever it belongs to might be looking for it, and if they created it to get to me, they won't hesitate to hurt you too."

Words. She needed to find *words.* The book didn't belong to someone else. It belonged to *her.* For the first time, adventure had crept into her life, and she couldn't ruin it.

"You're not," Ansel said. "Your adventure will come along, but this isn't it. Our paths weren't meant to cross." He didn't really buy the whole magical book thing and still figured it was some kind of weird tech, but he decided he'd try speaking her language. "Our lives are literally in separate books. You'll only get hurt if you continue to try to be part of my story."

Desperation at last freed the words trapped in Della's throat. She spoke softly, so no one would hear her from another room as she seemingly talked to herself. "But we've been given something miraculous."

"You found the book in the street," Ansel reminded her. "And now it's connecting us somehow, but who's to say if someone else found it, it wouldn't have started showing me their thoughts instead of yours?"

"My name is on the spine of the book you found," Della pointed out. "And yours is on the one I now hold. We were meant to find each other. Don't push me away the way you do everyone else."

"I don't push people away." Ansel scoffed.

"You forget I've seen everything you try to hide." Goodness, now that she'd started talking, she couldn't stop. "Do you even realize your crew loves you, foolish man? You don't know how lucky you are to have such close companions."

Ansel was nothing short of befuddled as he read her words. One moment she was melting into a puddle of embarrassment, the next she was ruthlessly picking apart his psyche? She was more cunning than she gave herself credit for. "Eryl is programmed to tolerate me," he grumbled. "Xaks gets paid for her loyalty. Yaggrel, our weapons specialist, loves anyone who gives him dangerous explosives."

"You know what I think?" Della asked, plopping back onto her bed.

"I am acutely aware," said Ansel.

"I think you've spent so long running that you don't know when to stop."

"Do you plan on scolding me all afternoon?" Ansel wanted to know.

"Well, I only have a limited amount of time until your ship freezes and you possibly die, so I suppose not," Della said regretfully.

"I have fond memories of that time five minutes ago when you were quiet."

Della blinked. Quite without realizing it, she'd stopped being nervous. How strange.

"Let's say you *were* in my book," she said. "What if you had been the one to step out of that carriage this morning instead of the Duke? Would things be different? I don't think so. You're so determined to be alone that I think you'd still deny that our paths were meant to cross."

"Well," Ansel said under his breath, "I wouldn't have left

you standing there, shivering and covered in mud; that's for damn sure."

A funny little thrill went through Della. There was something exciting about the notion of an arrogant space captain having the decency not to abandon her on the side of a road when a duke didn't. Eager to experience that pleasant rush again, she asked, "Oh?"

Ansel groaned. That *oh* was bait, and he was enticed. He liked that a ruined wretch like himself could still make a good, kind heart do something as innocent as flutter. It made him feel redeemable. *She* made him feel redeemable.

Oh hell, if she could read him thinking all that, he was in trouble. He should close the book now. Better to be a gentleman and dash her hopes to oblivion than be a bastard who led her on.

Della believed that being led on by Ansel Tulzok could be a wildly enchanting way to spend an afternoon, an illusion far lovelier than any daydream she'd concocted on her own.

"In case you haven't figured it out, I can see your thoughts plain as day. I know you intend to bid me farewell, but you should know that—" She faltered, then finished quietly, "If you wish to lead me on a bit longer, I won't object."

Ansel wavered.

"What would you do?" she dared to breathe. "If you met me on the side of the road as the Duke did, what would you do?"

"I'd at least give you my jacket." As soon as he said it, Ansel cringed, deciding Xaks was right. He was a moron. He'd told Della he was dangerous, yet here he was lending her his imaginary jacket like a total fool.

Della smiled. The jacket was a mere intangible thought, but no one had spared her a thought for so long, she'd cherish it like a priceless gift. She imagined pulling it on, feeling the warmth of him still clinging to the fabric as she buried her hands in its sleeves. How might it smell?

"Like pure, raw sex appeal," Ansel said dryly.

She blushed, realizing he'd seen her thinking about his warmth and his smell.

Because Ansel was—as he'd already established—a bastard, he instantly wanted to make her blush again. There was something achingly sweet about a girl blushing over him. He'd thought himself incapable of being sweet with anyone. He hadn't been in a long time, not since—

"After I chivalrously, selflessly, *heroically*, lent you my jacket," Ansel interrupted his own thoughts, "I would invite you into my . . . what did you call it? Carriage? Is that like a hoverkart?"

Della couldn't believe this strange man was indulging her daydream. More than that, she liked the idea that she could explain something to him for once, when so many things in his story baffled her. "It's a sort of box on wheels drawn by horses that you ride in."

Ansel tried and failed to visualize that. To be fair, he hadn't tried exceedingly hard. He didn't like to try exceedingly hard at most things.

Wheels he had heard of but had never seen used, for they were wildly impractical when you could simply hover over rough terrain without having to smooth it into roads. As far as what a horse was, he had no idea. Some kind of beast of burden, if he had to guess.

"Fine, then," he said, "after I expertly reined in the beasts, dismounted the carriage, *graciously* lent you my jacket et cetera, I would invite you to come with me."

"Why would I accept your invitation? You're a stranger. An odious man like you could be up to all sorts of nefarious activities."

"Odious, huh?"

She bit her lip. She was too serious; her jests tended to come out sounding too sincere to be funny. "I was only teasing," she said.

He knew. And what a captivating surprise that was. Ansel cradled his hands behind his head and crossed his ankles. "*Odious.* Bold accusation from a book thief."

"I didn't steal it. I found it. I intended to deliver it, but there was no address."

"Sure. You don't seem very remorseful. For a girl with a rebellious imagination, I bet always doing the right thing gets boring. You act like you want safety, but you want danger, Della Farley. I think you'd want my activities to be nefarious because I think you'd want to be nefarious right along with me."

Della's heart skipped a beat. It was true. At night, she replayed interactions she'd had during the day, imagining what would happen if she spoke the biting retorts she'd yearned to voice when she merely bit her tongue. Sometimes, she wished she could be truly diabolical.

She might not have the option to be wicked in real life, but she could be wicked with Ansel in this imaginary one. There was no reason to be afraid or timid. Even though he'd infiltrated the sanctuary of her mind, she was still safe. There was nothing he could do to her, trapped as he was behind a book.

Even if he weren't, Della almost thought—considered—maybe even *wished* she could trust him. She had no reason to do so, having seen very little of what was in his heart. She wanted to trust him because if you couldn't trust a boy in a magical book that had been placed in your path on the most random, dreariest of Tuesday afternoons, then you might as well not bother trusting anyone at all.

"What would we do once I got in your carriage?" Della asked breathlessly.

Ansel's lips twitched as he read her question. There were far more foolish ways to cope with life than indulging in a few

daydreams. He would know. "I'd sweep you away, of course, and then we'd—well, the details concerning what we'd do next are too salacious to recount."

"Now who's being shy, Captain?" Della asked innocently because *innocent* was the role she played best. Everyone thought being quiet meant being naïve, but the idea that the wisest people were those who talked the most was a chilling notion indeed.

"Well, I don't want to embarrass you." Ansel shifted, pulling at his collar. "Your stable boy hasn't prepared you for the types of pleasures I'm capable of delivering."

"Educate me." Della's pulse whooshed in her ears. She could hardly believe her boldness. "Unless you don't know yourself."

"Of course I know," he sputtered. Despite the dropping temperature in his cabin, he kicked off his blankets.

"Then tell me. What would we do?"

"Scandalous things!"

"Are *you* embarrassed?"

"I don't get embarrassed," he said.

Della was tempted to take that statement as a challenge.

***Della, you saucy minx,* Ansel thought. He cleared his throat. "What species are you? Maybe I can figure out what planet you're from."**

"Human?" Della said. The question would have been absurd a day ago. "Do you mean to come get me?" Della liked that thought a bit too much. She could picture it—a grand ship crashing from the sky into the center of her dreary village, wood creaking, sails flapping.

Ansel chuckled. "One taste of adventure and now dukes and carriages are too pedestrian. You'd rather a spaceship drop from the sky to abduct you? Also, the ship isn't wooden. It's metal. And there aren't sails. There are engines."

The image in Della's head transformed into gleaming metal, the chug of steam, and the scent of coal. Everyone would run screaming while she stood there in the ship's shadow, skirts billowing in the fumes. She'd climb aboard, they'd find her mother, and they'd leave her miserable gray world.

Ansel grimaced. "Della, I can't come get you. I only asked to try to figure out where the book came from and who it belongs to."

"How many times do I have to tell you?" Della asked. "It belongs to me . . . *us.*"

Ansel decided there was no use arguing. "All that aside, you might be galaxies away, and I'm not in the business of taking passengers." Everyone aboard his ship served a purpose. Things got messy when you started trusting more people than were strictly necessary. "Besides, you wouldn't be safe. There's a target on my back. That's why you should return the book where you found it."

"So that's it?" Della asked. "You'll throw my book away and never think of me again?"

Had Ansel once thought Della made him feel redeemable? She made him feel irredeemable. To say he'd never think of Della would be a lie. He would always wonder about her—if she found her bravery, her voice, her happy ending.

"Of course I'll think of you," he admitted, though he didn't know what made him say it. There was something about her. Talking to her made the weight on his heart ease, though he didn't understand it. There was peace in her spirit that soothed his. She felt like something remembered rather than something discovered.

Della felt it too. Speaking to him felt as easy as conversing with an imaginary friend—though far more interesting, as she couldn't predict what he'd say next. The books tore down the stiff decorum of first greetings, leaving her with a feeling of familiarity, as though their souls had been getting to know each other far longer than a handful of hours.

"Maybe we ought to hold on to the books a little longer," she said tentatively. “For further examination. You know, only until you figure out who’s trying to kill you.” Della didn’t truly believe the books belonged to anyone other than him and her, but she figured playing along with his delusion might convince him to do what she wanted.

Ansel snorted but couldn’t deny the wisdom of her words, even if she herself did not believe in them. Maybe it would be best to keep the book close rather than lose the only clue to figuring out who had tapped into his mind. “Fine,” he said, even as his instincts warned him that he was making a grave mistake. “For one more day.”

CHAPTER 5

Della didn't have a chance to look at the book again until later, after dinner was over and the family had gone to bed.

As she worked, she thought of a fairy tale her mother used to read her. "*The girl was lonely*," her mother's fading voice whispered as she read in the low sing-song voice parents reserved for bedtime stories. "*She wished a fairy godmother would appear and turn her rags to riches but feared her dreams would never come true . . .*"

Della shook her head. The childhood tale might as well have been her life. Except now something extraordinary *had* happened to her. She just needed to figure out what purpose the books served in her story, and how to use them for good.

It seemed to take forever for the house to go silent. She was acutely aware of the lost hours, knowing it meant Ansel's ship was about to dock, and that she might miss her opportunity to speak with him again.

When finally the last dish was washed, and the bedroom floors upstairs no longer creaked above her, Della sneaked into the back corner of the kitchen and settled herself onto her mattress. A small window above her bed let in moonlight, barely enough to read by.

She opened the book, only to find that there was little new material to read. Again, it seemed as though the book skipped over the insignificant parts of their days, recording only the information it deemed pertinent. Ansel must not have been doing much as he waited for his ship to dock. There was only a question from him, waiting for her:

"Why do they force you to do all the cleaning? That's what bots are for."

"Bots?" Della mouthed the word.

His response appeared on the page almost instantly.

Ansel had been watching closely for something new to show up in Della's pages. To try to learn more about who might have planted the book on his ship to spy on him, of course.

Her confusion over bots puzzled him. She must be on an outskirt planet, detached from the tech of the rest of the galaxy.

"Bots, robots, are like . . . machines," Ansel explained under his breath, hoping Yaggrel wouldn't notice him talking to a book.

They were both on the gun deck, the short weapons specialist zipping around as he outfitted Ansel in the gear he'd need to traverse the ocean floor. Ansel's flashlight was propped beside him, lighting the room. Yaggrel's arms cast shadows across the wall as he plucked masks and gloves and weapons off overflowing shelves.

"Machines that can clean?" Della asked blankly.

"Sure, bots are devices that can be automated—programmed—*persuaded* to do tasks for you," Ansel whispered, struggling to think of a way to explain. He sat and tucked Della's book next to his thigh to keep Yaggrel from seeing it as he bustled around the armory. "They're made out of metal and electricity—"

"Electricity?"

"Think of . . . lightning. That's a form of electricity."

Della gasped at the notion of being able to harness the power of lightning. "These *machines*, they move about of their own accord and do things for you?"

"Some do. Eryl is technically a bot but she's mostly just a pain in my ass."

"It's magic."

"It's science."

Yaggrel's judgmental face appeared in Ansel's line of sight. "I'd ask who you're talking to, but you're sitting there staring at your crotch, so I've decided I'd rather not know." He shoved a chest holster into Ansel's arms.

"I'm reading." Ansel held up the book from his lap.

"And you have to sound it out?" Yaggrel asked, clearly annoyed.

"Yeah," Ansel barked back. "I'm new to it." He decided it was better for Yaggrel to think he was illiterate than have to explain that he was holding onto likely dangerous spyware because the girl on the other end intrigued him.

"I intrigue you?" Della asked.

Ansel decided to pretend the books had failed to deliver her question and changed the subject.

So, what are you going to do about your mother? he asked in his mind, deciding to try *thinking* his words rather than saying them to avoid further scrutiny as Yaggrel continued to pass him gear.

Della had been alone with her worries for so long, she had forgotten how nice it was to have someone to share them with.

"I suppose I'll have to try asking Mrs. Loughty for next month's wages in advance." Della sighed heavily.

Or tell that duke he owes you for them, Ansel pointed out, once again in his thoughts. He was pleased that mentally carrying on the conversation seemed to be working.

Della said, "It was his driver's fault I lost my letter, not the Duke's."

Close enough, thought Ansel, half to himself.

Della decided it was even nicer yet to have someone annoyed with injustices on her behalf.

"I cannot knock on a duke's door and ask for money." Della shuddered at the embarrassment of it.

Then steal what he owes you.

"You're incorrigible."

Ansel began buckling on a tactical belt equipped with a commlink, flashlight, and backup charges for his blaster. ***What makes you think you're not good enough to walk up and talk to him?***

"Perhaps you cannot understand; you can fly across the heavens as you please, doing what you want, when you want. But things are different here. It's not my place to mingle with the likes of him. I am the person who sets the stage for everyone else. No one is aware of me, and one day, when I'm gone, no one will notice my absence."

Ansel pondered that a moment. ***Did you know that DNA carries memories?*** **And then he realized she might not know what DNA was.** ***Your memories are woven into your DNA, the very fiber of your being. They become part of you, so integral to your identity that traces of those experiences can even be found in the DNA of your descendants. What I mean to say, Della, is that the impact of you can be found in everyone you've crossed paths with, and that impact will influence generations. You exist more profoundly than you know.***

Della blinked back an unexpected prickling behind her eyes. "That feels uncharacteristically sentimental of you."

Ansel shrugged. ***It's just science. Although you may never get to see as much of the universe as you want, I'll carry something of you with me now, across the stars, until the end of my days. Part of your world has collided with part of mine, and all because you and I met.***

"I think you're wiser than you let on," Della said.

Nah. **Ansel stepped into his space suit.** ***We're just not that different. You say I can fly anywhere whenever I want, but I'm not free. I'm hunted. Most days, I'm barely holding on.***

***'Course, I've got to make sure I look like I'm fine, for the crew. Some days, I feel invisible too. I'm a captain to some, a criminal to others, and myself to no one.* Ansel couldn't believe he'd let all that out. He'd have to be more careful. Admissions slipped out far too easily in his thoughts.**

Della tried to think of a way to show him that the books granted her insight into him, that she understood him the same way he understood her. He seemed to effortlessly know just what to say to chase away her feelings of smallness, and she wanted to reciprocate.

"Maybe you don't have to keep up the performance," she said. "You believe those around you expect you to be an unshakable version of strength—a bold, daring fighter who always has a joke on the tip of his tongue and a spark in his eye. But perhaps there is a greater strength in letting yourself break for all to see."

Ansel shook his head. *It wouldn't do the crew any good to know their captain's a fraud.*

"You don't need to prove your worth by being something you're not," Della insisted. "Your kindness is the part of you I find courageous, not your skill with a weapon. I believe one displays more tenacity by being kind than being cruel, as kindness is scorned and therefore a much braver undertaking. If you were honest with your crew about how you're feeling, they would respect your vulnerability, not think less of you."

Ansel snorted softly and slid his feet into his boots. *It's a nice thought.*

"It's true," Della said. "You forget I can see your soul. And I happen to find it quite easy to admire."

Ansel froze. His heart did something funny that he couldn't make sense of. He couldn't remember the last time someone had paid him a compliment, if ever. And hers struck him deeply.

Direct, sweet, simple. *I find you easy to like.*

With the guilt of his past and the uncertainty of his future, he'd never considered himself a person easily loved. Maybe not even by himself.

He was saved from trying to figure out how the stars he was supposed to respond by the jolt of his ship as it touched the ocean floor. The ship shuddered, let out a metallic groan, then silence fell as the floor beneath his boots steadied.

"We're here, Captain," Yaggrel said, handing Ansel his helmet.

Worry nestled in Della's stomach. Instinctively, she flipped ahead in his book, to the end, the way she did as a child when she grew worried that characters wouldn't make it out of their latest scrape. But of course this wasn't any ordinary book where she could reassure herself with the black-and-white happily ever after printed on the last page. The ending to their books was yet to be written.

And then an idea crept up on Della, like a wolf stalking his prey. Slowly first, then with a great pounce that sent her reeling.

Maybe they had some power over their destinies.

She thought of the empty pages in her own book that Ansel held in his hands, the pages that would one day reveal her ending. The emptiness held infinite possibilities.

"What if . . ." Della said quickly, before Ansel could set her book aside and possibly never see this wondrous notion that had overtaken her. "What if we had the power to control our fates?"

Ansel paused, helmet in one hand, book in the other. *What are you saying?* he asked silently.

Tingles of excitement washed over Della's skin. "What if we can write in each other's books and give each other everything we've ever wanted? Everything printed in the books is true—real events that have actually happened. If we wrote things in them ourselves, would they *become* true too?"

***That seems like a bad idea,* Ansel thought, feeling Yaggrel watching him with impatience.**

"I thought you didn't believe they were magic," Della said. "Either we write in the books and nothing happens, or we write in the books and our dreams come true. You have nothing to lose by trying."

In my experience, things have a tendency to go wrong when you least expect them to.

"So we'll start with something small and see if it works."

In the stories Della's mother read to her, trifling with magic usually brought calamity into people's lives. Magic always came with a price. But the idea that everything she'd ever wanted could be a few pen strokes away was too tempting. She would no longer have to struggle. No longer have to fight for every word. No longer have to sweep, scour, and scrub.

Della dared to hope—and not the shallow hope she entertained when she daydreamed and knew it was hopeless, but real hope. A belief that reality wouldn't disappoint her this time. "Write something," she whispered. "Please."

Ansel hesitated. Then he decided Della was right; he didn't believe in magic. There was no harm in doing as she asked.

"Come on, no book is that good," Yaggrel said impatiently, prodding Ansel toward the door. "Let's not forget, we're on a bit of a time crunch. Freezing to death and all that. Put the book down and get to work."

Ansel clutched the book harder, some deep, primal part of his brain snarling a possessive *mine* that startled him with its viciousness. "Give me a minute." Ansel shone his flashlight in Yaggrel's eyes. "I'll meet you at the airlock to kiss you goodbye, if that's what you're worried about."

"I'd rather kiss a slippery flesh-eating zaaneir larva in the most putrid stage of its life cycle." Grumbling, Yaggrel prowled out the door, sparing a final suspicious look back over his shoulder.

Della couldn't resist commenting, "I don't know what a

zaaneir is, but I take it that was not a complimentary reflection of your skills as a lover."

"I assure you there's nothing wrong with my skills as a *lover*," Ansel bit back as he searched for something to write with. It proved to be a bit difficult, as he and his crew recorded most things electronically. But Ansel eventually found the end of a green scaleshader in one of Yaggrel's not-so-secret nooks—a colored stylus that the vain little snorble used to enhance the hue of his hide.

"All right," he said, "something harmless." He propped the book on his knee as he wrote, muttering to himself. "Wow, thank you, Ansel. You're so nice, Ansel. There's no one as selfless as you, Ansel."

He finished his sentence with a quick jab for the period. *Ansel's jacket appeared before Della,* his sentence read. The color melted into the page, which was weird but didn't *mean* anything. Maybe the paper was simply . . . defective.

The pigment faded away, and then—

Della waited with breathless anticipation, but nothing happened.

"There," said Ansel. "See? It didn't work."

"Try something else," Della insisted. "Maybe we can't write things into each other's worlds. Maybe we can only control things that already exist inside our stories."

She hurried to come up with an idea. As was often the case with Della's ideas, it soon grew from a little one into a big one.

Earlier, Della had thought that if she'd been clever or charming enough, she could have caught the Duke's attention. Maybe she could have a second chance. She'd assumed a great romance wasn't in her future . . . but now, she could ask Ansel for one.

For one wild, *ridiculous* moment, Ansel's idiotic heart ratcheted up a notch. It was rare for a woman to look to him in pursuit of happiness that lasted longer than a single night.

Then, realizing what Della meant, that she didn't want a grand romance *with* him but rather *from* him, he controlled his thoughts.

"You want me to write that the Duke falls madly in love with you?" He wasn't sure he could stomach writing Della a future with a man capable of wishing her a good day while she stood there, shivering in the mud.

"He apologized for his driver's error," Della protested. "What more could he do? He is a duke. He did more than most would have. He stopped. He . . . he saw me," she finished quietly.

He saw her. She had a point there. It was more than Ansel could do, trapped behind pages.

Della set her chin and said, "You write what I want, and I'll write you however much money you need to fix your ship."

Ansel's morals swiftly went out the window. He was not a man above bribery, though he doubted Della would succeed in doing more than defacing a book. Still, on the off-chance the magic worked, he'd be wise to get his cut. "I hope you have a lot of ink for all the zeros."

"I'm not writing you that much. Think of an achievable number."

He hesitated, then gave in. "Fine. What do you want me to write for you?"

Della drew herself up. "I would like you to write that I cross paths with the Duke again. I want you to write that I find the bravery to speak to him. I don't need you to write that we fall in love—that should be a thing a person does of their own volition. I only want one day where they treat me like one of their own. Once he sees me as an equal, maybe I can start by befriending him." One could-be fed into the next until she saw exactly how her story should end. "Perhaps he'll ask me to tea before the night ends. And then to a picnic after tea, and a ball after the picnic. Of course, he'll find out the truth one day, that I'm just a maid, but by then he'll know me on the inside, and it won't matter a bit. He'll probably even offer to help my mother too. Oh, I'll need a dress, though."

"A dress?" Ansel asked.

"Yes, a dress so I look the part when I see the Duke." She knew she'd imagined far more than what was likely to occur, but finding a book with a real man inside wasn't *likely* either, so she wouldn't limit her what-ifs. Magic was her only hope, and she was desperate enough to set aside her pride and *trust.*

Ansel began packing the last of his things. "I'll write what you want, but you write this," he said, voice muffled as he held the flashlight in his teeth while he jammed his blaster into its holster. "Write me fifty thousand credits, enough to fix the shields. Write that this mission goes well, that we catch Neegu, and he leads us right to Balor." He slipped his flashlight into his belt. "Write that we make it off this planet alive without freezing to our deaths. If your little books can manage all that, maybe I'll believe your magic."

CHAPTER 6

Della woke the next morning and went about her tasks, dusting mantels, airing sheets, and scrubbing floors, but her mind was far away in the stars. Every time the thought of the book brushed the back of her mind, a delicious tickle shot through her nerves, like the fluttery feeling of remembering a first kiss the day after it happened.

Her life had been knocked off kilter. Anything could happen. Anything *would* happen, thanks to the magic. Della anticipated it with the impatient excitement of a child the night before their birthday.

At last, while the Loughtys ate breakfast, she had a free moment to catch up on what had happened between the time she and Ansel parted and now. Worry lurked beyond her excitement. She feared for Ansel's safety, given the dangerous nature of his mission. He only had until this evening to find Neegu and make it back to his ship before it froze.

Ansel stood in his ship's airlock, having instructed his crew to guard the ship and leave if he failed to return within the next twenty-four hours. Trepidation filled him as an automated female voice counted down the final seconds until the airlock door would open and let in the ocean.

Ansel knew tracking down Neegu should be his only focus, yet he slipped out Della's book from the waterproof pouch on his hip. It was probably stupid to bring it along

when it could easily get ruined, but he couldn't quite bring himself to leave it behind. He peeked at the pages to see if she'd been up to anything new since he last looked.

He'd last looked approximately forty-five seconds ago.

There was nothing new—she was presumably sleeping—so he tucked the book away in the pouch alongside his other personal effects. The book was small, so it fit easily.

In case Ansel didn't make it back alive, he decided he should think of something witty for Della to read about later.

"Should I tragically die, I'd hate to deprive you of the details regarding our hypothetical salacious carriage escapades," he said into the tiny, echoey chamber. "You wanted an education. I'd teach you—"

"Captain," Xaks's voice said into his earpiece, "who the hell are you talking to?"

Ansel decided he was the one who needed an education—an education regarding the ins and outs of mute buttons. He'd forgotten that he'd kept the radio channel to his ship open in case he needed to contact the crew.

The airlock doors sprang apart, and water rushed inside, engulfing him. Coldness seeped toward his skin, even through his space suit, which could withstand the pressure of the ocean as well as the vacuum of space.

"Do me a favor and forget you heard that," he managed, his frigid lungs fighting for air.

"I have the sudden urge to sterilize the inside of my skull," said Xaks.

They'd landed on the outskirts of the city, the glow of which lit Ansel's surroundings. Craggy rocks formed a foreboding landscape. Beyond that, the city loomed, a breathtaking architectural wonder. Its lower levels consisted of the barnacle- and reef-crusted stone structures of those creatures native to the planet who didn't need additional life support to survive. The water over the sprawl of buildings functioned as a highway. The city was one large mound of doorways, windows, and shop signs. Lights shone at odd angles from crooked windows, sending little beams up into the water.

Opalescent figures rippled this way and that, bustling from shop to shop. They were so pale, they nearly seemed to glow. Feathery fins rippled off bodies that formed no distinct shape, but rather ghostly blobs centered around darker nervous systems.

Fish darted to and fro. A great mammal with triangular leathery wings made her way slowly through the center of the city with her calf, letting out a haunting song.

If only Della could see it all.

Ansel shook the thought away. The fact that her name would pop into his head without warning was troubling and distracting.

He squinted upward. The city accounted for the needs of its land-dwelling visitors with towering mushroom-like structures that ballooned over it, lights shining down from what would be the mushrooms' gills to illuminate the waters below. The domes of the mushrooms contained a secondary city suitable for air-breathers. That was likely where Neegu was.

As he swam toward the city, Ansel fiddled with the radio controls on his wrist, tuning his amplifier to pick up the sounds around him. The faint chatter of the locals began zipping in and out of his helmet's speakers as they swam by. High-pitched squeals morphed into fragmented sentences as his translator figured out the speakers' dialect of echolocation and interpreted it.

Ansel approached the stalk of one of the mushroom-like structures, which was even more massive up close. An airlock door rested in the middle, the eye of a camera mounted above it.

With his face downturned, Ansel hit the *open* button and

stepped inside. As the door shut, his heart rate kicked up. He'd dyed his hair dark, changed his name, and grown out his beard to keep people from recognizing him, but those felt like meager defenses—especially when the city would already be on the lookout for intruders after an unauthorized aircraft crashed into their planet.

The water drained from the airlock, then the floor shifted beneath him as the room rose, lifting him into the dome. Warm air blasted him from all sides, drying his space suit and chasing the chill from his bones.

He touched the pouch on his hip, ensuring his blaster was still safe inside. The fact that the motion also ensured Della's book was still tucked away was irrelevant.

The door opened, and Ansel stepped out into a vaulted arched hallway that circled the perimeter of the dome. Rows of green lights swooped up the wall to the ceiling, curving with the contours of the rotunda. The hall was occupied as if it were a city street, creatures of all shapes and sizes jostling as they went about their business.

Doors along the hallway functioned as storefronts, each room representing a building. The neon signs above them twisted into recognizable letters as Ansel's translator interpreted the words.

With so much ground to cover in very little time, the search for Neegu felt impossible, but Ansel gritted his teeth and began.

Della looked up from Ansel's book. There were no more words, which she took as neither good nor bad news. For if something dreadful had occurred, surely it would have been recorded, and if Ansel had been successful in his quest, it too would be in the book. Likely the book didn't feel the need to record hours upon hours of fruitless labor.

Della decided to send him another letter, hoping he might respond to it if and when he found time.

"Dear Ansel," Della whispered as she skimmed a feather duster over the parlor mantel, sending dust mites swirling into the morning sunbeams streaming through the windows. Speaking to him in the sleepy half-dreamworld of the empty pastel parlor felt as natural as talking to her own consciousness. There was no longer a need to organize her thoughts in written form. She simply let them flow in her head, the way he did the night before.

I very much enjoyed meeting you yesterday. If the magic works, and we decide to write ourselves happily ever afters, what would yours look like? I implore you to answer honestly and not insult me, as I'm sure you'll be tempted to, with false aspirations about wealth, perfect hair, fame, or other such tomfoolery.

Yours,
Della.

She wasn't able to read his response until a little while later when she sneaked into the kitchen for a quick peek at the book.

Ansel had been searching the city all night to no avail, and he was exhausted. Never before had he felt so close to and yet so terribly far from finding Balor.

At last, light-headedness forced him to stop long enough to purchase an unidentifiable lump of food for breakfast from a street vendor. As he wolfed it down, he checked Della's book.

She'd been worrying about him, which made him feel . . . weird—vaguely tender and raw.

He remembered how it was, talking to her last night. She saw his weaknesses and still thought he was *easy to admire.*

At once, Ansel wanted to write Della back. To bring to life, at least in a small way, the future that Balor had stolen from him. What would it hurt? He'd never meet her. Talking

to her was like thinking any other thought that would never see the light of day.

As he wove his way back into the flow of street traffic, he muted his mic, then triple-checked it because the thought of his crew overhearing him being *genuine* was far more mortifying than them overhearing him spouting flirtation.

He'd never composed a letter but decided to follow Della's lead.

Della dear, he began clumsily, unsure if he'd addressed her right because he'd already forgotten how she'd done it.

I have already achieved perfect hair, thanks to many years of mastering the art form, and won't require your assistance with the matter at this time. As for my happy ending, I think—

He shoved the long snout of a particularly pushy creature out of his way, snapping, "Watch it."

With a sigh, he returned to his mental note.

I am weary, Della. I want to stop running. I've been banished from Lumeria for nearly ten years, and I just want to go home. The planet was not particularly kind to me growing up, but it's my birthplace.

I've considered trying to make a home elsewhere, but I've realized there's no way around facing Balor again regardless. I must clear my name no matter where I settle because the alternative is I find peace for a few years, and then what? Bounty hunters knock on the door of my children's home and take their father from them?

Ansel couldn't quite believe he'd admitted that particular fear. Stars! What was happening to him? One sleepless night, and he was crumbling.

Enough about me. What type of ailment does your mother have? While I'm no doctor, I grew up on a planet known for its medicinal breakthroughs and may know of something that could help.

Once your mother is better, I know you want to travel the world, but what about after that? Will you go on wandering forever?

With all the irresistible charm in the world,
Ansel.

After reading Ansel's letter, Della tucked his book into her apron pocket. She couldn't help but admire the way he denied himself temporary happiness to protect his unborn children, but decided she'd better not remark on it for fear of embarrassing him further.

She thought up a response while upstairs, re-pinning Mrs. Loughty's hair after an unfortunate encounter with a door frame had knocked it askew.

Ansel,

Your correspondence has filled me with awe. I admire your unwavering tenacity. The way you think highly of yourself when there is little evidence to support your claims of irresistibility is commendable.

On a more serious note, as for what ails my mother, the doctors are uncertain. It's her heart, they say. She experiences palpitations and grows faint, and therefore must rest and avoid excitement and exertion. If you have any advice, I'm eager to hear it.

As for your other question, yes, I think I might be happy wandering forever. I want to see as many wonderful things as it takes for my waking world to become as magnificent as my dreams.

"Della, you clumsy girl," Mrs. Loughty scolded when Della dropped a hairpin. "If you don't have a clever mind, the least you could do is have clever fingers." She imparted the insult as though benevolently reciting an aphorism.

Della entertained a brief but satisfying mental image of accidentally stabbing a hairpin through Mrs. Loughty's ear-drum.

Yes, Ansel, I think I could be quite content wandering the world forever. The thought of a life without human companionship is not unappealing. If I am to feel small, I want to feel small because I'm standing at the foot of a mountain or beside the ocean or under a vast star-filled sky, not because I'm standing before a spiteful person.

Yours,
Della.

P.S. I find myself wondering what you look like.

It was only after Mrs. Loughty's hair was pinned and Della went downstairs that she was able to slip the book from her apron to see Ansel's response.

Ansel read Della's note as he caught his breath after an unpleasant confrontation with a six-fisted, eight-foot-tall individual who found his questions regarding Neegu's whereabouts suspicious. The creature, assuming Ansel was a Cooperation agent sticking his nose where it didn't belong, utilized his six fists to bodily heave Ansel from his black-market grocery store.

Devious Della,
If I'd known from the beginning you had such a sharp tongue, I would have fallen in love with you immediately.

If the duke is not on his knees at your feet by nightfall, he is a fool.

Speaking of fools, I hope you do not take the words of that insufferable Mrs. Loughty to heart. After years of exploring the universe's crustiest crevices, I've found the least intelligent life-forms are the quickest to bring others down in their attempts to claw their way up from the bottom of the food chain.

I hope you find peace in your wanderings.

Logically, I know you should get rid of my book, for safety. But a small part of me likes to imagine you standing by seas and mountains with my book tucked under your arm. I find myself curious to see your reaction the first time you see an ocean.

And now I'm afraid I'm getting too wistful for a ruffian, and since I have a reputation to uphold, I will leave off this letter here. See what you've done to me? You've infected me with your dreams, and now I've lost my mind to them.

As for your mother, I'd wager if I could bring her case to Lumeria, they might have a few medicines for arrhythmias she could try. Unfortunately, I will be shot on sight if I try to return. If I ever manage to clear my name, however, and if I can locate your planet, I will make the trip.

Yours,
Ansel.

P.S. Whatever P.S. means. I do too.

Della stared at the letter in bafflement. Just last night he'd said he wouldn't come for her, and now he'd *make the trip.* As though traipsing across who-knew-how-many galaxies to help her was as insignificant as lending a neighbor a cup of flour. Since remarking on his generosity would likely only result in him shrugging off her thanks with a sarcastic reply, she responded:

Ansel,

Oh dear. Sorry to hear about your run-in with the brute. Hoping your perfect hair remains intact.

Affectionately,
Della.

Della was overcome by the possibility that one day, Ansel might truly land his spaceship in the middle of Poling and step out with a cure for her mother. Of course, who knew how long it would take him to clear his name, or if he could even find her, but it was something.

After that, Ansel's book remained blank for a long time. The afternoon ticked by. Teatime came and went. The sun sank lower on the horizon. Still Ansel's book remained blank. He was running out of time, and trepidation gnawed at Della's insides.

Then a knock on the front door made Della startle so hard, she smacked her head against the brick fireplace where she'd been sweeping the hearth. Wiping her hands on her apron, she got up and answered the door. Outside stood a page boy, who handed her a letter.

"Who is this for?" Della asked. "It doesn't appear to be addressed to anyone."

The page boy shrugged. "Dunno. It came from the Duke of Eshford."

CHAPTER 7

A letter from the Duke. Della's heart scarcely had the chance to leap before a high-pitched squeal made it scamper away in fright.

"The Duke?" Miss Alma Loughty, the eldest Loughty daughter, rushed into the room in a flurry of lavender lace, her blond ringlets bouncing. She swiped the letter from Della and tore it open, sharp blue eyes darting as she read. "He's invited me to his dinner party tonight!"

Immediately, Della felt foolish for thinking the letter might have been meant for her. Thanking the page boy, she closed the front door while Alma dashed into the sitting room, calling for her sister. Della followed and reestablished her position kneeling at the hearth as the younger Miss Loughty, Phoebe, fluttered into the room.

Della did her best to sink into the brickwork. Chambermaids were not to be seen. Luckily, Della was good at being invisible. Once, when she was a child playing hide-and-seek with the other schoolchildren, she'd hidden in a tight spot between a large desk and a wall where no one else was small enough to fit. Excitement welled in her belly as she heard child after child being discovered until she was the last one.

Instead of looking for her, the other children began a new round, declaring the boy found before her the winner, and Della's heart had sunk.

Being noticed was all well and good. Being missed was something else entirely. All she could do was crouch there, wedged against the wall, listening as the children played three more rounds without ever thinking to look for her. It was only when a concerned teacher asked the children if they knew where Della had gone that they remembered her existence at all.

"What does it say?" Miss Phoebe asked, pulling Della to the present. She poked her snub nose over her sister's shoulder, trying to read the letter.

Miss Alma cleared her throat. "He writes: 'To the lady I had the pleasure of meeting yesterday afternoon'"—Della's ears perked up—"'I request the honor of your presence at my dinner table tonight. I hope our second encounter will be more pleasant than our first.'" The sisters exchanged a look. "Did you meet the Duke yesterday?"

A tiny line appeared between Phoebe's brows. "I was home all afternoon. You?"

"The same." Alma pondered this a moment.

Meanwhile, Della's heart raced. Could the Duke have meant that letter for her after all? He must have. She'd asked Ansel to write that their paths would cross again, and now here was a letter, inviting her to dine. The magic. It was working!

Alma tapped her chin. "You know, I did spy him while out and about yesterday morning. Do you think he made an error and was actually referring to then? I was being measured for a new gown, and when I exited the shop, there he was."

"Right there? Outside the dressmaker's shop?" Phoebe gasped as though the notion of a man walking past a shop was revolutionary.

"No," Alma said. "He was on the opposite side of the street, fifty or so yards to my right, turning down an alleyway, and I didn't see where he went because a wagon blocked my view."

Clearly, Alma's encounter with the Duke had been deeply significant and emotionally remarkable for both parties. It was no wonder the meeting left such a lasting impression on the dear Duke that he rushed home at once and wrote to Alma . . . over twenty-four hours later to invite her to his party.

"That must be it!" Phoebe exclaimed.

The letter is actually meant for me, a tiny voice in the back of Della's mind piped up. But of course Della didn't speak up. The attention would be unbearable. She'd once supposed that even if she were trapped under a carriage, she'd rather rot away than yell for help and make a spectacle of herself. Where was that bravery Ansel was supposed to write for her?

"Della?" Alma bellowed, craning her neck toward the doorway. "Where are you? You must help me dress for dinner. Make haste!"

The sisters bustled from the room in search of Della, who knelt by the hearth, mere feet away. "Actually, that letter's meant for me," she whispered inaudibly to the bricks, her imagination hushing, fading from glittering dining rooms and swishing gowns to soot and sweeping.

It wasn't until a half hour later, once Alma was dressed and sent on her way, and Phoebe retired to her room to sulk over not having a duke of her own, that Della had a chance to breathe again.

She found the letter on Alma's vanity. The girls had obsessed over it so much, the poor scrap of paper was a sad, wrinkled slip of a thing, soft from being folded and unfolded too many times.

Magic had orchestrated a second meeting, and Della managed to ruin it for herself anyway. Hot tears stung the corners of her eyes, which only made her angrier. Here she was, furious with herself, yet all she could do was cry.

Deciding to check on Ansel and see if he was having a

similarly disappointing day, she retrieved the book from her apron pocket.

In a final act of desperation, Ansel asked a local to recommend the seediest bar in town and paid the establishment a visit, hopeful Neegu might be there, conducting business. Ansel arrived with around an hour left before he had to return to his ship and found a seat at the sticky sandstone bar.

A bartender with long antennae spiraling out from his flat skull and six eyes protruding from the side of his face tilted his head sideways as he addressed Ansel. "What will it be for you?"

"Something strong, thanks."

The bartender slid Ansel his drink while he balanced several other glasses in the numerous clawed, fuzzy arms running the length of his torso.

Clutching his glass, Ansel hunched his shoulders, giving the illusion that he was absorbed in his drink. Surreptitiously, he scanned the room, searching the dark corners for Neegu.

If he retrieved Della's book from his belt and placed it on the bar, it was only to appear casual. The less alert he looked, the less suspicious.

If his eye happened to catch on a sentence describing Della fighting back tears, it was an accident.

If something behind his ribs burned because of it, he told himself it was only because the distraction was inconvenient and his drink was strong. He didn't have time for—

Confound it.

"What's wrong?" he asked before he could remember to think the words instead of speak them out loud. Hopefully, people looking would think he was talking into the comlink on his wrist. *Don't tell me your duke let you down,* he thought. *What a shocking turn of events after his impeccable first impression.*

Della realized the words on the page ended there. That

Ansel must right now be sitting at the bar, waiting for her reply. His sarcastic commentary on her life somewhat soured the wonder of the books.

"It's easy enough for you to tease me about my dire prospects when you've already had a great romance," Della said acidly. There were definite downsides to this connection they had. Gone were the days when she could cry in private. Now she had to endure him spying on her and saying, "*I told you so*." She wondered why she'd even bothered to worry about the vexing man. "Who is she, anyway, the girl you're always thinking of though you try not to? The one who saw through your supposed darkness."

Ansel choked. Alcohol burned his throat, making his eyes water. Sensations bombarded his weakened defenses. The smell of earth and greenery. The warmth of lips and shared laughter and whispered promises. Sunlight dancing through fluttering leaves and soft grass beneath his palms.

Ansel unclenched his fingers. "She was a friend."

Della didn't believe that for a second.

"What about your stable boy?" Ansel fired back. "He wasn't romantic enough for you?"

A lump formed in Della's throat, prohibiting her from answering. What they had was not romance. What they had was loneliness and desperation. They had gentle, inexperienced hands, dusty straw, and a handful of weeks. They held each other simply because they had no one and nothing else to cling to.

"Isn't that how you want it?" Ansel asked, because of course he'd shamelessly read her thoughts. "Gentle hands and mournful pining? Isn't that how all the great romances go?"

Della shoved the book back into her apron. Instead of a fairy godmother, Della had received magical intervention in the form of a criminal drinking at a bar on a completely different planet who considered the very thought of her name to be nothing more than an inconvenient distraction.

Scowling, she walked back to the kitchen, intending to read

between dinner preparations. As she turned the corner, all her frustrations melted on her tongue. Because there, on her mattress, was a dress. A beautiful dress.

It was delicate pink muslin with fitted sleeves and white lace flowers. Hope soared within her. The magic was still working. She'd have her one night of grandeur, just like the heroines in her mother's fairy tales. It felt impossible, naïve even. Except she had magic on her side now, so she had to trust that the Duke and his friends would accept her as one of their own, as Ansel had written. And Ansel—a small pang of guilt went through her that she would be at a party while he was still stuck underwater, but if the magic was working, then that meant he had nothing to worry about either.

The Duke's dinner would begin an hour before Mrs. Loughty took hers. Della wouldn't stay long. She'd be back before Mrs. Loughty noticed her missing. One hour. She had one hour to win the Duke's favor and change the trajectory of her life.

She wondered if Alma had made it to the Duke's. If she'd somehow been accepted into the dinner party, despite not being invited, Della would be gracious enough not to mention the mix-up. Surely, even after the Duke confirmed Della was the one he'd invited, he'd allow Alma to stay as well and spare her any embarrassment. Della didn't necessarily like Alma, but the situation was her fault for not speaking up about who was the intended recipient of the invitation.

Feeling a little silly, Della donned the dress. As she hastily wrestled buttons and ribbons, she half expected Mrs. Loughty to walk in and find her playing dress-up when she should be working.

Once the dress was on, though, Della found a little bit of bravery. She tucked Ansel's book under her bed, for the dress had no pockets, and left the house for the Duke's dinner party.

Della arrived four minutes late. She trembled as she knocked on the grand door to the Duke's manor, though she tried to remind herself that being late when you were a lady meant you were fashionable, and no one was likely to punish you for it.

The door swung open, and Della's tongue promptly tied itself in knots. A butler looked down his long nose at her, blocking the doorway with his tall frame. "Well?" he prompted. "State your business."

"I'm here for dinner," Della stuttered. "I've been invited."

The butler guffawed. "There's a streak of soot on your cheek, girl. I don't know what you're about, but be on your way and be thankful I don't alert your employer to your impudence."

Apparently, Della's altered appearance was fooling no one. If only finding a place to fit in were as easy as fitting into a dress.

Ansel once thought Della was capable of being a dangerous bounty hunter. A seductress. Someone he wanted to whisk away in a carriage and have scandalous adventures with. When someone else saw your dream, it meant it was in the beginning stages of becoming reality. This gave Della the hope that maybe, just maybe, she had a sprout of confidence—a small but growing capacity to be bold.

So Della gritted her teeth, ducked her head, and darted under the butler's elbow and into the manor. If she could just get inside and find the Duke, the magic would make the rest fall into place, surely.

A mixture of panic and elation thundered through her veins as she ran down the hall. Glossy woodwork blurred by. A plush burgundy rug dulled her racing footsteps. The smells of spices, roasted meat, and fresh bread made her salivate. She followed the scents farther into the house. The butler yelled after her, and she redoubled her efforts, desperate to find the Duke so he could confirm he'd invited her before she was caught.

At last, there it was: an opulent dining room shimmering

with candlelight and gilded cutlery. Della burst inside, chest heaving and skirts swirling about her legs. Her entrance prompted a surprised clatter of silverware. Each person seated around the long dining table—and there were a fair many persons seated there—looked up.

Fighting for breath, Della struggled to maintain an elegant posture even while inwardly she wished to melt into the ornamental rug. "I'm here," she said—unnecessarily, as everyone could certainly see she was there, judging by their stares. She looked imploringly toward the Duke. "It's me. Della. You invited me."

"Does every young lady in Poling mean to pretend they've received a dinner invitation tonight?" an older woman asked primly.

Della realized she must have been referring to Alma. A brief glance about the room showed her that Alma was not in attendance. She must have been sent away when everyone realized the Duke hadn't invited her. Della winced, thinking of how mortified Alma must have been.

"If you're referring to Miss Alma Loughty," Della said, "it isn't her fault she thought the invitation was meant for her. We . . . live in the same household, you see. When she read the post, there was no reason for her to assume it was meant for me."

A heavy hand clamped around her shoulder. "Apologies, Your Grace." The butler's voice rumbled behind her. "The wench slipped in, despite my best efforts. I will escort her out immediately."

"Wait." A chair scraped across the floor. Everyone turned as the Duke stood at the head of the table. "Della," he repeated her name. "We met before, have we not?"

She nodded, confused as to why he was asking when he'd said as much in his letter. "Yesterday, Your Grace."

Recognition dawned in his eyes. "Ah! The mishap with the carriage. I remember now." He said it without any sort of emotional inflection, as though they'd amiably bumped into each other at the market, and his carriage had not splattered her with silt.

The butler's hand lifted from her shoulder. An awkward silence ensued in which Della prayed for spontaneous combustion.

"I'm sorry," she said, though she didn't know why she was the one apologizing. "When I received your letter, I thought you wished me to attend your dinner party. I see now there was a misunderstanding."

A furrow appeared between the Duke's brows. "You keep mentioning an invitation. What invitation?"

A long, loud peal of boisterous laughter rang out. The man seated to the Duke's right stood, clapping his hands slowly as though he'd just witnessed a brilliant performance. "The invitation I sent her, of course." The new speaker was handsome like the Duke. But his smile was wooden, as though swarms of biting words had skittered through his teeth like termites and chewed a permanent path through his lips. "I told you if we stopped to check on the girl, she'd fall madly in love with you, and I was right. See? I wrote to her pretending to be you to prove it, and now look. The twit actually showed up."

Della's throat and stomach tumbled over each other until they coiled into one tight knot. "You sent the letter, not the Duke."

The man nodded. "Indeed. You didn't know it, but I was in the carriage, bearing witness to your blossoming romance. Tell me, pet, how'd you catch the fancy of our Laurence Moreland?" The man eyed the others at the table, inviting them in on his joke, and they willingly began smiling along. "Was it the fetching embellishment of dung in your hair? Or the way you dress in all the latest fashions? Why, I'd never supposed aprons were all the rage."

The gathering tittered, to which the man seemed to take an almost carnal delight.

"That's enough, Radcliff," the Duke said, turning to Della with an apology in his gaze. "I'm sorry, my dear. My friend is quite the jokester."

She didn't know what to say. If she tried to speak, she'd only release the sob burning at the back of her throat. Later in her bed, she would probably think of the perfect scathing retort. For now, all she could do was stand there. Her consciousness felt too small for her body, watching from a distance as her mind and mouth failed her.

The Duke's expression softened with pity. "You were deceived and came all this way. Let me make it up to you. Why don't you join us?" He nodded to the side, and a servant stepped out of the shadows with a chair, placing it at an empty spot at the table.

The way Radcliff beamed at her made her feel like his new favorite plaything to be used, abused, and discarded. "A grand idea," he said. "We should all get to know our future Duchess better."

More hesitant laughter.

Della did not want to sit down. The Duke likely thought he was doing her a service by asking her to stay, trying to make up for his friend's vile tricks. In truth, he was only prolonging her agony.

But what could Della do? A duke had asked her to sit. With every eye on her, she crossed the dining room, her shoes squeaking with every step, and sat.

"What fun." Radcliff topped off her wineglass himself.

The following half hour felt like an eternity. The frightful turn Della's evening took didn't make her stop believing in magic; it simply made her start believing magic was a diabolical monster. While everything could have been a series of unfortunate coincidences, Della still held magic responsible. Surely it wasn't chance that every dream she'd wished for had been turned into a joke. *She* was a joke—the wretched mud-covered girl who thought a royal summons was meant for her.

To his credit, the Duke tried to include her in the conversation, but it proved to be a mistake. Radcliff followed his lead in an exaggerated fashion, asking for her advice about investments and horse racing, acting as though she were also a highly respectable member of society. His manner toward her was so earnest and sincere, he almost seemed genuine. But Della knew if she responded to any of his inquiries, she'd only encourage him further.

If only she could ask him his advice on roasting a chicken, mending a dress, or polishing tarnished silverware and laugh at his clueless answers. But drinking spirits and betting on horses was considered a nobler activity than scrubbing chamber pots, and so his ignorance would be forgiven, whereas hers was mocked.

Della couldn't muscle food past the lump in her throat even though she knew it tasted wondrous and had taken the cooks countless hours to prepare. Her earlier plans to befriend the Duke felt foolish. She wouldn't mistake his pity for respect.

At least Radcliff kept her wineglass full, which was the only decent thing he'd done, even if he only did it because he found the idea of her inebriation funny. A distracting but not altogether unpleasant humming took up residence in Della's skull. She knew it was dangerous to drink so much, surrounded by these awful people, but if she could gain nothing from tonight besides expensive wine, then she would utilize the opportunity.

Everything had gone wrong. She'd put too much faith in magic, and it had tricked her. Could she have put too much trust in Ansel too? Was it possible he'd written something incorrectly that skewed her whole evening?

But no. She didn't believe that. In fact, he might be in as much trouble as she.

Oh heavens! If his night was going as poorly as hers, he might be in even *worse* trouble than she. Unfortunately, his book was home beneath her mattress where she couldn't check in on him.

Ansel, she thought, praying he would look in her book before it was too late, *if you're reading this, proceed with caution. The magic is malicious.*

No. That warning wasn't enough. She had to make sure he was okay.

Della tossed her napkin onto the table. "I'm afraid I must head home now," she whispered to the tablecloth.

She needn't have bothered. No one heard or noticed. By then, even Radcliff had grown bored with her. Past the point of caring what they all thought of her, Della stood up and walked out. She was tired of being their amusement for the night. The conversation behind her didn't so much as falter.

Della ran all the way home. The nights were growing colder, heading into winter, and the frosty mud crunched under her boots. Each impact of her feet vibrated her shinbones. Her lungs ached from the frigid air. Her heart ached from the frigid world.

She was foolish to think the book could better her life. She'd abandoned all her responsibilities only to be ridiculed and laughed at.

When she burst into the house, Mrs. Loughty stood in the foyer waiting for her, her arms crossed over her ample bosom. A scowl slashed across her face, any pretense of kindness finally gone. "Where have you been?" Her face went red with fury when she took in Della's attire. "Why are you wearing Phoebe's dress? I left that for you to hem."

Della went numb. She looked down and realized she was indeed wearing one of Phoebe's dresses from last season. She hadn't recognized it because Phoebe had only worn it once. It seemed magic was less magical than Della had hoped. It had to conform to reality's rules. Dresses couldn't appear out of thin air, and maids couldn't become ladies, not really.

"I'm sorry, Mrs. Loughty. It was a mistake," she heard herself say. "I'll begin dinner at once."

"You will do nothing but begin packing your bags, you flighty, unreliable girl. Always smiling like a dunce with your head in the clouds. Stealing my daughter's clothes. How long has this been going on?"

"Never, I promise." The insistence sounded weak, even to her own ears. Because the truth was, she was so, so tired of obeying the rules when nothing ever came of it. She was tired of apologizing.

"It doesn't matter." Mrs. Loughty drew herself up. "It won't happen again. You will leave this house immediately, and I hope you are not expecting my recommendation."

Della was not. People were rarely kinder than they appeared, least of all the caustic Mrs. Loughty.

And so, Della changed into her own dress, gathered her few possessions and Ansel's book, and headed into the cold night, leaving the last decade of her life behind her with nothing to show for it besides callused hands and a blistered heart.

CHAPTER 8

With nowhere to go, Della sneaked into a neighbor's stable, intending to spend the night in the loft before seeking new employment in the morning. She hurriedly settled herself on a pile of hay near a window, the buzz of wine still blurring the edges of her vision. The smell of horses and warm manure filled her nostrils, and animals softly snuffled below. The sounds might have been comforting if she weren't so preoccupied.

With frantic fingers made stiff and clumsy from the cold, she flipped open Ansel's book. Squinting in the near darkness and holding the pages up to the window, she barely made out the words.

Ansel could hardly believe his luck. Shortly after he'd finished speaking with Della, Neegu walked into the bar with a group of his friends. Barely three feet tall, Neegu had blue skin speckled with white dots. His neck was scrawny and heavily tendoned, little nubbed horns dotted his prominent brow like moles, and tentacles curled off his thin cheekbones.

Neegu and his friends joined a game of cards in the corner. Uninterested in making a scene by tackling him on the spot and hauling him back to his ship, Ansel walked over and asked to join the game. Neegu didn't appear to know who he was; he only grunted in the affirmative and indicated an empty seat. If Ansel ran out of time, he would resort to the tackling plan, but if he could pry the information he needed

from Neegu without resorting to brutality, ruining his jacket, and bruising his knuckles, he would prefer it.

Neegu's appearance was convenient, but Ansel didn't take it as a sign the magic was working, especially not after he'd gone a day without fifty thousand credits falling at his feet. It was just a coincidence. But then something peculiar happened.

Fifty thousand credits all but landed in his lap.

He began winning. Never had he been so successful at a card table. Over the course of the next half hour, players came, then left shortly after in defeat as Ansel laid down winning hand after winning hand.

He was unstoppable. At this rate, he'd win enough credits to fix his shields and have Balor in his clutches by the end of the week.

And yes, now part of him wondered if it was magic, but that would be ridiculous. Obviously, he was amazing at cards. That made more sense, even though it had never been true before. Maybe Della's stubborn optimism played a part in it. She practically radiated positivity, and it had made him confident. He'd thought he would win, and so he did. A self-fulfilling prophecy.

Now if only Neegu would be a bit more forthcoming with information regarding Balor's whereabouts. But Ansel was sure that was only a matter of time. He was on a winning streak, after all.

Between rounds, as the dealer shuffled the deck, Ansel leaned back in his chair and sneaked a peek into Della's book beneath the table. Before he flipped back to the place he'd left off earlier, his eye caught on a line on the newest page.

***Why are you in a barn?* he thought.**

Della blinked down at the question that had appeared as she'd been reading, which meant that just now, Ansel had opened her book and would soon flip back and read about her mortifying evening.

"I beg of you, please, don't go back and read my pages," she said in a rush. She could not bear the thought of one more person witnessing her embarrassment. Especially him.

***Did he hurt you?* Ansel thought darkly as the dealer flicked him cards.**

"I am unharmed," Della said to the empty hay loft, tucking her chilled fingers under her legs.

***Why are you cold?* Ansel thought as he read about her warming her hands, barely able to focus on the sticky cards in front of him. Out loud, he asked Neegu if he'd encountered any difficulties during his last job. "These clients act like selling product is as easy as giving away free yucket pups," Ansel said conversationally, shaking his head. "My last job took me to the Galvenstian belt. The place is crawling with hunters. You were recently near there, weren't you?"**

Neegu grunted. "Did a deal on Trestine for a longtime client."

Ansel's interest sparked. The longtime client might be Balor, which meant they might be close to pinpointing his location, which meant—*for stars' sake, Della, why are you in a barn?*

"I grew bored of my cot and wanted a change of scenery?" Della tried. "Just listen to me. Magic does not care for our best interests. It only wishes to undermine our wants. You should leave now and board your ship before things take a turn for the worse."

***One more hand,* Ansel thought.**

Della groaned. He wasn't listening. He still didn't believe in the magic.

She didn't know how to fix this, and the alcohol muddling her thoughts didn't help. All she knew was that she needed to get Ansel to safety before something dreadful happened. "You were wrong earlier," she said in a burst of resolve, needing a distraction, any distraction, that would pry him away from the table. "I don't want gentle hands and mournful pining."

Ansel's fingers stilled where they'd been fiddling with his credit chips.

"I've . . . often thought I'd quite enjoy being ravished against a wall." Della's cheeks flamed, but her humiliation was a small price to pay if it saved him from misfortune. If she embarrassed him too by association, all the better. If he were blushing at a card table, perhaps he would have the good sense to leave for the sake of his pride. "I want fierce passion—the drag of nails and the sting of teeth. I want desperation and—"

***Della.* He thought her name, nothing more.**

"If I were there, I might think to kiss you," she said, quieter. "I'd grab you by your stupid ears and rattle whatever lies between them, and then I'd kiss you if it would tempt you away from danger."

Even surrounded as he was by the worst ruffians and scoundrels on this side of the galaxy, Ansel was beginning to think Della was the most dangerous thing in his life. *You'll be begging me to forget you said all that tomorrow when you're sober. Who got you drunk?*

"I'm not drunk, you infernal man." She was a little drunk. "I'm worried about you."

Don't fret, love. I heard you.* Ansel knew better than to take any warning idly. He'd unholstered his blaster beneath the table the moment he read about her distress. Glancing at his wrist screen, he realized he had a mere fifteen minutes before his crew was scheduled to leave, with or without him. He was out of time. *Believe it or not, I was listening, even before you asked me to ravish you against a wall.

"I did not ask you, in particular, to ravish me against a wall," Della stammered.

Chuckling, Ansel slipped Della's book away, thinking,

Stay safe, before slapping his final hand onto the table. "Good game, friends." He began sliding his winnings toward himself. "But I'm afraid I must be going."

"Not so fast," a muscular, tusked brute across from him rumbled. "I've been watching you, I have. You keep looking beneath the table. I say you've been cheating."

Because he knew protesting would do no good, Ansel just shrugged and smiled as if to say *you might be right.* And then he forced himself to cope with the fact that he was probably about to get punched.

The beefy creature lunged across the table. Ansel sidestepped. His attacker slammed into whoever had been standing behind Ansel. The two went tumbling across the floor, knocking into several more patrons on their way. Those patrons took offense—as patrons of a bar were wont to do at any slight grievance. Their friends proceeded to take offense on their behalf, and the room descended into an all-out brawl.

After collecting his winnings, Ansel pinpointed Neegu weaving his way through the crowd toward the door. Stalking after him, Ansel shouldered his way through the mayhem, ducking under an airborne chair, recoiling from a misplaced punch inches from his nose, and stepping over a crunched cleaning bot that had been caught in the crossfire.

Maintaining a fair distance behind Neegu, Ansel tracked him out of the bar and down the indoor street, nearly losing him a few times in the bustle.

At last, Neegu stepped through the nondescript door of a hotel. After waiting a few minutes, Ansel stepped inside. The smell of stale smoke filled his nostrils. It took a moment for his eyes to adjust to the dim interior. The place was shabby, the lobby's dark green wallpaper peeling. A tiny receptionist the size of his fist buzzed behind the front counter, her minuscule wings a blur behind her. She began to greet him, but he held up a hand and shook his head,

thumbing the safety of his blaster. The weapon powered up with a faint, high-pitched whine. The receptionist zipped into a hole in the ceiling with a practiced flourish that indicated this was not the first time she'd hidden from rough characters handling their business in this establishment.

Ansel exited the lobby through a doorway and entered a hall in time to see Neegu enter a room farther down. Ansel crept closer, his footsteps muffled by a long, shabby rug that looked like it had seen a few bloodstains during its lifetime. The sconces along the walls flickered in the corners of his eyes. When Ansel reached the door Neegu had entered, he paused only a moment before kicking it open and raising his blaster. "Don't move—"

The words died on Ansel's lips. A semicircle of human thugs greeted him, their own blasters leveled at his head. On the couch behind them, with his ankle crossed over his knee as though this were a casual brunch and not an ambush, was Balor.

Della's heart dropped. The worst had happened, and it was her fault. Ansel had told her to toss his book away, but she'd convinced him to test the magic. She'd written that Neegu would lead him to Balor and damned him with her own hand.

Unable to tear her gaze away, she read the new words as they wrote themselves on the page.

Ansel's shoulders slumped. Nearly ten years fighting for justice, and this was how it would end. He wouldn't get his revenge. He'd be butchered in a dingy hotel room on the bottom of an ocean.

Ansel looked from one of Balor's henchmen to the next, waiting for an escape plan to hit him as they always did. None came. He was outnumbered. He might be able to take a few of the thugs with him, but he'd never fight his way out of this alive.

"Hello, old friend." Balor smiled pleasantly. "I heard a

ghastly rumor you've been hunting me." He stood and passed a wad of credits to Neegu. "When will you learn? You are not a hunter. You are prey—prey too hungry and desperate to notice the steel trap around the quarry you think you've caught. Dear Neegu here was only too glad to play the part of bait if it meant a cut of your bounty. Luckily for you, you're worth more alive than dead."

Ansel's breath came too quick, too shallow. He'd rather Balor simply kill him than turn him in to the Cooperation. He couldn't go back to prison after experiencing the vast freedom of space.

"Really, Tulzok," Balor said, "you should have seen this coming."

He was right. If Ansel hadn't been preoccupied with an impossible book and the whimsical dreamer within, he would have recognized things were falling into place much too easily. Instead, Della had him wanting to believe in magic and dismissing all signs of danger. Without realizing it, he'd let her get to him. At some point, between watching her dream and blush and cry, he'd become enamored by the idea of being the one to make her laugh. He hadn't done that yet, he realized. Maybe he never would. An irredeemable oversight.

Della gazed with wide eyes at the page. Why was the exasperating man thinking about her at a time like this? She needed to find a writing utensil—then she could save him, write him out of this mess.

Or maybe not. Considering how things had gone the first time they'd tried to change their stories, doing so again might be unwise. In trying to help, she might only make matters worse. She had indescribable magic at her fingertips, yet she was still powerless.

All she could do was helplessly read on.

Balor nodded to his men. They closed in. Before Ansel

could react, one lunged, knocking his blaster from his grip. The rest descended as soon as he was unarmed. A punch to the gut knocked Ansel off balance. Two men caught him before he could double over, wrenching his arms behind his back. The tendons in his arms strained as his shoulder sockets threatened to pop. The largest thug grinned as he backhanded him across the face. Ansel closed his eyes against the pain.

If Balor found the Della-shaped hole in Ansel's armor, he would exploit it. The only upside was that Balor was not much for reading. Hopefully, if he took her book, he wouldn't examine it closely enough to figure out what it could do. Because now that he was forced to face the facts, Ansel had to admit there was something weird about the books. If by some minuscule chance they actually did have power, with Della's book, Balor could control her entire life. Could use her against Ansel in any manner of heinous ways.

Ansel fought in vain against his captors, thinking only of escape—not for himself anymore, but for Della's future he held in his protection. He'd been stupid, bringing her book with him.

Della stood and began to pace across the loft, biting her fingernails until they bled, her mind racing for a solution to help Ansel, but there was nothing she could do.

At last, Balor's crew released Ansel. Not because he'd escaped their clutches, but because he no longer could.

Blood stung Ansel's eyes and coated his tongue. His knees buckled, and he collapsed to the floor. When they began punishing his ribs with their boots, some distant part of Ansel's consciousness urged him to utilize this opportunity, in case he ever managed to escape. He might never be able to get this close to Balor again.

Using the last of his strength, he latched onto one of the guards' boots, clamping it against his chest. With movements so quick that no one would notice, he slipped a tiny tracking device from his belt and jabbed its spike into the boot's rubber sole before its owner managed to thrash away, kicking Ansel in the chin so hard his teeth clashed together and copper flooded his mouth.

Balor approached, looming over Ansel with a leer. Flickering over the hard mask of the man who'd betrayed him were memories of the soft features belonging to a boy who had been his friend.

"Do you know what a friend is?" Balor had asked the day he noticed Ansel huddled and starving at the base of an oak tree. "Friends are people who'd do anything for each other."

He gave Ansel a stolen crust of bread, and Ansel gave him his devotion.

He'd followed Balor's rules of friendship, doing all the things he asked—far more bad than good—but in the end, Balor betrayed him. Abandoned him.

Vaguely, Ansel was aware of four of the men pinning him to the disgusting carpet and Balor pressing his boot to his windpipe. "I could kill you, you know."

Ansel rolled his eyes as well as he was able, considering one was swelling shut. He was determined not to let Balor hurt him again—not in the way beyond the physical, the way that ached long after bruises and bones healed.

"I won't," said Balor. "But I could. Perhaps you don't deserve mercy, but I always did cherish our friendship more than you did."

Ansel's vision darkened. No matter how he thrashed and writhed, he could not escape the pressure of Balor's boot grinding him into the ground the same way Balor had crushed his loyalty beneath his heel.

Don't read this, Della, Ansel silently pleaded. He'd never make her smile. Ultimately, the only thing he'd make her do was cry. For she would be the type to cry over a book.

"Let this be a reminder to never cross me again." Balor's

voice seemed to come from very far away. "You will never be free, especially of me."

Ansel felt the cold tip of a knife carving something into the soft flesh on the inside of his bicep. He shivered, throat too raw to scream.

Ansel's vision tunneled, his thoughts turning too slippery to hold on to. He thought of Della's letters, how open and trusting she'd been, laying her heart at his feet. He couldn't decide if she was unaware that she could get hurt or if she simply didn't care if she did. She had a quiet reckless streak, rebelling in small ways against a universe that wanted to break her—caring when she had no reason to, remaining soft when the world had done its best to harden her.

Ansel refused to look at what was happening to his arm, but he could feel the knife's slick drag, etching letters into his skin. In one last flash of stubborn spite, he ignored the letters by writing one of his own.

Della Dear,

Rest assured that I will still look devilishly handsome in an orange jumpsuit.

I once said that magic was just unexplained science. I still believe that's true, but you've shown me the beauty in leaving things unexplained. Instead of scrambling for answers, maybe we should pause and let ourselves enjoy that brief moment between discovery and understanding when anything is possible. When dreams have the opportunity to come true. When fortuitous card games aren't traps and happy endings are guaranteed. When you and I were destined for greater things.

Now, the moment between dreams and reality has closed. The fact is, there was no reason fate decided to throw us together. We are nothing more than a strange anomaly, a coincidence, a glitch in time and space.

You defied destiny by choosing to say hello, despite the fact that our paths weren't meant to cross. I think that means more than if we were written in the stars. The universe is cruel, and I detest the idea of being a pawn in its schemes. I would rather meet you despite fate than because of it.

Don't weep for me. Laugh at me, the foolish thief who let you steal a piece of his heart.

Your charming, majestic, glorious, et cetera acquaintance of twenty-four spectacular hours,
Ansel.

When blackness took Ansel, the last thought on his mind was:

P.S. I'm sorry.

CHAPTER 9

When Della finished reading, she did cry. She cried for Ansel, and she cried for herself. She cried for her stupid, spoiled dreams, for her shredded dignity, for her lost employment, for her ailing mother whom she had failed. She cried for the little girl she used to be who believed there was goodness, adventure, and joy to be found everywhere. Perhaps she was better off surrendering her destiny back to fate. For if she'd simply accepted her humble place in the world, none of this would ever have happened.

A little later—Della didn't know how long—ink bleeding onto the pages of the book in her lap caught her attention, forming new words. She wiped her eyes and read, the paragraphs blurry in her watery vision.

Ansel awoke to a prison guard hauling him out of an airlock and down a hall. Luckily, or perhaps unluckily, the atmosphere in the building appeared to be compatible with Ansel's biology because he had not yet dropped dead. The guard stopped at an empty cell and shoved him inside before slamming the door.

Ansel sprawled on the floor, staring at the ceiling. His every breath was strained and agonizing, his ribs jabbing his lungs with each shallow inhale. It took a few minutes

before he managed to lift his head and take in his surroundings.

These were not the bleached white walls of a Cooperation prison. The room was constructed of dark, dingy cement. No windows, though the prison door was transparent, made of a thick pane of foggy polycarbonate. He realized he must be in some local establishment, probably meant to hold him until a Cooperation warden came to collect him.

Della's heart throbbed painfully. Ansel was alive, thank goodness. She wished his story was like any other book that she could stop reading when the tale became too painful to bear. But she couldn't simply set his book aside; she had to help him somehow.

Perhaps she could try writing him free, but writing in the books before had resulted in catastrophe. While the things she and Ansel wrote came true in roundabout ways, if she wrote that Ansel escaped, he likely wouldn't magically blink and find himself transported out of prison. Instead, a dreadful accident might occur—Ansel might choke or bleed out from his injuries—and his exit from the prison might be made in a body bag. Any idea she came up with had a thousand ways it could go dreadfully wrong.

More words filled the page.

With a groan, Ansel rolled to his knees. Sharp pain pinched his rib cage. His head throbbed. His tongue felt dry and too big for his mouth. They'd taken his space suit, gear, and the winnings from the card game. He patted his hip only to find the pouch on his belt was empty. Icy fingers of dread clamped around his heart, and he cursed viciously.

Della's book was gone. Either some prison guard—or worse, Balor—had it now.

No.* It was the only thought in his mind. *No, no, no.

Ansel staggered to his feet and limped to the door. Gritting his teeth, he shoved his shoulder against the door with

all his might. Pain lanced through him as he jostled his injuries, and he let out a broken sound of frustration. His every nerve screamed at him to stop, but he slammed himself into the solid polycarbonate again. The door creaked but didn't budge. Sweat beaded over his brow, and his breaths turned ragged. His strength gave out halfway into his third shove. Collapsing weakly against the door, he slid to his knees.

Gasping, he rested his palms against the damp, sweating pane, squinting to see if there were any guards outside who might have seen his futile attempts at escape. He should have looked for them before, but his mind wasn't working right—too frantic and clouded with pain and desperation.

For a moment, Ansel thought the polycarbonate was old and hazy, making the hall beyond look dark and distorted. Then he realized that at some point after he'd been locked in his cell, the hallway had been filled with water. He'd seen safety measures like this taken in other high-security prison wings—filling the halls with substances uninhabitable to the prisoners within. Even if Ansel managed to get out of his cell, the swim down the water-filled hall to the airlock at the end was a long one. Probably impossible, especially in his state, and without his space suit. The good news—if there *was* good news—was that there weren't any guards out there. Why bother patrolling when he'd kill himself trying to escape?

Ansel let out a sound somewhere between a sob and a delirious laugh. Claustrophobia constricted his heart. The walls of his tiny cement air bubble seemed to press in on him. He rested his forehead against the door, knotting his jaw to keep from screaming in outraged defeat. His crew would be forced to leave when he didn't return. The only one who would bear witness to his fate was . . . Della. He wondered if she'd stopped reading when he'd begged her to.

No. Of course she wouldn't have. She would read about him weak and broken and giving up, and she'd worry over him.

If whatever had happened to her had been as unpleasant as what happened to him, she had no business concerning herself with his problems. She'd been in a barn for some reason, and he needed to find out why. More than that, he had to get her book back before anyone figured out what it was. Escape was vital.

Opening his eyes, Ansel reexamined the cell door, which remained as impenetrable as ever. Not a surprising thing for a prison door to be, but still disappointing. Furthermore, it didn't appear to have a digital lock like the ones at Cooperation prisons. Those, Ansel might be able to hack. The primitive contraption on the other side of the door securing it shut was something Ansel had only heard about but never seen: a padlock.

Della froze. Here, at last, was favorable news.

Because Della knew how to pick a lock.

Of course, it did her little good when she couldn't communicate with Ansel, and she wasn't there to help.

Unless . . . maybe she could be.

Maybe she could write herself into his story. Instead of trying to write the lock open, she could rescue him herself without needing to rely on magic's fickle whims.

It probably wasn't possible, though. Everything they'd written for themselves had only come true in a way that was feasible, given the laws of reality. No fancy dress had appeared out of thin air, nor had fifty thousand credits materialized in Ansel's pockets. Therefore, if Della tried to write herself to Ansel, it was likely nothing would happen at all, as was the case when Ansel had tried to write her his jacket.

Then again, maybe she and Ansel were the exceptions to the rules.

She had to try. Not only was Ansel in danger, so was she, depending on who held her book. Or perhaps part of her was just looking for a reason to dive into his story because she never felt at home in her own. Maybe it was her mother in her, compelling her to turn misfortunes into adventure.

Whatever the reason, it would be a quick thing. She would write herself into Ansel's story, free him, recover her book, and be home by morning to seek new employment.

Goodness. It was astonishing how greatly her mental checklists had changed. They had gone from things like *go to the market* to *visit another world and rescue a rakish starship captain.*

Grabbing the book, Della hopped to her feet and climbed down the loft ladder to the stables below, her heart beating wildly against her ribs. After some rummaging, she procured the nub of a pencil sitting next to a ledger.

She considered what she should write. Part of her thought she ought to be as specific as possible. Then again, including more details only provided magic with more ways to tamper with her wishes.

So, hunching over Ansel's book, in her best penmanship, Della wrote: *Della arrived at the prison that held Ansel.*

Plummeting into Ansel's book felt like the sensation of falling one might experience right before drifting off to sleep. Della dipped into blackness, and her stomach sank down, down, down. As her thoughts swam, a long-faded memory jostled loose, sharpening as it swirled before her mind's eye.

Della first picked a lock when she was seven.

She had been too sick to go to school, so her mother smuggled her into the kitchen of the home where she worked as a housekeeper.

Della soon grew bored. Knowing her mother often sneaked home books from the library without her employer ever noticing their absence, Della decided to fetch one to pass the time.

She found the library easily enough, thanks to the directions of a scullery maid, but when she tiptoed up to the door, it was locked.

It took her more than a few bent hairpins to manage the lock, but once she was inside, she was rewarded with shelves upon shelves of books. She knew she had to hurry before she was discovered, so she snatched the first book she came across and retreated to the kitchen.

It was about a young boy, Riktel, who must have been the size of a tiny insect because he lived under a bulging tree root protruding from a forest floor. His people lived like creatures of the forest. As soon as a child was able to survive on his own, he was thrown from the nest, expected to make his own way in the world. But the boy had no interest in finding a trade or building a home or one day taking mates of his own. He wanted more, though he couldn't vocalize what. All he knew was that the life expected of him felt empty, meaningless.

Every interaction he experienced with another person served only as a means to survive, nothing more. Mates stayed together only long enough to raise their young. Personal contact was initiated only to pick a bug from a neighbor's hair or to share body heat during a cold night. Farmers and bakers and tailors conducted their business with a smile, but as soon as they received their half of a trade, went on their way, leaving the boy's half-spoken question of "How are you today?" dying on his lips.

"You ask too many questions." He'd heard it his whole life. No one understood him. They laughed when he invented a device that could play a tune like a songbird out of a reed or stained a sunset onto a canvas with berries, asking him what purpose such nonsense served.

People thought him odd, and once he was on his own, no one would take him as an apprentice. It was for the best. He couldn't bear the thought of becoming a docile, compliant part of the circle of life. So he lived on the outskirts of civilization, surviving off the land when he could, swiping food from those who cast him out when he couldn't. And still, he wished for more.

After reading about the boy, Della returned the book to its place before her mother came to fetch her, and no one was ever the wiser.

That night, when she slipped into bed, she dreamed that she was in Riktel's world. The trees plunged into the sky, so high she couldn't see the tops, for she too had shrunk to the size of an insect. Her bare feet padded over soft pine needles, a cool breeze teased the ends of her hair, and she smelled rain and earth—and then she met a dirty little boy about her age sitting on a tree root.

She asked him, "How are you today?"

Riktel gazed at her with wonder and tears glimmering in his eyes and said, "Better now."

She taught him what a friend was. They played hide-and-seek, and he always found her.

PART 2

OUTSIDE OF TIME AND SPACE, a young librarian fell in love with a book.

More specifically, she fell in love with a man in a book. The son of a poet, his dry wit in the face of his misfortunes never failed to brighten her spirit. But his story was a tragedy, and she could only helplessly watch the pages filling day after day as he raced toward his predestined ruinous end.

As he sank into deeper and deeper despair, she longed to do something to ease his suffering. She knew changing the books was forbidden, but she simply wanted him to know he was not alone.

A librarian must never deface a library book, but she did the unthinkable and penned a letter into his story. Though they were from different dimensions, she knew he'd be able to understand her words, for there was one power the library granted its keepers, and that was the gift of language. To read, speak, and understand any tongue in any world.

It wasn't long before it was discovered what she had done. Her letter had given the man hope, too much hope. It bolstered his resolve, and soon his ending twisted into something new, altering the trajectory of his life until his book no longer fit in the genre that destiny had assigned.

The library suffered. Shelves began to crack, ink to bleed, pages to tear. The order of the library had been disrupted, and realities blurred together.

The situation had to be rectified, the apprentice taught a lesson. In normal circumstances, librarians were never allowed to write themselves into stories, but this was a special case.

The elders sent her into the book so she could undo all the good she had wrought. To ensure the story ended how it ought. To be the man's undoing.

CHAPTER 10

When Della's eyes snapped open and she tried to reorient herself back to reality, reality had shifted. Gone was the scent of hay and horse. Gone were the rough barn wood and soft moonlight.

The air here, wherever *here* was, was stale and cool. As her eyes adjusted to the dreariness, she could make out a tiny dark room. The walls were some kind of stone, smooth and flat. She still had Ansel's book clutched to her chest, which confused her, seeing as they hadn't been able to transport Ansel's jacket through the books before. Perhaps since she was holding the book, she was able to carry it with her. That would explain why her clothes also made the trip—thank heavens.

As she caught her breath, she pondered the snippet of her childhood she'd remembered. She'd forgotten about Riktel's book—likely thanks to the fever that muddled her memories. She used to be so lonely that she dreamed of making friends with book characters, and now here she was *literally* in a book. Ansel's book.

"Who are you?" A low voice behind Della sent a shiver down her spine. It rasped over an edge of unmistakable pain.

Slowly, she turned. On the other side of the cramped quarters stood a man. Since the room was only about eight feet wide, he was quite close. Close enough that he could reach her in moments if he decided to act. He wore a leather coat, dark trousers, and suspenders. Half his white shirt was soaked with blood. Where the shirt was open at his neck, his chest glistened with a sickly film of sweat. And his face . . . She gasped a little. A purple bruise marred half of it, swelling his eye shut. A cut slashed across his stubbled jawline, a trail of dried blood tracking down his neck. His eyes held the wild sheen of a trapped animal. In a way, she supposed he was.

"Ansel?" she breathed.

Though his expression was one of confusion, the words that left his mouth were as cocky as ever. "If I'd known angels of death looked like you, I might've gotten myself killed years ago."

He had to be delirious if he thought she was some divine being come to spirit him away. Of course, the first thing Ansel *would* do upon encountering a goddess of death was flirt with her. Then again, he probably wasn't a stranger to flirting with death.

"Oh heavens" was all she managed, words escaping her grasp.

"We both know I'm not going there. Don't be a tease."

Della couldn't stop looking at him. She couldn't have imagined him even if she had tried.

Ansel was too rugged to be considered handsome in any conventional sense. He would look like a wild boar sitting next to the Duke of Eshford's aristocratic friends. Judging by the bumps of his nose, it had been broken a few times, and the challenging set of his jaw looked like an open unspoken invitation to fight, yet there was an allure to his tangle of curls, wild dark brows, and expressive mouth. She could hardly believe this hardened outlaw had lent her his daydream jacket and called her *Della dear.*

Without the pages translating his words, she wondered briefly how it was that she could understand him, considering their books were written in different languages. Then again, of all the impossibilities of the last few days, this one peculiarity was rather minor. The intricacies of magic defied comprehension.

"Say something." Ansel's voice drew her from her thoughts. "Am I dying or not?"

"It's me," she squeaked, sounding less like a bold, adventurous heroine and more like a field mouse. "Ansel, it's me, Della."

Ansel's lips parted, and his expression fractured. "*Della?*" His gaze swept up and down her form. He took a cautious step forward—and goodness, he was rather a hulking man, muscular and broad. "Tell me you haven't died too." The knot in Ansel's throat bobbed. "You shouldn't have ended up here, in the same place I did."

She shook her head. "Neither of us died. I just—I wrote myself into your book?" She phrased it as a question because she could hardly believe it herself.

"That's impossible." He lifted a hand as though to touch her, before he thought better of it and curled his fingers back. She noted the way he kept his other arm tucked against his injured ribs.

He blinked rapidly, his eyes glassy and feverish. Then he shrugged out of his jacket and handed it to her as though he couldn't have done anything else in that moment, even if the earth had opened and the sky had fallen.

"What is this?" she asked.

"You're cold."

Was she? She supposed she was. The cell was hardly warmer than the loft had been. The skin of her hands was pink and raw from the chill, and she realized her cheeks must be in much the same state. She slipped the jacket on, and—oh my. It did smell nice. Behind the musk of sweat and blood, there was a hint of faded cologne that made her want to close her eyes and inhale.

"Why were you in a barn?" he demanded, causing her to refocus.

"I hardly think the inconsequential details of my evening

are the most pressing matters at hand." She had no urge to relive the events that landed her in the stable.

"Why are you here?" he asked, like he couldn't make sense of his own thoughts.

"I've come to break you out?" she said timidly, again as though it were a question. Inwardly, she groaned. Only she could make a grand rescue sound like *could you pass me a scone, please?*

"But *why*?" He shook his head, arms dangling limply at his side.

"I have hairpins," she whispered.

"That's . . . commendable?" Ansel's voice was strained, whether from extreme physical pain or the mental agony of having to endure a conversation with her.

At the very least, couldn't he manage a *thank you*? Here he was, looking at her like she was the reason his day was ruined, which was really saying something considering the man had crashed his ship into an ocean, won and lost fifty thousand credits, and been captured by his mortal enemy, whose men proceeded to beat him soundly before tossing him into prison.

"The hairpins are why I needed to come here," Della explained. "I know how to pick locks with hairpins, you see." She stole a look at the door and grimaced. "Of course, little good they do us when we're trapped on this side of the door. I should have known the book wouldn't have landed me in the most ideal of conditions. Though I suppose being landed underwater in the hall would have been far worse." She was babbling. She never babbled. She did the opposite of babbling.

It was Ansel's steady, dark gaze. It was unnerving. Most people looked through her, only sparing her a brief glance when they needed something. He wasn't just paying attention. He was focused, as though she were his one concern, despite his aforementioned misfortunes.

"Why are you here?" he asked helplessly for a third time.

That was when she realized what he meant, and her heart

softened. He could not comprehend why anyone would *bother* going to the trouble of rescuing him. Several responses came to mind, but none felt quite right. *Because I like you. Because I got you into this. Because you're kind.* "Because you lent me your coat," she said, proud of the fact that her voice only wavered a little. "I owed you a favor."

"Stars above. Those books really are . . . something." Ansel let out a long breath. "But look, you and your hairpins don't belong here. Whatever you did to get yourself here, undo it now before it's too late. If you're found helping me, they'll lock you up too."

"I'm not leaving until we recover my book."

Ansel's eyes flew open. "Wait—the books. You have *my* book." With two long strides, he closed the distance between them and slipped the book from her limp fingers. "And you still have a pen, clever girl." He whisked the pencil from her other hand while she was preoccupied, blushing over his unexpected praise. "Never mind your hairpins. I'll write us out. Then we'll find your book, and you can go home."

Oh. Oh no. Not the magic again. Della opened her mouth. Croaked. Wet her lips. Tried again. "Ansel." It came out far too hushed. "I don't think that's a good idea." Again, too quiet.

And too late. He'd already flipped the book open and scrawled a few lines, his grin confident. "There. Fixed."

A metallic groan sounded throughout the room, the screeching amplified to unbearable decibels in the cramped space. Della and Ansel's eyes locked. Mixed with her feelings of impending doom was the realization that he had lovely eyes—dark, striking, exquisite. The sound of rushing water swiftly drowned out that realization and replaced it with a new one: As soon as she had a chance, she was going to shake Ansel senseless. It wouldn't take terribly long; his actions indicated he was already mostly there.

"What have you done?" Della's gaze flew to the door, which

had unlatched a few inches, though the chain and padlock kept it from opening all the way. Water rushed through the gap, reaching her shoes in moments and swiftly coating the entire floor.

"I wrote that we escaped," Ansel said. His cringe was trying valiantly to look contrite, but he couldn't quite pull it off. "No matter. I'll just write the door all the way open." He lifted his pen once more. "Don't worry, Della. A quick swim to the airlock, and we'll be free."

Della darted forward and wrenched the pencil from his grip, frigid water swirling about her ankles. "You will do no such thing. Suppose the door flies off its hinges and crushes you against the far wall? Haven't you noticed everything we write goes poorly? We must think things through."

"What other choice do we have?" He tried to pluck the pencil from her fingers.

She held on. "Stop panicking."

"I'm not panicking. Everything is fine." He gave the pencil another tug.

She yanked it back. "I've noticed the more you insist things are fine, the less likely it is to be true."

Ansel's grip slipped unexpectedly, causing the pencil to go flying from Della's hand. It tumbled end over end until it landed with a plop in the knee-deep water. Della's stomach dropped right along with it.

"You foolish, hasty man!" Sinking to the floor, Della groped beneath the freezing water, searching desperately for the pencil. "Your mind is obviously muddled, leaving you in no state to be making decisions."

"Don't act like all of this isn't your fault." Ansel's voice rose as he stowed the book into a pocket on his belt before dropping down beside her.

"*My* fault?"

"I can't stop thinking about you!" he shouted, as though it

were an accusation. "If I hadn't been distracted, I would have seen the ambush coming."

"You are horrid," she decided.

"Quite!" he yelled before lowering his voice to a reasonable volume. "Here's an idea." He'd clearly decided to ignore her implication that all his ideas were complete rubbish. "Once we find the pencil, we write that nothing terrible happens to us ever again. Magic won't be able to make us miserable after that. Besides, who says magic is all bad? You managed to write yourself here without suffering too much, right?"

"Yes, I'm having a marvelous time," Della snapped with more venom than she thought herself capable. "You realize a request like that would get us killed, right? Nothing terrible can happen to us if we're *dead.*"

"If we write that nothing terrible happens to us, then we won't die," Ansel argued.

"Death isn't terrible when we're both too dead to realize we're dead!" Della's skirts billowed in the water. It was impossible to see past the surface. The room's dimness made their hunt a blind effort. Della's hands began to shake. In her squatted position, the water was nearing her neck. "Just . . . keep looking." She rose to her feet and tugged her hairpins loose. "I'm going to work on the door."

With limbs made heavy from the cold press of water, Della fought her way to the door. It was open just far enough that she could reach her arms through the gap. Water gushed against her chest, doing its best to pummel her away. Fighting against it, she latched her fingers around the padlock on the other side of the door. The current tried to rip the hairpin from her hand, and salty water sprayed into her eyes and mouth.

She jammed the pin in the keyhole, but it was impossible to feel or hear the tumblers. With her numbing fingers, her efforts to work the hairpin were flailing and clumsy. Della couldn't quite remember why she'd ever found the idea of oceans appealing.

As she worked, the water crept to her chin, and she had to crane her neck to keep her head above the surface. A coil of fear wound tightly in the back of her throat, but she refused to cry. Desperation kept her on task as she twisted and worked the hairpin.

"I can't find the pencil. Please tell me you've nearly got the door open." Ansel's voice grew muffled as waves licked at her ears. "I hope you're ready to swim."

"I *can't* swim, you wretched man," she spat.

"*Oh.* Fuck me," he muttered.

She didn't turn to see his face, but the tone of his voice indicated it had finally dawned on him just how much trouble they were in.

When Della could no longer stand with her nose above the water, she took a deep breath and plunged beneath. Her lungs burned as she fought the padlock. A few seconds. A few more seconds and maybe she'd have it.

Strong hands wrapped around her arms and hauled her to the surface. She coughed and sputtered, her head bumping against the room's ceiling. She was shocked to find a mere foot of air remained.

Ansel pushed hair away from her face, his big palms warm against her cheeks. "Della, you shouldn't have come. You dreamed for me and hoped for me and now you'll die for me."

"Do you truly think now is the ideal time for a soliloquy?" Della asked, the situation making her far more brash than she'd ordinarily be. "Let me go. I've almost got it!"

He blinked in surprise, like he'd been fully ready to deliver a farewell speech, then lurched back into action. "Then take the jacket off so it doesn't drag us down once you get the lock open." He was already pushing it over her shoulders and yanking the sleeves down her arms.

Rather unused to being manhandled and efficiently undressed by men with gorgeous eyes and roguish smiles, Della slightly lost her train of thought.

"Once we're out, I'll need you to kick, okay?" Ansel's voice was strangely both muffled by water and too loud in the tight space.

She nodded, took a few gulps of stale air, then wrenched herself free of Ansel's grip and let her skirts drag her back down to the bottom of the room.

The hairpin was still jammed in the lock, and she went right back to work. The current had calmed now that the room had nearly filled. When she opened her eyes, she could just make out her surroundings, the light beneath the waves tinged greenish. Her pulse throbbed behind her eardrums. Her chest ached.

The padlock sprang open in Della's hands.

At first, she thought her mind was playing tricks on her, providing her with one last daydream, but no. The door was unlatched.

And then Ansel was there, grabbing her wrist, shouldering the cell door the rest of the way open, and tugging her into the hall. She tried to turn around, to get one more gulp of air from the cell, but he shook his head, and her spirits sank. He must have drawn his final breath right as the water swallowed up the rest of the air pocket, then dove down to her.

The only path was forward.

Following Ansel's lead, Della kicked her feet and churned water with her free arm as he swam toward the door at the end of the hall. Her skirts twisted around her legs, weighing down her movements. The excursion siphoned the oxygen from her body.

Bubbles spewed from her nostrils, dancing before her darkening vision. She would never make it. They were only halfway there.

Della's lungs devoured whatever oxygen was left in her

blood. Her eyes and muscles and chest burned, burned, burned. She had to fight to keep her jaw locked as her body demanded she breathe. More bubbles escaped. It felt as though her rib cage was turning inside out. It was no use. She had to breathe. *Had* to.

Ansel's hand around her wrist gave her a firm tug. She drifted into him, their bodies colliding, legs tangling together. She tried to flail, to get out of his way so that he might at least have a chance to make it, even if she couldn't. His hand slipped from her wrist. For a moment, she thought she'd succeeded, that he understood her unspoken message and would leave her behind. Then his palms cupped her face and he dragged her flush against him, the press of his body warming her skin. Quite before she knew what was happening, his mouth was on hers, hot and demanding.

The shock of it jarred a few more bubbles loose, but he gripped her tighter, and she forgot about breathing altogether. His mouth pried hers open, and he forced air into her lungs, reminding her in no uncertain terms that she was to breathe, and he would show her how.

Recognizing the kiss for the rescue it was, she accepted his breath with relief. The air was stale and nearly spent, but as they passed it back and forth, it fooled her body into thinking it wasn't suffocating. That final breath he'd taken while she'd still been working the lock was just enough to steady her. It was not a kiss. There was no passion or love. It was simply necessary. Yet she couldn't help noticing how surprisingly soft his lips were, how skilled and intentional.

He parted from her on an exhale, leaving her lungs full. When cold water again touched her lips, she had to be careful to keep them sealed, even though she immediately missed his presence.

Weaving his fingers with hers, Ansel pulled her onward. Della kicked after him, finding herself quite revitalized.

Nonetheless, by the time they reached the door, her head

throbbed. Her lungs once again grabbed desperately for air, clawing at her throat, demanding she breathe.

Ansel punched a glowing orb next to the door, which caused it to whisk open. They swam inside, and the door shut. A half second passed in which Della thought she surely wouldn't make it a moment more.

Then an oddly lifeless female voice said something unintelligible, her words distorted by the water, and a drain opened in the floor. Della kicked for the ceiling as the water swirled downward. The current tried to suck her with it, but she fought her way past, her face cresting the surface just enough that she could gasp and cough against the dripping ceiling tiles.

Ansel broke the surface next to her. It took him a moment to manage to fill his lungs, as though they were stuck together. When he at last found air, his breaths were shuddering and broken.

The water drained swiftly, carrying them back down to the floor, where they crumpled into gasping, choking heaps. With a mighty creak, the walls around them opened, revealing large windmill-looking contraptions. They spun to life, blasting the pair with warm gusts so powerful, they nearly knocked Della off her knees. Within seconds, they were both dry, and the walls closed back over the devices.

Della and Ansel staggered to their feet, still fighting to catch their breath. Before they could though, the door on the far wall whooshed open, making Della jolt with surprise. A strange figure in uniform charged through, a knife raised in his taloned fist. Della let out a squeak, bracing for impact. It came in the form of Ansel's hand shoving her behind him as he stepped between her and their attacker.

Della heard a solid, wet thud and let out a soft cry, expecting Ansel to collapse dead. She opened her eyes to instead find him pulling a knife out of his shoulder and, without a second thought, as if such things happened to him every day, he buried that same knife into the guard's thigh. He was reaching for her nearly before the deed was done.

She grabbed his hand because she had no idea what else to do. As they darted around the wailing guard, Ansel snatched a rectangular card hanging from a ribbon off his neck. Della's gaze snagged on the strange gray contours of the guard's elongated snout and long, pointed ears. She wished she had time to study him longer, but as he was bellowing and reaching for another weapon on his belt with murderous intent, that seemed unwise.

She and Ansel ran to the door through which the creature had entered. Ansel waved the card he'd stolen from the guard in front of some kind of glowing panel on the wall, which seemed to cause the door to unlock, because it opened. Once they were through, he elbowed another panel on the opposite side to shut it again, trapping their attacker inside.

"Are you dying?" she asked, feeling as though it was a perfectly reasonable question, given the knife incident.

"I don't appear to be, but I bet you'll know if that changes." Ansel sounded a bit too surprised by his self-assessment to be comforting.

A long, low tone wailed through the building, and lights began flashing, illuminating the narrow hall in red. "What's happening?" Della asked.

"Alarms," Ansel grunted without slowing his pace as he dragged her along. He shielded her face as he pointed to a red blinking orb tucked high in a corner. "They have cameras. Don't let them see you." She began to ask what those were, but he was already explaining. "They're like eyes that other people can watch you through."

Fascinating. If she had extra eyes, Della would scatter them throughout the world so she could slip away whenever she wanted. Her real eyes could be looking at Mrs. Loughty as she ordered her about, but Della would be far away, gazing across a field of wildflowers in a mountain valley.

"May I have one—a camera?" she asked right as another guard burst around the corner, a glinting black weapon raised. For a moment, Della couldn't figure out what it was, but then she realized it must be some kind of pistol, though it looked far sleeker than the heavy flintlock handguns gentlemen waved about when they pretended to duel each other back home.

Ansel slammed the guard against the wall, pinning his wrist by his side and wrenching the weapon free of his grip. A swift knock of the butt of the pistol to the guard's temple, and he collapsed to the floor. Ansel aimed the gun at another one of those eyes mounted to the wall and fired. Della jumped as a bolt of light shot from the pistol and exploded against the eye, shattering it to pieces. An immense wave of heat washed over her in the blast's wake. The experience was far different from the crack and gunpowder of the muzzleloaders she was familiar with.

"I suppose that answers my question about the camera," she said under her breath.

Ansel tugged her down a second hall. "We need to get out of here and find a ship."

"Your crew is still here," she said.

He shook his head. "If that clock on the wall is correct, we're long past the time we agreed they'd leave if I hadn't returned. They're gone."

"They wouldn't abandon you. They care about you too much for that."

He snorted. "Right. I forgot."

"You infernal man." She nearly stomped her foot. "What's more important, your own stubborn self-pity or our survival? I demand you find a way to contact your crew so they can come pick us up."

"You think that'll work, huh? That they can just swing by and pick us up? It's a prison break, not a night out with friends."

"You're far more pleasant inside your head than you are outside of it," she remarked.

The clatter of boots on a hard floor pounded toward them. Ansel whisked her into a half-open door, huddling her inside a room that appeared to be a closet. It was cramped, and she found herself pressed against him, her forearms to his chest.

She didn't know what to make of him face to face, this man who groused at her one second and gave her his last breath the next. Attempting to read his book was difficult enough when he tried to hide certain facets of his consciousness, but it was nothing compared to the impossible task of reading his body language in the flesh.

"Oh dear, you're bleeding," she whispered, registering the warm dampness seeping through her sleeves.

He pressed his hand to his shoulder and coughed out a wry laugh. "Knife wounds have an annoying tendency to do that."

"You know, I think meeting while our lives were in danger was fortunate. It spared us all the awkwardness, don't you think? I wouldn't have known how to speak to you if I had to politely introduce myself instead of saying things like, 'Goodness, you foolish man, must every decision you make lead to mayhem?'"

"Every decision I make does not lead to mayhem."

"You nearly drowned us." Della bent over, reaching for her hem. When she found her petticoat, she deftly tore a strip off the bottom and straightened. "Pull down your shirt."

"If you're intending to ravish me against a wall, know that I won't object, but I do prefer to be dined beforehand."

Della flushed. "I only mean to bind your wounds."

He sighed, but took the strip of fabric from her and clumsily started wrapping it around his injured shoulder with one hand, over his ruined shirt. Remembering what Balor had done to Ansel's arm, Della assumed he didn't want to face the mutilation just yet.

"You didn't kill that man who attacked us," she noted, feeling his warm breath on her neck as she helped him tie the binding.

"I don't kill when it can be helped." His voice was low in her ear. "None of the crew do—well, we're still working on Yaggrel."

Della finished tying and pulled away. "Then why is it you have such a high bounty on your head? Surely there are worse criminals in the galaxy than a thief."

"The Cooperation is not a fair justice system."

"Justice systems rarely are. What makes yours unjust?"

"The Cooperation is an infrastructure of prisons funded by the citizens of the galaxy for its protection. Bounty hunters enforce the laws of each planet and are paid by the Cooperation, which keeps a percentage of each bounty. How long a criminal spends in jail depends on how long that percentage can pay to keep him there."

Ansel fell quiet as another group of guards thundered past their hiding place. When they were gone, he continued. "Some planets collect taxes and use the funds to post predetermined bounties, based on the crime committed. Some planets, like Lumeria, don't have governments, and the citizens collect credits to post a bounty themselves. Since I angered a great deal of people by supposedly stealing their protection, a lot of people donated."

"What if a poor person is wronged on Lumeria?" Della asked. "What if the victim is someone without community support and no funds to pay for justice?"

Ansel didn't respond, which was answer enough.

After listening to ensure the coast was clear, he opened the closet door and stepped back into the hallway. "Let's just say it's a good thing you rescued me, else I'd be spending a very long time behind bars."

"It *was* fairly heroic, wasn't it?" she asked timidly, feeling rather pleased with herself.

"A feat of remarkable bravery." He studied her, something dangerously close to a smile curving the corner of his mouth. It was as though he himself was just now taking in the full scope of what she'd done to get there.

A little flutter went through her at the force of his full attention and that smile, but she managed to keep her senses about her as they continued on their way.

Ansel nearly opened two more water-filled hallways before Della stopped him, incapacitated five more guards, and shot dozens more of those *cameras* he'd told her about before finally managing to find the storage room where his personal effects were held.

He rummaged through the bins arranged on the shelves until he found the correct one and set it on the counter, which was only the height of his knee, as the creature who worked behind it—who they stowed in a closet—was very short. He pulled out what Della assumed were his confiscated items: another pistol, some other unidentifiable gear, a helmet, and a small leather-bound book identical to the one Della found in the street.

"Thank the stars," he breathed.

"Is that . . . ?" she began, but he'd already handed it to her, and she read the spine: *Della Farley, vol. 84.*

How strange. His had been titled *Ansel Tulzok, vol. 5*, implying the previous years of his life were chronicled in four other books somewhere. Surely there was not enough material about a simple housemaid to fill eighty-four volumes.

"I'll find a pen, and you can write yourself back into your book." Ansel's voice drew her to the present.

That had been the plan, hadn't it? Break Ansel out, recover her book, and return home to find new employment.

Except, in his letters, Ansel mentioned there could be medicine on his home planet, Lumeria, that might help her mother.

She could try simply writing herself to Lumeria, but the book's magic always came with a dreadful consequence. Writing in the book the last time nearly drowned them, and Della wouldn't do her mother any good dead.

But maybe she could get to Lumeria without magic. She

could help Ansel defeat Balor and clear his name. In exchange, he could grant her passage aboard his ship. He'd take her home with him to Lumeria, where she would collect the medicine for her mother and return to Poling, all her problems solved. True, she might have to use magic, in the end, to write herself home if Ansel couldn't find a way to sail her back to her planet, but better to risk her life once instead of twice.

The chance of finding new employment back home with no references was slim, and anyway, the medicine in her own world might treat her mother's symptoms, but it wasn't enough to cure her. As preposterous as the idea might be, gallivanting across the universe with Ansel was her most promising chance of saving her mother.

It was time to take her future into her own hands.

"I'm not leaving," Della said.

"You're not *what*?" Ansel seethed.

"I'm not through rescuing you yet," she said, deciding there wasn't enough time to explain her plan and undoubtedly argue with him about it. "I'm not leaving until you're safe."

He snorted humorlessly. "Then you might as well consider my story your new home."

Della decided that was invitation enough for her. "Thank you."

"Della, I'm begging you to see reason. You can't just decide to stay."

"Oh, well, since you've told me I can't, I suppose that changes everything," she said. Little did he know that being told not to do something only tended to make Della more inclined to do the thing.

"You're a bit of a brat, aren't you, Della Farley?" But he said it with begrudging appreciation that made a warm glow of happiness bloom inside her chest. "You're determined not to leave until you see me off this planet?"

"Correct."

"*Then* you'll go home?"

"Absolutely." *Not,* she thought but didn't say.

All her hopes were here with him, but now didn't feel like the best time to introduce him to her plan. He saw her as a pitiable distraction at worst, a liability at best. Even if he enjoyed her company in his mind, he clearly didn't consider her fit to remain here by his side.

"Fine." He sighed.

"Truly?" she asked, surprised, knowing he could likely just take her book from his belt and write her home himself.

"We've both had enough people dictating our lives. I don't care to be one of them. I won't force you to do anything, even if that means you die a senseless death down here with me." He gave her a pointed look.

"We're not going to die. Your crew can help us. You can communicate with them now, can you not? With your helmet, or perhaps one of your other items?"

"I'm telling you. They're gone." But he lifted a strange cylindrical object from his gear and pressed something on the side that made a tiny green light blink on top. "Xaks? Are you there?"

Silence followed for a few moments before a reply came crackling back. "Captain? Is that you?" a smooth female voice issued through the speakers. "I'm freezing my circuits off. Have you almost made it back?"

"Not quite, Eryl," Ansel said. "Are Xaks and Yaggrel all right?"

"They're huddling for warmth, sir."

Ansel grimaced. "I'm sure they're thrilled."

"In your absence, Xaks has drawn up a full-course menu that features your testicles, fried and served three ways."

"A real pioneer in the culinary arts, isn't she?"

"On the contrary. Testicles are already considered a delicacy in multiple systems."

Ansel lowered his device long enough to give Della a look and say, "You're right. They adore me. Only your truest friends fantasize about chopping off your delicate bits."

When she'd read about him, Della had pictured Ansel delivering his quips with a quick, easy smile and a twinkle in his eye. In reality, that was not the case. His responses were spoken with a straight face and a wry tone that betrayed no true emotion. Briefly, she wondered what it would take to get his smooth, arrogant control to snap, and if she could be the one to do it.

"Look, Eryl," Ansel said into the speaking device. After a glance at Della, he turned his shoulder and muttered in a low voice, "Could you maybe . . . come pick me up?"

"Pick you up? You want me just to swing by and pick you up? To clarify, are you in prison, or enjoying a night out with friends?"

Della's smile broadened. Ansel noticed and rolled his eyes, though the corner of his mouth twitched. "Both."

CHAPTER 11

Ansel wrapped up his conversation with Eryl by delivering a rapid-fire rundown of instructions that included alarming sentences such as "Just blast the doors off the place," and "Of course you won't accidentally hit us with the plasma cannons, probably," and "Yes, you'll be detectable as soon as you fire up the engines—assuming they'll fire up—so you'll just have to do as we discussed before and outrun their missiles."

Della barely understood any of it, but from what she gathered, their chance of survival was not particularly high. Ansel's plans seemed to rely heavily on chance, which meant he was either very brave or very stupid, seeing as chance rarely favored him.

As soon as Ansel bid Eryl farewell, he began moving about the storage room, sliding containers off the shelf and digging through them, tossing them aside when he couldn't find what he wanted.

"What are you searching for?" Della asked. "Maybe I can help."

He dumped out the contents of one of the tubs and moved on to the next. "Since you refuse to write yourself home, we'll need a second space suit. Without one, as soon as Eryl blasts a hole in this place, the pressure of the ocean will crush us instantly."

"What an uplifting visual that is."

Fists began pounding on the door to the storage room, guttural voices shouting things like "Halt!" and "Open up!" The door shook in its frame, threatening to give out any second.

From the depths of the storage room, Ansel let out a sound of triumph and returned a moment later, a wrinkled, shabby-looking article of clothing in hand that looked like a pair of breeches and a shirt had been sewn together into one garment. "Jumpsuit," he said, noticing her confusion. "Other names include *space suit* and *uncomfortable.*" He found the bin holding all his effects and shoved it toward her. "Put mine on. I'll take this one."

With no time to argue, Della did as he asked. With much hopping and wriggling, they fought to wrestle on their garments. Ansel was hampered by his injuries, Della by her yards and yards of skirts. The knowledge that the prison could blow apart at any moment made her movements hurried and clumsy. In hindsight, it would have perhaps been easier to lose a few petticoats before attempting to cram them inside the suit, but it would take too long to start over now.

Ansel appeared before her, his suit on already. He shoved the last loop of her skirt down the leg hole of her jumpsuit before grabbing an eyelet on the front and pulling it up to her neck with a *zip* noise that fastened the whole suit together. Before she had time to blush over his knuckles grazing her collarbone, he'd grabbed his helmet from the table and slipped it over her head with an easy movement that indicated he'd done this enough times that it was second nature.

"Stay close." Ansel gave the helmet a little tap, jarring her head a bit. "If you see a bright ball of plasma barreling toward you . . . duck."

A distant rumble shook the floor beneath their feet. "What was that?" Della asked.

Ansel grinned. "They're here."

The wall in front of them exploded. Rubble, fire, and ocean

smashed together in elemental confusion. Water won out, scattering the debris. Ansel's hand latched onto Della's as the shock wave hit them, sending them tumbling head over heels in the churning current.

A large chunk of rubble knocked Della sideways, and her hand nearly slipped from Ansel's. She held on by her fingertips. Another dull boom vibrated her helmet as a blast of bright purple and blue shot past, instantly heating the water around her. A second explosion rattled the ocean. She looked over her shoulder but couldn't see much beyond bubbles and carnage. Fear coursed through her blood, yet she'd never felt so alive.

"Pinging you now, Eryl," Ansel's voice said into her ear, strangely tinny and distant. "Come to our location."

Della shook her head, unsure how she was able to hear him, then remembered reading about how helmets here were equipped with some sort of communication device. "Do hurry," she breathed.

"Who was that?" a new female voice asked, dry and gruff where the first was smooth and polished.

"Xaks, you're alive," Ansel said. "How unfortunate. I should have known I needed to wait a few minutes longer before calling Eryl. That cold heart of yours has strengthened your immunity. You've been unknowingly preparing for this day your whole life."

"Captain, respectfully, shut the fuck up," Xaks said. "Who are you bringing aboard?"

"Perhaps it's a strumpet," Eryl suggested helpfully.

"Ansel can't afford strumpets." Xaks dismissed that notion. "They upcharge him because of his personality."

Della didn't mind being called a strumpet. If she had a more charming disposition, she might consider the occupation herself. She was more concerned with how she would convince everyone to let her stay. Xaks didn't seem keen on the idea of welcoming a newcomer on board, and she didn't want to cause a rift among the crew.

"Well?" Ansel asked her, and she blinked to realize he'd swum them to the top of a large boulder overlooking the city. "There's an ocean for you."

She stared, unable to comprehend what she saw through her helmet's visor. There was a small cloud of destruction, sure, but beyond that, ocean plants swayed in the currents, their transparent gossamer fingers reaching toward the surface, and city lights sparkled in the distance. The explosion of color was blinding compared to Poling's monochromatic landscape.

Della turned to find Ansel looking at her, a strange, vulnerable expression on his face. It was as if . . . even though his story had subjected her to near drowning, mildly hurt feelings, and an explosion, he still held out hope that she didn't find her time in his universe completely miserable.

Della opened her mouth, but for the first time in what felt like ages, words failed her.

A shadow dropped over them, and she looked up to see the steel belly of a massive man-made creation. It was shaped vaguely like a ship, though it split into two cruelly pointed bows, and the masts were missing. Turrets poked out from all sides like the thorns of a honey locust. Blue lights glowed across the hull, casting the ocean floor in flat, otherworldly light. Windows recessed into the ship's various facets glinted wickedly. As the ship sank lower, Della could make out a patchwork of mismatched panels across the hull. Someone had painted a skull on the side, though it was doing a poor job of covering a string of numbers and the word *Cooperation*.

"There she is," Ansel's voice crackled through her helmet, inflated with pride he wasn't even trying to hide. "Miss Demeanor."

"Captain's special name for our D3-Meanor class starship," Eryl interjected before Della could ask. "He thinks he's clever, though my programming suggests wordplay is one of the lowest forms of humor."

"D3-Meanor sounds soulless," Ansel said. "We should address her like the lady she is."

"Adorable," Della said.

He sputtered. "*Adorable?*"

"Why, yes. The poor thing is doing its best to look intimidating, isn't it? But it can't quite manage it." Della purposefully didn't specify whether she was referring to the ship or Ansel.

"It manages it just fine," Ansel grumbled.

Truth be told, Della was more impressed by the (likely) stolen, (very) beat-up ship than she had any right to be but didn't think it would hurt Ansel to be knocked down a peg or two.

"I *am* rather adorable. Thank you for noticing, strumpet," Eryl's voice butted in. "I've been trying something new with my cannons."

"They do hold themselves rather jauntily," Della said. "Very fetching."

Ansel let out a peeved breath. "For the last time, Eryl, you are not the ship." He turned to Della and said, as an aside, "Being synced to the ship's computers has given her a bit of an identity crisis."

A distant *boom* rumbled behind them, followed by a streak of red light that arced over the city and zipped past the ship, causing it to shudder in the water. A prickle of trepidation ran down Della's spine, and she found herself reaching for Ansel's hand. More booms echoed after the first, filling the sea with deadly blurs of light.

"There are the missiles again," Ansel said. "Hurry up, Eryl."

The ship continued its descent, sinking rapidly until its side was level with their boulder. One of the missiles clipped the hull, knocking the ship into the boulder. Steel squealed against rock. Della lost her footing as the ground shook. Ansel caught her elbow before she could float away and urged her toward the ship. A door on the side slid open. A few powerful strokes of Ansel's arms sent them careening inside the opening.

As the door closed and the water drained from the room, Della struggled to keep her footing, thanks to the shuddering ship and her heavy space suit.

More rumbling booms threatened to rattle the ship apart. She was distantly aware of Ansel's voice in her helmet, yelling at his crew, "Fly, fucking *fly*. Go, go, go!"

A roar vibrated through the ship, so loud Della could feel it thrumming inside her rib cage. The floor tilted, and she fell to her knees. Ansel dropped down beside her, his hand finding the small of her back for support. The roar grew louder, then an immense pressure sent them sliding against the airlock wall in an awkward heap as the ship took off.

"This is going to be a rough ride," Ansel shouted in her speaker over the racket as she peeled herself off his chest. "Hold on."

Having nothing to hold on to besides Ansel, Della did just that, winding her fists into his space suit and squeezing her eyes shut. Her body began to feel too heavy, pinned back against the wall as though bricks rested upon her chest. The ship shook harder, rattling her teeth. She wondered if it was normal or if something was the matter with the vessel.

Ansel grabbed her elbow when she started to slide away. His fingers were hard around her arm, but no one had held her in so long, she liked that he gripped her as if he didn't want to let go. In his arms, she was finally able to catch her breath, even while the chaos reigned on.

Squinting an eye open, Della looked at the big, gloved hand gripping her so tightly. Ansel's thumb twitched, feathering over her space suit's sleeve. Della froze. The twitch softened into an unconscious caress, his thumb tracing a gentle curve against the inside of her elbow. A flutter tickled her belly. She glanced up at him, but he was staring ahead, jaw clenched. Since he didn't even appear to notice what he had done, she fought to compose herself.

Then all at once, everything went completely still.

With the absence of the missile fire, the silence was so absolute that for a moment, Della thought her ears failed her.

Ansel released her, and Della sat up. "Have we stopped?" she asked.

Wincing, Ansel peeled himself away from the wall. "No. We've only broken through the planet's atmosphere." He wearily took off his helmet and set it aside.

"Oh." She decided not to bother asking for a science lesson regarding *atmospheres*, or why they seemed to hold a particular animosity toward Ansel's poor ship. A pause ensued, then, "Sorry, I don't know what to do now." Looking down, she noticed her hands trembling. She'd scarcely had a chance to breathe, much less feel awkward, but now she had no idea how she was supposed to act.

Ansel stood stiffly. "You're coming down off adrenaline. It's normal."

"Pardon?" Her brows pinched.

He walked over to her and began unfastening her helmet. "Adrenaline. That fight-or-flight feeling you get in dangerous situations that increases blood flow, sharpens senses. Once your body isn't focused on survival anymore, it can leave you feeling a little lost."

"What do you do when you feel this way? Am I to have a little cry?"

"If you want." He lifted her helmet off, and cool air touched her too-tight lungs.

"Does it help?"

"Not really." Ansel hung the helmet on a hook on the wall.

"Then I suppose I won't bother."

For the first time, Della realized how cold it was in the ship. Her teeth chattered, and their breaths formed frosty clouds in the air. With fumbling fingers, she began working the rest of her space suit loose. Beside her, Ansel did the same, and her ears went hot at the sound of his undressing, *both* of them undressing in the same room. Scolding herself for being ridiculous, she began shaking out her space suit and folding it into crisp rectangles.

She heard Ansel's steps as he walked over, though she was finding it difficult to meet his eyes. He took the garment from her hands and stretched past her to hang it on a hook behind her. Tucked between him and the wall, Della went completely still, her pulse slow and hard. His close proximity made it difficult to breathe.

"I'm sorry I blamed my imprisonment on you," he said gruffly.

"And I'm sorry I called you a vexing gollumpus with a brain as smooth as marble and wits duller than a cantaloupe."

Slowly, the corner of his mouth curled upward into an appreciative smirk that had her body feeding her that *adrenaline* all over again, as though it sensed that smile was trouble all on its own. "You didn't call me that."

"Oh. I must have only thought it. I rescind the apology."

Free of her helmet and in the bright lights of the room, she was able to see him more clearly than before. He had faint lines around his mouth, but it was impossible to discern if they had been created by smiling or frowning.

Her stomach tingled as she recalled the warmth of that mouth against hers. Was Ansel thinking of that moment too? Probably not. He had done what he needed to for them to survive and probably hadn't spared it a thought since.

He'd thought such lovely things in his book, but now that she stood before him, he was barely able to look at her, as though now that danger had passed, and he was no longer morally obligated to protect her, she wasn't interesting enough to hold his attention.

As always, she was fading into the background. Even though she stood right before him, it was as though he had to continuously remind himself she was still there. His gaze kept dropping from her eyes—*oh.*

Oh.

Oh heavens. He hadn't stopped noticing her at all. He was staring at her mouth.

With a start, she realized she'd been doing the same thing, gazing at his lips and remembering the moment in the hall. He must have noticed her looking and gotten the impression that she was signaling her desires. She hadn't been. Not intentionally. Though the desires were certainly there, she preferred to keep her thoughts safely inside.

But fate had shown that it liked picking at the vault of Della's secrets. It had her stumbling through coincidences, mistakes, and accidents that all added up to this: a girl stumbling upon a book and meeting a boy, a series of lonely, desperate confessions, and an unintentional look at a set of entrancing lips that couldn't be sure if they wanted to smile or frown.

Coincidences could only be coincidences for so long before they became destiny. Perhaps there was no one better suited for a girl with her head in the clouds than a boy who lived among the stars.

CHAPTER 12

If Ansel mistook Della's wayward glance as a brazen advance—one he seemed amenable enough to entertain—she wouldn't correct him. For once, she'd been bold, even if it was by accident. So, in the greatest act of courage she'd managed thus far, Della lifted her chin and didn't look away. It was like living something she might have imagined late at night, when she thought about all the instances during the day when she could have been brave. She vowed that tonight, she wouldn't have to wonder what she might have missed out on because she was too embarrassed to display what she wanted.

"Good evening," she said timidly because, in actuality, wobbly eye contact was as far as Della's confidence stretched. She blushed. *Good evening?* What kind of ridiculous person waited until the tail end of a rescue mission to say *good evening*?

"Hi." Ansel rested his hand against the wall next to her head. Somehow, even his swollen eye found the tenacity to glitter rakishly.

Della couldn't be sure, but she thought he might be laughing at her—though not in the way other people laughed out of derision; there was a fondness to the soft tone of his voice that made her feel charming and . . . pretty. Somehow, the way he looked at her made her feel *pretty*. And special. And wanted.

"It's been nice meeting you," she whispered.

"Don't be polite. You know it hasn't been nice at all."

"But it could be, don't you think?"

As his smile faded, Ansel's head tilted in the ghost of a nod, like the phantom of a thought he'd tried to bury.

She took a tiny step so her toes bumped his.

He wet his lips, his gaze roving over her face. "Yeah?" He wasn't answering her question but asking one of his own, the weight of it heavy in his eyes.

She nodded.

It was unclear which one of them reached for the other first. Maybe it happened simultaneously. It felt inevitable. All that mattered was that, in a great rush, they found themselves in each other's arms.

Ansel grabbed her by the jaw and neck and brought his mouth down, hard, onto hers. Her fingers tangled around his suspenders as she melted against him, her curves pressing against the hard planes of his body.

He did not kiss her like she was some timid, breakable thing, nor did he treat her as though he thought she was shy. His lips moved, hot and urgent, against her own, and at last, there was no need for words. Della was no longer embarrassed or awkward. Her lips parted for him eagerly, able to show him what she wanted far easier than she could ever tell him.

Ansel approached kissing with the same egotistical overconfidence he approached anything else. He threw his whole being into the endeavor without the slightest hint of uncertainty. He knew what he was doing, and more than that, the arrogant bastard seemed well-aware of his own proficiency. Heaven help her, she liked that.

Kissing him felt wild and out of control, yet each of his movements was intentional and certain. He tasted like whiskey tinged with the faint metallic tang of blood from the split lip he'd apparently forgotten, though it had to sting, the way he was abusing his mouth for the sake of hers.

His tongue swept across hers in a slow, purposeful thrust. The act exuded carnal suggestions that had her cheeks flaming and her mind reeling with erotic images—the flex of muscle in the darkness; soft gasps muffled by silky sheets; hot, slick mouths gliding over skin.

Della traced her fingers down his suspenders. His shirt was thin and soft against her knuckles, warm with his body heat. That shirt did something to her, the way the thin material hugged Ansel's broad shoulders and stretched across his muscular chest before falling loosely to his waist, hinting at a taut stomach beneath.

Gliding her hands around his back, she clenched the shirt in her fists and tugged him tighter against her. His bottom lip was surprisingly soft—plush and velvety—as she sucked it between her own lips.

A low, broken groan escaped Ansel's throat. He stumbled forward, pinning her against the wall. His fingers dug into her hair, deliciously rough as he trailed kisses across her jaw and nipped at her earlobe. He guided her thigh around his waist. The pressure of his hips against hers awakened a dull throb of want within her, and she found herself shifting against him to ease the empty ache.

With a ragged curse, Ansel broke away just far enough to whisper, "Stars, Della," against her lips, and she liked how he said her name like that, somewhere between awe and utter misery.

And then his lips were on hers again, and she was clutching his shoulders, needing him closer, closer, closer—he let out a strangled grunt of pain, and her hands flew off him.

"I'm so sorry." She gasped. "Your shoulder. I forgot. You're bleeding out. Dying, possibly. We must fetch help immediately."

But he was already reaching for her, shushing her. "Dead is the only state I'm leaving this room."

And then his mouth was on hers again. In Ansel's kiss, she

felt every lonely, longing confession that had ever passed between them. She felt his hurt and her own melding together to create a new kind of ache, one that was something beautiful now that they shared it. It was a pleasant mournfulness, like crying over your favorite book—revisiting it over and over again simply because it made you *feel*.

"Captain?" Eryl's distant voice called through the wall. "Captain? Has the airlock door malfunctioned? Are you trapped? Shall I override the system?"

Ansel pulled away from Della, blinking as if he were waking from some kind of trance. She braced her hands against the wall behind her, panting for breath, her lips tingling and kiss-swollen, her body still desperate.

Ansel took a few moments to compose himself before answering. "No, Eryl. We're fine. We're coming"—he grimaced—"out soon."

Della couldn't help the quick glance that told her Ansel might need a little longer than *soon* to be fit for the eyes of polite society.

She fussed with her hair, trying to organize it into something presentable, even though the water, helmet, and Ansel's hands had done a thorough job of ruining it, perhaps forever.

"Here."

Della looked up to find Ansel handing her a book. She caught a glimpse of the title on the spine. It was her own, not his.

"What are you doing with that?" She shivered, the warmth of his kiss fading from her lips.

"It's yours. You might as well use it to write yourself home. Take it with you so you can look after it," Ansel said stiffly as though his body hadn't been molten against hers moments before. "Eryl can find you a pen."

Della didn't take it. She wasn't sure how she felt about him trying to ship her home moments after he'd kissed her like he needed her to stay. Had that been the only reason he had done it? Because she was here and willing, and she would be gone soon, so he thought, *why not?*

She wished Ansel were handing her *his* book. She would grab it, fling it open, find his thoughts, and discover the truth. But her book would show only her own confused feelings, and little good that would do.

No. No, she wasn't confused. She was . . . she was furious? The rage boiled in her chest, melting away her hurt. She was unfamiliar with the emotion, which was why it had taken her a moment to place its name. As a rule, she didn't get angry, not really. Frustrated, annoyed, yes, but not angry. Generally, it got her nowhere and wasn't worth the trouble. Until now.

Della shoved away the proffered book and marched past Ansel for the door. "I'm not leaving."

He scrambled after her. "I won't let you endanger yourself because of me any longer. You promised you'd go home after you helped me escape."

She jabbed at the glowing rectangle next to the door, the way she'd seen Ansel do to open doors in the prison. "I lied. I'm not going anywhere. I'm staying on this ship. I'm going to help you clear your name—oh do be quiet, you fretful hen. I'm not endangering myself for *you*. Once we clear your name, I'm going to ride with you to Lumeria so I can fetch medicine for my mother. Only after all that will I return home." The door still hadn't opened, so Della went to jab another glowing orb.

Ansel caught her finger midair. "Easy. Do you want to send us hurtling into space?"

The fact that his touch made a little zing travel up her arm made Della livid. He'd proven his touch meant nothing, and she wouldn't let him reach for her on a whim again. "Unhand me."

He did so with a fierce glare. "You can't just invite yourself on board. You don't know what it's like out here. Space is a cold, cruel place, especially when you're constantly being hunted by the universe's deadliest mercs."

"I don't know what it's like?" she retorted. "I've been beaten and spat at. I've been mocked and degraded and groped. My society's finest are far crueler than your universe's deadliest."

Ansel blinked, looking stunned and a little horrified on her behalf.

"You surely don't mean to forbid me from saving my poor, ailing mother." Della gazed up at him innocently, though her question was a thinly veiled test of his character.

After a pause, he melted a little, letting out a long sigh through his nose. "I suppose, if you want to subject yourself to danger for your own cause, stopping you would make me a . . ." He searched for the right word.

"A cad?" she offered with a side of venom to let him know exactly what she thought of how he was treating her in the aftermath of their kiss.

Scowling, Ansel pressed something on the glowing surface of the wall that made the door slide open. "You are a conniving person, you know that?"

"You owe me. I rescued you."

"I saved your life. Twice! I'd say we're even."

"It was only in need of saving because you—" Della drew up short outside the door, her mouth falling open as she gaped up at the humanoid figure towering above her in the dim hall.

The figure was constructed out of white metal plates and rods, gleamed to a high polish. It had a slender upturned nose, intricately constructed eyes that swiveled and glowed yellow, a pleasantly formed mouth, and a hinged jaw, part of which was cut away to expose the bronze mechanisms within. The back of its head was crafted with some kind of clear shell that revealed flickering gold and green panels. An overwhelming sense of wonder consumed Della. And to think she'd once thought waterfalls were an extraordinary notion.

The impossible being lifted a gangly arm and fluttered

seven bizarrely long fingers. "Greetings. I'm Eryl. Are you the strumpet?"

"I'm just Della." Della gave a little curtsy. "Della Farley. I'll be joining you."

Ansel provided another deep sigh from somewhere behind her that no one concerned themselves with.

"So glad we'll have the pleasure of your company, Miss Farley," Eryl said. "I will find some blankets for both of you."

"Blankets?" Ansel asked. "Why?"

Eryl cocked her head. "My ambient air temperature sensor indicates the ship has reached a degree your species may find uncomfortable. It may take some time to warm back up. Aren't you cold?"

Ansel frowned. "Not in the slightest."

"But you're always cold," Eryl began to protest, but she was interrupted.

"You've got to be kidding me," a dry, female voice Della recognized as Xaks's intoned. A new figure stepped around the corner to join them outside the airlock door.

Della tried to refrain from staring. Xaks wore a dark jumpsuit and gloves, and her head was encased with a water-filled helmet that purred softly as bubbles flowed through it. She was striking, with high cheekbones, purplish skin, and delicate fins that curved from her ears. Perhaps Della ought to be frightened, surrounded by these strange criminals, but at least they were honest about who they were, unlike people like Mrs. Loughty who hid their cruelty behind smiles.

"How do you do?" Della asked, dipping into a curtsy.

"You can understand Xaks?" Ansel asked in surprise behind her. "I didn't know you spoke judrax."

"I suppose I do now," said Della, assuming this must again be the magic of the book.

Xaks looked past her, clearly unimpressed, regardless of

whatever languages Della did or did not speak. "Captain, what is this?" Della supposed she was the *this* Xaks referred to. "We can't afford freeloaders."

"I can work," Della said hurriedly. "I can't pay you, but I will earn my keep."

Ansel placed himself between Della and the other two—an act that caused Xaks to raise a bald brow. "Let's take a minute to discuss this like civilized people."

Della found the suggestion to remain civilized amusing coming from the man who'd had his hands halfway up her skirts moments before.

"Della, do you mind if the crew and I speak privately for a minute?"

She shook her head, wondering how many details about their unusual meeting Ansel would tell his crew. If he told them about the books, would they believe him?

Ansel led her to another door at the end of a hall. He opened it and then rested a hand on the jamb when it tried to close of its own accord. "Wait on the bridge, make yourself comfortable, but for comet's sake, don't push any buttons."

"Buttons?" She twisted one of the buttons on the front of her dress.

Ansel pointed to one of the glowing orbs on the panel near the door. "These kinds of buttons. Pushing certain ones controls the ship in different ways, and I'd rather not crash into a meteor because you got curious."

Della still didn't really know what he was talking about but made a show of removing her fingers from her button. "Understood. I will leave all the handling of buttons to you."

His eyes dropped to her buttons with a heated look, then he seemed to shake himself. "Good," he grunted, and she walked past him into the room.

The door shut behind her, leaving her alone. She climbed the few stairs up to a platform, on which sat two chairs behind semicircular tables that housed dials, levers, and blinking red lights. *Buttons*, she supposed. Beyond the chairs was a vast window. Filling the window was an even vaster view of space. Stars. Stars as far as she could see, brighter than she thought possible.

Her eyes gorged themselves on the view. Her plan had been to collect the medicine and go home, but how could she ever leave this place? Even if she would be free to travel once she healed her mother, how could she be content with oceans and mountains when she could see *worlds*?

With a start, she realized tears were rolling down her cheeks, chilling in the frigid air.

She had never been more out of place than here, in her black maid's dress and white apron, standing silhouetted in the massive window of a spaceship—yet the infinite expanse of cold space was the most welcoming place she'd ever visited. It didn't care about her, or if she were too plain or quiet or ungraceful. It was easier to navigate the cosmos than it was to tiptoe her way through social circles. For the first time, her mind went silent, no longer urging her to act the least like herself in order to fit in.

A tremendous crash outside in the hall made her jump and spin around. A few moments later, Ansel, Xaks, and Eryl entered the room, accompanied by a fourth person.

"This is Yaggrel," Ansel said casually, as though there had not been a mighty racket beyond the door moments before. "He's our weapons specialist and part-time cross-stitching enthusiast."

Yaggrel opened his maw and clenched his rows of needle-like teeth into an unnerving smile. He was maybe four feet tall, with a wiry frame and four spindly arms he kept folded at his chest. A sinewy tail undulated behind him like that of a coiling snake. He had a domed head with wiry hair, large black orbs for eyes, and his fingers ended in long, wicked talons.

"A pleasure meeting you," Della said politely.

"I only cross-stitch when it's upon the flesh of my enemies as a torture technique," he said in a chilling, rasping voice.

"Blazing asteroids." Xaks sighed wearily.

Ansel pinched the bridge of his nose. "See, we talked about making a good impression. Can you understand how maybe you've failed to do that?" He turned to Della. "He doesn't do that—good impressions, but also the cross-stitching thing—he's not allowed. He's making it sound like it's a regular thing, but it was only one time. We were trying to find him a creative outlet to channel his anger that didn't involve dismemberment."

Yaggrel let out a displeased growl.

"Anyhow," Ansel said, "back to the point. You *did* save me and we *do* owe you. So . . . we've agreed you may stay."

Della beamed, a thrill of joy rushing through her.

"But," Ansel went on, "you will not be involved with anything dangerous. No helping us catch Balor, no more prison breaks, no more interfering."

Xaks muttered something under her breath behind Ansel's back.

Ansel shot her a look over his shoulder. "She is not a freeloader. In return for passage to Lumeria once we clear my name, Della will work on board as a maid. She has prior experience, and I think we'll all come to appreciate her being here."

"Very timely, your arrival," Xaks told Della dryly. "Our cleaning droid recently malfunctioned."

Some unspoken conversation passed between their glares that Della couldn't make sense of, but it didn't matter. She could stay.

CHAPTER 13

While Eryl took Ansel to the sick bay to tend to his injuries, Yaggrel showed Della to her room. As they walked, Della tried to catalog the layout so she could navigate the ship herself, but it was no use. There were too many doors and halls to keep track of. It became a blur of gray steel, blue lights, hissing vents, and too many gauges, levers, and blinking *buttons* to count. She wondered if Ansel even knew what they all did.

"And this is where we torture our prisoners." Yaggrel pointed into a nondescript room. He seemed to think making up false and horrific usages for each room they passed was a valuable use of his time.

Della hummed, feigning polite interest. She wouldn't tell him, but she found Yaggrel's dark sense of humor oddly endearing. The spirited fellow did his best to appear scary, but considering no one else seemed to take him seriously, she suspected his behavior was one big ruse meant to frighten her. At least she certainly *hoped* the creature did not actually keep a collection of decaying entrails in his room, the way he claimed.

As the unsettling tour progressed, each room they encountered solidified the fact that A, Ansel's ship was in terrible disrepair, and B, his barren decor aesthetic inspired the same sort of feelings one might experience from stepping into a damp crypt. A film of greasy dust covered every surface, the wall panels were rusting away, and exposed pipes oozed glowing gelatinous substances.

"Here we are." Yaggrel tapped a button on the wall with his claw, and a door slid open. "Your room."

Della's lips parted as she stepped inside. The room was small but felt endless, because the walls and ceilings were constructed out of octagonal panels of glass to create a stunning observatory. If she looked up at night, she would feel as though she were sleeping among the stars—which she supposed she was. A bed three times the size of her cot at Mrs. Loughty's stood in the center of the room, piled with layers of blankets and numerous pillows. A dresser, a full-length mirror, and a few storage chests took up the rest of the space.

Della hurried to the edge of the room and looked out. Down below, the rest of the ship sprawled, a landscape of man-made brutality.

"We call it the crow's nest, in honor of ancient days," Yaggrel said from behind her. "It's not much, but the Captain said to give you the room with the best view."

As Yaggrel left her to explore, Della's heart warmed at the knowledge that Ansel remembered her desperation to see as much of the universe as she could.

Behind her, she heard her bedroom door whisk back open. "Do you like it?" Ansel's voice asked.

Della turned and went a little breathless at the sight of him put together and cleaned up, leaning against the doorframe. His hair was combed, and he wore fresh clothes, including a striking black coat that billowed around his knees as he straightened and walked over to her. A whiff of expensive-smelling cologne wafted off him, something vaguely floral and musky.

"Of course I like it." She spun in a circle. "But where am I to sleep?"

"On the bed, generally."

"*That* bed? It's all for me?"

Ansel cocked an eyebrow. "Unless you plan on inviting someone to share it with you."

She blushed. "And the chest and the mirror and the dresser?"

"Yours to use."

"But I don't have things to put in them."

"We'll find you some."

"Thank you." The words felt too flimsy to express her gratitude.

Ansel shifted his weight in an uncharacteristic display of discomfort. "We should talk."

A spike of apprehension shot through Della. Was this about the kiss?

"Indeed, we do have matters to discuss." Nervous energy had Della practically wringing her hands. All she wanted was to deflect the conversation she knew was coming. "No one has told me what my duties will be yet. I will clean, of course." *Does the crew hate me?* "I'll wipe the walls, mop the floors, dust every surface." *Do you view what happened as a mistake?* "I can scrub laundry and draw baths." *Did you change your mind, and you're going to ask me to leave?* "And I'm an excellent cook."

Ansel held up a hand. "We have machines to wash laundry, sterilization chambers that cleanse us in under five seconds, and nutrition tablets that negate the need for food. Honestly, just pretend to look busy enough that I don't have to listen to everyone else complain that you're not pulling your weight."

"Nutrition tablets?"

"A simple pill—capsule—you swallow that accounts for all your dietary needs. Saves time."

Della let out a little half-laugh. "But food is one of the most enjoyable parts of living—not just the act of eating—gathering together for meals feeds the spirit as well as the body. In trying to make your lives easier, I fear you have only succeeded in making yourselves more miserable."

"It's fine. The tablets are easier."

"Sometimes the best things in life are difficult." *And headstrong and snarky and devastatingly gorgeous in the way that makes a girl's knees go a little weak.* She cleared her throat. "A good life is not necessarily an easy one, Captain."

"You don't have to call me *Captain*."

"I'm part of your crew now. The rest of your crew calls you Captain."

"The rest of my crew haven't read my mind." Ansel wandered farther into the room, keeping space between them. "Actually, that's why I'm here." He drew the books out of an inside pocket of his coat. "Now that you're part of my crew, this thing between us isn't appropriate. My thoughts are my own, and yours are yours. It's not right for us to read these. It's better we keep our own books. You're responsible for your story, and me for mine."

Della recoiled. A few hours ago, he was willingly sending her bits of his consciousness, addressed to her and signed off with a *yours, Ansel,* as though he were giving her himself right along with them. Now he wanted *his thoughts to be his own*?

Maybe he regretted the kiss. It wasn't good, and he didn't enjoy it, and he was letting her down gently.

But no. Della brushed off those insecurities. She knew her faults, and being a poor kisser wasn't one of them. Ansel hadn't acted as though he didn't like the kiss. He hadn't *felt* like it either. She went warm, thinking of how he felt pressed against her, big and hot and hard.

So he was being stubborn, then. There was likely some insufferable moral dilemma involved, some entirely nonsensical reason why he wouldn't allow himself to feel anything for her even though he clearly wanted her—at the very least in a physical capacity. She was too sweet for him, too inexperienced, and he'd convinced himself he was a horrible beast, unworthy of her. Either that or he was under the delusion that staying away from her was somehow protecting her. Men always did think they knew how to take better care of a woman than she did herself.

Whatever the reason, Della wouldn't put up with it. She was unwilling to throw away what they'd been given.

Della steeled herself. "I don't mind if you don't share your book with me. I'd still like you to have mine." She marched up to him, took her book, flipped it open, and then shoved it back into his hands. "You reading my thoughts is terrifying, mortifying, but when you found my book, for the first time in my life, I felt seen. I'm not good at speaking, but you could see what I was saying on the inside, and I thought, maybe, someone could finally understand me. Don't take that from me."

Della was close enough that she could see the twitch of Ansel's irises as his gaze flicked down to the page and read a few lines. Perhaps it was cowardly, letting him read her thoughts instead of saying them out loud, but it was the bravest Della could be at the moment.

"You're not, you know," he said quietly. "Too sweet for me."

Her palms grew sweaty. Of all the things he could have read, why did it have to be that?

Slowly, he tucked both books back into his coat. "I might be honorable enough to give you my coat when you're shivering, but don't think I'm so noble that I wouldn't happily corrupt you in every way I know how. Though I haven't totally ruled out the notion that you'd be the one corrupting me."

Flushing, she lifted her gaze to his, silently pleading for him to close the gap between them.

"But, Della," Ansel said in the way he had that made her name sound like it pained him, "what happened between us wasn't what you think." He began moving about the room, developing a sudden and deep interest in the furniture. "I don't know why it happened or what came over me. There I was, in prison, wondering if I'd ever get out again, and then you showed up, and—and we *survived.* All I could think was, here is this marvelous, nonsensical, extraordinary creature who saved my life and once mentioned wanting to be ravished against a wall, and there happened to be a wall *right there*, so I guess I felt obliged to do something about it all."

Della blinked. He'd delivered the entire speech matter-of-factly, as though the string of words was logical and not a complete mental spiral. "You're speaking of the kiss?" she asked with forced restraint as her thoughts exclaimed: *You think I'm extraordinary?*

Ansel ran a hand through his hair before continuing in a careful tone. "Sometimes, when adrenaline is high, you think the emotions you're feeling are something . . . else. It'll have your heart pounding and your breaths quickening, and it's easy to confuse one feeling for another. What happened between us, whatever we felt—those emotions were simply brought on by circumstance."

Della's whole life, she'd been made to feel small, and now here he was, diminishing their kiss. How dare he act like what they did was nothing more than a reckless moment of passion, as though he had not bared his soul to her, telling her she'd stolen a piece of his heart?

If she had not witnessed how Ansel's mind worked, he might have fooled her into thinking he did not care for her, but she had seen too much of him to let doubts take root. He pushed everyone away the moment he felt something real.

It was too soon to tell how she felt about him in return, but she knew it was more than brief, passing lust. She felt attraction, certainly, and wild girlish infatuation—the kind that made her want to rest her elbow on a windowsill and gaze wistfully across a field of heather, daydreaming about what it would be like to make him smile. But there was also more. She admired all that single-minded determination—and especially liked it when it was directed at her. She cared about him, this lonely man who didn't understand love—frustrating dolt though he was.

She wanted to yell some sense into him but couldn't muster

up the courage, fearing she'd lose her nerve halfway through and stutter, or worse, cry. She'd never be able to convince him he was the most exasperating man she'd ever encountered if she stood there *crying.*

So Della said, quite conversationally, "I suppose during other high-stress situations—for instance, when you're lounging in your bed—it's once again the adrenaline taking over your body that compels you to write fantasies to women, detailing how you would lend them your coat and rush in on a white horse to save them from their miserable lives?"

"I don't recall the color of the horse being mentioned," he grumbled, color rising to the high points of his cheeks.

Extraordinary. The man who claimed he didn't blush—who flirted mercilessly and shamelessly—grew pink the moment she stepped a toe in the direction of his heart.

"Look," Ansel said, "you'll eventually have to go home to your own world. So," he went on brightly, as though the matter were settled, "while I might not be opposed to a fling for the duration of your stay, you want a grand romance, so obviously it can't happen again."

"Please, do continue telling me what I do and do not want," Della said mildly. "An epic romance is not necessarily a lasting one, you know."

"You deserve someone good." His voice dropped to a soft, placating tone that didn't convince her for a second. "I don't want to break your heart."

Della all but snorted. "Says the man who, not two minutes ago, declared he'd happily corrupt me. You're far too much a rogue to concern yourself with a few broken hearts. I bet you could break three before breakfast without batting an eye, if you set your mind to it." She jabbed a finger at his chest. "You're scared for your own heart. In the books, you opened up to me because you thought we would never meet, but things are real now. You're backtracking because . . . you're terrified."

Ansel made a face, his placating expression vanishing. "I'm not worried about my heart."

Della clenched her trembling fingers into fists and lifted her chin. "Then prove it."

His body weight shifted forward. For a moment, she thought he would reach for her. But then he stepped away with a shake of his head. "I know what you're trying to do. You can't tempt me."

"Is that a challenge?"

"Do your best," he snapped, and Della realized that somehow, inexplicably, they were close again. He glared at her through dark spikes of hair, his scowl hovering above her parted lips.

Deadly calm spread through Della. Had he told her he did not want her, had he asked her to put the matter to rest, she would. Yet he'd only dared her to try. And try she would. Everything Della had ever wanted was at last within reach, as though she'd finally caught up to the lost pages of her story. She refused to let such a momentous part of her life be rendered meaningless.

"Well then." Della squared her shoulders. Ansel had once ventured into her daydreams and found her, and now she would find him again. "If you're so worried about protecting me, all the more reason for you to hold on to my book so you can keep an eye on me. Though I do apologize if you read about me thinking of you at night. My dreams tend to run uninhibited, and I have a vivid imagination."

Later, after Ansel left, muttering something about how they would reconvene tomorrow to discuss strategy, a knock sounded at Della's door.

Della answered to find Eryl on the other side, holding a stack of linens in her arms. "The Captain instructed me to bring you fresh clothes and teach you how to use the sterilizer."

After thanking Eryl and inviting her inside, Della placed the stack of clothing on the bed. She lifted the top item and unfolded it to reveal a man's white linen shirt, much like the one that had driven her to distraction on Ansel's body all day. "Are these—" she began.

"Ansel's, but I promise they're clean," Eryl assured her. "Your options for clothing are limited at the moment, with only one other human on board."

Della was not in a position to be picky, so she simply nodded and refolded the shirt.

"Once you've changed, I'll take your own clothes to be washed, and you can have them back in the morning," said Eryl.

"Oh, I can wash them myself," Della hastened to say.

"No need," Eryl said. "We have a machine that does it."

This place seemed to have a machine for everything. Della wondered if there would be anything left for her to do at all.

"I don't know what standard of time you're used to on your planet, but the ship runs on universal time." Eryl pointed at a little metal ball sitting on the bedside table. Numbers created entirely of light floated above the ball, displaying the time. Della felt her eyes widen, but Eryl acted as though the floating clock was nothing out of the ordinary. "That means a twenty-four-hour day. If you want to wake up at a certain time, just tell the time bot, and it will rouse you. But don't be alarmed by its methods. Yaggrel continuously sets all the bots to deliver rude morning greetings, no matter how often we reset them."

Beckoning Della to follow, Eryl showed her a small washroom in the hall. Inside, there was a closet Eryl called the sterilizer. She instructed Della to strip down, walk into the closet, and flip a switch on the wall.

When Della did so, a quick spray of steam blasted her from all sides, followed by a gust of warm air that dried her skin. The whole affair took mere seconds. Walking out of the closet, she felt clean, yes, but much less relaxed than she would have been by a bath. She slipped on one of the shirts Ansel had lent her, which fell to her thighs like a nightgown. Having no underthings, Della felt the soft material caressing her skin with every movement. The fact that the shirt was Ansel's made each brush feel significant.

Thanking Eryl for her help and bidding her a good night, Della darted back across the hall before anyone could see her so scantily clad.

Back in the—*her*—bedroom, Della slipped beneath the plush bedclothes. They smelled deliciously fresh in the way only clean linens could. The mattress and pillows cocooned her body as though she lay upon a cloud. She politely asked the ball on the bedside table—the time bot—to wake her at five. The ball spun once before falling still, which startled Della, but she decided to take it as an acknowledgment.

Dear Ansel, she thought, her eyes growing heavy. He probably wouldn't even read her book, either because he couldn't be bothered or because his newfound integrity wouldn't allow him to sift through her thoughts.

She hoped he would, though.

It is okay if I scare you, for you make me brave.

We mustn't let good and wonderful things float by as though they are meant for someone else. My mother taught me there's magic in the mundane. It's those quiet, small joys that will have you falling head over heels for your own marvelous existence.

I want to show you how it feels to be wanted—and not in the way that involves your face on a poster and a monetary number attached to your name. Admittedly, I hardly know how that feels either, but perhaps we could figure it out together. Our time is limited, but I don't think that means we are doomed to inevitably experience heartache, should we grow close.

Instead, we can explore whatever is between us the way one might take in a grand waterfall or majestic mountain range—we will see the beauty, experience the wonder, then return home, not heartbroken, but with a greater appreciation for the world, and a precious memory.

Yours,
Della.

CHAPTER 14

When Della awoke the next morning, she did not realize it was morning at all, for stars stretched above her as far as she could see. Then the previous day came rushing back to her, and she bolted upright, a broad smile spreading across her face—until she realized the time bot was yelling at her.

It had grown appendages sometime during the night and was now using those tiny limbs to jump onto her mattress and paddle her arm. "Wake up, you lazy slimeball!" it bellowed in a tinny inhuman voice. "If I had to list things you're slower than, they'd be, in no particular order: decay, bureaucracy, Ansel doing his hair—"

"All right, all right." Della scooped the bot up and plopped it back onto the table. "I'm up."

Its limbs snapped back around its round little body until it resembled a ball once more. A compartment opened on top, revealing the light that shone the time into the air. Goodness, it was ten past five. Della was running late on her first day.

With no time to waste, Della bounded out of bed and straightened the sheets. She desperately wanted to be so much more than a maid and was slightly disappointed that was her position once more after breaking free of her old life, but she had to start proving her capability somewhere. Then maybe everyone would see that she could contribute in more important ways.

Outside her door, she found yesterday's dress and apron, clean and dry, as Eryl had promised. After dressing and pinning up her hair, Della took approximately twelve wrong turns before she found the galley. It was in a sad state of disrepair. The space was small, nothing more than an aisle between cabinets, a sink, and a stove. The countertops were rusty, the stovetop covered in something sticky Della would rather not identify. Worse, there was no food to be found, only a cabinet that held jars of what must be the nutrition tablets. Making a face, Della shut the cabinet.

Luckily, she discovered cleaning supplies shoved in the back of a pantry. The bottles of solution had handwritten labels such as:

Grime Grenade
Yaggrel's, hands off
(no, really, it will melt your hands off)

Shitsplosion Potion
Cleaning Shit for cleaning shit

Gunkinator 3000
For gunky stuff

And, finally, one that simply read:

THE GOOD SHIT

She had to smile, imagining which members of the crew had named which bottles. Perhaps they'd all gotten in on the project one night, bonding as they worked together to clean up some unfortunate accident, and the ordeal had dissolved into a boisterous competition to see who could come up with the most ridiculous name.

The amusing mental images kept Della company as—armed

with rags, a bucket, and *THE GOOD SHIT* (which was somehow the least alarmingly named cleaner)—she faced the mess, rolled up her sleeves, and got to work.

"My eyes," Xaks groaned as she entered the dining area attached to the kitchen. She flopped onto one of the stools at the metal table. "Why is everything so bright?"

"Because it's not covered in scum." Della cheerfully fetched Xaks a nutrition tablet and placed it on a metal tray next to a napkin she'd folded into the shape of a flower.

"I prefer things scummy," Xaks grumbled. "Look at this table. I can see myself in it. Who wants to look at themselves while they eat?" She visibly recoiled as Della delivered the tray. "What the fuck is this?"

"Breakfast," Della said. "I know it's pitiful. A sprig of fresh greenery would have been a lovely addition to spruce up the plating, but there were none to be found."

Xaks held up the folded napkin as though it offended her. "Why do I need a napkin to swallow a pill?"

"I have no idea," Della said honestly. "I'm not sure how you swallow pills at all with a mask on."

Xaks glared, unscrewed a small porthole at the top of her helmet, and plopped the pill inside. They both watched it slowly sink in front of her face. In a flash, a long, serpentine tongue darted from Xaks's mouth and snatched the pill from the water. Her jaws snapped shut, and she bared her small, pointy teeth.

Della wondered if that was supposed to look intimidating. "Fascinating." She supposed she ought to be frightened of the otherworldly beings she'd encountered. The fact was, compared to humanity's capacity for evil, a few sharp teeth and extra eyes didn't faze her.

"And what if you wanted to eat real food?" Della asked Xaks.

Xaks pointed to the corner, where a large clear pod gathered dust. Inside the pod was a chair with its own small table. "I fill that with water and eat inside, where I don't need to wear my helmet. Or I eat in my room, which is water-filled too."

"I see." Della picked up a small notepad from the gleaming countertop beside her. "And what kind of food do you like? I'm making a grocery list."

"The blood of my enemies," Yaggrel growled, entering the room and hopping—not onto a chair, but onto the table itself. He perched there with his knobby knees pulled to his soft chin.

"So you'd say you're a carnivore?" Della took notes.

Xaks snorted. "He wishes. To his great embarrassment, his gut can only handle leafy greens."

Della struck a line through *blood of enemies* and replaced it with *salad?* "And what do you like, Xaks?"

Xaks leaned against the wall. "Not to be bothered first thing in the morning. Forget your list. The tablets work fine."

"Nothing brings people together like food and companionship," Della called as she withdrew into the kitchen to retrieve Yaggrel's nutrition tablet. "Everyone seems uptight, so working on group morale is especially important."

"I think we're appropriately uptight, considering we're on the run," said Xaks. "Besides, it's not like Ansel will want to spend credits on something as unnecessary as food."

"I like to spend my credits on lots of unnecessary things. Why draw the line at food?"

Della couldn't see Ansel from her vantage point, half inside a cabinet, but as soon as she heard his voice, her stomach did a little dip.

Quickly, she arranged Yaggrel's tray and stepped back into the dining room.

Ansel stood in the middle of the room, gaze flicking about briefly at its altered state. If he had any opinions on the kitchen's transformation, he didn't voice them. If he read what she'd thought to him last night, he didn't indicate that either.

Blood rushed to Della's face. How silly her letter felt in the starlight of day.

Ansel's swollen eye was turning vibrant shades of purple and yellow, and the cuts on his face were an angry, inflamed red. The whole effect was strangely intimidating. If it weren't for his book, she would have no reason to suspect there was something soft behind this imposing brick wall of a man. He seemed distant and unapproachable. It hardly felt real that she'd been in his arms the day before.

"Get off the table." Ansel shoved Yaggrel onto a chair.

The spindly creature let out a squawk and nearly toppled over. "One day it's '*Sure, Yaggrel, you can clean out the waste particulate filters on the table,*' and the next it's '*Don't sit on the table*'?"

Della eyed the table she'd cleaned twice and decided she had better fetch *THE GOOD SHIT* and make it three.

"Now that we're all here, what's our plan?" Xaks was all business. "Neegu was a dead end. We've lost Balor and our only lead."

"Not quite." Ansel took a seat. "We can still track him."

"How?"

"With a tracking device."

Xaks threw up her hands. "Wow, that's a really groundbreaking idea, Captain. I'm so glad we have you as our fearless leader."

Della wrung out her washcloth and worked her way around the table, wiping it down once more. Yaggrel didn't spare a glance as she leaned around him, Xaks glared, and Ansel—Ansel did nothing, but she was acutely aware of the proximity of his knee as she slipped between him and Yaggrel to clean the last bit of table. His hand rested on his thigh, flat and open, but when her skirts brushed his leg, his pinky twitched away from her as though she had scalded him.

"How extraordinary," Eryl boomed as she entered the room. "Everyone, look at the wonders Della has worked on my insides. If only everyone cared for my bowels thusly, they might not have been reduced to such a state."

"I'm begging you not to refer to the inside of my ship as your bowels again," Ansel said.

"Didn't Della do a good job?" Eryl tilted her head. "Why is no one singing her praise? Is my programming malfunctioning again? Am I mistaken?"

"She did fine," Xaks muttered.

"Passable," Yaggrel said.

But it was Ansel's quiet "Very well done" that made Della flush with pleasure.

"Thank you," she said, so awkwardly and so quietly she doubted anyone heard. They all resumed their conversation as she slipped back into the kitchen to prepare the last breakfast tray for Ansel.

"As I was saying." Ansel set a small black cube onto the table and pressed something on the side. "We can find Balor easily enough. I inserted a tracking device into the sole of one of his men's boots."

Della returned from the kitchen as a glowing transparent map sprang from the cube into the air, displaying countless rotating planets and a million stars, as though a miniature galaxy had come to life above their breakfast table. A red dot blinked in the midst of it all, making its way slowly across the map. She tried to stifle her gasp of awe.

"There he is." Ansel pointed at the dot. "After what he did to me, he won't be expecting us. Hopefully we can track him down and get a few shots off with the new SPM-500 before we drain the Miss Demeanor's grid too far to support that kind of firepower. All we need is to break through the Shield Stone's forcefield enough to allow us to board. Then we'll recover the Stone and return it and Balor to Lumeria for justice."

"We need a better name for the Megacannon besides SPM-500," Yaggrel grumbled.

"That is its name," Eryl said logically.

"It's the highest-power laser cannon on the market," Yaggrel protested. "It deserves a more ominous name. Like Pulse Ender, or Crushinator, or Lucinda."

"Lucinda?" Eryl asked. "The name of your ex-nestmate?"

"Like I said, a name with the power to chill you to the bone."

"Let's focus, please," Xaks snapped.

Doing her best not to interrupt, Della gingerly snaked an arm around Ansel with his tray. His hand shot out and wrapped gently around her wrist. The tray slipped, clattering to the table with more force than she intended. Della flinched. Her knuckles tingled, anticipating punishment.

"Would you sit down?" Ansel asked. "We've managed to keep ourselves alive so far without being hand-fed our breakfasts."

Shaking her head, she pulled her hand away and went back into the kitchen, feeling Ansel's lingering gaze on her back. She was the maid. It wasn't proper for her to sit with them.

Across the room, Yaggrel let out a phlegmy burp to the accompaniment of the crew's disgusted protests.

"You're repulsive, you know that?" Xaks asked conversationally.

So perhaps there was no reason for Della to concern herself with propriety aboard the Miss Demeanor.

Still, she'd promised the crew she'd make herself useful, and sitting around all morning wasn't the way to do that. Until a new opportunity presented itself where she could prove her worth, she must remain on task. Besides, she had already eaten. Eryl had popped in earlier while Della was cleaning and helped her calculate which tablet was best suited for her, based on her nutritional needs.

"I don't think it's a good idea to go after Balor without shields of our own," Xaks was saying. "If we're unprepared, things will get hairy fast. He could shoot us down before we could even board."

"Can the ship support running the shields and the SPM-500 at once?" Yaggrel asked.

"That's why the element of surprise is so important," Xaks said. "We'll have to get as many shots fired as possible before we have to focus all our energy on maintaining the shields as we initiate boarding. Right, Captain?"

Ansel rubbed one of the petals of the prettily folded napkin on his breakfast tray between his thumb and forefinger, seeming to forget the conversation around him.

Yaggrel audibly gulped down his nutrition tablet. "Well, if we want to fix the shields, we'll need credits. Fastest way to get those would be to collect a bounty."

"The moment any of us go to turn one in, we'd be arrested right along with our prisoner," said Xaks. "Maybe if you spent your formative years in school instead of building illegal weapons, you'd still be eligible to work as a hunter."

"Don't act like I'm the only wanted criminal here," Yaggrel said.

"What about me?" Della hardly realized she'd voiced the question until everyone's stools squeaked as they turned to look at her. At last, here was her chance to show the crew she could add value to the team. She twisted her washcloth in her hands. "I'm not wanted."

"You?" Yaggrel scoffed. "Track down a dangerous criminal?"

"It's a good idea," said Ansel. She'd expected him to protest immediately, but he only regarded her, a calculating look in his eyes, as though he were fully taking her plan into consideration as a valid option. Pride swelled within her chest.

"She wouldn't even have to be involved in the capturing," he went on. "She'd only have to turn the criminal in. We could draw her up some fake papers. I kept her face pointed away from the security cameras during our escape, so no one would suspect or recognize her."

Slowly, Xaks nodded. "That new gambling moon, Creqreon, is two weeks' travel from here—don't light up like that, Captain. It scares me. We're visiting for work, not play. There's sure to be someone there worth capturing."

"How soon do you think we can get to Lumeria?" Della asked, thinking of the precious little time her mother had left.

"We have several parsecs of travel ahead of us," Ansel said, "but with any luck, we could be on our way to Lumeria within a month, maybe two."

Two months. Della did her best to keep her spirits from sinking, but she feared her mother might not have that much time.

The following week passed in a blur. Despite her worries for her mother, Della couldn't help but enjoy her time aboard the Miss Demeanor. It was paradise compared to the years of lonely, thankless toil at Mrs. Loughty's.

Yes, Della worked hard from the moment the time bot aggressively woke her in the morning until she lay down at night, but there was something satisfying about working with people you cared for, for a cause you supported. Especially when those people showed their appreciation, which they did, thanks to Eryl's insistence. After Della polished every nook and cranny on the ship until it shined, patched rusty panels, and oiled every hinge until nothing creaked, including Eryl herself, the android pulled her to her metal chest in a bone-crushing hug and declared she might believe Della hung a moon or two, if she hadn't been programmed with enough scientific knowledge to know better.

From then on, the android was Della's fiercely loyal ally,

demanding everyone else treat her kindly. She spent hours upon hours explaining words, tech, and customs that even Della couldn't have imagined mere days ago.

As far as where things stood with Ansel—well, Della was fairly certain he was trying to avoid her. Whenever they bumped into each other, he was always cordial—*cordial*, never straying outside the bounds of appropriate behavior. It was all dreadfully silly. His respectfulness was ludicrous, considering he'd shown himself more than capable of handling her in all sorts of lovely *dis*respectful ways—something that they both seemed to enjoy immensely but were now denying themselves for reasons Della had yet to fully decipher.

Why, just last night, she'd stepped out of the washroom and spotted Ansel walking toward her from the direction of the bridge. She'd blushed fiercely; she hadn't expected him to be up so late, and she wore only his shirt, her dirty laundry tucked under her arm.

Ansel had taken one look at her, spun on his heel, and begun walking the opposite direction.

"Don't redirect your course on account of me," she'd called politely, despite her embarrassment. Eryl had shown her an intergalactic fashion magazine the other day, so she knew the way she was currently dressed wasn't really all that scandalous, even if it felt that way.

Meanwhile, Ansel wore only a pair of loose black pants and a white undershirt that clung to his biceps, one of which was still bandaged. His hair was disheveled as though he'd been running his hands through it, the color in his cheeks high. He looked delightfully debauched, and part of her wished she could have been the cause.

"Shall we walk together?" she asked nervously, wondering if she'd done something wrong.

"I can't right now." His gaze locked onto her bare legs.

Heat flickered its way up Della's body. Every inch of exposed flesh burned. The brush of cotton over her skin as she breathed turned excruciating.

But Ansel had only tipped his head and bid her a brusque "Good night, Della," before continuing on his way.

So, since he seemed intent on avoiding her, she wrote him letters in her mind as she went about her chores, or at night before she fell asleep—some short, some long, some daring or ridiculous, in hopes that if he were reading them, he'd have no choice but to let it slip and reveal the fact during the day.

CHAPTER 15

Precious Ansel,

If you had not been so embarrassed over your subpar kissing techniques as to give up on the whole ordeal altogether, I would have found it in my heart to forgive you. There would have been a long road ahead to achieve excellence, but I am a patient teacher and would have graciously provided numerous hands-on demonstrations for the sake of your studies.

Alas, you decided not to pursue higher education.

With regrets,
Della.

Dear Ansel,

I'm slowly becoming acquainted with the other crew members as my daily tasks lead me to their sections of the ship. For instance, today I visited the gun deck to find that Yaggrel's method for organizing his various bombs, guns, and poisons involves leaving them scattered over the floor in a chaotic minefield in which one wrong step might cause a person to disintegrate, melt, and explode in one fell swoop. I of course offered my services to help him organize the chaos.

I was telling him about my mother as we worked, and Yaggrel tried his best to contribute to the moment of recollection by announcing, with a heartfelt look in his eyes as though he cherished the moment, that his own mother tried to eat him as a larva.

I feel as though this explains much about Yaggrel.

My experience polishing tarnished cutlery came in handy when it came to restoring Yaggrel's collection of knives. Though I must admit that every so often, when Yaggrel wasn't looking, I launched his more unsettling poisons out of the airlock. Don't tell.

When we were done, Eryl came down, beheld the shining armory, and promptly picked Yaggrel up by his ankle, letting him dangle there until he expressed his thanks. I've never had as fiercely loyal a friend as I have in Eryl.

I'm enjoying my time here immensely. Though I must admit, when I lie down at night, the sheets are rather cold and empty. Is your bed similarly chilly? Perhaps we could workshop some solutions and come up with a mutually beneficial way to remedy the situation.

Your shivering companion,
Della

P.S. You wore your shirt inside out all day today.
P.P.S. You didn't, but I hope I made you check.

Dear Ansel,

In regards to your shirt, inside out or otherwise, I find it far more promiscuous than any scrap of white linen has the right to be. How dare you wear such a scant little thing? I wonder if you make yourself look debauched on purpose, the way your sleeves are always rolled up to your forearms, your top buttons undone as though you forgot how to navigate the fasteners halfway through the ordeal. You're fooling no one, you know. We all know you spend your nights alone, me most of all. I find your appearance ridiculous, infuriating, and altogether captivating. Please stop.

Thank you in advance,
Della.

P.S. Never stop.

Ansel,

Xaks is proving to be the most difficult crew member to win over. She constantly mutters things like "Liability" and "Weak, puny human" whenever she absolutely knows I'm within earshot.

Today, I retrieved a ladder and spent a great deal of time cleaning the haze from the bridge's windshield in an attempt to win her approval.

However, she refused to even acknowledge me until Eryl showed up and stood in the middle of the room with her arms crossed, demanding Xaks thank me. Eryl made the entire ship shake while Xaks yelled, "Boiling hells and damnation, Eryl. I'm going to remove your consciousness from the ship's mainframe if you don't cut that out."

Eryl did not "cut that out," though Xaks did not end up removing her consciousness from the mainframe either.

I got the distinct impression that the whole ordeal did

not help my case when it comes to endearing myself to Xaks.

Any guidance would be appreciated. For the sake of creating a united crew, of course. Not because I want you to pull me aside into some dark corridor and speak firm words to me about how I shouldn't provoke my fellow crew members.

Della.

P.S. I noticed you walking stiffly today. A warm bath—if such a thing exists here—might ease your bruised ribs. Say the word, and I will draw one for you.

My obstinately distant Captain,

Though we have not talked at length since the day of my arrival, I feel as though I've gotten to know you. I've observed the way you always have a word of encouragement for the crew, even if it is wrapped in jest.

You are fiercely protective of those in your care. I saw it in the way you defended me as we fought our way out of prison. I see it in the way you bark at Yaggrel not to blow us all to smithereens while he tinkers with his newest explosives.

You are the friend to others you never had. I note the way your brow creases when Xaks speaks longingly of the mercenary she will become when she has enough money to change her identity and start over—how she will hunt unposted bounties and accept payment in the form of "thank yous" from those the Cooperation has failed. I see it in the way you spent four hours tracking down a bug in Eryl's mechanical brain. (I never did see the bug, though you claimed you found it. So strange that an insect managed to find its way onto your ship in the middle of space.)

It fills me with awe that Balor's betrayal did not break the part of you that bothers with loyalty. Instead, it's as though you fight to prove every day that integrity exists, as though you alone can cure the unfairness of the universe with your decency. I only wish you might believe that others feel the same devotion toward you.

I think of you. Often. I wonder what you're thinking during the day, if you look out across the stars and dream about the home you might build on each one, if only you could.

I think about you at night most of all, in ways I shouldn't.

—Della

P.S. Have you noticed I haven't returned your shirt? I still wear it at night, and it makes me miss you, which is odd because I never had you to begin with.

My Ansel,

You called me Della dear yesterday in passing, and then you smiled, as though the smile itself was your letter, meant only for me. It only needed a "Love, Ansel" for it to be complete.

Yours—

Something in the cargo hold where Della had been cleaning caught her attention. It was a small rucksack tucked behind a stack of pallets piled with broken ship parts and forgotten crates. While a blanket of dust cloaked everything else, the canvas sack was clean, as though it had recently been displaced. Didn't Ansel discover her book in a rucksack? Could this be the same one?

Hiking up her skirts, Della tiptoed through the rubbish until she reached the pack. She plucked it from its spot before settling onto a pallet, her legs crossed. Something rattled inside the bag, so she lifted the flap and emptied the contents into her apron.

Out tumbled a necklace, a disk-shaped device the size of her palm, and a simple threadbare baby blanket. Why was Ansel hiding his childhood mementos down here? Lifting the necklace by its leather cord, Della examined its pendant in the dim hull light. A teardrop of rough amber hung from the cord. A ring of braided grass was encased within, suspended in the amber.

Though she knew she should stop snooping, she picked up the strange disk next, turning it over in her hands. It was unexpectedly heavy, the metal cold. A few tiny knobs protruded from the side. For a moment, Della debated throwing everything back into the bag and leaving it as she'd found it, but her curiosity got the better of her. She gave the knobs a few experimental turns.

The disk let out a crackle, shattering the silence of the cargo hold. Della yelped and dropped it. It skittered across the floor and came to rest a few feet away. A sheet of dim blue light rose into the air above the disk. It wavered like an apparition, standing the hairs on the back of Della's neck on end.

A face appeared in the light, ghostly and pale, and Della nearly screamed. The man had dark, slicked-back hair and sharp cheekbones. He looked about with an expression like cautious hope, but then his gaze landed upon her, and confusion shrouded his face.

Della would have thought the transparent man was a ghost if she had not seen Ansel conjure a projection of the stars at the breakfast table her first morning aboard the ship. Perhaps this was a similar phenomenon, and this man was not truly here, even if his image was.

But then the man spoke. "Who are you? How did you get this holocomm?"

Della's mind whirred. The disk had to be like the commlinks Ansel and she had used during the prison break to communicate with the crew. Only this device allowed a person to see as well as hear their conversation partner. How marvelous!

"I'm Della. Who are you?" Della asked eagerly, her fear forgotten. She scrambled closer to kneel before the projection.

The man's eyes narrowed, and he took a moment to reply, as though calculating his response. His hesitation put Della on alert, though surely if a way to contact this man was kept aboard the ship, he must not be nefarious.

"I'm a very old friend of Ansel's." He smiled warmly. That smile was so full of sincerity, it urged Della to forget her suspicion. "Do you know him?"

"Indeed, I'm aboard his ship."

The man brightened. "I admit, I thought the mate to my holocomm had long been lost, so when I heard the alert, I was quite shocked. More so when I thought the device had been given to a stranger."

Della blushed. "I confess, it was not given to me. It was lost, as you said, and I happened upon it. I shall return it to Ansel at once. If he hasn't been able to contact you in so long because it was missing, I'm sure he'll be eager to have it back."

"No need for that," said the man—had he told her his name? She couldn't remember, and now it felt awkward to ask in case she'd simply forgotten. "Here's an idea." The man leaned in, a playful glint in his eye. "Why don't we surprise the Captain?"

Helping an old friend plan a surprise for Ansel might be a nice gesture, a thank-you to repay him for his generosity in allowing her to stay aboard the Miss Demeanor.

Of course, if Ansel were reading her book, she supposed it wouldn't be much of a surprise. But since he'd given no indication he'd done so, she asked, "What do you have in mind?"

"I would love to drop in and say hello. It's been so long since we last had a chance to catch up. Wouldn't it be fun to plan an impromptu visit?"

Della nodded, but unease suddenly gripped her.

"Good, good. Give me your coordinates, and I'll let you know when you can expect me, so you can make preparations."

Time slowed, and an immense feeling of dread washed over Della. Ansel had said bounty hunters were after him, not to mention the Cooperation and however many other people he'd managed to make his enemy. This man who seemed a little too eager to know their location might not be the friend he claimed he was.

Della's heart beat once, twice, dull and slow in her ears. She knew she had to respond quickly, lest the man realize she was beginning to fear his intentions were not as pure as he'd like her to believe. She didn't know their coordinates, even if she wished to reveal them, but she had heard Xaks and Ansel rattling off numbers on the bridge, so she knew how many numbers comprised a coordinate.

Della drew in a breath. Time rushed back into place and her senses sharpened. She smiled excitedly and rattled off a string of random numbers as though she were all too willing to tell this man exactly where in the universe they were.

The man beamed, glancing down as though jotting the numbers into a ledger she couldn't see. "Wonderful! You've been such a help. With any luck, I'll be seeing you soon, Delilah."

"Della," Della corrected stupidly, but the projection had already gone dark.

Della's whole body trembled as she snatched up the disk—the holocomm—and dashed out of the cargo hold. She needed to find Ansel and tell him what had happened. Guilt gnawed at her belly at the possibility that she'd endangered them all by speaking to the man, even if she *had* given him false coordinates.

She checked a few rooms, but there was no sign of Ansel. Then she raced down the hall toward the infirmary. Pausing outside the sick bay door, lest she walk in on anyone in a state of indecency, Della listened to the low rumble of Ansel's voice intermixed with Eryl's unnaturally smooth cadence.

"She mentioned cleaning the cargo bay today," Eryl was saying. "I don't think you should presume she's in bed languishing from a deadly plague just because you haven't seen her in twelve hours."

Della froze. Were they talking about her?

"I never said she has a plague," was Ansel's disgruntled response. "I swear, if Xaks installed another sarcasm mod into your processor, I'm going to dump vinegar into her helmet."

"You seemed worried, so I assumed you feared she was ill," Eryl said soothingly, her perpetually even tone somehow borderline patronizing, though perhaps that was in Della's head.

Della fell against the wall. Had Ansel been *checking up on her*? It certainly sounded as though he . . . he noticed her absence.

Unexpectedly, a hard lump rose in her throat.

Ever since that day she played hide-and-seek, when ducking behind a desk was all it took for everyone to forget she existed at all, she'd yearned for just one person aside from her mother to notice her absence.

Della gathered herself. She had more important matters to attend to. It was embarrassing to think that Ansel might read of this moment later. Really, it was pitiful that such basic human decency should move her so.

Deciding that snooping had already gotten her in enough trouble today, Della lifted her chin and stepped into the infirmary. She immediately averted her eyes when she saw Ansel sitting on a cot, his top half stripped down to a fitted undershirt. Eryl was re-dressing his wounds, winding a fresh bandage around his bicep where Balor had carved the knife into his flesh. Della glimpsed two angry red lines slashed into the soft skin on the inside of his arm, right above his elbow. The lines met at a right angle, like half a cube, or perhaps a capital L. Before she could study them further, Eryl looped a swath of white linen over them, blocking her view.

"Della?"

Ansel's voice made her jump. She snapped her gaze to his face, blushing when she realized he'd noticed her peeking.

He raised a brow, prompting her to state her business. How was he so calm and collected? Was this uninterested man really the same one who'd thrust his tongue into her mouth only a week before?

Perhaps she felt awkward around him only because she'd been writing him letters—letters that he clearly still hadn't read. For surely he would not act so unbothered if he'd read her telling him things like *I wear your shirt at night.* At the very least, he would look at her like she had lost her wits. Which, perhaps she had.

Focus, Della, she chided herself.

"I fear I've done something dreadfully foolish." Della withdrew the holocomm from under her apron. Ansel's eyes went wide, and she rushed to explain. "I know it's yours, and I had no business touching it, but a man appeared, and I talked to him, and—"

Ansel shot off the cot and crossed the room to her in a few quick strides. He tugged the device from her hands and pushed past her.

Della trailed after him down the hall, a sick feeling festering in her gut. She had to have made a grievous mistake for him to be so distraught. "He asked for our location," she called, desperate to confess everything. "I didn't tell him, though; I assure you."

They turned the corner to the bridge. Ansel punched the

mechanism to open the door and marched up the steps to the command deck, Della behind him.

"Captain," Xaks greeted him mildly, her feet kicked up on her control panel.

Ansel ignored her, heading for the airlock on the other end of the room. He opened the door, tossed the holocomm inside, and shut it again, pressing a few more buttons until an automated voice announced, "Depressurization initiated." A countdown ran, and then the outside door flew open, and the device pinwheeled into space.

Ansel turned on Della then, breathing hard. "What did he say to you?" he demanded, voice hard. "Are you hurt?"

Della shook her head in confusion. "He told me he wanted to pay you a surprise visit. Who was he?"

Xaks swung her feet to the floor. "What's going on?"

Ansel squeezed his eyes shut and sighed. "Della just met Balor."

CHAPTER 16

"I still don't understand," Della said, but no one was listening. They were all talking over each other, voices rising as they discussed what to do next. "Why ever would you have a device on your ship to contact Balor?"

Everyone was seated around the dining room table, the three-dimensional map of space glowing between them. Well, Della was seated. The rest of the crew were rising out of their chairs as their voices grew more impassioned.

"I told you to throw out that blasted holocomm years ago," Xaks was snarling. "You represent the profoundly simple-minded nature of your species with excellence, Captain."

"And I told you to stop being a cantankerous, condescending wizzlefiend years ago, Xaks, but we see where that got us," Ansel bellowed right back.

"It's really brave of you to use your entire vocabulary in one sentence," said Xaks.

"We should all take a moment to breathe, except for me, because I cannot," Eryl droned on diplomatically, which only made everyone testier. "Studies have shown anger draws resources away from the areas of your brain responsible for rational thought and critical thinking. Of course, I always think rationally, as I do not get angry, nor do I have a brain."

"Everyone shut up, or I'll set off another one of my putrid powder bombs," Yaggrel finally roared, and everyone immediately fell silent. Whatever a putrid powder bomb was, it was evidently unpleasant. "There now," said Yaggrel in a much quieter voice. "No harm has been done. Della didn't tell Shithead where we are, and he apparently believed her false coordinates." He pointed to the map where the blinking dot that represented Balor's ship moved through the tiny replica of space, *away* from the Miss Demeanor.

"That was quick thinking, Della," Ansel allowed gruffly.

"Why was there a device to contact Balor in the cargo hold?" Della asked tentatively, scared the question would set off another volley of frustrations.

Letting out a long sigh, Ansel took a seat opposite her. "Balor and I stole those holocomms when we were kids. They came in handy during our years of thievery; I'd hacked them so they'd jam any nearby devices that tried to trace us or record our correspondence." Ansel scrubbed his hands over his face. "I was stupid to keep it. Sentimentality, I guess. I'd told myself it was harmless, because I'd disabled the receiver in mine so I could contact him but he couldn't contact me. Not that I ever wanted to get ahold of him, obviously. I figured he'd thrown his away long ago anyway."

"He didn't," Della said quietly. Perhaps Balor, too, held onto a fondness for the past, despite what he'd turned into.

Her heart softened a little. It wasn't such a silly idea that Ansel would keep what few possessions he had from Lumeria, but why in the cargo hold? And what about the necklace that had been in the rucksack too? She wondered if it had anything to do with that girl who was *just a friend*.

"Well, at least Balor can't trace us," Xaks was saying. "Assuming your hacking skills are as good as you think they are, Captain."

"They are," Ansel said shortly, and Della was irritated with herself for finding his arrogance attractive.

"If that's true, then he also couldn't have captured and

shared an image of Della's face, since you say messages sent on the device aren't recordable," Yaggrel chimed in. "So she can still collect a bounty for us next week at Creqreon without the Cooperation nabbing her."

"Balor doesn't even remember my name," Della assured them, thinking of how he'd called her Delilah. "Perhaps truly no harm has been done?"

Ansel shook his head grimly. "The problem is that now Balor knows I escaped. Those false coordinates won't fool him for long, and he has eyes everywhere. He'll find us. We need to get our shields fixed, and quickly, so we're prepared when he comes."

PART 3

IN ANOTHER TIME AND SPACE, the son of a poet farmed a dying planet. The words his father had spellbound him with as a child did him little good now. Words did not fill bellies. Like all the other poets, artists, and musicians of the old world, his father had starved.

And so, the son of a poet, now a man, had callused hands that spent more time wielding a shovel than a pen. Words, reading books . . . it was all useless now. The hard, sandy ground his planet had been reduced to was unforgiving, the people who occupied it even more so. And, as was tradition with those who populated crumbling civilizations, absolutely nobody cared about reading. Perhaps, if they had, their civilization wouldn't have crumbled in the first place—though individuals being aware of history had, historically, never stopped it from repeating before, so maybe all empires were doomed regardless.

And then he looked up one day from his withered, dying crop, and he saw a woman standing on the field's dusty horizon. He thought she was a mirage brought on by hunger and thirst, but she approached, and when she touched him, her fingers were cool and soft.

She called herself a librarian, a keeper of words, though

there were no books left that he knew of. She said she existed outside of time and space, that she knew the ending of his story, and it was not a happy one. He asked if she was Fate. She said that if she was Fate, he'd tempted her. And then she vowed that she would change his destiny, no matter the cost.

CHAPTER 17

That night, Della awoke to a knock on her bedroom door.

She shot upright in bed, her first wild thought being that it must be Ansel deciding it was time to stop avoiding her. She swung her legs over the side of the mattress, the floor cool against her toes. Quickly, she tiptoed over to the door.

But no one was on the other side.

Tap tap tap.

The sound came from behind her.

She turned, eyes scanning the room, then catching on a strange swirl of golden light outside the window next to her bed. Squinting, she approached, her mind struggling to make sense of the sight beyond the glass.

A shadowy form came into focus. It was Ansel, *outside the ship.* He smiled at her through the thick lens of his helmet, lifting one gloved hand in a wave.

Della tapped on the glass. "What are you doing out there?"

Of course, he couldn't hear her. He merely kept smiling as he pointed at something. Craning her neck, Della followed the direction of his finger to the airlock door on the side of the bridge, which she could just glimpse from her vantage point.

"You want me to go to the bridge?" She mouthed each word exaggeratedly so he would understand. "To the airlock?"

His smile broadened, and he nodded. She'd never seen him smile so much. How odd. It was a little unnerving, like an entirely different version of Ansel had taken up residence inside his body.

She shook off her apprehension. Maybe he wanted to show her how to swim through space like he was doing. Something to lighten the mood after the day they'd all had.

Quickly, she exited her room and hurried for the bridge. She made her way down a windowed hall, then drew up short when she saw Yaggrel floating outside.

Only he wasn't smiling.

His long, pointed teeth were bared, his fathomless eyes wide in horror, his wispy hair flying around inside his helmet. When he noticed her, he dove toward the glass, making her jump back. Her heart leaped to her throat as he began making frantic gestures, mouthing, "*Help!*"

Dread rushed up Della's spine. "I'm coming!" She sprinted for the bridge. "Xaks, something's wrong!" She punched the button to make the bridge doors spring apart. "Eryl?" But calling for Eryl was futile; the android had powered off for the night to perform something Xaks called a *software update*.

Della flew up the stairs to the command platform. It took her a second to comprehend the horrific sight in the windshield. When she did, it struck her like a blow. Her legs buckled, and she crumpled to her knees at the base of the vaulted windows. Shock paralyzed her, numbing her extremities.

Drifting past overhead, on the other side of the glass, was Xaks. Without her helmet.

Her fins ruffled slowly in the uninhabitable vacuum of space. Her lips were pale, bloodless, her eyes milky and unseeing.

"Xaks!" Della screamed, her voice breaking. "*Xaks!*"

Tears burned in her eyes, but she blinked past them. Ansel and Yaggrel were still out there for some unfathomable reason. Whatever happened to Xaks could happen to them.

Della staggered to her feet and raced for the airlock. It was all too awful, too strange, like a nightmare one might have while sick with a fever, but the terror she felt was too visceral for this not to be real.

She grabbed a space suit hanging in the airlock and began stepping into it. She'd only done this once, while escaping prison with Ansel, but she thought she remembered how to fasten everything. It was no harder than lacing a corset or threading a hundred pearl buttons down the back of a ball gown.

Once the jumpsuit was on, she shoved a helmet over her head, secured it, and closed the airlock door. She punched buttons at random until a female voice began counting down the seconds until depressurization.

She pressed her mask against the porthole of the outside door. There was Xaks, stiff and cold, drifting farther and farther away.

"*Xaks!*" Della's breath fogged her helmet's visor. She repeated Xaks's name over and over, pounding on the airlock door.

She jolted as Ansel swam into the porthole's view, uncomfortably close, still smiling away as though he had no idea of the trouble the others had found themselves in. Della pointed frantically behind him. "Something happened to Xaks. Help her. *Help her!*"

But he didn't seem to notice her panic. As she watched, he lifted his hands to his helmet and began unfastening it, his smile never wavering.

Della's stomach roiled, and bile tinged the back of her tongue. "Ansel, no. Ansel!"

"Depressurizing initiated," the airlock's voice said.

"*Della!*" a muffled voice bellowed behind her.

Della whirled to find Ansel's face pressed to the porthole of the door on the opposite side of the airlock, the one leading back onto the bridge.

She blinked hard. "Ansel?" She looked outside again. And Ansel was there too, unbuckling his helmet. Panic clutched her heart in an icy grip.

"Della, it's not real!" Ansel from the ship yelled behind her right as the airlock doors lifted.

With no time left to hesitate, Della jumped into space, launching herself at the Ansel outside. She reached for his wrists, intent on stopping him before it was too late. The distance closed between them, and then—

Her hands went right through him. Ansel's form rippled around her fingers, dispersing into a million tiny orange and purple sparks. With nothing to stop her propulsion, Della flew into empty space. Horror flooded her veins. *"It's not real!"* ship-Ansel had said. Had the crew outside all been some kind of hallucination?

Panic throbbed behind her ribs. Della tried to twist around to look behind her for the ship, but the space suit was too bulky, and she had no leverage. Just an endless void of nothingness.

Lights flickered at the edges of her vision. The sparks. They zipped around her in a flaming coil of energy, spiraling from her feet to her head. They alighted on her arms, a few at a time, then multitudes, faster and faster until they completely coated her limbs. She tried to brush them off, fear clamping around her lungs. They crept across her visor next, engulfing her view. Soon, all she saw was orange and violet.

Della felt heat next, everywhere the suit was thinnest. At her wrists, her ankles. Pleasant at first, then searingly hot.

"No." She gasped. "No, please, no!"

She felt the pressure of her space suit give way with a sighing *pop.* A spot on her wrist, which had burned moments before, now turned frigid. Air hissed over her skin, rushing out of the hole at her wrist like a cascading river. Della clapped her other hand over the leak, but another sprang open at her ankle. And her opposite wrist. Whatever the sparks were, they had somehow impersonated the crew, lured her out here, and now they would kill her.

Gulping down a few last breaths before she ran out of air,

Della squeezed her eyes shut. *Dear Ansel,* she thought, but made it no further before a heavy body crashed into her and a strong arm looped around her waist, hauling her backward. The sparks flew off her visor like a swarm of disrupted fireflies rising off a hayfield, but it was too late. The air evacuated her lungs. The moisture boiled on her tongue. She surrendered to blackness.

CHAPTER 18

Della woke wrapped in soft sheets, the smell of cold metal and something unnatural and medicinal in her nostrils. She stirred, cracking her eyes open. The gray ceiling of the infirmary loomed above her.

"Della?" Ansel's blurry face came into view, his voice raw and scared like she'd never heard it before.

She rubbed her eyes, clearing her vision. She lay on a cot piled with blankets. Ansel knelt at her bedside, his elbows resting on the mattress, his hands clutching hers.

"Hi," she whispered, the short greeting she'd heard the crew use numerous times feeling funny as it slipped off her tongue. It was strange and wonderful how groups of people adopted each other's ways of speaking until they created a dialect of their own. Even after she left, she'd still carry their words with her, a constant reminder that she was once a part of something.

Noticing the vulnerability in Ansel's expression, Della shakily sat up, the cobwebs melting from her mind. "What's wrong?"

"I—" He shook his head. Then, after a second of hesitation, he leaned over and wrapped his arms around her, tucking his face into the crook of her neck as though he might never let go. Here at last was Ansel, *her* Ansel, the man from the book, stripped of the ironclad armor he put on for the rest of the universe.

Ansel's chest was deliciously warm and solid against her

own, his hands achingly tender as they stroked her back. Yet just as Della decided his arms were her new home, he pulled away.

"What happened?" she asked thickly.

"Cosmic dust." He squeezed his eyes shut. "I never thought to warn you about it. I'm so sorry. For everything today. I haven't prepared you for all the dangers here, and I was a fucking idiot for keeping that holocomm. I should have protected you better."

"Cosmic dust?" Della repeated. The moments before her world went black came rushing back to her like a cold slap of water. "I saw you outside the ship. You took your helmet off! You—"

Ansel repositioned himself to sit beside her, the mattress sagging under his weight, shifting her against him. "It was all an illusion created by the dust. It will use everything you care about to draw you from safety. You can't trust the things you see out of your window in deep space."

It was rather like the fairy tales her mother read her as a child, the ones about avoiding dark enchanted forests. "Is the dust magic?" she asked.

He smiled a bit at that, shaking his head. "Science, Della dear. The dust is made from dead planets, crushed meteors, exploding stars. It contains the elements of life, carbon, ice, hydrogen, and is just intelligent enough to possess the desire to live, to evolve. It wanted to tear you apart, learn your genetic code, and use you for parts. It almost did, too. If I'd jumped out after you a few moments later . . ." He winced.

"How did it know exactly what to show me to lure me outside?" she asked.

"That's how it hunts. All it needs is a taste of your DNA to decode what makes you tick. It knows your deepest fears and can calculate how you may react to any given situation. As far as how it got your DNA in the first place, the sterilizer vents into space."

"Why did it target me?" Della asked, but she knew why. She remembered Xaks's words. *Liability.* She was the easy target.

"It didn't target only you," Ansel said gently. "We all see the illusions. Ignoring it becomes second nature once you're used to it." He rubbed his brow. "I never even thought to warn you. I'm so sorry, Della."

Della realized his hands were shaking. This giant man's hands were trembling because of her. He would likely claim it was due to adrenaline—his favorite excuse to dismiss emotion—but the stricken look in his dark eyes told the real story. He'd been terrified for her.

Della reached over and squeezed his fingers, stilling the tremors. "What do you see? When the dust shows you what you fear most?"

He grimaced. "It's sort of an unwritten rule in space not to ask. If you see a crewmate's visions, it's considerate to avert your eyes. You'll catch on."

"You can see other people's visions?" Della asked. "You saw what I did?"

"Yeah." The compassion in his eyes made her think he'd seen his fair share of horrors in space too. "The visions exist outside your mind. The dust bends light to turn into the images that haunt you, so anyone can see them." A grim smile curved his mouth. "Not that the visions are always terrible. Sometimes, it shows the thing you want most, whatever it thinks might lure you out. It's best not to look. It can become addicting, staring into space, allowing yourself to be tortured by your own fantasies."

Della's gaze traced the contours of his stubbled jaw and cheekbones, and she tried to read the thoughts behind his fathomless dark eyes. *What is it you want most, Ansel Tulzok?* she wanted to ask. Justice? A home? Or something else she hardly dared to hope for.

But there had been a grit to his voice with that final sentence that told her he wouldn't elaborate further. Instead, she only said, "Thank you for jumping out after me."

He tucked stray strands of hair behind her ears and gently kissed her temple as he stood. "Guess the dust knows my weakness." The innocent brush of his lips against her skin made her blood course hot. "I'll get Eryl to examine you. She should have rebooted from her software update by now. With some rest, you should feel better by morning."

Shortly after he had gone, Della noticed something warm and fluttery tickling the inside of her wrist. Frowning, she pulled up her sleeve—then let out a strangled cry. There, embedded in her skin, was a fine sprinkling of cosmic dust, glowing gold and purple. It must have gotten lodged there after the dust burned a hole in her space suit.

She knew she ought to call Eryl and have the dust removed and destroyed, yet something made her pause. She couldn't fault the dust for desiring more, for wanting to *live.* Wasn't that what Della always wanted? The difference was that the dust was [illegible] to do whatever it took to get what it yearned for, and [illegible] always let something hold her back.

Sometimes, I wish I were truly diabolical, she'd once told Ansel. Life would be easier if she didn't care so much. If she could just do what she wanted, like this space monster. Maybe that was the choice. Freedom or goodness.

Della stood and crossed the room, finding an empty glass vial among the medical instruments. She uncorked the top. Using a small scalpel, she gently scraped the skin of her wrist, the dust flaking away and swirling into the vial. When she was finished, she recorked the glass and held it up to the light. Disturbing the dust seemed to awaken it. It clustered around the dry flakes of her skin that had landed in the container, pulling them apart and consuming them. The sparks glowed brighter before breaking apart and multiplying.

Then, something strange happened. The dust formed an

image in the glass, the particles reflecting light to project a scene. It was fuzzy and a little shaky, as though she were viewing a room through someone else's eyes.

A flash of cherry blossom wallpaper made her gasp. She knew that wallpaper. It had decorated the apartment where she grew up. As Della watched, a low bookshelf resting against the wall came into focus. The titles greeted Della like old friends—the fairy tales her mother had read to her since she was a baby.

The scene was a memory.

"Choose a story, Della. Make it a good one." Her mother's voice issued from the glass as a mere whisper, yet it struck Della like a blow. Della hadn't realized how much she'd forgotten that voice. The soft cadence filled her with such mournful longing that tears pricked in her eyes.

The view inside the glass turned to the apartment windows, revealing a picturesque courtyard adorned with vining floral corbels. Tall, spindly towers rose from beyond the walls, obscured by low-hanging candy-floss clouds.

How was this possible? Ansel had said the dust could show her what she desired as well as what she feared, but how could it possibly know what her childhood home looked like?

Thanks to the fever that had turned Della's memory fuzzy, it seemed the dust had a sharper recollection of her past than she did. She'd forgotten that wallpaper. Those towers. And likely more.

The sick bay door banged open, and Xaks strode in. She took one look at the glowing vial in Della's hand and rolled her eyes. "You cannot keep a dangerous space monster as a pet."

Della held up the container. "It's showing me a memory I myself had nearly forgotten. How is that possible?"

"It's fed off you. Things you experience leave a map imprinted on your DNA. Your body can remember things long after your brain forgets."

Della hugged the vial closer to her chest. If she kept feeding the dust, perhaps it would show her more of her past. She'd give anything to glimpse her mother's face again.

"Just promise me you won't let it out," Xaks said wearily. She must have seen something in Della's expression that made her realize Della wouldn't give up the cosmic dust.

"Did you need something?" Della asked, for Xaks lingered by the door.

Xaks's gills flexed. "You've known us for a week, but the thing most likely to draw you out of the ship is the sight of us in danger." She shifted her weight. "What I'm trying to say is . . . while your puny human sentimentality is pathetic, it's also . . . touching." A look of something that might have been either nausea or respect passed over Xaks's expression.

A smile spread across Della's face, which only seemed to fuel Xaks's aggravation.

"Don't think I'm not going to tell Ansel about your little pet." She hmphed.

Della raised a brow. "You honestly think he'll ask me to throw it out?"

"Doubtful. I've asked him to throw *you* out numerous times to no avail." She snorted, bubbles spurting from her nostrils. "Puny human sentimentality. It will get us all killed."

CHAPTER 19

Eryl came in to check on Della one last time before letting her sleep. She'd just finished her poking and prodding when the sick bay door slid open and Ansel stepped through. He wore only a sleeveless undershirt and a pair of loose pants, and his feet were bare. He crossed over to them and swung himself onto the cot next to hers.

"Are you ill?" Della asked, averting her gaze and feeling her ears go hot.

Ansel eyed the jar of cosmic dust sitting on the table beside her bed. "Xaks told me you picked up a stray. I came to make sure it doesn't murder us all in our sleep."

"You're not making me throw it out?" Della asked, picking up the jar and tucking the stardust a little closer.

"I'm not. Because I am a fool, apparently."

"You're not," Della protested.

"I am," Ansel said cheerfully. "I've just been informed of my condition by Xaks, who used a lot of colorful and hurtful language to describe my idiocy."

Eryl shut down a few beeping machines and dimmed the room's light, interrupting their conversation. "You look to be in good health, Della. The most important thing you can do is sleep. I will check on you again in the morning."

"Good night, Eryl," Ansel, said, pulling back the sheets of his cot and making himself comfortable.

Della looked from Ansel to Eryl and back again. "Surely you do not mean to stay here all night."

"It's my duty as Captain to make sure any feral pets brought on board don't devour my crew. It's written in the bylaws. I'm afraid you're stuck with me." Ansel propped his hands behind his head. The way his biceps flexed struck Della as gloriously scandalous. Which was silly. There was nothing so provocative about an arm.

Eryl cocked her head. "Perhaps I should look you over once more, Della. My sensors indicate your pulse has elevated."

Della fought the urge to hide under her sheets.

"Go away, Eryl." Ansel yawned. "It's all your fussing and mothering that has her on edge."

"No!" Della exclaimed, then cleared her throat. "No, Eryl, maybe you should stay." The thought of being alone in this room with Ansel and all that bared skin and toned muscle—and oh heavens, his collarbone. She hadn't known the sight of a man's clavicle could make her blush. She blushed even harder when she considered how Ansel could read these thoughts of hers whenever he had a mind to.

"I will leave," Eryl said. "It's obvious my presence is causing you distress."

Della began to protest again, but Eryl shook her head ruefully. "You're fidgeting and sweating, your pupils are dilated, and your heart is pounding. It might be best if I leave and let the Captain soothe your nerves. I'm sure he can think of some way to help you relax."

A mortifying wheeze escaped Della's lips as Eryl breezed off, seemingly oblivious. Della wasn't completely convinced. Surely such a high-tech piece of equipment knew the physical signs of discomfort from the physical signs of, well, *something else.*

"The dust cannot escape, you know," Della insisted as the door whisked closed behind Eryl with an ominous clunk. "There's no need for you to stay."

"You *hope* it can't escape, you mean." Ansel kicked off his blankets and swiveled to sit on the edge of the cot and face her. "As it turns out, keeping stubborn women from getting killed by the stray monsters they insist on adopting is the one great joy in my life. You can't take this from me without irrevocably crushing my soul. Do you want to irrevocably crush my soul, Della?"

"I suppose not," she breathed, even though she knew she should say something about how improper this was.

"You do look pale," Ansel said, eyeing her. "You work too hard. Forced rest will do you some good."

"I don't mind work," Della said, doing her best not to hyperventilate. "Cleaning gives me an excuse to explore the ship. And there are all sorts of things you can learn about people by sorting through their possessions day after day."

"Oh? What have you learned about us?" The way Ansel looked over at her like that, propped up by pillows and a sleepy smile in his eyes . . . it made her want to tuck herself into his side and whisper into the night.

Then Della noted the greedy gleam in his eye. "Oh no. I'm not going to spill everyone's secrets so you can mercilessly mock them." She primly adjusted her blankets.

Ansel lifted his hands in a sign of surrender. "Fine, then what is it you believe you've learned about *me*?"

Della hesitated. Was this truly happening? He was going to sleep next to her in that bed all night long?

"Della?" Ansel drew out her name, and she let out a surprised laugh. "Which of my deep, dark secrets do you think you've discovered in my sock drawer?"

"Well . . ." Della sat up and scooted to the edge of her cot, mimicking his position. It struck her how close together the cots were. Their knees were less than a foot apart.

Considering his question, she thought of the rucksack, of the necklace that had been inside. She wasn't sure she wanted to ask about it. Maybe there were some things better left in the past.

"I suppose there is the way you leave your bed unmade," she allowed, deciding to keep the conversation light, since he'd only just stopped avoiding her. "I believe that indicates a predisposition to chaos."

His eyes glinted. "There's no point in making it when I'm only going to use it again."

"With that logic, one might as well not bother keeping anything tidy—which, now that I think about it, is perhaps your exact philosophy, given the state of your ship upon my arrival."

"Look at you with your jokes."

The mild appreciation in his tone made her toes curl, for which she immediately felt ridiculous. His praise did peculiar things to her insides. She couldn't help but think of those lecherous acts he'd alluded to when he talked of whisking her away in a carriage, and what sorts of hushed praise he might whisper into her ear when she pleased him then.

Della blinked away the mental images that thought aroused. "I'm only saying, if you made your bed as soon as you woke, it would look neat all day, and you could return to an orderly bedroom in the evening."

"What if you want to use your bed in the middle of the day?" The way he asked was innocent enough, but the twitch of his lips betrayed his suggestive intent.

"I don't have time for . . . naps," she stammered.

Ansel chuckled. "I don't have time for naps either." The way he was leaning forward, his shirt gapped at the neck, displayed a view of that tempting collarbone she wanted to bite. She could smell his lilac cologne, and it made her oddly feral.

"Do you think I'm dreadfully silly?" she blurted out, her skin burning hot. "Is that why you tease me like you do? Because I'm so easy to fluster?"

He lay back down, crossing his ankles and studying the ceiling. "I like making you blush, but I don't think you're silly. I think you have the capacity to *be* silly when you want to be, and I admire you for it."

She blinked. "You *what*?"

"After the life you've lived, the fact that you can still be sweet and funny and yes, a little silly, is admirable."

Della's stomach did a little flip. Most people scorned her soft nature. She never supposed someone would see it as a positive trait. "And I think you're—" the words rusted in her throat because she wasn't sure where to begin. *Tenacious? Noble? Unexpectedly kind?* "I admire you too," she finished, the words far too feeble to express the swell of emotion he inspired in her. She enjoyed his company. No, *enjoy* was too small a word. She ached with this beautiful, comfortable sensation she didn't quite know what to do with.

She simply . . . liked him. A great deal. She liked the whole crew, which was revolutionary because, aside from her mother, no one had ever given her a reason to like them before. She already mourned the day when she'd have to leave.

Then again, Della knew she shouldn't dread the prospect of leaving Ansel and the crew when it meant saving her mother.

A crease appeared between Ansel's brows. "Why do you look sad?"

She twisted her fingers together in her lap. "Do you think it is wrong to feel happiness when others are suffering?"

Ansel turned on his side and propped his head on his elbow. His gentle teasing was sweet, but the way he now considered her question with such serious deliberation made her feel . . . cherished.

"It's not one person's duty to carry the grief of the universe," he finally said.

"Not the universe. My mother. What kind of person does it make me if I can enjoy my time here while her life is in danger?"

"I don't think it makes you a particular kind of person. I think it just makes you a person." Ansel sat back up and brushed a knuckle over her knee—barely a touch, yet it sent tingling warmth spiraling through her veins. "She'd want you to be happy. Feeling bad won't get us to Lumeria faster. You can't survive life's miseries without allowing yourself to experience its joys, whenever they might come. You are good, Della, and you deserve to feel goodness."

"If I deserve to feel goodness, what do you deserve to feel? Badness?" Lifting her foot, she teasingly nudged his shin with her toes, hoping to break the somber mood. "Because you're such a big, bad outlaw? Or is it that you prefer being tortured and alone?"

Rolling his eyes, he lay back onto his pillow. "Eryl's right. You're unwell."

Biting back a giggle, Della followed his lead, pulling the soft blankets to her chin. She could hardly believe her forwardness, but he made her reckless. She was unimpressed by the sinister reputation the universe had concocted for Ansel. Something about him made her want to poke at him like he was a sleeping bear. She might enjoy the thrill of his bite.

Oh, heavens. If you read of this later, Ansel, please skip over that paragraph.

Della studied the flickering lights of the machines around her as they bounced off the ceiling, waiting for her eyes to grow heavy.

"Some part of Balor misses you, you know," she said quietly after a while. Now that she wasn't looking at Ansel, it was somehow easier to talk to him. Secrets traveled more easily in darkness. "I think your friendship was real to him, in some twisted capacity. He couldn't throw out that device. He appeared so quickly in the projection when I unwittingly summoned him. As though he'd been waiting for years to hear from you."

"Don't, Della," Ansel said softly. "I've wasted a lot of time looking for redeeming qualities in Balor. He didn't hold on to that holocomm for sentimentality. He likely held onto it in case it one day proved useful in hurting me. Which it did. I should have thrown that rucksack away years ago."

"It holds everything you have left of home," Della said.

"It's all I have left of a place I spent the first eighteen years of my life, but that place wasn't a home, no matter how much I like to lie to myself. I had no reason to hold on to items that remind me of pain." His voice went soft so she could hardly hear him. "I'm playing make-believe, cherishing the daggers that stabbed me in the back and pretending they're family heirlooms."

Della's heart ached for him, this man who stuffed the emptiness in his heart with pain instead of love because it was all he had. He called her good, but he was too. So good it hurt to think about. Part of her wanted to slip out from under the covers, crawl into his bed, and hold him. But of course, that would be terribly improper.

Instead she only said, quietly, "I missed this. How we were in the books."

He rolled onto his side, away from her. She thought he wouldn't say more, but then she heard his soft, "Me too."

"You don't have to keep avoiding me," Della said.

His back was to her, but she could see his shoulders stiffen. "I haven't been avoiding you. I just haven't been—" Though he didn't finish the sentence, she could guess the rest. *I just haven't been ravishing you against walls.*

Why? she wanted to scream. *Why deny this? What is the real reason?*

His unfinished sentence loomed restlessly above them all night, even after they both finally drifted to sleep.

CHAPTER 20

After she'd recovered from the incident with the cosmic dust, Della spent the next five days on board the ship in much the same manner as she had before, only now she had a tiny monster in a bottle to care for. (It had not, much to everyone's relief, feasted on the crew in the night.)

Della had taken to feeding the stardust the contents of her dustpans and, on occasion, plucked strands of her own hair, hoping it would show her more of her memories. Unfortunately, it only displayed images of her companions in various states of distress—or, more often, Ansel in various stages of *und*ress—an alarming new development that spoke to her unquenchable and growing attraction toward the Captain.

If one of the other crew members happened to look the dust's way, it showed their fears and desires instead. She tried to avert her eyes, but she still caught glimpses of them, which ranged from terrifying to, in Yaggrel's case, downright disturbing. Ansel, meanwhile, refused to rest his gaze anywhere near the thing.

On the morning of the sixth day, Della's time bot woke her with a rude, "I'd tell you to rise and shine, but you'll only do what you normally do and rise and *whine* about everything all fucking day."

Della silenced the bot and went to the window to find their ship approaching an enormous city floating in space. A *space station*, the crew told her. It was one large disk with buildings rising off the top, creating a sort of skyline. A long, pointed rudder jutted down from the bottom of the entire thing, perhaps to stabilize it. The sight was rather chilling—this huge chunk of metal floating in the middle of space. Ships darted to and from the structure like tiny gnats buzzing about a fruit bowl. Here, they would refuel, make small repairs, buy supplies (groceries included), and—Ansel insisted—purchase her new clothing.

It took an agonizing few hours to actually reach the station; distance was deceptive in space. But at last, they landed and disembarked, each of the crew members going their separate ways to explore what the station had to offer. Eryl, however, insisted on sticking by Della's side as they went in search of supplies.

"This is truly the current fashion?" Della called out to Eryl now, from a dressing room inside one of the space station's shops.

Della was hardly able to recognize the person standing before her in the mirror. She had traded her heavy skirts for a simple tunic over a pair of fitted leggings. Instead of pinning her hair up, Eryl had persuaded Della to let her braid it in complex ropes that gathered at the crown of her head before falling to the center of her back in a long plait. She looked smaller without her skirts, but she felt stronger, no longer suffocated by the world's idea of what she should be.

Della walked out of the dressing room into the cramped shop. It was packed full of clothes fit for all types of species. The smell of cotton and laundry stuffed the air, and multicolored fabrics draped over racks and dangled from the ceilings.

When Eryl swiveled her head toward Della, she let out a metallic twang that might have been a gasp. "You look wonderful, Miss Della."

"I'm still not sure I feel right about Ansel paying for all this when he can't even afford to fix the ship," Della said.

"He cannot afford to pay a fifty-thousand-credit repair. A

few articles of clothing won't break him." Eryl walked to the counter at the front and swiped her wrist device under a red beam of light, which Della had learned somehow transferred credits from account to account.

After the items were paid for, Della followed Eryl back into the hangar. The space was unfathomably big, its vaulted ceiling soaring so high it felt like a steel sky. Ships of all shapes zipped in and out like birds nesting in barn rafters, from tiny two-person vessels to cargo transports that needed every inch of the hangar's height to land. Down on the floor, crews bustled to and fro, and all throughout were food carts and hawkers selling their wares, calling out merchandise, from trinkets to weapons and beyond.

If Della closed her eyes, she could almost imagine she was back in Poling, the sounds of the market swirling around her. Of course, the smells were different—the metallic scent of fuel and steel instead of the stench of stale mud—but the energy was similar. When Della opened her eyes, the dreary memories of Poling shriveled under the blinding reality before her, cravats and bustles melting into jumpsuits and helmets.

"There you are." Xaks hurried over, holding a brightly colored bag of candy. "We're nearly ready to go. If there's anything else you want, you'd better get it." She plopped a candy into the top of her helmet and snapped it up with her tongue.

Della eyed the candy, her taste buds tingling. She had a sweet tooth she never got to indulge, not since the days when her mother brought home treats from the grocer's. She thought about asking Xaks for a piece but lost her nerve. "Where's Yaggrel?"

"Yaggrel doesn't like people. He tends to start blowing them up after prolonged exposure. I admit I can empathize with the urge, but it's best if he stays on the ship."

"Shouldn't we do our business here with more caution?" Della asked. "What if there are bounty hunters? Won't they recognize you?"

Xaks popped another candy into her helmet. "We're careful about where we dock. This station is safe, at least from bounty hunters."

"Well, that's comforting," Della said. "I just need to select a few more proteins before we go."

They made their way through the haphazard maze of booths and canopied shops. There were fish with multiple tails resting on ice, huge slabs of meat with ribs larger than she, fruits with flaky purple centers, and herbs with strange, wonderful scents.

Xaks followed them around, taking every free sample offered her way and providing helpful commentary like "Why are you taking so long?" and "Can't we go yet?"

Della rounded a yellow-and-white-striped tent selling tonics. She was reading the label of one that read *Gasoff, for the gas giant inside us all* when she spotted Ansel by the Miss Demeanor, growing increasingly frustrated as he called out instructions to a group of grubby maintenance droids. The zip of wrenches, the clang of hammers, and the crackle of welders could be heard across the hangar.

There was something inexplicably endearing about the way Ansel was fighting to maintain his composure as the knee-high droids completely disregarded his orders. The man had more patience than Della would have originally given him credit for, even if he was prone to grumbling.

He happened to look up while she was staring. Their gazes caught for a moment before his raked down her body. She felt every place her new clothing clung to her curves. She wished she could read his thoughts for a change.

"I should assist the Captain," said Eryl. "He might understand computers, but mechanics elude him. Without direction, I fear what the maintenance droids might do. I doubt they have a gigabyte of RAM between their audio receptors, combined. I believe I can feel one of the runts fusing my joints together as we speak."

"Don't spoil the fun, Eryl," Xaks practically whined, eating another piece of candy. "It's so entertaining, watching the Captain flail about pathetically."

Something tugged at Della's heart. She wished she had people who would talk behind her back like this—with the type of tender insults that actually declared the person's adoration of another's oddities.

"You're all so fond of Ansel," Della said quietly. "Does he even realize it?"

"I derive joy from watching the Captain make a fool of himself, and your takeaway is that I'm deeply fond of him?" Xaks asked.

"Of course you are," Della said dismissively, her words dissolving into a sigh as her gaze tracked Ansel's activity across the hangar.

Shoulders sloped in resignation, Ansel squatted to take a repair bill from the claws of a droid. As he stood, the ludicrously long receipt uncoiled nearly to the ground. Ansel scratched the back of his head, looking distinctly overwhelmed.

Della found his distress alluring. She wasn't sure why. Perhaps because he so often liked to insist that he had everything under control. Was that why he was so determined to disregard their moment in the airlock? Because one could not groan helplessly into another's mouth one moment and pretend to have sole control over one's life the next?

"Why won't he ever allow himself to love and be loved?" Della realized she'd spoken the thought out loud when she noticed the reactions from the others.

Xaks hesitated a long moment, exchanging a look with Eryl, whose golden eyes glowed steadily.

"Oh, puny human," Xaks said, not unkindly. "He will break your heart. Don't even try it."

But Della was already trying. She was certain he felt something for her, even if he didn't admit it, even to himself. A man did not give his last breath to a woman he felt nothing for. And if he did, then she admired him all the more for it. She would respect his rules if he wished to remain distant, but she herself was in too deep to escape unscathed.

She didn't *want* to escape unscathed.

For so long in Poling, she'd numbed herself to her surroundings. Now, she wanted to live, vibrantly and fearlessly. She opened herself to whatever pain or wonder or joy might come. Any scars she received as a result would serve as evidence that she'd experienced extraordinary things.

If Ansel broke her heart, she would be devastated for a while. She would miss him for a while. For a while, she might even hate him. But then she would go right back to feeling tenderness for him once more, when he was nothing more than a tale of great love she told when she was old.

"Perhaps," Della said, "it's better to experience heartache than never feel anything meaningful at all."

Xaks cocked her head, her gossamer ear fins rippling in the currents inside her helmet. "When I first saw you, I thought you were a sniveling coward."

Della waited for her to continue. "Was there supposed to be a 'but' after that, or are you just sharing more rude observations?"

Xaks sighed. "*But* you keep proving me wrong. Are you scared of nothing?"

Della smiled softly. "I am. Terrified of it. I am scared of nothing, of going my whole life *feeling* nothing, being nothing, seeing nothing."

"Well," Xaks said around a mouthful of candy, "if you want your heart broken, he'll do it soundly enough, I'll give you that. I've only seen him hung up on one woman, and she was his wife."

His wife.

His *wife*?

Air evacuated Della's lungs. Her insides coiled as though to protect themselves. Perhaps she'd been too hasty to open herself up to all the heartache the universe might have to offer.

She'd seen Ansel's mind, known he'd occasionally recollected a girl with vague fondness and lingering pain, but she assumed her to be nothing more than a long-lost love. Not his *wife*.

"*She was a friend.*" That was what Ansel had told her when Della asked him about the girl he kept trying not to think about.

"Oh no. You're looking clammy," Xaks said. "Relax. They were really young. The marriage was impulsive and short. They split up before his arrest."

The knots in Della's stomach eased, but only a little. She forced her legs to move, continuing to meander the market, even though she could hardly pretend to be interested in the wares. "I wonder what broke them apart," she mused, more to herself than anyone else.

"She betrayed him," Xaks said frankly. Her words were followed swiftly by a grunt as Eryl elbowed her. "*What?*"

"Humans are particular about where they obtain their personal data about one another. The Captain should be the one to tell her."

"That seems inefficient," Xaks grumbled.

"Yes, well," said Eryl. "That's the human experience. They love making their lives as difficult for themselves as possible."

Della subconsciously vowed never to tell Xaks a secret, considering the way she obliviously overshared everyone's business without a second thought.

"Good luck getting the sordid tale out of him," Xaks said. "It usually requires several pints of spirits and an unbearable amount of sad, sappy music."

"Does—does he still love her?" Della couldn't stop the question from leaving her lips, even though she felt cowardly, probing Xaks for information behind Ansel's back.

"She . . . did a number on him," Xaks said. "But no. He refuses to care about *anyone*."

Because he got hurt the first time? Or was there more to it than that? Those questions and more darted around Della's mind, but she sealed her lips, vowing to speak to Ansel personally about the matter when she next had an opportunity.

Xaks turned to Eryl, breaking the melancholy mood with a smirk. "Imagine if the Captain ever met someone he actually liked."

"The horror," Eryl said, her monotone pleasant as ever.

"He'd act like it was the biggest catastrophe to occur since that meteor knocked Wrythior out of orbit," Xaks said gleefully, slugging Eryl's arm, which resonated like a wind chime. She really was a terrible gossip. "He'd be a miserable wreck—would probably spend all his time moping about and annoying the rest of us with his foul mood."

"Imagine if that person started living on his ship," Eryl said conversationally. "It would drive him to distraction."

"Imagine if she were even able to look past the fact that he's a vain, arrogant philanderer with terrible spending habits and no prospects," Xaks said with relish.

"He'd desperately wish he could fall for her, but he wouldn't let himself because"—Eryl's voice shifted to a chillingly accurate imitation of Ansel's—"he's a tragic, brooding captain who can't experience frivolous things like *joy* and all-consuming passion."

Heat rose to Della's face. They were clearly teasing her. Was she that obviously moon-eyed? She suspected Ansel felt some level of attraction and perhaps even fondness for her, but this? The way they acted, the poor man's entire existence was in shambles, and that simply couldn't be true.

Could it?

"Imagine if she wore her socks tied up by little ribbons above her knee," Eryl went on. "He would probably be compelled to deliver an entire monologue about them to his poor android when all she did was ask him if he wanted her to change the air filters."

"Oh, oh, I've got an even better one," said Xaks. "Imagine if her name was Della."

Eryl tilted her head. "I sense this is one of those instances where you have lost the spirit of banter, Xaks. To communicate in the custom of humans, you must say everything aside from what you actually mean."

Xaks turned to Della and, wonder of wonders, *winked.* Della's chest filled with warmth because she realized . . . they were treating her as though she were one of them. True, their jabs were gentler versions of the scathing barbs they lobbed Ansel's way, but the kind spirit behind them was the same. They were letting her in and trying to tell her something, something incredible and marvelous and—

Impossible.

It had to be impossible, didn't it? It didn't matter that Ansel had kissed her like a depraved scoundrel in that airlock or if he'd done any of the things the crew claimed. For if he felt something genuine for her beyond superficial attraction, wouldn't he have been forthcoming and told her about his *wife*?

Della decided it was time for answers. She could not sit by agonizing any longer, wondering how he felt. If Ansel wanted her as badly as Xaks and Eryl implied, it was time for him to tell her himself.

"We need to go." Ansel's voice behind her made her jump so hard she nearly choked. "Yaggrel just contacted me. According to the signal from the tracking device, Balor reversed his trajectory and is advancing our way. Someone here must have seen the Miss Demeanor and tipped him off, and he realized those coordinates Della gave him were false."

So much for this station being safe, Della thought, but she held her tongue.

"There goes our element of surprise," Xaks said grimly.

"We'll just have to be ready for him when he comes and hope the Miss Demeanor's power supply can hold up long enough for the SPM-500 to disable his ship," said Ansel.

"How long do we have?" Xaks asked.

"He's faster than us," Ansel said. "Even if we run, he'll catch us in less than a week."

"What does that mean?" Della asked.

"It means if we don't collect that bounty tomorrow and get our shields fixed, we're fucked," said Ansel.

Dear Ansel,

I admit it stung a little to learn such a crucial piece of information about you from someone else, but I suppose I cannot blame you. It's my fault I've chosen to be so transparent, and I cannot expect the same in return. You told me as much when you asked to keep your book, and it wouldn't be right for me to expect more.

I am beginning to feel silly, writing you these letters as though I'm under some delusion they mean something to you. I fear this has become another game of pretend, and I'm having trouble distinguishing where the dream ends and reality begins. That is not your fault either. You warned me I shouldn't start falling for you. The trouble is, I'm rather clumsy and have tripped.

With Balor encroaching, perhaps it is better we refrain from distractions anyway, however pleasant they might be. Unless you give me some sign that you wish for me to continue, I will not bother you with these letters anymore.

Regards,
Della.

CHAPTER 21

He'd bought her candy.

After they departed the space station, Della felt as though she were writing a farewell letter—until she found a little unopened bag of candy that matched the one Xaks bought. She'd gone into the kitchen to sort through the strange, unfamiliar foodstuffs, and there it was, on the cold stove where she couldn't miss it.

Della approached it as though it were a frightened animal who might dart away the moment she offered it affection. It sat upon a torn piece of paper with a note written on it, signed by Ansel. His handwriting was truly horrendous, all slashing lines and giant scrawled vowels.

Dear Della,

I don't advise asking Xaks to share her candy. She tends to cut people.

Yours,
Ansel.

Her heart palpitated, and her hands grew clammy. Had Ansel looked over in the hangar and noticed her eyeing Xaks's candy?

Or had he *read* about her wanting it?

If he'd read about it, then he must have also seen her wishing for a sign from him that her letters meant something. Maybe the candy was his admission that he'd been reading. A hesitant request to resume what he'd once withdrawn.

The possibilities filled her with giddiness, though she tried to rein in her racing imagination. She should show some restraint and not go throwing her heart around like a schoolgirl because a handsome captain bought her candy.

She slipped one of the hard candies between her lips as she set about sorting the food for that night's dinner. Sweetness burst across her tongue as the outer shell cracked, allowing fizzy syrup to dance across her mouth. The candy was unlike anything she'd had before. It had a mind of its own, drops of it bouncing from taste bud to taste bud, setting each one alight before it trickled deliciously down her throat.

She resisted the urge to try another, intent on preparing the menu, which would require a clear palate to familiarize herself with the unidentified slabs of meat and multicolored fruits. The prospect of navigating all those odd, bristly vegetables was especially intimidating.

She'd told everyone dinner would be served at six. The announcement was met with many complaints, but she was determined to seat the crew around a table where they would eat a meal like civilized people instead of darting in and out of the kitchen at all hours.

Good food was the reprieve the crew needed after the bad news about Balor, and they were set to arrive at Creqreon the following morning, which made tonight feel momentous somehow—the last night of peace before a dangerous adventure. She needed to create a meal worthy of the occasion.

Following an afternoon of simmering, kneading, boiling, and chopping, Della heaved a tray containing the main course—

something that resembled a roasted six-legged chicken—and entered the dining room, fully expecting it to be empty. She'd already mentally prepared herself for the task of tracking down the reluctant crew and dragging them to dinner.

Instead, there they all were in their places at the set table, waiting politely. Not one elbow was on the table, much less anyone's backside. It even looked like an attempt had been made to slick down Yaggrel's wiry comb-over.

Unexpected tears pricked at Della's eyes. Gathering herself together, she placed the tray at the center of the table and unveiled it to appreciative sounds of hunger and awe. Not even Xaks, out of her helmet and sitting in her special water chair, had anything sarcastic to say.

Eryl helped Della bring out the rest of the food, then took her place at the table. Before her sat a special plate of electronics cleaner and high-grade oil. Xaks was served in her chamber through a mini airlock and expressed her thanks via a speaker on the side.

After placing the last bowl, Della turned to retreat to the kitchen, where she had plans to listen in on their conversation and take full credit for every sigh of contentment.

Ansel caught her wrist. "Don't try that ever again. Sit."

Della's pulse thundered. "It's wrong."

"But it feels so right," Yaggrel muttered obnoxiously under his breath, which earned him a vicious kick under the table.

Ansel's exasperated look gave Della the distinct impression that he was solely responsible for everyone's timely attendance at dinner, and that it had taken much encouragement and possibly a few threats. She was touched.

"It's not my place," said Della when Ansel continued to hold on to her wrist.

Ansel stood and pushed Della down into his chair. "We're a bunch of fugitives, Della. If you don't have a seat with us, you don't have one anywhere."

She'd always sort of assumed that was the case. But then Ansel went to the kitchen and brought her a plate, fork, and utensils. He dragged over the kitchen's quintessential wobbly stool no one else liked and sat on it next to her. Everyone started heaping their plates before piling food onto their neighbor's, shouting enthusiastic things like "Have you tried this yet?" and "Holy shit, these tarts are like an orgasm in my mouth" and "I don't want to hear about what's orgasming in your mouth, Yaggrel" and "Would you all watch your fucking language during Della's fucking dinner she worked really fucking hard on?"

Something strange began to happen.

Della began to feel like she belonged.

She couldn't help but remember that awful dinner party at the Duke's. It was objectively nicer with crystal flutes instead of tin mugs, and high-class lords and ladies instead of misfit criminals, but in her eyes, it fell short in every way.

The crew were discussing their plans for how they were going to apprehend the criminal they'd found who was visiting Creqreon tomorrow—a human named Gyrund, wanted for grand larceny with a fifty-thousand-credit bounty on his head. (Eryl, being practical, suggested handcuffs, Xaks an overly elaborate plot only she understood that involved false identities, a code language, and some kind of bird, and Yaggrel described a bloody, gruesome affair that no one found helpful.) Della couldn't tell if they were in earnest or if the entire conversation was a series of inside jokes, but it didn't matter.

Xaks's blunt insults were like affectionate hugs. Eryl's smooth voice felt like having your closet checked for monsters. Yaggrel's crude comments and violent tendencies felt like—well. She supposed every family had a strange uncle.

Ansel's elbow bumping against her own felt like butterflies, candy, and stolen kisses. Every so often, he'd look over at her, his eyes dancing with mirth, as though they were in on something the rest weren't. Della could hardly focus on the rambunctious conversation. She was distracted by his mouth, by those lines that formed around it like brackets. Nestled in a world full of disappointment and heartache, his smile was set apart in parentheses, like a slice of happiness reserved just for her.

"Remind me why we gave up food." Xaks groaned at last, pushing her empty plate away and belching, bubbles swirling up through her water pod.

"We've been so focused on surviving that we forgot to live," Ansel said, his gaze never leaving Della.

The kitchen was quiet in the aftermath of the dinner, but it was not the cold silence Della was accustomed to during those long nights at the Loughtys. It was warm and full, as though the room still held the laughter of those who had occupied it.

She hummed as she washed dishes, the tune accompanied by the gentle chink of silverware, swish of bubbles, and squeaks of her rag.

"What's that song?" Ansel asked behind her.

Somehow, she was both bewildered and unsurprised by his presence. Bewildered because the idea of someone willingly seeking out her company still felt bizarre. Unsurprised because Ansel at her side felt exquisitely inevitable.

"I don't know the words," she said, in response to his question. "My mother always hummed it." A sudden wave of memories crashed over her. Her mother, humming as she tucked Della in, or as she placed a cool washrag on Della's brow when she was sick, or as she clattered around in the next room as Della fell asleep at night.

The sudden sound of the kitchen door swishing shut startled Della from her thoughts.

"Oh no," Eryl's distant voice called through the wall. "The

door appears to have malfunctioned. I fear the two of you will be stuck in there until I can rectify the situation."

Ansel scrubbed his face, utterly drained, and Della held back a laugh. Instead of demanding Eryl open the door, Ansel walked over and leaned against the counter next to the sink, facing Della.

"That song. It sounds like one I heard once. Isn't that weird? That someone in your world put together a series of notes in nearly the same order as someone from mine?"

"I'm not sure I believe in coincidences anymore," she said.

Some distant clanking could be heard from beyond the door. "I fear this may take all night to fix," Eryl called. Since the android quite literally did not have a life of her own, she must feel the need to meddle in other people's. "You two had better get cozy."

"Where did you hear the song?" Della asked.

"Lumeria. Balor played it incessantly on this annoying little flute he had. He used to distract people with it while I swiped their wares right out from under their noses."

Della wondered if the song had resurrected Ansel's memories the same as it had hers, if his mind was far away in a home he'd long ago lost. "Despite everything, you miss him, don't you? The friend you used to have?"

"More like the friend I never had." Ansel began rolling up his shirtsleeves, and a cup nearly slipped from Della's hands as he bared his forearms. "I looked up to him like he was my older brother, but the whole time he was manipulating and exploiting me. That's what hurts the most, missing something that never really existed."

"I'm sorry," she said, the two words far too feeble to express the painful compassion swelling in her heart.

"Not your fault." Pushing off the counter, he closed the gap between them. He gently took the sudsy cup she'd been washing out of her hands, nudged her aside, and finished scrubbing it himself.

Della stood there with bubbles dripping off her fingertips, entranced by the sight of Ansel up to his elbows in dishwater. A simple act, yet it made her feel doted upon. "You really shouldn't do that," she said softly. She meant the dishes, but she also meant *You really shouldn't make me fall for you.*

He tossed the dishcloth over his shoulder, grabbed her waist in his soapy hands, and hoisted her onto the countertop before she could react. "Who is the captain of this ship? Me or you?"

"You." Her heart beat wildly. She felt the heat of his body where he stood between her knees. In her new clothing, his every touch felt new, unmuffled by thick skirts and a corset.

"If I want to wash dishes, then I will wash dishes," Ansel said. "I'm not sure where you get off telling me what to do. You should be disciplined for insubordination."

"Then discipline me." Her cheeks flamed as soon as she said it, but her parted thighs ached with want.

"Careful." Ansel's eyes darkened. "You might want to behave. When I inflict a punishment, I don't stop until I hear screams."

"I never scream."

"Begging, then." His gaze dropped to her mouth.

"Best of luck."

"Stars," he breathed. "I'll have to brush up on my water-boarding skills."

He didn't lean closer, but Della's lips tingled in anticipation. She shifted forward infinitesimally, her every nerve urging him to close the gap between them.

"Della," Ansel said, his lips inches from hers. "I need to tell you something."

"Your wife." Della squeezed her eyes closed.

Slowly, he pulled away. "Xaks told you." It wasn't a question.

"Why didn't *you* tell me?"

"I didn't think I needed to because I didn't plan on this happening—me and you. But now I'm struggling to deny that it is."

"Why do you want to deny us?"

"I don't . . . trust people easily."

Deep sadness went through Della that Ansel hadn't felt safe enough to confide in her. Where the books provided her comfort in the way they helped her communicate thoughts and feelings that she struggled to convey on her own, they did the opposite for him. Revealing his heart only caused him discomfort.

"It was short-lived, the relationship," Ansel said. "We don't have things like marriage on Lumeria, so when she told me about this vow of unwavering love and trust . . . I'd never wanted anything more."

"But she ended up betraying you?" Della winced, remembering what Xaks had said.

Ansel shifted to lean on the counter beside her, crossing his arms. "I was with her while Balor was stealing the superconductor." His tone was cold as he relayed the tale, as though he were telling a stranger's experience instead of his own. "When Balor framed me, I thought everything would be fine with her as my alibi. But when the time came for her to vouch for me, she didn't show up."

"But why?" Della gasped.

"Balor paid her off."

Another surge of primal protectiveness went through Della, as though she should have been there to help Ansel, even though she had quite literally been in another world. He had been betrayed by the only two people he'd ever trusted with his heart. No wonder he was reluctant to trust her too.

"You still love her?" Della forced her voice to remain even.

"No," he said quickly.

"But you don't trust me." She slid off the counter and went back to the dishes. She understood why he was wary, but she was not a thing he could literally place on a shelf and expect to still be there when he was ready to return to it. "You can read my mind with my book, and you still worry I would hurt you like that?"

"You'll have to go home eventually," Ansel said, eyes full of misery, "for your mother. I've had Eryl search every database to try to figure out where in the universe your planet is, and we can't find it. The only way to your reality is through your book."

So it was as she suspected. The only way home was to risk magic again.

"And what if you can't come back?" Ansel went on. "What if you don't want to? I couldn't ask you to leave your home and the only family you have left. And besides, how can I make any kind of commitment to anyone when I could be caught and thrown into prison any day? It's not that I can't trust your character. It's that we're doomed."

Della felt the story she wanted with him escaping her clutches yet again. If only she could catch a few shreds. "You don't—" Della stammered. She set a dried plate on the counter and tossed the dishcloth on top before facing him and trying again. "You think you know what I want, but you don't. I know you feel the attraction between us, but it's not as though we must fall in love. This can be temporary. It is my understanding that you've managed other such . . . arrangements before, without deeper commitment?"

"I can't touch you and feel nothing." Ansel's jaw knotted, and she might have thought he was angry with her if it weren't for the words he was speaking.

"Oh." How odd it was for a heart to break and swell all at once, like a balloon filling so full it burst.

"I'm sorry," he said, allowing her to see the pain in his eyes. "Maybe you were right about me being scared for my own heart. I don't think anything I've experienced will have prepared me for losing you, if I let this thing between us continue."

"I'm glad you told me." Della scrubbed pointlessly at a spotless spoon. She'd wanted this, for him to be vulnerable the way he was in his book, but it hadn't turned out the way she'd imagined. She understood now why he kept it all in, hoping to spare them both this helpless anguish.

"Please go," she said, blinking back hot tears. He was scared to love, and she was terrified she'd never get the chance to.

"Let me help you finish the dishes at least."

Della shook her head. It hurt too badly for him to be so near and so distant all at once. If he stayed any longer, she would cry, and she didn't want him to see her do that. "Eryl," she choked out, "please open the door."

The door immediately whisked open, and after a moment's hesitation in which Della hoped Ansel would change his mind and pull her into his arms, he was gone.

And she was alone. As alone as she'd ever been after Mrs. Loughty's house parties, when she was left cleaning up scraps, each discarded ribbon or half-eaten confection a mockery of a life she could never have. Perhaps she would never be more than this. A maid. An observer, nibbling at the crumbs left behind after everyone else's adventures whisked past. It was foolish to think a simple hop into a book could turn her into someone she wasn't.

CHAPTER 22

Della finished the dishes, because she was a reasonable woman who completed the tasks she set out to do. If she stacked them with more force than necessary, it was only because it was late and she was tired, not because a frustrating captain had driven her to the brink of desperation before telling her they could not be together.

No. She wasn't being fair. Since the airlock, he hadn't done anything to encourage her feelings aside from showing her kindness. Well, perhaps he'd flirted with her a bit in the kitchen, but he stopped it before anything further happened.

Continuing to invite him into her heart was futile. She should find him and calmly, coolly, ask for her book back. He would give it to her because he was polite, and also probably incapable of feeling as shut out and confused and utterly *unraveled* by her as she was by him. He may have admitted that he fancied her, but if he felt as much for her as she felt for him, he would not have been able to turn his back on her.

Oh goodness. She could not face him again without either crying or screaming. Perhaps it would be simpler to retrieve her book from his room herself. He surely wouldn't mind. It might take him a few days to even notice its absence.

Della dried her hands and walked swiftly out of the kitchen and down the hall, stopping only when she reached Ansel's bedroom door. She jabbed the correct button on the rectangle—

which Xaks had taught her was called a *screen*—next to the door to get it to open. Once she had her book back, she would feel better. Safer. Composed.

Before the door even slid all the way open, Della was whisking through. She didn't fear that Ansel would be in his room, for he spent his evenings on the bridge, only retiring late at night, long after everyone else had fallen asleep.

There her book was, lying on his desk, lit by a beam of starlight like a beacon guiding Della's path. She crossed the room and snatched it off the table. The pages fell open. Before she could close them, her eyes snagged on the words inside and she realized—

It wasn't her book at all.

It was Ansel's.

Before she could stop herself, her eyes caught on a few more lines. It was enough to tell her he thought about her. Often. Her heart fluttered. She should close the book and leave. Maybe it was better not to know his opinion of her. He probably thought she was desperate and naïve, throwing herself at him left and right.

Yet her self-control cracked. She was ravenous for his thoughts, his feelings, his secrets, and before she knew it, her greedy gaze had devoured two whole pages.

Ansel thought he was capable of maintaining a distanced relationship with Della. That notion lasted right up until the morning after their kiss when she leaned around him to place a breakfast tray on the table, and his entire body completely rebelled against the idea of her serving him. *She'll work as a maid in exchange for passage to Lumeria.* Whose stupid fucking idea had that been? His. It was his stupid fucking idea. She'd saved his life. He should be serving *her.*

He wanted to be serving her. On his knees. However she wanted him.

He was suddenly struck with the strong desire to brush his thumb along the inside of Della's delicate wrist. To gently

tug her onto his lap. To take his time kissing her because he'd made the mistake of not doing that before. She had a constellation of beauty marks down the left side of her face, and he had the indecent urge to whisper a dirty secret to each one as though he were making filthy wishes to the stars.

It was not the first time he'd felt a strong physical attraction toward someone. That wasn't what had him worried. Obsessing over the memory of her desperate lips and her soft thighs around his hips was one thing. Experiencing joy because she'd done something as preposterous as fold his crew proper little flower napkins for breakfast on their stolen battleship was something else entirely.

She was more in person than he could have imagined when he'd spoken to her in the books. That stubborn tilt to her chin when she told him she was staying. The way she selflessly tossed aside everything to save her family. To save *him,* when she'd only known him for a day. The bravery she displayed by boldly wearing her heart on her sleeve. Most of the universe scoffed at love as something primitive, a trivial and embarrassing pursuit. She sought and protected it as though it were a treasure to cherish.

The problem was that Ansel's ship was relatively small, and Della was *everywhere.* On the bridge, dusting control panels. In the armory, nodding politely along to Yaggrel's gory stories. Even in Ansel's *room.* He'd ducked in there to expel a sexually frustrated scream, and there she was, *welding* of all things, in her stately, puffy-shouldered dress and apron. She'd flipped up her visor and smiled at him, telling him all about how Eryl had taught her how to patch the rusty panels of his "positively revolting" ship, and all he'd wanted to do was wipe the soot off her nose and carry her to his bed.

That very night he'd been reduced to needing to do something depraved to himself and was on his way to his quarters to attend to that when she stepped into his path

half dressed, wearing only *his* shirt, and looking like temptation incarnate.

Every cell in his body was begging *please, please, please.* He didn't even know what he wanted, only that he *wanted.* Trying to keep himself from mauling the poor woman when she was just trying to go to bed, he'd choked out a moronic and dickish "Good night, Della," as though he had the galaxy's largest stick up his ass.

Ansel's biggest problem, aside from the fact that his brain short-circuited when Della was around, was her book. And the fact that Ansel couldn't keep his hands off it. He'd made the idiotic decision to dare her to tempt him, and she gamely rose to the challenge. He supposed he could tell her to stop at any time, but if he had to refuse himself every other pleasure when it came to her, he was allowed this one vice.

She'd turned him from a man who often forgot that the alphabet was a thing into a bookworm. Every free moment, he was ducking into a secluded alcove to see what she was thinking. He might feel bad about it if she hadn't explicitly given him permission. If she wasn't encouraging him with every letter to continue looking.

It was agony, and he couldn't stop torturing himself.

"Find what you were looking for?" Ansel asked wryly from somewhere in the room behind her.

Della squeezed her eyes shut. Of course he was here. She hadn't even checked to verify he wasn't, barging in here with single-minded determination. There was no use pretending she hadn't read his book.

Slowly, she turned, yearning to spew her frustrations but unsure how to begin. Maybe: *Pretending you don't already have feelings to keep your heart from breaking is as silly as closing your eyes at night to hide from monsters.*

Or: *I simply demand that you cease your mental self-flagellation and stop standing in the way of your own happiness.*

Or: *Oh heavens, he's naked.*

And he was, bathing in a freestanding tub in the middle of the room, cool starlight glowing off his wet, muscular shoulders.

"You have a bathtub on a spaceship," Della said with incomprehension.

Ansel had a book in one hand. The other dangled languidly over the side of the tub. One arm and shoulder were still wrapped in bandages. Della did her absolute best to wrench her gaze back up to his face, but not before she noticed the fading yellow and green bruises blotched across his broad chest.

"Someone suggested I try taking a bath for my ribs." Ansel turned a page without looking up. "The walk from the kitchen took you longer than I thought it would."

The book wasn't just a book. He was reading *her* book. In the *bathtub.* Casually, as though her falling apart because of him was nothing more than entertainment. For heaven's sake, if he knew she was coming, why didn't he make himself decent?

"I would have dressed if I'd known I'd have enough time before you barged in here and snooped through my private possessions." He smirked, looking across the room at her through the damp strands of hair falling over his brow.

Was he really going to sit there, having a conversation with her thoughts as he read her mind?

His gaze flicked briefly to the book, then back to her. "Correct."

You ass, she thought.

"Correct," he said again, softer.

She could ask him to put the book down but let him see her wanting him and annoyed with him at the same time. Let him see her noticing the muscled slope of his shoulders and the scent of his stupid floral, musky, *intoxicating* soap permeating the humid room even while she debated which facet of his face was the most punchable.

"Aren't you going to ask me for your book?" he asked. "Isn't that why you came?"

"Do you *want* to give it back to me?"

He behaved without urgency as though her standing there, while he reclined naked in a tub, did not affect him in the slightest. "You wanted to take it back because you thought it didn't mean anything to me. And you've just read that isn't the case. So, it seems you've wasted a trip." He feigned nonchalance, but he was not nearly as suave as he thought he was, for she noticed the way he held her book a little tighter. Confounding man. He would not have her, yet he could not let her go.

Della's fingers twitched to reopen his book and discover what it was he wanted from her, for he revealed very little of himself, aside from his bare chest, bare arms, bare *everything*—and blast it all, he was looking at her book again. How much of this could he read? Judging by his interested expression, all of it.

She straightened her shoulders. "Tell me you want to keep it, and I won't take it."

"I want to keep it." His throat lurched. For the first time since she'd entered the room, his smooth control slipped. "Why'd you sign your last letter off with *regards*? Fucking *regards.* Like we didn't—like we don't—like we aren't *us.* I don't know how we can be together. I only know I can't ever have you telling me you're writing me your last letter ever again."

Della's heart beat faster, shaking itself free of the bands of tension containing it. Perhaps there was some way they could have each other, at least in a small way.

It wouldn't be the first time they'd shared a fantasy.

Setting Ansel's book back where she found it, she took a hesitant step closer. The bathwater wavered in her peripheral vision. "When I write my next letter, I'll be sure to think of an ending far more pleasant than *regards.*" Della leaned close, and Ansel's eyes widened, his pupils expanding to darken his gaze. She plucked her book from his hands. "Though perhaps I shouldn't write to you tonight. I wouldn't want to keep you up, with so much riding on tomorrow's success."

"I rarely sleep anyway." His voice dropped, and she shivered. "May I mention you in my letter?"

"What are you asking?" She liked the way he sounded both a little scared and like a ravenous beast circling its prey.

"I have many extensive thoughts on the subject of you and me, but if you are uninterested in the topic, then perhaps I shouldn't think of you in . . . explicit detail."

"I'm very interested," he managed, wetting his lips. His lust-glazed eyes bore into her. Each soft lap of water as he shifted in the tub haunted her ears. "Think of me however you like."

"Wonderful." She opened her book to the last written page and placed it back in his hand. "Don't you dare leave this bathtub."

"What are you—"

"You said you can't touch me without feeling something. This way, you don't have to touch me at all."

Dear Ansel had already written itself onto the page.

Della hardly remembered returning to her room. Her mind raced, her heart fluttered, and her fingers trembled. The idea of Ansel dripping wet in that tub, reading and savoring each of her thoughts and actions—it was both electrifying and frightening. She shed her tunic and leggings and pulled on his shirt. The soft linen scraped over her goose-fleshed skin as she slipped between her sheets.

"Dear Ansel," she repeated, her voice a whisper in the darkness as she slid her hand beneath the blankets.

She closed her eyes and pictured him in the tub, the way the room's warm lights flickered off his skin. The scent of him was imprinted in her nostrils, heady and clean and singularly sensual. She imagined herself back in the room and what could have happened if he'd spoken the two-word request she might have found lining the inside of his book like patterned wallpaper, had she dared to open it. "*Come here*."

"If you start reading one-handed, please don't drop my book in the bathtub," Della whispered, stifling the nervous giggle that threatened to fracture the fantasy.

She forced herself to focus before she grew self-conscious and lost her nerve. Her skin flushed with a mixture of slight embarrassment and divine anticipation. *If things could be different,* Della thought, continuing her strange sort of letter, *I might have shed my clothing and joined you . . .*

She could practically feel how the humid air of the room would blanket her bare skin, could practically see Ansel looking up at her with darkened eyes and a devilish curve to the corner of his mouth. She imagined stepping into the tub, the steaming water enveloping her skin and soothing the needy ache between her legs.

In her room, Della glided her hand lower, over the curve of her belly, past her navel. She wished the press of her own fingertips were his touch instead, that they could exist together outside of daydreams and parchment. Pleasure tightened and relaxed her muscles all at once. Her imagination blurred into a haze of soap-slicked skin and steam-plumped mouths.

She painted the scene in her mind for Ansel, showing him how things might have been.

He would have pulled her to him, his skin hot against her own as she straddled his hips. The image strengthened until Della felt as though she were there, Ansel winding a strong hand into her damp hair, urging her down to claim her lips in a sensual kiss.

Squeezing her eyes shut, she pictured him capturing her thighs in his hands, his deliciously rough fingertips digging into her flesh as he guided her rolling hips. His head would roll back, and he'd groan as she kissed the column of his neck.

Della became consumed by the tingling pleasure tightening

her body. The fantasy fragmented into a kaleidoscope of images and sensations—languid kisses and soft sighs crescendoed into desperation, into the rhythmic shifting of muscles and soft broken cries, water splashing over the side of the tub. If only it could be real. But if this was all they could have, it would be enough.

Ansel. Della thought his name as the pressure in her body released. Her lips parted in a silent cry before sensation wracked through her in shuddering waves that left her boneless and gasping.

Her hand flopped to the side as she lay catching her breath, her skin flushed, her legs tangled in hot sheets.

"*Yours, Della*," she whispered.

CHAPTER 23

Creqreon—or the armpit of the galaxy, as Ansel had lovingly referred to it—was one of twelve small moons orbiting a massive orange planet with gossamer rings. When Eryl woke Della before her alarm the next morning to tell her they'd arrived (which made her time bot extremely indignant: "*Oh, you're too good for me now, you lump of space trash?*"), Della rushed to the bridge to take in the view. It was too beautiful, the sun bursting over the massive planet like bubbling lava, the smaller moons like spots of soot cast in its shadow. One of those moons glittered with lights and the facets of man-made infrastructure.

A little shiver went down her neck when she heard the weight of Ansel's footsteps behind her. He stepped beside her, following her gaze out the window. Della studied his expression in the glass's reflection, feeling herself blush from head to toe at the memory of what she'd done to herself the night before. Dark smudges had taken up residence beneath his bright, wild eyes, and his hair was more mussed than normal.

"Stay up too late reading, Captain?" she asked innocently, secretly hoping she'd contributed to his rumpled appearance.

"As a matter of fact, I did." When he faced her, his look was scorching and displayed that this time, he would not pretend he didn't read her letters. "The book I'm reading is a literary wonder."

Something fluttered behind Della's ribs. She searched his

expression, trying to determine if he'd engaged in similar activities as herself the night before or if he had simply enjoyed reading about her risqué pastimes. "It must be quite good indeed, to keep you so engrossed."

The corner of his mouth twitched. "My new favorite."

They docked in a private hangar only an hour later, but Della's anticipation of seeing the moon made it feel like a small eternity. Originally, Ansel had brought up the loathsome notion of her staying on the ship for safety, but Eryl pointed out that they'd all be much safer together than apart, so thankfully the idea was abandoned.

As Della followed the crew down the gangplank, she turned in circles, taking it all in. The hangar's dark walls gleamed, and their shoes sent echoing taps across the polished floor.

They were greeted by a sleek humanoid droid who welcomed them to Creqreon, offered them drinks, and whisked them through a door into the casino's lobby.

Della gasped as the room opened before her, cool recycled air brushing over her skin. Dice thudded over felt, wheels ticked as they spun, and machines dinged and clattered. Laughter punctuated the hum of servers taking orders and dealers calling bets.

While the act of gambling didn't look all that different from what Della had glimpsed in Poling, Creqreon made even the most luxurious of gambling houses appear dim and shabby. Black gleaming tile squeaked beneath her shoes. Neon lights outlined the bars, colors flashed from backlit machines, and transparent screens floated everywhere, displaying scrolling numbers. Mirrored walls reflected the glitz to infinity. Della caught glimpses of strange, wonderful creatures at each table they passed, all punching buttons, drinking, and placing bets.

Della made her way to the floor-to-ceiling glass wall at the end of the room. Below her stretched an endless landscape of glittering lights and towering buildings. Tiny, enclosed ships zipped to and fro, keeping their passengers safe from the moon's thin atmosphere as they carted them from place to place. Beyond, the hazy outline of the distant planet loomed on the terra-cotta horizon, its rings like sideways ghostly rainbows.

"Are all those buildings part of the casino?" Della asked when Eryl approached, her loose gait and towering form unmistakable, even with the long-hooded cloak she wore to disguise her identity from bounty hunters who might recognize her as one of Ansel's crew.

"It's all connected, yes," Eryl said. "Creqreon is a network of restaurants, brothels, hotels, gambling rooms, and bars."

"And it is *glorious*," Ansel said with relish, joining them. His voice was muffled behind the black mask he wore that transformed his face into a series of sharp angles and spikes.

"We're here for work, not play." Xaks called out the reminder from a short distance away. Her face too was concealed. She wore her typical helmet but had dimmed her visor so no one could see her features. Yaggrel, meanwhile, wore a pair of thick goggles and a cloth mask that veiled the lower half of his face.

"How do we know who to arrest?" Della asked, turning to face the room. She looked from face to face, wondering which might be Gyrund, the man wanted for grand larceny.

"*We* will not be doing anything," Ansel said. "You will stay with Xaks while Eryl, Yaggrel, and I find Gyrund."

Xaks muttered something about babysitting, and Della cringed. Xaks wouldn't continue to respect her if she was a burden. But Della also didn't want to be difficult, so she kept her mouth closed.

"Eryl, search the crowd," Ansel said. "In case we can't find Gyrund, run face scans on everyone to see if anyone else pings a bounty. While you're at it, jam any incoming signals so no one else's droid can do the same to us. Doesn't mean they can't still recognize us the old-fashioned way, but let's make it difficult for them, shall we? Xaks, you and Della go enjoy yourselves. Yaggrel, remove that bomb from under that couch cushion immediately."

Sheepishly, Yaggrel slipped a massive round grenade out from under the couch. Where the little fellow had smuggled in an explosive of such magnitude, Della would really rather not consider.

"Keep your commlinks on," Ansel said. "With any luck, we'll meet back here within the hour."

Four hours of forced one-on-one time demolished whatever progress Della had made with Xaks. Della could feel the dislike oozing off Xaks across the table where they sat. They had not *enjoyed themselves* as Ansel suggested. Xaks paced and grumbled, lost bets, grumbled some more, bought drinks she was never satisfied with, and finished things off with a twist no one could have predicted by grumbling yet again.

Della spent the time observing the sights, smells, and sounds. She found that she could understand everyone around her, even without the translation device Ansel had offered her. She still wasn't sure how it was possible. The books must have blessed her with some kind of gift for words when she traveled through their pages.

When she grew bored of eavesdropping, Della withdrew the vial of cosmic dust and set it on the table. It hadn't seemed right to leave it behind, so she'd stuck it in her pocket that morning. A good thing too, for the dust must be hungry by now.

Plucking a hair from her head, Della removed the stopper from the glass long enough to slip the strand inside before corking it again. The sparks stirred to life, clustering along the strand of hair and consuming it until it had disintegrated and joined their masses.

"That dust is going to escape and kill us one day," Xaks muttered.

"The only one you're making miserable is yourself, you know." Della tucked the glass away. "It's not like I wanted to be left behind either. You might as well not bother feeling any ill will toward me and spare yourself the mental turmoil."

Xaks turned up the light of her helmet enough for Della to see her glare behind her visor. "Being miserable makes me happy."

"Oh. Well. Then you're welcome, I suppose. I'll continue being insufferable."

Xaks rolled her eyes.

Della loved that none of the rules of decorum from her own world applied in Ansel's. Among his ragtag crew, behaving improperly was the only proper way to behave, which made things much easier. Taking jabs at people was acceptable, even encouraged.

"I could develop an irksome habit if it would increase your irritation and therefore your happiness," Della offered. "Maybe bouncing my knee or sniffling." She demonstrated both.

"I cannot fathom what the Captain sees in you," Xaks said.

Her every thought, mostly. "Yes, well, it's taken him a while to come around to the idea of me too."

"Sure, if by 'a while,' you mean ten seconds." Xaks snorted. "The day you arrived, we brought the matter of you staying to a vote. You lost, and he pulled rank—something he's never done, by the way—and said he was the Captain, and you were staying, and that was that." Xaks waved over another drink, shoving aside her collection of empty glasses. She jammed a tube connected to her space suit into the beverage. Her tongue coiled around the other end of the straw where it protruded into her mask, and she took a long slurp. "When we continued to point out all the reasons your staying was a terrible idea, he shoved our cleaning droid in a closet, declared it unfit for service, and cited your experience as a maid as the reason you needed to stay."

Della remembered the crash she'd heard while she'd waited on the bridge as the crew discussed the matter of her staying. "Oh," she said breathlessly, her skin tingling warmly all over.

"Your existence has become very inconvenient for me," Xaks went on. "If you break the Captain's heart before he manages to break yours, it will destroy him, and then I'll be obligated to avenge his pitiful human feelings by destroying you in turn, which is an annoying prospect because I don't completely dislike you. On the other hand, if he breaks your heart first, I suspect some part of me will feel obligated to avenge *you*, which poses the same issue because unfortunately—and for some incomprehensible reason—I like the Captain. So you see the dilemma?"

"Most vexing. Utter misery. You should be thrilled." In truth, Della had no idea Xaks felt such devotion toward her—if a slight reluctance to eviscerate someone into dust could be considered devotion, which, from Xaks, she believed it could. "Why is everyone so certain someone will break a heart during this venture?"

"Because human hearts are feeble," Xaks growled in disgust. "The Captain's is particularly soft. It's his most shameful quality. Nearly as embarrassing as the way he wears his hair."

Xaks's impassioned opinions had Della holding back a laugh. "How long have you known Ansel?"

"Years. Since prison. He helped me escape. I owe him my life, which is mortifying. Eryl was the Cooperation warden droid in charge of our wing. She's only the delightful know-it-all she is today because the Captain hacked her to help get us out. Yaggrel is the newest. The little runt tried to kill us a few years ago, so creatively that the Captain was impressed enough to offer him a job."

"What landed you in prison, anyway?" Della asked, fascinated.

"Murdering annoying little humans who ask too many questions."

"I cherish our little talks."

Xaks grunted, but at least she was past grumbling. "Are you ever going to disclose how *you* met the Captain?"

"He didn't tell you?" Della asked carefully, unsure how much to reveal.

She was saved from having to respond by the arrival of the rest of the crew. Eryl stood guard at the end of the table, her towering presence keeping any curious onlookers at bay while Yaggrel hopped into Xaks's side of the booth, and Ansel slid in next to Della.

"Well?" Xaks asked. "Can we go now?"

"We found Gyrund, but he has security." Ansel wearily took off his helmet and set it on the table. "He's in a VIP booth surrounded by guards. Unfortunately, there aren't any alternative candidates here with a high enough bounty to bother with. Most criminals are probably avoiding this place for now while it's still new and in the spotlight. We need Gyrund."

"I suggest we just blow the place wide open," Yaggrel growled.

"No one's blowing anything," Ansel said.

"Unless—" Xaks began, eyeing Della, who resisted the urge to sink into her seat. "What are his sexual preferences?"

"Humans," Eryl said. "Women, if the company he keeps is any indication."

"I'm going to give you a second to tell me you're not suggesting what I think you are," Ansel said dangerously.

Xaks leaned across the table. "She's our in. Have you ever seen anything in your life look less suspicious? We give her a different outfit, a little zhuzhing—"

"No."

"Oh, come on. All she has to do is get him out of that VIP booth. We'll intercept them before anything happens."

Della couldn't decide if she was horrified or flattered that Xaks wanted to use her as some kind of sexual bait. She'd never supposed anyone could look at her and suppose, *Now, she would make an excellent temptress.* They mostly thought things like, *Who is this girl in my house? Oh, yes, my maid. I forgot about her.*

Ansel made a face of disapproval, but it didn't matter what he thought. She was part of the crew. She couldn't allow herself to be coddled or shown special treatment. She had to contribute.

"I'll do it," Della said, with no idea how she would *do it,* unless the man found discussions about removing wine stains from rugs stimulating or chapped, callused hands arousing. "But I do fear someone will have to teach me the art of seduction."

"To attract a mate, you just have to climb atop a large boulder, howl at the sky, and bare your genitals," Yaggrel said, lounging on a large, scooped chair beside Della in the shop Xaks had called a beauty parlor. Yaggrel flexed his seven long toes, admiring the silver sheen an attendant was painting his claws.

"I don't know what mating rituals humans prefer, but I don't think that's it." Xaks glared out of one of the room's many windows with obvious impatience, the orange sunset silhouetting her slender, angular figure.

The salon encircled an upper floor of one of Creqreon's tallest buildings—*skyscrapers,* Xaks had called them. The outer walls held gold-trimmed windows that looked upon the gleaming city. Inside, mirrored surfaces of pink and white—from the floors to the counters—sparkled so brightly, they hurt Della's eyes. The sound of the little wind contraptions called *dryers* hummed in her ears, and mingling odors of perfume and pomade made her nostrils tingle.

Gripping the mauve upholstery of her chair, Della winced as her own beautician—a rather lovely woman with large ears like a cat's and a snow-white pelt dripping with bejeweled piercings—buffed at the calluses on her feet. Over the past hour, Della had been scrubbed, trimmed, shaved, and waxed until her skin was shiny and nearly raw. Yaggrel had taken part in many of the same treatments with her, saying he was studying them to use as new interrogation techniques, but Della suspected he secretly enjoyed the pampering.

As the beautician wrapped up her treatment, the crew continued coaching her (rather ineffectively) in the art of seduction. Della was practicing saying the phrase "Hello, stud" in various tones while Yaggrel collapsed to the floor with laughter and Eryl patiently repeated two "Hello, studs" per each of Della's, trying to demonstrate the proper inflection but failing because her programming forced her to say it in the exact same way every time. Meanwhile, Xaks was shouting alternative suggestions through it all—"'Hello' sounds too formal. Try 'Hey, stud,' or, 'Hi, stud,' or, 'Greetings, stud,'"—when Ansel threw open the door, entering the salon.

Xaks's shouted "Salutations, stud!" died on her lips.

Ansel gave her a crushing look.

She cleared her throat. "Captain. The plan is coming right along. We're hard at it in here. Progress is . . . progressing."

"You're wasting your time with these lessons." Della scarcely had time to feel the sting of Ansel's words before he added, "She doesn't need them."

Everyone in the room exchanged glances. Xaks was doing her best to look nauseated, but her eyes danced with merriment, Yaggrel held back a grin, and even Eryl's stoic face carried an air of excitement.

Ansel ignored them all and hung a dress off the back of a

mirror. "Gear for the job." He made a face of distaste. "Yaggrel, choose some weapons she can conceal. I want her armed."

Yaggrel's pointy ears perked up. "With pleasure."

Ansel gave a curt nod. With that, he exited once more, the door smacking sharply behind him. Della held back her amusement at his foul mood. A thrilling suspicion had begun to take hold of her that *she* had contributed to his current temperament—more specifically, the fact that she would be seducing another man. There was something wickedly gratifying about that.

"Well then." Xaks clapped her hands together. "As I've been saying, enough screwing around. I think a practice run is in order."

CHAPTER 24

Della found her practice target sitting at a bar, gripping a glass with tight knuckles.

"Remember," Xaks had said before they parted ways, "if anything goes wrong or you feel uncomfortable, yell for backup. Or just stab the guy."

"I feel as though I ought to warn you," Della said as she approached, "I've been instructed to stab you, should you make me uncomfortable."

At her voice, Ansel looked up. His eyes widened and dropped over her body once, twice, three times before he dragged them back up to her face. "Della." Her name left his lips almost inaudibly.

Her ensemble consisted of a long-sleeved blouse with a high ruffled neck. A leather corset was layered overtop, cinched under her bust. Her skirt was a long brown and black flouncy thing, trailing in the back and cut ludicrously short in the front, leaving her garters on display. It was far more risqué than anything Della could have imagined back in her world, but she'd never been particularly self-conscious about her body—it was perhaps the one thing about herself that didn't make her feel awkward. The way she saw it, it was just skin, flesh, and bones, the same as everyone else had. While she knew her breasts were likely too modest to be considered desirable, her hips too slim, her face too plain, there was nothing she could do about them, unlike her mind and tongue, which she really felt as though she ought to be able to control better.

Swallowing a flurry of nerves, Della forced herself to relax. "Hello, Captain," she said, in a voice a little lower than her own. This was the voice, after much trial and error, the group decided was the least ridiculous. "What are you doing out here all alone?" She pulled up a stool next to his and sat, resting an elbow on the bar to lean in close.

His hand flexed around his drink. "I do believe I'm . . . sulking," he said as though he were baffled by his own revelation.

"Whatever for?"

"I'm still working that out." His cheekbones cast sharp shadows in the bar's neon lights, making him look more unapproachable than normal.

Confidence, Della reminded herself. Luckily, they were seated at the darkened end of the bar. Everyone else was occupied a fair distance away, including the bartender, so no one would witness her embarrassing herself.

"I could help you feel better." Della placed a hand on Ansel's thigh, right above his knee.

Ansel cocked his head, and then his expression cleared. "Oh, I see. You're seducing me."

"It's for practice." She hesitated. "Would you rather I didn't?"

The corner of his mouth twitched with mild amusement. "I suppose you might as well try."

Della bit her tongue before she could snap at him for acting like being pursued by her didn't matter one way or another, as though he had to *endure* the interest of women day in and day out.

Slipping from the stool, she stood between Ansel's legs, gazing up into his eyes in the way Eryl had called "irresistible" and Xaks had declared "disturbed." She was beginning to wonder if she should follow Yaggrel's advice and either scream or begin shedding clothing.

"Tell me how to make you feel better." Della toyed with a brass button on his jacket, feeling his eyes on her. "What do you like?"

"I've gotten really into reading lately."

Della couldn't tell if he was being serious or holding back a laugh. She felt tremendously ridiculous. Groaning, she pulled away, hiding her face in her hands. "I can't do this, and now I can never bear to face you again. Please, don't look at me."

"Della," he said gently, pulling at her hands. "It was a valiant effort. Really."

She moaned again, sinking into her chair. "Don't laugh at me. I cannot bear it."

He stood and bent over her, bracing his hand on the bar as he tilted her chin so he could murmur in her ear, "How can I laugh when I can't breathe?"

A heady, tingling rush swept through her.

"You should stab me, preemptively." His thumb tracked a path across her jaw.

"Why?" She swallowed hard.

"Because I'm going to say something that might make you uncomfortable."

"All right," she whispered. "Proceed, and if I feel any discomfort, I shall stab you at my leisure."

His knuckles tightened around the bar. "When I picked that dress for you to wear, I wasn't thinking of the mission. I was thinking of myself—my own selfish desire to see those stockings of yours again. Then I went from imagining how that dress would look on you to imagining how it would look off. I imagined removing it myself. With my teeth." His lips brushed against her ear, sending a pleasant shudder down her neck. "I obsess over the way you moaned when I held you in that airlock. I wonder if you'd make that sound again if I let you ride my—comets, woman, feel free to stab me any time now."

She felt the brush of his hand against her thigh before he

jerked the knife out of its sheath, shoved it in her hand, and pointed it toward his own sternum.

Then, smirking, Ansel released her hand and eased back onto his stool, reaching for his drink. "See? Just be direct." He shrugged, as though they were having any regular conversation.

Della looked down at the knife in her trembling grip, contemplating where in Ansel she'd most like to stick it. *Egotistical man*, acting as though the whole speech was a lesson in seduction.

"Tell him you want to be ravished against a wall, and it will be all he can think about." Ansel watched her with apparent disinterest, but his eyes sparkled, betraying him.

And—wait a moment. He wasn't being blasé about what was happening between them at all. His eyes were focused, sharp. He was completely captivated, and he was—

Was he . . . was he *teasing* her?

He was. And he was enjoying it, judging by those impish lines forming around his mouth as he bit back a smile. Oh goodness, he was doing exactly what she had in her letters—attempting to flirt and coax and tempt. He was *engaging* in her very game, and what a revelation that was.

This playful side of Ansel was hardly something Della believed could exist, but last night had erased some barrier between them, and now they were tiptoeing across the border where it had been, testing how far they could go.

Della jammed the knife back in its sheath. Reaching into her pocket, she withdrew the vial of cosmic dust and then clunked it on the bar between them, being careful not to look at it herself until he had. She was pretty sure she knew what his strongest desire at the moment was, and that it currently outshone even his darkest fears.

Mouse, meet cat.

Ansel's gaze instinctively settled upon the glass when she placed it between them. The dust swelled and darkened.

Inside the vial, Della saw herself—how she might look if viewed by someone else. Her surroundings were murky, but she made out a few smoky shapes in the coiling blackness that surrounded her. A bed. A dresser. As she watched, a pair of hands came into view. She'd know those hands anywhere. They were his, corded and strong, tangled in the ties crisscrossing the front of her corset, loosening them one by one. With one final, slow pull, the fabric gaped open, a patchwork of shadows concealing the pale curve of her breasts ever so temptingly out of view.

A gentleman might have made the pretense of averting his gaze from the glass. Ansel did not. He only leaned back and watched the scene, taking another long, slow drink. "It's very comforting to know the mistress of a monster is a fiend herself," he said dryly.

"I would not have to resort to such measures if you didn't provoke me." She gave a breezy shrug.

Ansel's blatant gaze fixed several degrees southward of her face before lifting to meet hers. And—oh my. The lustful sheen glazing his eyes made her heart pound. He unabashedly adjusted himself beneath the bar. She should probably be appalled by his crudeness. She definitely shouldn't like it.

Between them, the scene in the bottle continued in a lazy blur of entwined limbs and sweat-sheened skin. Della fought the irrational urge to laugh. It seemed his little game had backfired. She whisked the cosmic dust off the bar and shoved it away as it began moaning.

"Well, thanks to your tutelage, I know exactly how to seduce Gyrund." She stood and brushed invisible lint off her skirts.

Ansel straightened a second after. "I don't like that you have to do this."

"Oh, petal." Della tsked, patting his cheek. "Careful. It seems your emotions are high, causing you to say things you don't mean. One might almost think you're jealous."

As she turned to go, Ansel caught her jaw in his hand, his

ring and pinky finger curving gently around her neck. "I *am* jealous." He'd dropped the game, and her heart skipped several beats. "Write to me tonight."

She loved it when he told her what he wanted her to do because she knew it wasn't an order, not really. It was a plea. Obey she would—of course, always—but not before she made it difficult for him. "Do you really need more reading material already? You know, I always mark my favorite passages in books, so that I might return to them. Maybe you could try that."

The look he gave her was fierce and honest and made everything fade around them. "I already reread my favorite parts. Twice last night and once this morning."

"The book must have affected you greatly," she breathed.

He coiled a strand of her hair around his finger and gave it a little tug. "It took an unexpected but captivating turn that left me spellbound."

CHAPTER 25

Ansel informed the crew with an impressively straight face that Della was more than ready for the mission.

While Della took a lift to the floor where Gyrund's VIP booth was located, the rest of the crew took the stairs—the plan being to hide in the stairwell until the moment Della uttered the code word that would alert them she'd gotten Gyrund away from his guards, and they could move in. Her ear was fitted with a hidden communication device to contact them, and under every ruffle of her outfit, Yaggrel had hidden weapons—knives in her sleeves and a knife on her thigh under her skirt. As a final touch, Della slipped the vial of cosmic dust into a hidden pocket. For some reason, she felt safer having it near, as if the mere memory of her mother could protect her.

This floor was quieter than the main lobby. The soft carpet dulled Della's footsteps as she made her way past roped-off tables of serious-faced gamblers playing high-stakes cards. The nerves tightening her stomach were unpleasant, unlike the exhilarating tingling she'd felt earlier with Ansel.

Servers drifted from table to table, murmuring low so as not to disrupt the players' concentration. Ice clinked gently in drinks, and only the occasional squeak of a chair or the shuffling of cards penetrated the hush. The cloying scent of smoke and alcohol clogged the back of Della's throat.

"Have you located him yet?" Xaks's voice asked in her earpiece.

"I believe so." Della had just spotted a curtained-off section in the corner with a VIP sign pinned to the velvet curtains. Two human guards stood stationed outside.

"If you need help, we can be there in seconds," Xaks said.

"I won't need help." If Della sounded sure of herself, maybe she'd start to feel it.

As she approached the curtains, the guards straightened, resting their hands on the blasters at their sides. "State your business," one said gruffly.

Her heart tapped inside her chest like it was trying to prod her away from danger. "I'm here to see Gyrund."

"He's not expecting anyone. Be on your way." But then he touched an earpiece, pressing it against his head as he listened to someone on the other end. "Really?" he asked. "Her?"

The guards exchanged a look. The one who hadn't spoken turned away and muttered into his own commlink. When he turned back, he tilted his head toward the curtains. "Come on."

Paranoia spiked through Della, barbed and swift. Surely things could not be progressing as easily as they seemed.

One guard stepped forward and grabbed her roughly by the arm. The other followed as the first forcibly escorted her through the curtains. The air around her transformed from cool to stuffy. Sweet-scented smoke clouded the space. The shadowy figures of a half dozen gamblers seated around a table rose through the haze. Della's skin prickled, her legs aching to run.

"Here she is." The guard holding her shoved her forward.

A thin, reedy man who must have been Gyrund looked up from the head of the table. He might have been in his forties, with a long, shrewd face and curling mustache. Gyrund considered her as though he were perusing a dessert tray. "She's smaller than expected."

It was then that Della noticed the small screen sitting off to the side, displaying the space outside the booth where the guards had been stationed a moment before. Gyrund must have one of those cameras Ansel told her about hidden outside to keep watch.

"What did a little thing like you do to be worth so many credits?" Gyrund asked almost absentmindedly as he continued to play his hand of cards, and alarm shot through Della as she realized instantly something was wrong.

"Pardon?" Della tried to inconspicuously take a step toward the tent's opening but backed right into the solid chest of one of the guards.

"Couldn't believe my luck when I saw your face outside my tent," Gyrund continued. "Della, is it? How'd you manage to break into a high-security prison without detection?"

No. No, that wasn't possible. "You must have me mistaken for someone else."

"It's strange," Gyrund went on. "Your name's been kept off the public Cooperation wanted boards. Someone powerful wants you for themself. An anonymous reward was offered to only the most elite hunters in the galaxy for your capture. What's even stranger is the reward is to be doubled if we turn you in with a certain book spotted in your possession. So tell me. What's so special about this book?"

Della's gut plunged to her toes.

"It's Balor; he knows about the books somehow," Ansel said in her earpiece, his voice almost hard enough to mask his worry. "Shit, I must have missed a camera during our prison break. If Balor watched the footage, he could have realized there was something unusual about the books. He could have used the footage to plaster your face across the private wanted boards. Get out of there, Della. We're on our way."

"No, stand your ground," Xaks snapped. "Stick with the plan. Tell him you'll take him to get whatever book he's talking about. Whatever it takes to get him alone. You'll never make it if you run, and we can't take on all of them."

Della darted her gaze from Gyrund to the guards to the exit.

"Don't even think about it," Gyrund said.

Before Della could make a move, the guard behind her wrapped his arms around her biceps while the second trained his blaster on her. He flicked something on the side of his weapon, and a high-pitched whine filled her ears as lights blinked up the side.

Gambling chips clinked. Cards flicked across the table. No one spared her a look. They tossed their money around as easily as they played with human life—*her* life.

"Take her to the ship," Gyrund said, rolling the dice with a lazy flick of his wrist.

Della might not be a gambler, but she was good at bluffing, especially when it came to hiding her feelings. "Let me go. I have a team of highly trained soldiers waiting outside."

"You expect me to believe that?" Unalarmed, Gyrund produced a blaster from beneath the table and placed it on the felt, barely looking up from his cards. "Don't fight. I don't feel like dealing with a difficult prisoner, even if you are worth more alive."

"Killing me really isn't worth the mess. Do you know how hard it is to get bloodstains out of carpet?" Della forced her voice to steady as she tried to buy time. "I'm only a maid. It's Ansel Tulzok, the man I broke out of prison, you want."

He chuckled. "I don't care about Tulzok's bounty. Yours is higher."

Higher? Why would hers be higher? Unless Balor knew he could control Ansel if he had her.

Gyrund nodded at the guards. "Take her weapons."

Della's palms sweat as the guards roughly searched her. One by one, they found the weapons Yaggrel had planted. A guard snatched the cosmic dust from her pocket and lifted it to inspect. "What the—" The dust flared white hot, and he let out a yelp of pain and dropped it.

The glass shattered against the floor.

Cold fear gripped Della as gold and purple sparks flared at her feet like a rearing cobra, their crackle drowning out the whine of a second blaster.

One of the guards fired.

Della saw the bright red missile rushing toward her, and then a veil of sparks lifted before her, consuming the missile, burning brighter as it absorbed its energy. Shielding her.

Della gaped at the wall of sparks standing between her and the guard, a chill traveling across her skin. She turned to face the card table. Forgotten chips rested in extended hands. At last, the dice were silent, the cards ignored.

The sparks began to swirl slowly around Della, but none of them touched her. Perhaps the cosmic dust had consumed too much of her to want to devour her, as though it saw her as an extension of itself. Or perhaps this was its way of thanking her for the hearty dinner before it.

"Did you know," Della said calmly though her heart drummed with power, "dust is a maid's worst adversary. It creeps into every crevice and consumes every surface. Fighting it is futile. Dust is my nightmare. But today, I think it's yours."

Golden light streamed around Della. Hot air billowed her hair and whipped her skirts around her body. Chairs clattered to the side as the gamblers fell over themselves trying to escape. Vague outlines took shape in the dust as it fed on their fears and desires. A shadowy animal like a wolf snapped its jaws, its lower half dissolving into trails of sparks. A clustering swarm of long-legged insects skittered up a man's leg. A beautiful woman led another into the shadows with a tempting smile.

"It seems you've caused a bit of a ruckus, Della dear." Ansel's voice came through her earpiece, his tone holding the carefully light nonchalance he'd employed in every dangerous situation they'd found themselves in. From reading his book, Della understood what that tone meant—that he was panicked and barely holding it together. She wondered if she was the only person alive who knew about the pure fear hiding behind his cocky smiles.

"Casino security heading your way," Ansel said. "The crew went to get the ship. You and I will meet them there."

"Why aren't you with them?" Worry clenched Della's chest as she imagined all the horrible things that could have happened to split him from the rest of the crew.

"For you, Della." His no-nonsense voice broke into something devastatingly tender. "Of course for you."

"Oh." She was still a little baffled by the feeling of being cared for.

"There are guards between us," he went on, all business once more, "but if you can get to the next floor, I'll meet you there."

Della was already moving, pushing blindly through the curtains and into the main room, which had dissolved into chaos. Patrons ran this way and that, their furtive glances darting to the shaking, glowing VIP booth.

A gambler tumbled out of the curtains, a ghoulish monster taking shape and pouncing onto his chest, stray sparks dripping off the beast as it formed. One person screamed. Then another. Tables crashed to the ground and chips rolled beneath chairs in everyone's haste to escape.

Tearing her attention away from the scene behind her, Della darted through the crowd.

"Head down the corridor to your left," Eryl said in Della's ear. "I downloaded the floor plans, and Ansel managed to hack into the building's security cameras, so I have eyes on you."

Della did as she was told and turned left, leaving the sounds of destruction behind her. She entered a busy hall, dodging elbows and wings and pincers.

Her chest burned with exertion as she burst into the next room—a darkly lit upscale restaurant. Her intrusion caused the occupants of several tables closest to her to scrutinize her with distaste, though the rest of the room remained oblivious to the disruption outside. Soothing music played in the background, and patrons leaned close over gleaming tables, murmuring low.

"You there," a guard shouted from across the room, shattering the tranquil atmosphere. He wove swiftly through the tables toward her, pointing. "That's the girl."

Della's heart rate kicked up a notch, reaching a sickening tempo. She whipped her head this way and that, searching for a path through the dining room, but spotted two more guards closing in, cornering her against a wall.

"Where are you?" Ansel's voice asked in her earpiece.

"I don't know. A restaurant?"

"Stall for five minutes," came his steely reply.

Della had no idea how she could possibly evade the guards. She was not a fighter, nor was she a mastermind. She was a maid. Her skills involved serving tea, mending clothes . . . disappearing into the scenery.

Acting on instinct, she ducked her head and slipped in amongst a cluster of servers. They carried sparkling, flaming desserts, drawing the attention of everyone in the vicinity. Gasps of awe and polite applause surrounded her. She plucked one of the servers' hats from his head, ducked under a flaming dessert, then crouched and lifted a tablecloth before diving under the table. She crawled over a tangle of legs—there were far more feet jammed under that table than she expected, as everyone seated there had at least three. She emerged on the other side, tugging the server's hat over her hair. She swiped someone's coat off the back of a chair and pulled it over her conspicuous outfit. Luckily it was white and blended in with the staff's uniforms.

Acting as casually as she could, she swiped a few dirty plates off a table. Keeping her head low, she followed another server toward the kitchen. She might be in another universe, but there was a universal familiarity to the polished flow of the staff that she fell into easily. The servers were an undetectable but powerful undercurrent that propelled the room's operation. There was an ease to the fast-paced rhythm of the staff—checking in on a customer here, collecting a payment there, shuffling old plates with new, all while juggling dozens of requests, orders, and complaints with a smile. And no one noticed them.

Surreptitiously, Della looked over her shoulder to find the guards looking about in confusion. She might make it out after all.

"Two more minutes," Ansel said in her ear, the roar of some kind of engine in the background.

A hand closed over Della's wrist. She turned, expecting the dark visor of a guard, but it was only a man sitting at the head of the table behind her.

He nearly looked human, except his nose was barely more than two slits for nostrils and was located between his violet eyes, and spiraling horns curled off his brow. "Excuse me, I'd like to file a complaint. My food was horrible."

Della glanced down at the man's plate, which had been picked clean. Only a bone remained. "What was wrong with it?" she asked, gaze flitting around the room to note the guards' positions. Two were across the room, but the third had wandered dangerously close, his masked head swiveling this way and that as he looked for anything out of place.

"It was overcooked, too salty, and cold," said the man, and his entourage nodded in agreement, their plates similarly empty. "Inedible."

Apparently, only *nearly* inedible, for they had managed to finish it, poor souls. Futilely trying to pull her arm away, Della said, "I'll let the cook know."

"I demand a refund." The man raised his voice. He slipped his wrist device off and shoved it into her hand. "Take this to your manager and have them cancel the charge placed on my account at once."

Della's blood bubbled with frantic impatience. "All right, yes, of course."

"Impudent human," the man snarled, still without releasing her.

"What's going on over here?" The guard's voice, distorted from the mask, sent shivers down Della's body as his shadow dropped across her.

Della didn't give him time to recognize her. She ripped her arm from the irate customer and ran.

"Ansel," she said, pronouncing his name around a pant. "I hope whatever escape plan you have in mind is ready."

"Do you trust me?"

Footsteps thundered closer behind her as the guards shouted to one another, joining forces in pursuit.

"I can't say your history of poor foresight and impulsive decision-making fills me with assurance, but I do trust that you try your best," Della said as she tore across the dining room, dodging patrons, leaping around chairs, and crashing into tables. Dishware clattered in her wake.

"Good. Then I'm going to need you to find a blaster, shoot the third window down the hall to your right, and jump out of it."

"Oh, well, if that's all." Bursting out of the restaurant, she raced down the hall he'd indicated, one side of which was lined with windows overlooking the city.

She didn't realize how high up she was until she glanced over and saw the hazy drop. Her throat went dry. The ships near the moon's surface looked like nothing more than ants.

"Ansel," she whispered. "I'm scared."

"I've got you, sweetheart," he said, voice softening even though she could hear him struggling with something in the background. A few muffled grunts made her wonder if he was involved in some kind of scuffle.

Before she had a chance to ensure he was all right, two dark figures stepped out of a doorway in front of her, their blasters raised at her head. Della skidded to a stop and attempted to backpedal, only to find the guards behind her had caught up. She panted, caught between them.

"Now, Della!" Ansel said in her earpiece. "Jump!"

But there was no way she could get one of the guards' weapons to shoot the window without being caught or killed first.

Just when she thought all hope was lost, a strange, flat light flickered along the windows, faint at first, then brighter and brighter.

"What's that?" A guard turned to look just as a great wave of purple and golden sparks crashed around the corner like water over a broken dam.

The guards screamed. One ducked, though he needn't have bothered. The dust flowed around them with disinterest to reach Della. Della's heart skipped as it gathered into a swarm. It had grown substantially and now towered above her. She wondered if she was next, if it had consumed enough of everyone else that it now wanted her.

But it only spun around her in a glittering swirl, teasing the ends of her hair, brushing her cheeks, as though checking that she was okay.

One of the guards fired his blaster, but it missed wildly, ricocheting off the floor and bouncing down the hall. The dust glowed bright, as though angered, coiling itself into a tight ball over Della's head.

"Don't harm them," Della said impulsively. They were only doing their jobs. From their perspective, she *had* caused a great deal of needless calamity. "Break the window instead." She pointed to the third window.

Nearly before the words had left her mouth, the dust shot toward the glass in a blinding blur. The glass imploded, and cold, thin air gushed into the hallway. The guards ran one way, and she ran the other. *I hope you know what you're doing, Ansel,* she thought as, with two hard pumps of her legs, she sent herself hurtling out of the window into empty air, glass and sparks glittering around her like exploding stars.

CHAPTER 26

Della's stomach flew to her throat. She plummeted fast, faster than she thought possible. Her breath was snatched from her lungs. Orange sky and gleaming buildings blurred around her. Wind whipped her hair back, and thin tears streamed from her eyes.

And then she landed flat on her back onto a couch. At least, that was what it felt like.

Fighting for air, Della blinked up from where she lay on some sort of leathery divan to see a glass dome closing over her. The cosmic dust condensed into a near-solid form, sitting on her chest like some small animal made entirely of glowing stardust. It had no weight but was vaguely warm.

"Thank you, Ansel. You're so brave, Ansel. Never has anyone led such an inspiring rescue, Ansel." His voice came from somewhere in front of her, and she realized the couch was *moving*. Very swiftly. Careening this way and that in a nauseating manner.

Air entered her lungs in a mighty gulp. Gasping and blinking back tears, Della dizzily sat up to find she was in a tiny ship made up of two rows of seating and encased by domed glass. It was one of the hover vehicles she'd seen zipping around the city from the casino. Ansel must have been waiting in the vessel beneath the window.

The cosmic dust trickled off her like sand before reforming

into a small blob on the seat beside her, where it stretched like a cat before curling up.

"It seems as though Eryl and I did most of the work, and you were just *there* at the end," Della said through coughs.

"But I was *there* very cleverly." Ansel sat in the front row, hands flying over the controls as he guided them through a maze of buildings at a breakneck speed.

"Were you fighting someone?" she asked. "I thought I heard you struggling mightily through the earpiece."

"I was not struggling *mightily*," he said indignantly. "I was *heroically* commandeering the ship."

The last of Della's fear melted away, and she laughed, her giggles tumbling over one another until she hiccupped and snorted. It might have been embarrassing if Ansel didn't look over at her with extreme fondness.

All at once, Della felt a great surge of affection toward the absurd wonderful man, and she realized, right there in the back of a hijacked aircraft, moments after leaping from a skyscraper, that she had fallen a little bit—or perhaps more than a little bit—in love with Ansel Tulzok. The timing was nonsensical, but feelings rarely occurred when convenient.

Ansel spared the backseat another glance, oblivious to her emotional enlightenment. "Just to recap, that dust is the terrifying space monster that tried to murder you a week ago?"

"Indeed," Della managed, as though her heart were not palpitating, her mind reeling. "It seems we've come to an understanding. I give it other people to eat, and it doesn't eat me."

"The stuff of lasting friendships," Ansel muttered, and she wanted to kiss him soundly.

"Actually," Eryl said through Della's earpiece, "reviewing the security footage, the dust didn't kill anyone. It terrified and distracted them. Granted, it might have taken a few nibbles—some hair here, an elbow there—but everyone is very much alive."

Ansel gave the dust a double take. "I must have misheard. You're telling me Della *tamed* the terrifying space monster?"

"More likely, the terrifying space monster is simply less terrifying because it is more Della than monster now. She's been feeding it a fair amount of herself, you see."

"Normally I'd say that seems like an unsettling and ill-advised pastime," Ansel said, "but since it saved you, I guess I can't fault your disturbing fixation."

"Perhaps the dust saved me, but that doesn't help us in the long run," Della said, sobering. "Gyrund got away." She'd failed. Balor was going to catch up to them, and they'd be defenseless without their shields.

Ansel glanced at a screen on the control panel that displayed a view out the back of the craft. Two other small ships painted with Creqreon's insignia had peeled around a corner and fallen in pursuit behind them. "All we needed were credits," Ansel said, accelerating. "Gyrund was just a means to an end."

"But I haven't managed to collect any credits either," Della said.

"Haven't you?" Ansel swerved, sending one of their pursuers crashing into the side of a building.

Della glanced down and realized she still had a white-knuckled grip on the rude man's wrist device from the restaurant. Slowly, she smiled. She wouldn't mind spending his money. There was a sort of sweet justice to it, a small amount of payback on behalf of all mistreated waitstaff.

"We'll stop to fix our shields in the morning. Balor's not going to get his hands on you or the books," Ansel vowed grimly.

Della climbed over the backs of the seats and, with much yanking of her skirts, managed to settle herself beside Ansel in the front row. Heavens, he was beautiful—brutally handsome in the way a storm was breathtaking, with wild lightning flashing in his eyes and willpower thundering through his veins.

"Don't look at me like that. It's distracting." His gaze flicked her way before he schooled it back into place and continued navigating the rooftops.

She braced a hand on his thigh. "Like what?"

The aircraft clipped the side of a building, knocking her against his shoulder and jarring them even more wildly off course. "Stars, woman," he grumbled under his breath.

Della held back a smile, then remembered they were running for their lives, and she really ought not to think about leaning over and kissing away the tension in his neck.

Ansel sent their vessel diving downward, and Della's stomach leaped to her throat. Just as suddenly, their descent leveled, and they slipped gently under an awning protruding from a darkened lower level of one of the buildings. He flipped off their lights, shrouding their hiding place in shadows.

Their soft breaths took up the silence as they waited to see if the security ship would follow. Several tense beats passed, but nothing appeared.

"We'll wait them out, then make our escape," Ansel said. "The crew has the ship parked out in the dunes outside the casino, waiting for us."

Della leaned back, letting out what felt like the first breath she'd taken in a while as she prepared for the wait.

Ansel regarded her, his brows raised. "What's that smile for?"

She only shook her head. "Just adrenaline."

Reaching over, he brushed a loose tendril of hair from her face.

"What was that for?" she asked, expecting him to take the excuse she offered and claim his actions too were fueled by adrenaline.

"I don't want you to write me another letter." She would have felt hurt if he didn't quickly follow that shocking declaration up with, "It's not enough. I want to touch you."

"Because of adrenaline?" she clarified.

"Because I want to."

"Oh," she breathed, soaring with impossible hope.

"And I want to remind everyone this is an open communication channel," Xaks's voice butted in, though Della could hear the rest of the crew shushing her.

Wordlessly, Ansel leaned over Della and pressed a button above her head labeled *speaker output mute.* Then he checked the light was on approximately three additional times before sliding her across the seat.

"What are you—" she began, but his intent became clear as he swung her over his lap and arranged her knees on either side of his hips. His blaster dug into the side of her knee, but she couldn't be bothered to care. "What, *now*?" She found herself out of breath all over again for an entirely new reason. After weeks of brushing hands, his deliberate touch was a little overwhelming, but she loved the boldness with which he pursued her now.

"The guards could find us any minute," he said, nuzzling her neck and removing her commlink from her ear, switching it off.

"Exactly. We should prepare." She wound her arms around his neck, trembling over the fact that she could finally do so after aching to for so long.

He moaned softly. "I agree wholeheartedly. If I don't kiss you, I'll be distracted with wanting to, which might prove problematic if I need to employ rational thought during the fight to come." He pressed her back into the control panel, placing a slow kiss to the hinge of her jaw. "Kiss me, Della. Kiss me because we're not dead. Kiss me because that could change any minute. Kiss me for kissing's sake."

A kiss for the sake of kissing. She brought her lips down onto his. She didn't fool herself into thinking one stolen kiss would mean anything in the end, but if all Della's life could be was a series of stolen moments, then she'd rob all she could.

"Are you sure about this?" She pulled away briefly. "I thought you said you couldn't touch me without feeling something."

"I feel nothing," he said tenderly between kisses as he trailed his mouth down her neck. "I am a cold, heartless criminal."

She moaned as he gently bit the skin where her shoulder met her neck. "Oh yes. Somehow, I'd forgotten about your great terribleness."

Each of his touches was a lie, contradicting his weak insistence that he felt nothing more than physical passion. Yet she would let him continue fibbing. The way he held her made her feel wanted. Adored. She would revel in his falsehoods, in the achingly attentive glide of his tongue and the silky strokes of his lips.

"Della," he whispered, and her heart gave a vicious twist that a ruffian such as he could say her name so sweetly. "You terrify me."

She knew he was more scared of this moment than of any of the dangers they'd faced earlier. They could pretend that none of the games they'd been playing were real, but she'd already fallen for him. He'd realize it the next time he read her book—and he would likely throw his walls back up in a ridiculous attempt to protect them both.

Della clutched him tighter as though hopelessly trying to hold on to a wave before it slipped back into the ocean. Ansel rocked forward, their hips grinding together, eliciting a gasp from them both. His hands slipped under her skirts and skated along her legs, and she bit back a groan that dissolved into a heartbroken sigh.

"Is something wrong?" Ansel lifted his head.

"Of course not." *It's only that I think you're wondrous.* "It's only that—perhaps we should stay alert." *And you refusing to care about me hurts worse than if you simply did not.* "And keep a lookout lest harm befall us." *And I hate that you won't just let people love you when it would save yourself and others much heartache.* "And of course there's the fact that you're an insufferable, obstinate man who thinks far too highly of himself and possesses an uncanny ability to make poor choices nine out of ten times, and the way you purposefully make yourself look like you've just rolled out of bed after a long night of debauchery is ridiculous, and you have this annoying habit where you never fully finish a beverage but leave half a drink in the bottom, and you—you drive me to distraction, and you have a lovely smile, and—" *And I think I love you*, she thought but didn't say.

Ansel sat back, his eyes wide, as though he knew what her outburst truly meant, as though she bore the declaration all over her face. He opened his mouth, and she knew what was coming. The gentle rejection, the *I can't, you shouldn't.* The merciful suggestion that they needed to stop.

Della slid out of Ansel's lap and resumed her position beside him. "We should get going," she said quietly because she was a coward. "It's too dangerous to linger."

CHAPTER 27

Della did the only rational thing she could after essentially confessing her feelings to Ansel and ruining everything. She hid.

As soon as they reconvened with the crew and vacated Creqreon, she handed over the stolen wrist device to Xaks, then retreated to her room, where she stayed for the remainder of the evening, the cosmic dust hopping after her like some kind of, well, living dust bunny. Its freedom was something Xaks had not seemed entirely comfortable with, but as the dust had not murdered them all, Della saw no reason to keep it contained. It had surely consumed enough of Della to see the crew as friends.

Della knew she was being foolish. Ansel could be reading her book at that very moment, but so long as she didn't know if he had or hadn't, she could pretend she'd never have to face the consequences.

When it was late enough that everyone should be in bed, Della got up and visited the washroom, leaving the cosmic dust resting on the foot of her bed in a blob the size of a large cat.

After stepping out of the sanitation chamber in a cloud of steam, Della donned Ansel's shirt, the thin material sticking to her skin. On her way back to her room, she heard the low drone of voices from the bridge down the hall. Trepidation filled her as she wondered what the crew were up so late discussing.

Steeling herself, knowing she could only avoid the inevitable for so long, Della reversed her course and headed for the bridge.

The door whooshing open as she entered made it impossible to conceal her presence.

She mounted the stairs to the platform where the control boards sat. Ansel and Xaks were in their captain's chairs. Yaggrel perched on a control board, and Eryl loomed to the side. They all watched her in the pitying way everyone looked at someone who'd just been discussed behind their back.

"Ah, you're up," Xaks said without preamble. "We're making arrangements to have the shields fixed in the morning. There are extra credits left over, so we purchased you a spot aboard a passenger vessel to Lumeria. It only seemed right, considering you procured the credits."

Della's heart sank. Down, down, down. She knew she ought to be grateful. Getting to Lumeria as quickly as possible was the right thing to do. Yet somehow their aid felt like betrayal. "Whose idea was this?" Della's voice wavered embarrassingly.

Ansel looked up with bloodshot eyes. Without him even having to speak, Della knew the answer to her question.

"Balor is tracking us," Xaks went on, either oblivious to or ignoring the tension between Della and Ansel. "Based off the speed of his ship, he'll be upon us in three days. You're safer on your own."

"Balor's looking for me too," Della protested. "I'm safer here than alone."

Xaks shook her head. "Your involvement with us put a target on your back, but you're still ambiguous enough that you should be fine if you keep your head down and don't crash any more high-stakes card games filled with the galaxy's most wanted. As long as Balor has us in his sights, you can slip away and return home without him ever knowing."

"Home," Della repeated.

"Your home," Xaks said deliberately. "Ansel told me about the books."

"What books?" Yaggrel asked, but everyone ignored him.

Della glared across the table at Ansel. "There it is, then. You read my book, didn't you?" He must have seen her feelings, panicked, and now he was getting rid of her the only way he knew she couldn't fight.

"Reading?" Yaggrel asked. "That doesn't sound like the Captain. He's not very good at it. One time, he tried to read directions to what he assumed was an intergalactic eatery, but he misread the name. He was convinced we were going to a smokehouse called Flint's, and I was so looking forward to a juicy Sichetian flank."

"Your constitution doesn't allow you to eat red meat," Eryl reminded him promptly.

"You stormed off." Ansel held Della's gaze. "You obviously didn't want to talk. I couldn't read your mind after that."

"Anyone in my position would have stormed off in a fit of rage," Yaggrel said. "I didn't need you to read my mind. Stars, Ansel, you had to know I'd be disappointed. I'd been dreaming of steak all day only to discover you docked us at a place called *Flirts*, which, Della, as you can imagine, was an establishment of a far different and unexpected nature from what we'd been promised."

"All you do is push people away when they get too close," Della said.

"Exactly." Yaggrel waved his spindly arms at Ansel. "I trusted you."

Ansel rose abruptly from his chair. "This was about taking care of your best interests."

"While I do appreciate the sentiment," Yaggrel said, "surely even you realized my best interests at the time involved steak, not erotic dancers."

"The only person you care about is yourself," Della snapped, staring Ansel down.

"Yeah!" Yaggrel stood.

Xaks shoved him off the control panel, and he flew off with a yelp in a wild tangle of limbs. "They're not talking about the steak, you imbecile."

"You only want me to go to protect yourself," Della said, feeling every eye now intensely focused on whatever was happening between her and Ansel. "You care about me, about all of us, and we care about you. You can be as prickly as you want, but that's not going to change anything."

An awkward beat passed before Ansel said, "Everyone get off my fucking bridge," his voice deadly calm.

Of course. When things got too difficult, he was doing what he always did. Running. Pushing. Fighting. Della turned to go.

"Not you, Della." Ansel flinched. "Stars, of course not you."

So she stood there as the rest of the crew filtered off the bridge until only the two of them remained.

"This isn't about my feelings." Ansel sighed in defeat. "Here are the facts. We may not survive it when Balor finds us. Your mother is suffering back home. She needs the medicine you set out to retrieve as soon as possible. Every moment on my ship endangers you, true, but it also endangers her."

Hot tears pricked at Della's vision, but she knew he was right. This wasn't only about her, and she mustn't be selfish. Her throat felt thick, constricting her emotions, stifling them the way she used to be so good at doing. It would be easier and perhaps kinder to leave without confessing her feelings.

But she was tired of swallowing her emotions, of being painfully aware and self-conscious over every one. If she didn't value them, no one would.

"There is something I need to tell you before you send me away. Continuing to deny what I feel for you would diminish what is between us." Her voice wavered, but she pressed on, speaking to the wall past his head because she couldn't quite meet Ansel's eye. "I need to tell you that I—"

"Don't."

"You cannot simply demand my feelings away. It's too late. I already—"

"I know you do," he burst out, rounding the control panel. "But I can't let you bare your soul to me yet again while I say nothing."

"You don't have to placate me. I know you do not care for me the way I care for you."

At that, his countenance fractured. Something broke within him as he closed the remaining distance between them and touched her jaw. "To hell I don't."

"If you cared for me half as much, you could not let me go so easily."

"Easily," he repeated. Golden light from the window behind her traced the angles of his face and carved shadows beneath his cheekbones. "Look behind you and tell me again how easy this is for me."

Though confused about his request, she did as he asked, turning away from him to face the window. As gold and violet light bathed her in color, she fell back a half step, bumping into Ansel's chest. He steadied her as she took in the cosmic dust filling the vaulted bridge windows. It wasn't *her* dust, of course—hers was still back in her room. This dust was wild and malicious, preying on whatever fears and desires it could find. And it had found Ansel's.

One vision swirled into the next, sparkling light forming and reforming into scene after scene in a glittering swirl. Della in Ansel's embrace on this very bridge, their lips interlocked and their arms entwined. Della in his bed, sleep-mussed hair sticking to her cheek as she slumbered with his arm over her waist.

Della in his future—curled on his lap in his captain's chair and chatting about nothing while stars whisked by. Della coming out to greet him from a small cottage tucked away in the woods. Della crying his name as Cooperation wardens tore him from her arms and two children who had her hair and his eyes clung to the edges of her tunic.

"Don't tell me I don't care for you when I literally cannot see a future without you in it."

She turned in his arms. The emotion in his eyes struck her with its earnestness.

"I'm not good with—this stuff. But I . . ."

"But you what?" Her heart lifted, but Ansel, the man who always had a comeback, was at a loss for what to say. "Are you . . . trying to confess your feelings?"

"Shit," Ansel cursed under his breath, running his hands through his hair. "Yes, and you turn me into the biggest damn coward. I've wasted so much of our time being an idiot. Denial won't save either of us. My heart's already decided it's yours anyway. Make a liar out of me. Let me promise you forever tonight, knowing you'll leave me tomorrow."

Warmth blossomed in her chest before tingling all the way to her fingertips. A smile curved across her face. Finally, finally, *finally*. Her smile turned into a stifled giggle as he yanked away and began pacing. "Fuck, this isn't the time or the place," he was saying. "It should be romantic, like by a waterfall or something."

"I'll be certain to have one on standby the next time you decide to declare yourself."

Ansel ceased his pacing and faced her. She fought her curling lips, but he noticed them, and his anguished expression softened, then turned grim. Determined. He marched over, took her face in his hands, and said, in a voice that was anything but cowardly, "I am in love with you, and you know it, you fiend."

And then he kissed her. On and on he kissed her until she could hardly stand it. His tongue parted her lips to stroke over hers. Aching, Della arched against him, needing to feel the scrape of his body against hers.

"I'm sorry," he groaned against her mouth, pressing her against the control panel.

"Whatever for?" Della gasped.

"I'm not a duke," he said through desperate kisses. "If I were, I'd probably take you on quaint picnics and throw you parties and kiss you tenderly under the light of the full moons."

"Gracious, how dull," she said. "It's a good thing you're not a duke. I'm far more interested in what a good-for-nothing rogue might have in store."

"I'm not good for *nothing*," Ansel growled against her collarbone. "I do have one or two talents."

"Of course you do," Della said soothingly.

"Easy." His eyes blazed. "Don't torment me unless you want me to prove it to you right now."

"Of course I want that, you absurd man."

Nearly before she'd finished talking, he was kissing down her neck again, muttering, "Good," and, "Thank the stars," and "I want to be good for you, Della."

She wound her fists in his hair. "And I want to be incredibly wicked for you, Ansel Tulzok."

He let out an indecent, helpless sound she liked quite a bit. "Stars above. How can you be so sweet to everyone else and say such filthy things to me? Do you have any idea what it does to me?"

Della grinned. "It makes you press me against things and kiss me, which is generally the objective."

"I want to do more." Pulling away, he cupped her face in his big hands. "I could make you feel so good. Please let me."

She nodded as well as she was able. "Yes, *yes.*"

His eyes darkened. "Get on the control panel." The command was hungry and immediate, as though he'd been thinking of nothing else for days. "And let me see you."

Hoisting herself onto the panel behind her, Della slipped one button of her shirt loose with shaking fingers, then the other. She wore nothing under the shirt, and the metal was cold beneath her legs. The cosmos swirled behind her in a blur of stars and sparks. Her heart drummed hard in her chest, and her skin tingled with anticipation.

Ansel watched her with lust-darkened eyes as her last button slipped free, and she leaned back, propping her hands behind her, letting the material gape open.

Ansel swore. "Look at you."

Della couldn't believe the man who endured beatings without betraying pain was crumbling at the sight of her. She felt desirable, powerful, the least shy she'd ever felt in her life. There was something wildly erotic about him fully dressed, studying her, laid bare.

Ansel's ravenous gaze roved her flesh, the knot in his throat lodging along the column of his neck. He took a step toward her, then another. "Tell me I can touch you."

"Please." If he didn't, she would weep from the empty, aching agony.

Ansel's hands found her thighs as he groaned her name into her mouth. She leaned into his hands as they explored her, lingering in all the places that made her gasp. The startled look he gave her when he dipped his fingers between her legs and found how badly she wanted him darkened into primal need. She reached to start undoing some of his own buttons, but he sank to his knees before her.

"I must admit this isn't how I pictured my evening going," she said breathlessly.

"Your imagination isn't as good as mine when it comes to this, Della dear." Ansel kissed the side of her knee. "Let me show you my dreams this once."

And show her he did.

"Ansel." She gasped his name, trying to convey everything she felt in a single word.

He didn't stop what he was doing to respond—thank heavens, and bless the man—but his thumb stroked her hip as though he understood, as though he were telling her it was all right to break because he promised to painstakingly collect every shattered fragment.

Della had gone her entire life holding herself together, tying everything she felt into a strong knot, securing it away so no one could use it against her. But this was Ansel. She'd spent her life lost in daydreams, and he'd visited them, found her, and drawn her out.

His every touch conveyed vehement approval, chasing away any notion of self-consciousness. All she felt was seen, understood, as he responded to every sigh and shudder of her body. He devoured her like pleasing her was his sole purpose, the pressure inside her mounting higher and higher.

She bit back a cry as waves of bliss coursed through her, muscles quivering along her inner thighs and her elbows buckling. Ansel rose and caught her, kissing her long and deep, his mouth warm and soft.

Wrapping her legs around his waist, she pulled him against her, sighing contentedly. "Do you think you could do that again?" she mumbled against his lips.

Ansel *did* think he was capable of doing such a thing again, judging by the way he promptly buttoned her shirt back up, albeit very crookedly, and dragged her to his bedroom.

Shushing each other's laughter, they tiptoed down the hall, bumping into each other, pausing to kiss every few steps, drunk on happiness.

They fell through the door into his room. Della laughed and spun to kiss him so that he stumbled backward toward the bed. The mattress hit the back of Ansel's knees, and he fell onto it, dragging her on top of him.

Then Ansel paused, his expression growing earnest. He sat up, brushing her hair off her face. "I'm sterile, just so you know.

I mean, not naturally. We have medicine here to make us infertile until we stop taking it. And I don't have any diseases you might catch. Eryl mentioned you don't either, after she tested your blood after the cosmic dust incident, which was a terrible breach of medical privacy, but you know Eryl. So whatever happens between us, you'll be safe. Not that anything more has to happen between us, but—"

Della pressed a finger to his lips. "Okay."

She nudged him further onto the bed. He let her push him back against the headboard. Let her straddle his hips and gently remove his shirt, minding the bandages he still wore around one shoulder. She'd controlled so few situations in her life, and she liked that he allowed her this one. Her gaze wandered over his bare torso. He was splendid. Not overly defined, but there was a definite power in the slope of his shoulders, the flex of his stomach.

"Take what you need from me," he told her. "Tonight, you're the thief."

"And when I leave tomorrow?" Sadness bled into her incandescent joy. He was giving her everything he had to give right before he had to give her up, and there was nothing she could do to change the situation.

"Then you'll take my heart with you, you pretty little burglar." He gently touched her cheek. "But don't let yourself leave before you're even gone. Stay with me here, now."

So she blinked back her sadness and saved her grief for later.

"I'm curious," he said, voice low. "What will you do with me now that you have me?"

Her blood rushed hot in her veins. Truly, she didn't know where to start. There was so much she wished to do and precious little time.

She began by re-shedding her shirt, enjoying the animalistic spark that lit his gaze and made his expression go a little wild, as though he'd not seen her laid bare only moments ago. She helped him shimmy out of his breeches. Then, ever so slowly, she leaned in to kiss him, stroking her tongue over his, reveling in the low whimper he made in the back of his throat as she ground against him.

"I think my first impression of you was correct after all. You *are* trying to kill me," Ansel groaned, his fists winding into the sheets as though he were physically restraining himself from urging her onto him.

She loved him like this, his restraint on the verge of snapping, the way he gave over his body to her mercy. Hadn't she wondered if she could be the one to make him lose control? Her body wound tighter just thinking about it, and she desperately wanted him to enact whatever depraved plans swirled behind his hungry eyes.

"What do you need?" he asked, apparently sensing the shift.

She felt her face flush hot.

Ansel leaned forward and took her face in his hand. "Don't go quiet now. We both know you're capable of telling me what you want."

She wanted to feel him reveling in her, consumed by her, his focus narrowing until she was his entire world. She wanted to be his pleasure, his purpose, his everything. That was when she felt the most powerful, the strongest. "I want what I've always wanted," she whispered. "For you to stop holding back. Show me how you feel."

His gaze blackened as his pupils dilated. The next thing she knew, he'd spun her around, his large hands enveloping hers as he roughly guided her to grip the bedpost. She felt the warmth of his chest against her back as he knelt behind her. He kissed the curve of her shoulder, sending delicious shivers down her spine. His arms wrapped around her, his fingers playing and teasing until she was arching against him. When he chuckled smugly against her temple, she elbowed him for his arrogance, which only made him moan and kiss the curve of her ear.

Confused that he'd rewarded her for shoving him, she looked over her shoulder. "What, you aren't going to tell me to be good?"

"No." His smile was wicked as he rolled his knuckle over that place so desperate for his attention. "I like you bratty." And he showed her just how much he liked it by notching himself at her entrance and easing inside of her.

She sighed his name, the pressure almost unbearable but utterly divine. He gently bit her shoulder, stifling a broken grunt. He let her grow accustomed to the feel of him, until she was matching his movements for more.

"Stars, I love you," Della murmured, nearly incoherently.

But he heard her. For at last, at *last,* he stopped holding back. With a rough jerk, he braced his hand above hers on the bedpost, his knuckles going white and his breaths coming out in ragged half-curses and jumbled praise.

"You're mine," she gasped, half in wonderment that he'd at last given himself over to her, half in realization that she was no longer alone. That she finally had another person to call *hers.*

His fingertips dug into her hip, his jaw scraping against her spine as he growled, "*Yours,*" in agreement against her skin. Her body tightened around his, and her nails scratched the bedpost as she hit her peak.

He let her ride out the waves of pleasure before repositioning her to face him. She was pliant and content and willing. She might have let him lead her into a volcano at that moment. Luckily, he only reclined against the pillows and positioned her over his lap. He lowered her back over him with a sigh, and she moaned, her body somehow reawakening and urging her to seek more, more, more.

He let her set the pace now, her hips finding a languid rolling rhythm, her thighs still shaking.

Her climax was slower this time, a gentle, sleepy build peppered by tender kisses and soft smiles. She wound her arms around his shoulders, their mouths matching the pace of their hips, their tongues caressing lazily and their lips kiss-swollen.

When Della cried out, her body shuddering and pleasure pulsing through her veins, Ansel followed, mumbling nonsense against her skin. She collapsed against his glistening, heaving chest as he trailed gentle fingers down her back.

The evening bled into a haze of whispered promises that could only last until morning came. Of delicious dozing and gentle waking. Of middle-of-the-night kisses that heated into desperation. Of frantic hands and roving mouths, of gasps and hushed confessions and giggled secrets. Of pretending this was a beginning and not an end.

When morning came, Ansel stroked his fingers through her hair, and they said nothing at all, for they both knew the other was wishing it could last forever.

And then Ansel's time bot woke up and ruined the moment by saying something incredibly long-winded and lewd that didn't bear repeating, but it did make Della realize how nice Yaggrel had made her own bot in comparison. She dissolved into giggles as Ansel snarled, "I'm going to fucking murder Yaggrel," diving across the bed for the bot, which blithely hopped off the nightstand and scuttled to the safety of the closet.

PART 4

OUTSIDE OF TIME AND SPACE, a librarian returned from a book, heartbroken.

She wiped a tear from her eyes even as the other librarians told her *well done.*

Well done indeed.

She had broken her promise to the son of a poet and betrayed everyone she loved. In the end, she could not change his fate.

She had shattered hearts. Ended lives. Wrought tragedy.

Yet in the librarian's eyes, her worst crime was that she'd fallen in love. She would pay for that for the rest of her life. For she touched her belly and knew her troubles were not yet over.

CHAPTER 28

During the night, Xaks brought them to the space station where they would fix the ship's shields . . . and where Della would depart.

Della stood with Ansel and the crew (including Yaggrel, whom Ansel had refrained from fucking murdering) by the gangplank of the passenger vessel that would take her to Lumeria.

She looked up at the sleek, rounded vessel she was to board, so different from the spiky contours of the Miss Demeanor. Other passengers pushed around her, chatting happily as they walked up the gangplank.

"I know the captain." Ansel broke the melancholy silence, his hand brushing her lower back. "She'll get you there safely. With the speeds her ship is capable of, you'll be there in three days."

Three days. She'd be reaching Lumeria around the same time Balor would reach the Miss Demeanor. Della wanted to lean into Ansel's touch and fall back into his arms, but if she did, she wouldn't leave.

Della blinked hard, letting one fat tear roll down her nose before swiping it away.

Every crew member looked at her in horror, a single tear rendering the hardened fugitives helpless.

"Stars, don't cry," Ansel said, sounding a bit broken up himself.

"Yes, stop," Xaks commanded gruffly in what she probably thought was a comforting manner. "No one has died yet."

"I, for one, am inconsolable," Eryl said in her usual, pleasant voice. "We will miss you, strumpet."

"Use this if you run into trouble." Yaggrel solemnly pressed a walnut-sized bomb into her palm with the air of someone gifting a family heirloom. "And this." He passed her a messenger bag holding the cosmic dust. Its flap was closed to avoid alarming other passengers, but a faint glow still seeped out from under the leather.

After everyone else had said goodbye, Ansel approached her. He reached into an inner coat pocket and withdrew a familiar leather-bound book. His name was inscribed on the spine. "This is yours."

In a way, she thought he was saying *I'm yours.* She clutched it to her chest. "Are you sure?"

"I don't plan on giving you your book back, and you'll need some way to visit me." He winked, then tilted her chin and kissed her right there in front of his crew and everyone else in the hangar. The crew made various noises of approval and revulsion. He brushed her tears away with his thumbs as she settled back on her heels. "Besides, you'll need some reading material for the trip. I bookmarked all the places I fell for you."

She smiled, noticing all the tabs sticking from the pages. There were a great many. She hugged the book to her chest, refusing to allow herself to feel sad. For if she were sad, this would feel more like a *goodbye* rather than a *farewell for now.*

Ansel pulled her into a desperate embrace, and she kissed him once more, fiercely.

"I will be back," she whispered the vow to him and him alone, "and you and I shall write ourselves the most wondrous of stories."

The trip to Lumeria passed quickly enough. Della spent a great deal of time caring for the cosmic dust, which had taken to showing her more of her memories. Most were mundane—her studying in school or preparing dinner with her mother. But there was a particular scene the dust liked to show Della over and over again of her mother uttering the words, "*You have the power to choose your own story, Della. Make it a good one.*"

The last time the dust had shown her the scene, the words were said lightly, lovingly. Now they were twisted, dripping with sorrow. Her mother's face wavered in the dust's light, tears tracking down her cheeks. The setting around her was their apartment, just as in the earlier memory, yet her mother's countenance radiated fear.

None of it made any sense, and the memory always faded shortly after her mother spoke. Della had no recollection of her own of the incident, which seemed strange. Surely such a shocking display would have stuck with her, no matter how young she might have been at the time, but it was yet another memory she'd lost to her fever.

When Della wasn't losing herself in the dust, feeding it her fingernail clippings and the contents of her hairbrush, she and Ansel exchanged countless letters, ranging from an observation they'd made during the day, to something funny they overheard from the crew or Della's fellow passengers, to softer late-night confessions ranging from greatest fears to favorite colors.

Dear Ansel,

I was thinking of the way you declared your love for me—very eloquently and with many flowery words, truly an inspiration for many future poets—and I couldn't help but feel concerned regarding your heart. I do hope I will not break it. I do not want to become a memory you despise.

Yours,
Della.

Dear Della,

I think there is very little I could not forgive you for. Break me, if you wish. It will hurt less than if I never let myself have you.

Yours,
Ansel

P.S. I don't need eloquent words. When I see you again, I'll think of a few creative ways to show you how much I adore you.

Ansel Dear,

Don't strain yourself. I'm happy to provide suggestions.

For instance, I happened to glance at my bed the other day and briefly considered how pretty you would look laid out upon it while I had my wicked way with you.

Looking forward to your thoughts on the matter.

—D

Della Darling,

It's been one day, and the Miss Demeanor is in shambles without you here (and, if I'm being honest, so am I).

Eryl's processor is lagging, Xaks is scowling even more than usual, and Yaggrel—well, he found out you threw away his poisons, and he's pissed about it, to be honest, but I can sense that he misses you too. Very deep down, beneath all that rage.

Love,
Ansel.

P.S. I have considered your proposition at length. After a particularly pleasant solo brainstorming session in the sterilizer, I've come up with an alternate suggestion. It involves my desk, you, and a compromising position.

A,

I'm touched by your letter. Tell Yaggrel I left him a week's supply of his favorite veggie pies in the preserver. If you really want to delight him, tell him I slipped those poisons of his into one of the pies—he's so dearly fond of daily activities that come with a side of possible death and will likely spend days trying to determine which pie is contaminated, which will keep him out of everyone's hair.

Yours,
Della.

P.S. A captivating notion that I counter with: You, taking me against the windows in the bridge. Though we mustn't leave a smudge, lest Xaks figure out what we were up to.

Della love,

Tomorrow we face Balor. I'm not sure what the odds are that we make it out of the confrontation alive, much less with Balor in our clutches. Eryl would probably be overjoyed to run the calculations, but I won't ask her due to the undoubtedly soul-crushing nature of her answer.

The optimistic part of me—which is a brand-new part of me I hadn't realized existed before you shone a light on it—has evidently already decided we will succeed, because I've found myself dreaming of "after." After we apprehend Balor and return the superconductor to Lumeria. After you return to me.

Does your "after" look the same as it did when I asked you about it all those weeks ago?

Yours, always,
Ansel.

P.S. Don't fret about smudges, sweetheart. After we're through defiling whichever surface—or surfaces—you choose, I will happily scour the entire ship on my hands and knees with THE GOOD SHIT to eradicate every last smudge.

My Dearest Ansel,

This reminds me of the first time we dreamed together, except this time, it seems more possible that our dreams will come true.

I don't know what my "after" looks like anymore. I just know that I don't ever want there to be an "after" you.

Maybe you will whisk me away and we will travel the stars forever, doing our best to chase down each one. Maybe we will build a little cottage on Lumeria where we will rock in our chairs until we're old and simply watch the stars swirl freely overhead.

Or maybe we'll find something in between that

suits us both equally. We can spend whatever season on Lumeria is the most miserable traveling and return home for the nicer bits.

Or perhaps you could cook and clean and keep our house on Lumeria, where you would spend a significant amount of time staring mournfully out windows, writing love sonnets and longing for my return, while I smuggle something dangerous across the galaxy, coming home to you only infrequently, when we will spend a week of passion together before I'm off again once more.

Your dashing adventurer,
Della.

Della Dear,

During these past few days, I've spent enough time pathetically staring out windows longing for you to last a lifetime. If you want to smuggle something dangerous across a galaxy, I will keep ship for you. I don't need a house because you make any place feel like home.

Love,
Ansel.

At last, Della awoke the third morning to the captain announcing their arrival at Lumeria over the ship's intercom. They entered the planet's atmosphere with a slight jostle that was nothing like the chaotic entries of Ansel's ship—the rattling and shaking that made her wonder if the whole thing would fly apart. The thought of Ansel made Della's belly tighten as she considered how he would likely confront Balor before the day was through.

She wanted to say something more to him now, but everything she thought of sounded too much like a goodbye. Instead, Della simply whispered a short *I love you* before she ran to the main deck, joining the other passengers eagerly looking out the windows as they approached the big green planet.

They sank down, down, down, the ship finally brushing past the treetops to settle—

Except the ship didn't settle onto the forest floor. It kept sinking down, down, down, because the forest floor was still miles and miles below. They navigated around a twisted bramble of limbs, the bark of one branch eclipsing the window for several long minutes before they made it past—for the trees were impossibly large, entire cities carved into their sides. Creatures as big as cows with spines running down their backs and long, fleshy tails grazed on pastures of moss swathed across large boughs. Switchback roads snaked back and forth up tree trunks, twinkling lanterns tucked into their bark lighting the path.

The trees were so gigantic, Della felt as though she were the size of an insect.

Something prickled at the back of her memories. A chill washed over her, and she realized—

"I've been here before."

CHAPTER 29

Della first picked a lock when she was seven. She broke into a study to read a book about a young boy named Riktel, who was the size of a tiny insect and lived on a bulging tree root protruding from a forest floor. That night, she dreamed that she shrank to the size of a bug and visited him in his world.

A world that looked a lot like Lumeria.

At least, she'd assumed she'd shrunk, but what if she hadn't? What if the trees were simply so large, she'd felt as minuscule as a beetle?

And what if it hadn't been a dream at all?

A cold chill ran down Della's spine. Was it possible she could have written herself into a book when she was a child, long before she ever found Ansel's? She could have dismissed the whole thing, chalking the experience up to nothing more than her vivid imagination.

The same way she'd dismissed other such daydreams.

Unless those hadn't been dreams either.

As the ship alighted on a landing pad constructed off the side of a tree limb, Della shivered, taking a dizzy step back from the window. She couldn't trust her own thoughts, her own *mind.* Her thoughts reeled as she questioned every dream about every book she'd ever read.

"Welcome to Lumeria." The captain's echoing voice came through the intercom over the buzz of shuffling passengers as they collected their belongings and pressed toward the gangplank.

Della hardly noticed them. As she sifted through her memories, they turned fuzzy, and she soon lost track of which were real and which she had previously assumed were her own imagination. Her thoughts ceased to have meaning, like the phenomenon of staring at a word too long until it began to look like nonsense.

Della drew a few calming breaths. She knew she shouldn't jump to any conclusions. Perhaps her imagination had only concocted a dream that happened to look eerily similar to a real place. Besides, she didn't have time for existential crises at present.

Gathering her things, Della followed the crowd of passengers down the gangplank. Misty forest air filled her nostrils with the scent of wet leaves and rich earth. The network of landing platforms perched disjointedly in the tree's branches were joined together with swinging rope bridges. Ships came and went, weaving their way through a cage of twigs and leaves like clumsy bumblebees.

Clutching her pack, Della ran her hands over the material, ensuring Ansel's book was still in place. The faint glow through the fabric reassured her that the dust, too, was still tucked away. She gave Ansel's book a quick check, relieved when she read that Balor had not yet reached the Miss Demeanor. Shakily, Della walked across one of the bridges toward the city that spiraled up the tree's trunk. Though she tried to ignore it, she couldn't help the feeling of familiarity as she took in more of her surroundings.

The narrow path swung beneath her feet as she stepped out from under a canopy of leaves to cross over the vast nothingness between the outer branch and the trunk. The humid air was stifling in her too-tight lungs, smelling of decomposing leaves and pine needles. Below her, fuzzy clouds gave the illusion of a soft landing, concealing the hard earth far, far beneath. The sun was doing its best to break through the fog, casting the forest in pale green light.

At last, Della stepped from the bridge to the road carved into the side of the trunk. The streets winding up the tree were broader than she would have imagined possible, wider even than the main cobblestone roads of Poling back home. On one side, cheery shop windows winked at her. On the other was a cold drop to nowhere, partitioned off by a flimsy rope fence.

The city's inhabitants—mostly humans—didn't seem to notice the wonder of their world. Heads down, they bustled from one task to the next, like a colony of ants scurrying about their hill. Though the street was busy, it was hushed, the only noise an occasional scuff, clatter, or bang of people going about their tasks. No small talk. No laughter. No arguments.

Though she had been very young when she read Riktel's story, Della remembered his book's depiction of the people in his world, how they went through life like forest creatures, intent on survival, disregarding emotional connection, art, and love, considering it unessential. Her scalp prickled at this second confirmation that she'd been here before.

Maybe it wasn't such a stretch to believe she could have visited another book in the past when she'd already done so once, but it was a strange coincidence to have seemingly visited two books set in the same reality, the same planet.

Della stepped in front of a man passing by. He drew up short and regarded her with a look that was neither pleasant nor unpleasant.

"Excuse me," Della said. "Could you direct me to the nearest apothecary?" Dissecting her memories would come later. For now, she needed to focus on the most pressing matter: her mother's heart.

The man nodded, gave her a few quick directions, then went on his way without a goodbye or any other well-wishes.

Della entered the apothecary, ducking under bundles of herbs hanging from the ceiling, their clean, fresh medicinal scent tickling her nostrils. Books, glass vessels, and strange instruments were packed on rows of haphazardly placed shelves. She wove among the maze toward the clinking and rustling issuing from the back of the shop until she emerged before a heap of clutter that might have, at one point in time, been a front counter.

"Good morning?" she asked uncertainly.

A pouf of curly gray hair shot over the rubbish, attached to the round, wrinkled face of an elderly woman. Thick glass lenses reflected over her eyes. At first, Della thought they were spectacles, but they weren't. They were twin monocles attached to separate chains pinned onto the woman's plain brown blouse. The lenses must have had different strengths, for one of the woman's watery blue eyes was magnified so it nearly filled the monocle while the other was considerably smaller.

"Good morning," Della said again. "I'm Della. Della Farley."

The woman cocked her head. "Healer," she said by way of introduction.

"Do you have a name?" Della inquired.

"What use are names? They serve no purpose, tell you nothing about a person. Titles explain quickly what you're good for. They're all we use here on Lumeria."

Della's heart gave a hard throb. She'd known Ansel's childhood had been cold. Had he grown up without even a name of his own?

"Isn't a person good for something beyond what they can offer others?" Della asked.

"Like what?" asked the healer.

Della had no idea how to respond to that. If this was indeed Riktel's planet too, she supposed it made sense why a boy like him might be an outcast here—someone with nothing to contribute to a place where entertainment, love, and art had no value. He would be like a songbird in a beehive, unable to fit into any of the roles around him essential for the colony's survival. His song would be considered useless, no matter how sweet it might be. She thought of Ansel, too, how lonely his childhood must have been.

"Did you need something?" the healer prompted. As with Della's encounter with the man outside, the question was not asked with any rudeness intended. It was only frank, to the point.

"I was hoping you might have something to help my mother's heart."

The woman settled onto a stool behind the counter, popped a monocle out from between her cheek and brow bone, and listened as Della told her about her mother's ailment.

"Her heart never beats at the proper rhythm. Sometimes, her chest aches so much she cannot breathe. She grows faint, feels sick to her stomach, and even struggles to eat and sleep. It pains her so much, she weeps. Her life is shrouded in shadow, and until I find a cure, she cannot live properly."

The woman's countenance remained unchanged throughout Della's summary.

"Well?" Della asked. "Can you help her? A friend of mine mentioned you may have some medicine for arrhythmias."

"She doesn't have an arrhythmia," the woman said matter-of-factly. "She has a broken heart."

"A broken heart?" Della repeated. "That's ridiculous. She has experienced no great loss or tragedy that I know of. How could I even fix such a thing?"

"Bodies we can heal here on Lumeria. Minds? Hearts?" The healer shook her head. "Those are different matters entirely, beyond our comprehension."

If Della's mother had a broken heart, then that meant there was no cure. Della's hopes teetered, threatening to plummet. Did her mother even know what ailed her? She must not, or else she never would have let Della fruitlessly toil for years to purchase medicine that would never work.

What could have made her mother slip into sorrow so profound? Perhaps it was a descent so slow that her mother didn't even realize it was happening until she could not escape the darkness.

"Please, may I have the medicine anyway?" Della rasped out. "I do not know what else to try."

The healer shrugged. "If you're certain. It makes no difference to me. It won't hurt her if she's not sick, but don't be surprised if it does no good."

The woman ducked behind the counter, then returned with a large jar filled with tiny white capsules. "Have her take one tablet twice daily after food. This is a year's supply. Come back when you need more. If it works." The healer's tone made it clear she doubted it would.

Della transferred over some credits, and it was done.

In her hands she held the thing that should have given herself and her mother their lives back. Yet now she was filled with worry that reality would once again disappoint her.

Della forced away her doubts. Surely this could not all have been for nothing. The medicine *would* work. She would have to return for more eventually, of course, but for now, all she had to do was go home.

But she hesitated. "Do you by chance know a boy named Riktel?" She knew it was a far-fetched question. This world was a large one, and even if this was indeed the same planet from Riktel's book, it was unlikely she'd happened to land in the city was living in. But she had to ask.

The healer had wedged her monocle back in, and her mismatched eyes blinked in tandem. "Ah, that's an old word. Hardly a name, more of a title, really, much like Healer."

Della's breath caught at this third indication she'd been

here before. She couldn't deny the facts any longer, impossible though they seemed. "What kind of title is it?" she asked.

"Riktel is old-tongue, slang. There's no good translation for it. Essentially means 'useless one.' There are several loitering around the roots at any given time. Shouldn't be hard to find one."

Useless one. The Lumerians had declared a little boy useless before he had even reached ten years of age. But he wasn't useless at all. If nothing else, he'd eased the loneliness of a sad little girl.

"I'm looking for one in particular . . . about my age." Della wished she could describe Riktel, but her memory was too fuzzy. She'd been only seven at the time.

"One's as useless as the next. What does it matter which you find? Just as you could have sought out any other healer in the city and gotten the same thing you got from me. See? Titles. Much more convenient than names."

Della clutched the jar of medicine a little closer. She would get nowhere with this conversation. Before she tried to write herself home, she'd travel down to the roots and look there herself. "Thank you for your time."

As Della wove back through the shop, her eye caught on a poster board hanging by the front door. The fliers there were dusty and jumbled, layers upon layers covering each other so it was hard to tell what any of them said.

But half a name stuck out from the rest, prompting Della to walk up to the board as though in a trance. She moved aside an advertisement so she could see the entire sign that had caught her attention.

It was an aged wanted poster, displaying a grainy picture of a much younger Ansel, clean-shaven with sandy blond hair; she'd nearly forgotten that he mentioned he'd dyed it dark to hide his identity. She stared at his face. There was something heartbreakingly familiar about it.

There was a niggling at her brain, like the sensation of having forgotten something behind after leaving home. Her gaze flitted back to the top of the poster, which read: *WANTED: Electrician last known using the pseudonym Ansel Tulzok.* The poster went on to list his supposed crimes, ranging from the petty crimes he must have committed in his youth to the theft of the Shield Stone, stealing Cooperation equipment, assaulting wardens, and escaping prison.

Why did the photo of this young man cause tears to prick at the back of her eyes, as though she were mourning someone long gone?

"I don't understand," Della murmured to herself.

As if in response, something went hot against her side. Della looked down to find the messenger bag containing the cosmic dust flaring brightly. Before she alarmed the healer, Della ran outside and ducked into a little divot between two lobes of bark. She made it just as sparks began cascading over the side of the satchel. She fell back as they rose before her and showed her a memory.

Della always thought she'd had a fever when she was sixteen that left her childhood memories blurred.

Now, the dust showed her a different story. The dust showed her the fever wasn't a fever at all.

It showed an image of a teenaged girl in a classroom. Della knew she was looking at herself even though the girl looked completely different from Della's reflection. This girl was shorter and blond with sharp features whereas Della was brunette with softer features, but Della *knew* she was her. Somehow. Some way.

The answer floated outside her brain, just out of reach.

In the dust's picture, the old version of Della reached out to take a book her teacher handed her, only to vanish into thin air as soon as her fingertip brushed the spine.

CHAPTER 30

As soon as she blinked her eyes open, she recognized the forest around her.

She was in the same small clearing nestled next to a tree root where she'd met Riktel years ago. The root towered next to her as high as a three-story building. The grass swayed like a choir, and the wildflowers released their fragrant pollen.

She did not find the boy she'd met the first time. She found a different boy—a young man, really, maybe seventeen or eighteen, sitting against the root, his long legs crossed at the ankles. His tawny hair shone golden. On his sun-washed face lingered a slight smile, as though he were not only content with his life but life in general.

When he cracked his eye open and spotted her, that smile broadened. "What's a pretty, high-bough thing like you doing in the roots?"

She looked up into the tree. The inhabitants of the world had carved a city into the trunk—bark awnings protruding from shop fronts and tiny fairy lights hanging along the paths, nestled into the bark like flickering fireflies.

"I'm not from up there," she said. "I'm from a different place, very far away." The grass was cool and soft beneath her bare feet as she walked over and introduced herself.

He stood and took her hand. "Electrician."

"Electrician?" she said slowly, trying not to be rude over the strangeness of such a name.

"Is something wrong with that title?"

"I'm simply accustomed to names like Peter or Rupert or Ansel."

His eyes twinkled in the sunshine. "Now, now, could anyone named Rupert possess my charm?"

"You think highly of yourself."

"No, but I suddenly find myself in fierce competition with this unknown Rupert for your attention. I must flaunt what assets I have."

"Are you flirting with me?"

"Obviously."

How odd. She had never flirted with anyone before. But this place was made for flirting, surrounded by delicate forest flowers, earthy red-capped mushrooms, the sweet symphony of birdsong, and sunbeams streaming through the canopy above like satin ribbons. And the golden-haired boy was made for flirting with, with his mischievous smile made for stealing first kisses.

"Are you hungry?" he asked. "I have enough lunch to share."

"Sharing a picnic is a sweet gesture for a ridiculous flirt such as yourself. You're less of a scoundrel than you'd like people to believe, aren't you?"

He was indeed. They sipped fragrant sassafras tea, split an herby loaf of bread, and carved pieces off a wheel of sharp cheese. He told her about his life, how he came from nothing and spent his youth stealing to survive, but recently earned an apprenticeship at an electronics shop where he spent his day tinkering with gadgets, because he had a knack for gears and circuits. He made her laugh with his tales of eccentric customers and inventions gone wrong that led to mild electrocution and staticky hair for weeks. In turn, she told him about herself, how she always felt out of place, how books were her friends instead of people. Remem-

bering the last boy she'd visited here had no concept of friendship, she began to explain it to him, but he cut her off.

"I know what a friend is," the young man said. "I have one. Well, maybe two now." He winked at her.

How things had changed since she last visited. Perhaps Riktel had told his world about friendly companionship, and it had spread throughout the land. The idea pleased her, that she'd helped Riktel help so many.

Soon, he told her it was time for him to go, that he had to return to work. "Are you staying here long?" he asked.

"How long did you have in mind?"

He walked backward toward where he'd left his pack against the root. "For dinner. For the afternoon." He grinned cheekily. "Forever."

"How forward of you." She linked her hands behind her, her skirts catching on the wildflowers. "Are you proposing marriage? Why, we've only just met."

"Marriage?" He frowned. "What's that?"

She supposed she shouldn't be surprised he didn't know that when his world only knew about friendship, thanks to her. Maybe her influence could bring even greater love to this world. What an overwhelming prospect that was. "Marriage is when people vow to love each other forever."

He regarded her with curiosity. "What is love?"

She blinked. "You can't know friendship and not know love."

"Love is undying devotion?"

"Friendship is so much more than just devotion." Had she not taught that to Riktel? "Love can be platonic too, the simple joy, caring, and appreciation you feel toward another person. Don't you feel that toward your friend?"

He hesitated. "Maybe."

"The love in a marriage is different," she went on. "It's romantic. It's—" Well, truthfully, she didn't know how to describe it, seeing as she'd never been in love, but she had read a great deal

of epic love stories in her sixteen years, which she felt qualified her in some small way to explain the subject. "I think it's deep affection, attraction, happiness you experience just from being around another person. It's comfort and acceptance. It's knowing you don't have to face the world alone anymore."

His gaze was full of such a deep yearning as she described it, it broke her heart a little. "And it's simple as that?" he asked. "Deciding and promising to love someone forever?"

"Maybe not simple, but so long as both people in the marriage trust each other and are determined to keep their word, it can be wonderful."

"How does it work?" A look of stubborn resolution settled over his face as he set his pack aside, all other responsibilities forgotten. "We should get married right now, you and I."

She giggled because obviously, he was being ridiculous. She'd never met a young man like him, so eager to love, so open with his heart. Most young men her age were standoffish and snide, as though the very things that made life worth living—affection, joy, and kindness—were beneath them.

"Well," she said, "you have to have a wedding, for one thing."

"Show me how."

Though she was far too old to have pretend weddings with boys under oak trees, that was what she did. She hoped that showing him the ritual would enable him to teach it to others, the way Riktel had spread friendship throughout the land.

She twisted a crown of flowers for her hair and braided blades of grass into wedding rings. They stood facing each other with their hands linked as twilight settled, and an explosion of fireflies awoke to flicker around them like hundreds of candles.

She taught him the vows and laughed as she struggled to fit the makeshift ring over his first knuckle, feeling silly about the whole game. He played his part well, though, face solemn and palm warm and sure when he slid on her ring. "Now what?" he asked, his breath feathering the hair at her temple.

"The couple shares a kiss to seal their vows." She tried to wriggle her hand free, thinking he surely would want to end the game there.

"A kiss?" he repeated. "What's that?"

Her gaze snapped up. "You don't know what a kiss is?"

He shook his head.

She stammered the response. "It's when you press your mouth to someone's skin, or their lips, to show affection." A hot flush traveled from her cheeks to her toes. "Would you . . . would you like me to show you?" As though she, a girl who had never been kissed, had any business displaying authority on the subject.

"If you must," he said, as though bearing a great burden.

She couldn't fault him for that. She supposed the notion would sound very odd for someone who had never heard of kissing.

Her stomach fluttered, but she rose on her tiptoes, rested her hands on his shoulders, and gently pressed her lips to his. His skin smelled of pine and something a little smoky that might have come from being electrocuted a few too many times.

When she pulled away, his countenance remained unchanged.

"Of course, it can last longer than that," she said apologetically, feeling as though she'd very much failed to introduce him to the thing so many poets spent their lives writing about.

"Can it?" he asked with interest, the color high in his cheekbones.

"Would you like to try?"

In response, he stepped forward, placed his hands on her waist, and dipped his head, kissing her in much the same way she had him. One tentative press, pulling away ever so slightly before initiating a second, longer one. This time, she parted her lips under his to stroke his mouth with hers. She felt the nervous tremor in his hands as they wrapped around her lower back to pull her close. She slid her arms around his neck, sighing as his mouth became pliant against hers, until their lips found a rhythm as natural as breathing that made her toes tingle.

When they pulled apart, breathless and wide-eyed, he said, "We should get married every day. Twice."

She giggled and had to explain that kissing was something people could do anytime they wanted, which seemed to make him regard the entire world with new wonder and appreciation.

Over the next several months, the two of them met every day at the same clearing where they'd had their fake marriage, having picnics, sharing their every thought, idea, and plan. He said he lived with his friend somewhere among the roots and told her she could stay with them if she liked, but she preferred to live in the forest, sleeping under a fig leaf and surviving on the fruits she foraged in the woods.

They spent many hours with their hands linked together, her head resting on his stomach as he reclined against the tree root and listened to her describe her world to him, how the only trees she saw were pressed into pages and scrawled with ink. Occasionally, the young man grew troubled, saying he feared his friend was hatching a scheme that might land him in trouble.

"If he is your friend, he would not risk your future," she said gently.

"He noticed me when no one else did. That has to mean something, doesn't it?"

There were lots of ways to be noticed, she secretly thought. Hawks noticed mice, too, right before they dove in for the kill. "Love doesn't mean you must lend the other person your unquestioning support," was all she said. "Sometimes, the most loving thing you can do is disagree."

And then, abruptly, it all came to an end one morning when she awoke to find herself in her own bed, surrounded by cherry blossom wallpaper, and her heart broke for the boy she'd left behind.

Her mother's face came into view. Behind her stood a semi-

circle of robed figures. Elders, her mother called them, there to draw her out of the book she'd been lost in for months.

Della gasped, and the cosmic dust blinked out. She had no recollection of her own of the dream, or of her mother being there when she woke. She'd always thought—*knew*—she'd been in Poling by then, hadn't she? She had awoken to a disgruntled doctor telling her she'd had a fever and Mrs. Loughty asking when she might be well enough to return to work. *Hadn't she?*

Which was real?

Ansel had told her that her experiences left an imprint on her body. Xaks told her the dust had the power to show her things she'd long forgotten. If the memories the dust showed her were real and not just illusions it created to toy with her, it meant her own memories—the ones existing in her head—weren't accurate. Della didn't think the dust would show her something so shocking just to frighten her. It had proven itself time and time again, in the way it protected her and seemed to care for her. But if the scene it showed her was real, that meant her whole mind was a lie, full of missing pieces and false information.

Until today, she'd thought meeting Riktel had only been a dream. But that dream had always been so vivid in her head. As if it actually had happened. And the dust showing her it was real somehow made more sense than if it wasn't, even if it brought about far more questions than answers.

In the memory the dust showed her, her past self seemed to know her visit to Riktel's world wasn't just a dream. If that were true, how had her memories grown so corrupted? Maybe her journeys through the books muddled her mind. But why did she look so *physically* different in the memory the dust showed her, as though she'd been a completely different person?

And that young man. *Ansel.*

She'd visited Ansel when he was a teenager, so different from how he was now, so eager to trust, desperate to love. They'd been friends, and they'd gotten fake married under an oak tree, and then she'd vanished from his life altogether when she woke, and—

Oh. *Oh no.*

Della shivered, chilled from the inside out. And now she knew with certainty. The memory the dust showed her was real. Because Ansel remembered it too, even if he didn't recognize who she was now.

To her, their wedding had been a game. But to a boy who might latch onto the first promise of love when he previously didn't know such things existed—

It might have been very real to him at the time.

The hairs stood up on the back of her neck. When she'd found Ansel's rucksack of childhood possessions from Lumeria in the cargo hold, there had been a necklace inside, and preserved inside the pendant of amber, a ring of braided grass.

Ansel had said his wife abandoned him when he needed her most. But she hadn't abandoned him. She'd been dragged out of his story at the exact moment he needed her.

Della's fingertips prickled with foreboding, and guilt churned her stomach. Surely this wasn't possible. Surely *she* wasn't the girl who'd betrayed Ansel. He would have recognized her when they met again, wouldn't he? Then again, her appearance was significantly different in the memory the dust showed her. Still, Ansel should have remembered her name, at the very least. That thought gave her a sliver of hope.

Desperate to talk to him, she scrambled to her knees and dug through her pack as the cosmic dust condensed back to the ground and nestled next to her knee. Finding Ansel's book, she hastily flipped through it, her eyes flying over the pages.

Ansel gripped the bridge control panel with white knuckles, watching the blinking dot move across the holomap projected before them. The navy and gold blur of space slowed around them as a large ship came into view in the distance: Balor's vessel, twice the size of the Miss Demeanor.

"Shields up," Ansel announced. His mouth twitched as, for the first time in months, the order was actually able to be carried out.

"We'll be in range any time now," Xaks said tensely. "You sure about this?"

"No, I've been spending the last eight years getting to this moment on a whim," Ansel snarked, his heart pounding hard behind his ribs.

"Yaggrel has readied the SPM-500. We're nearly in range. Permission to proceed?" Eryl asked in his helmet's speaker.

Ansel glanced down at the book lying open on the control panel. Should he say something to Della? Or was saying goodbye a sure way to tempt fate?

He slid the book a little closer to see if she had made it to Lumeria and—

His gaze locked on a name. Riktel.

That wasn't possible.

Della shouldn't know that word.

Ansel read a little further, and something cold tightened around his heart. He sank into his chair, fingers clenching the sides of the book.

No. It wasn't true. He'd never seen Della before she appeared in his prison cell. The girl he met in that clearing on Lumeria had looked completely different—and in more ways than what came from the passing of nearly ten years. She *was* an entirely different person. She'd introduced herself as *Delilah.*

Della having that memory was impossible.

The dust must be manipulating her. Because otherwise it meant Della, *his* Della, had abandoned him. Betrayed him.

Did she? a little voice asked. She didn't choose to leave when she fell into his book all those years ago.

Balor was the one who told Ansel that Delilah accepted his bribe and fled Lumeria. At first, Ansel thought Balor had hurt her, done something to her so that she couldn't come to his aid. But then, a few days later, Ansel received a hologram and a dried ring of braided grass. The hologram showed Delilah in perfect health on a different planet, saying she was sorry, but she saw an opportunity to escape Lumeria and pursue her own life, and she took it. Ansel had taken off his own ring, which he wore encased in an amber necklace, and shoved it in the bottom of his rucksack, where it had stayed ever since.

Ansel had read the conversation Della had with Balor when she accidentally contacted him with the holocomm. "*I'll talk to you soon, Delilah.*" At the time, Ansel thought it was a little joke Balor was making to himself, calling Della by the name of Ansel's old infatuation, but maybe Balor knew something Ansel didn't.

"Captain?" Eryl prompted. "We must act now. When he begins firing on us, we'll have to divert too much power to maintain the shields to be able to use the Megacannon. Shall we advance or retreat?"

"Yes, yes. Advance," Ansel rasped. Closing the book, he bent over and rested his head in his hands, squeezing his eyes shut as though he could block off the panic threatening to overwhelm him. He just needed a second. "I'll be right back."

Jerking away from the control panel, he strode off the bridge into the hall. His knees buckled, and he slid down the wall to the floor. This shouldn't be affecting him like this. Of course he'd known for years his so-called marriage was nothing more than a game. But at the time, he'd been ignorant. His entire understanding of marriage had come from Delilah.

The moment he explored the universe outside of Lumeria, though, he'd seen the concept of marriage practiced on other planets. Though the customs varied from place to place, he'd come to understand love was not something you could just decide to do upon first meeting a person.

But on the night he finally opened up to Xaks about his past after a few too many drinks, he'd told her he'd had a wife, even though he never did, not really. It was simpler. Less embarrassing than admitting he'd been naïve enough to get his heart broken over a childish game. It made his hurt feel less pathetic when he explained how she'd abandoned him. How *Della* abandoned him.

His skin burned, and his insides churned with the sick sort of anger that was more hurt than rage. He knew the feeling well. The feeling of betrayal.

No. He didn't know for certain Della and Delilah were one and the same.

But somewhere in his heart, he did. He didn't know how or why, but he knew it. It made a horrible kind of sense.

He scrubbed his knuckles over his dry, gritty eyes. He couldn't think about this now. He had things to do. And after he hauled Balor's miserable hide back to his ship, he was going to drink himself into oblivion so neither he nor Della could see his thoughts at all. He was not going to let himself feel like this again. Would not let *her* make him feel like this again. Time and time again she'd played with his life as though it were a game, and he was the fool who fell for it. *Her.*

Ansel stood, tucked the book under his arm, and walked back onto the bridge.

"All right, Captain?" Xaks asked, letting more worry than she'd ever displayed before lace her voice.

He hated that. He was starting to despise affection. Its sweetness was only a sign of the bitter aftertaste of betrayal sure to follow.

"I'm great, Xaks." Ansel forced an easy smile to his face.

He slapped the book onto the control panel and found a pen. Even though writing in Della's book when she hadn't asked him to felt wrong, her returning home to deliver the medicine had been part of the plan all along. What did it matter if he sent her there or if she did it? Her lingering on Lumeria was doing no one any good. Once she was home, he didn't have to think about her ever again.

Now that she'd gotten the medicine, he owed her nothing. That had been the deal. She helped him, and he got her to Lumeria. No need to overcomplicate that. Maybe once she was a few universes away, he'd stop feeling so suffocated.

After scrawling a quick line in the book—*Della returned to Poling*—he slammed it shut, tossed it aside, and turned to face Balor's approaching ship.

CHAPTER 31

Della's stomach dropped out from under her, and everything went dark.

Before she even opened her eyes, she smelled the stench of stale mud and knew she was back in Poling.

Groaning, she sat up and took in her surroundings. She was sitting in a muddy alleyway. Snow flurries stuck in her lashes and turned to slush on the ground. Everything she'd been touching had made the journey with her. She still held Ansel's book and the bag containing the medicine, but the cosmic dust had been sitting beside her in Lumeria, and now it was nowhere to be found. It was a silly thing to be upset about in comparison to everything else, but she would miss its company.

Poling looked even more drab compared to the glitter of space, the glamor of Creqreon, the whimsy of Lumeria. The distant sounds of the market met her ears, giving her a vague sense of where in the city she was.

As she thought over Ansel's reaction to her memory, she considered the way he'd said she'd introduced herself to him all those years ago as Delilah. She didn't understand why her past self would give him an alternate name.

There were still too many missing pieces. And without the dust, she had no way to coax more memories to light to explain the past.

Della didn't know why the book had dropped her in this

alley, but as it rarely seemed to have her best interests in mind, she didn't think she ought to stick around and find out.

Slipping Ansel's book into the pack, she stood. Cold air cut through her thin tunic and seemed to pierce her heart, the way it ached.

Ansel had sent her here. He was rightfully confused and hurt. She'd unintentionally contributed to turning him from a boy eager to trust and love into a man whose heart was buried in betrayal. All she wanted to do was explain that it was a misunderstanding, that her feelings for him weren't just a game, and she hadn't left him on purpose. But he'd read her book, so he should already know that.

Della resisted the urge to dig out Ansel's book. He needed, *deserved*, time to consider his feelings without her reading his mind. Going into a battle with Balor in his current distraught state couldn't be good for Ansel's focus, and she couldn't make it worse. She would check in on him soon to make sure he was all right, but until then she'd—

She'd what? Della turned in a circle. Should she mail the medicine to her mother in Reftshire, then return to Mrs. Loughty's and beg for her job back? No. That was a useless waste of time.

Della would deliver the medicine herself, on foot if she had to. It couldn't take longer than a handful of days if she set her mind to it. She needed to speak to her mother face to face. Maybe she could answer the rest of the questions racing around Della's head. Why did her past self look nothing like her current self? Why did she have a memory of being sick when she never was? Who were the elders? Did Della's mother know her daughter had spent her childhood slipping in and out of books?

Della ducked her head and began walking toward the alley entrance. The winter air was honed sharp with cold, lacerating her cheeks as it sliced past. As she walked, she thought of what she wanted Ansel to know, the letter she'd write him, if only he'd read it.

Dear Ansel,

I am so sorry for the inexcusable hurt I caused you. I don't know how this works yet, only that I've traveled into books long before yours. Dozens. Hundreds, maybe. It is possible that my every daydream was real.

Goose bumps prickled along her flesh. How did she even know the world she currently occupied was her true home? Poling might be nothing more than a story too, and Ansel's world a story within a story.

A horrible feeling pooled in the bottom of Della's stomach. Her whole life, she'd felt as though she didn't belong. Maybe it was because she didn't. Maybe it was because she'd hopped from one world to the next so many times, she no longer knew which was hers, which was real.

Ansel, there is so much I don't understand, and I can only hope my mother might be able to provide clarity. Until then, I can only tell you what I know. I don't have memories of my own of that day under the oak tree, yet I'm certain I never thought of you as a joke.

Yet if you were a joke, you'd be the one I keep at the ready at all times—the one that makes me smile every time I think of it, the one I want to tell the entire world, the one that makes people roll their eyes a little when they hear me recounting it yet again, and I notice but don't care because it's too dear for me to ever let go.

Love—

Della drew up short as a shadow peeled away from the alley wall ahead of her. It was a man in a fine suit that likely cost more than a year's worth of her wages. The glow of a pipe pulsed in the darkness, illuminating his face and glinting off a golden watch chain looping from his pocket.

She stifled a gasp. It was Radcliff. The Duke's cruel friend.

He was half turned away from her, so she doubted he even knew she was behind him. She was about to slink away before he saw her, when her gaze again caught on the pocket watch. If she had a bit of money, she could purchase a ride to Reftshire, perhaps on a mail coach. That would shorten her trip to a few days at most.

Ansel's words from one of their first conversations resurfaced in her mind. *Steal what they owe you.*

Didn't Radcliff owe her for what he'd put her through? This at least was a small sliver of her life she could control. And she was so profoundly unnoticeable, she was confident she could slip the watch free without him even feeling it.

Reckless and a little desperate, she tiptoed closer, careful that her shoes would not slap the wet stones underfoot. When she was near enough that her throat began to tighten from his overpowering cologne, she delicately plucked the watch from his pocket.

Slowly, she backed away. She was nearly out of reach, almost far enough away that she could sprint out of the alley to disappear into the crowded streets—when Radcliff's hand shot behind him and clamped viciously around her wrist.

As he turned, his long fingers gave her arm a sharp twist. The pocket watch slipped from her grip, and Radcliff caught it neatly with his other hand.

"Hello, pet." Della's stomach plummeted as Radcliff stepped into the light, his horrid smile glinting like the sharp curve of a scythe. She tried to run, but he wrenched her hands behind her back. Sharp pain shot through her shoulders, and she cried out, fighting fruitlessly against his hold.

Radcliff chuckled as though this were all an amusing game. “Don't run. The city constables are in no shape for a foot race.”

Della's blood curdled in her veins. She'd seen what the constables did to thieves. Or, more accurately, she'd seen the aftermath. The gray hands forgotten in muddy ditches, discarded like rotten produce along with all the other waste.

She thrashed, kicking wildly behind her. Radcliff slammed her roughly against the wall, her chin scraping the freezing stone. She tried to twist away, but he pinned her with his weight.

“Shh, none of that,” he snarled in her ear. “The audacity, seating yourself at our table. Look at you. A thief *and* a whore? Such indecency should not be permitted to roam the streets.”

For the first time, Della realized how her current attire of leggings and a tunic might look to the people of Poling. She strained against him, her muscles feeling as though they were ripping in her efforts to get free.

“Stop that.” Radcliff's breath was rancid against her neck. He drew a blade from his jacket. “Unless you'd rather I take justice into my own hands and get it over with?”

Della squirmed. She had no way to defend herself. Even the cosmic dust was gone, and Ansel—Ansel was an infinity away. He wouldn't know what was happening to her unless he read about it later.

Radcliff pinned her kicking leg to the wall with his knee, and pain lanced up her thigh. “Have it your way.” He tutted, wrenching her arm above her head and crunching her fingers against the stone with the heel of his hand, forcing her to bare her wrist for his knife.

Unintelligible words spilled from Della's lips—curses, pleas, apologies, she wasn't certain. Her wrist went cold, as if it could already feel the kiss of his blade, and frantic tears burned at her eyes.

A high-pitched whine filled Della's ears. At first, she thought it was her own fear, but then her brain identified the now-familiar pitch of a blaster charging up, so out of place in Poling, and her breath caught.

"I'd suggest getting your fucking hands off her, right now," Ansel said behind them, his tone chilling in the way it delivered the threat as though it were a cool pleasantry.

Ansel. Della's chest unwound, and she nearly released a sob of relief.

The pressure of Radcliff's body eased slightly as he looked over his shoulder. "Ah, good man, I appreciate your concern, given the position you've found us in, but you've misinterpreted the situation entirely. This little rat was attempting to pickpocket me." The edge of his knife grazed the skin of Della's wrist, drawing a bead of blood.

Ansel thumbed the blaster's safety, reflected green light blinking along the damp stone walls. "It would be a shame to lose one of the two kindest hands this side of the galaxy over a trinket, don't you think?" Ansel's tone dripped with apparent indifference, but Della knew better. He was the most dangerous when he feigned nonchalance.

Radcliff snorted, though he eyed the blaster's glow with wariness. Even he could likely recognize the weapon as some sort of pistol. "Step aside. This doesn't concern you."

"I'm afraid it does." Ansel's voice went cold. "Move. I'd rather not get your blood on my—" Words seemed to fail Ansel for a moment before he figured out how to finish the sentence. "Wife," he said wryly, and the fact that he'd attempt an inside joke *now*, after everything, was so inexplicable, Della almost laughed.

"Your *wife*?" Radcliff asked incredulously.

Della used the distraction to wrench free of his grip. She scrambled out of reach, swiping at the blood from the scrape on her chin.

"Are you all right?" Ansel lodged his blaster against the back of Radcliff's skull. The green glow of the weapon lit Ansel's face in a ghoulish light, revealing the casual smile he employed when his inner being was falling apart. With his eyes rimmed in red and glassy with hurt and fury, he looked downright demonic.

"I'm fine. Don't kill him." Della was unable to bear the thought of Ansel killing on her behalf when he was so against it, when he tried so hard to be good even though the whole universe called him evil. She'd already destroyed him enough.

After a moment in which he seemed to undergo great inner turmoil as he contemplated whether or not to ignore her request, Ansel eased away from Radcliff, though he kept the blaster pointed in his general direction. "Empty your pockets."

Radcliff did as he was asked, glaring with righteous anger the entire time. The watch and a handful of coins clattered to the pavement at his feet. "You will hang for this. Do you know who I am? How dare you assault me in this manner! You really want to die for this miserable bitch?"

Ansel shot Della a pleading look. "Can I kill him, just a little bit?"

"Afraid not."

"Fine," Ansel said with bitter disappointment before addressing Radcliff once more. "Do you have a hovercraft or some other type of transportation we can borrow? I need to pay a visit to my mother-in-law."

CHAPTER 32

They left Radcliff tied up in an icy puddle before searching for his carriage. There was a determined set to Ansel's jaw as he moved from task to task, and Della dared not interrupt, even though countless questions bombarded her thoughts. What happened with Balor? Were the crew all right? Would he ever forgive her?

As they walked, Ansel turned in a circle, taking in the dingy town center. Through his eyes, Poling had to appear even more drab. Irrational embarrassment swept over Della, as though she were somehow responsible for the stench and grime. Would he think less of her, seeing where she came from?

"That's a carriage?" Ansel gazed doubtfully across the road where Radcliff's coach sat parked. "And . . . horses?" he made a face at the beasts.

"Indeed."

Ansel strode across the street and Della trailed after him, receiving a fair number of scornful looks from passersby thanks to her form-fitting leggings and tunic. When they reached the carriage, Ansel flipped one of Radcliff's coins up to the coachman. "Have a drink on me, friend. Your employer is a little tied up currently."

The coachman's eyes darted as he tried to decide if Ansel's words contained a thinly veiled threat. Seeming to decide that they did, he scrambled off the carriage, gave each of them a nod, and scurried toward the pub.

"Can you drive a carriage?" Ansel asked Della. His tone was detached and all business, and it stabbed her straight through the heart.

Della shrugged. "It seems straightforward enough."

With a sharp nod, he held out his hand to help her onto the box seat. "You'll pilot for us, then."

"Us?" she repeated, hesitating. "You can't come with me. Shouldn't you write yourself back to your crew? Balor—"

Ansel's shoulders stiffened at the name. "He got away," was his curt reply.

"Got away? How is that possible?"

Ansel ran a hand down his face. "We caught him by surprise with the new cannon. It worked perfectly, tearing a hole in his shield, but I regretted setting your book aside as soon as I did. All I could think about was how everything goes wrong every time we write in our stories. I needed to make sure you made it back okay, and then I saw— Well. I called off the attack. Maybe the crew could have boarded his ship without me, but I couldn't risk their lives like that, so I told them to retreat."

"How could you?" Della breathed, thinking of all he'd given up.

"Stars, Della, you can't think I'd abandon you in favor of some stupid revenge plan."

"It's not a stupid revenge plan," she whispered. "It's justice. It's your life, your freedom. You need to go back, before it's too late."

"Not until we find your mother and find out where those books came from and why you have no memory of your past and why you used to look like a completely different person"—Ansel's voice built in volume—"and why you *came into my life only to leave it.*" His jaw flexed as though he was physically forcing himself to swallow back words.

Della winced. “I wish I could explain.”

“Well, you can't.” His voice held an edge that made her realize how soft it had been every other time he spoke to her, and she flinched. “It broke me at the time, and you don't even remember.”

“You're not being fair.” Anger prickled behind the ache of guilt in Della's throat. “My memories are not my own. My mother may have lied to me my entire life, and *you*—after everything, you think I would ever purposely hurt you?”

Ansel closed his eyes and let out a long breath. “No. I know you don't understand what happened any more than I do. If you are Delilah, I have hated you for much longer than I have loved you, and I don't know what to do with that or how I'm supposed to feel.” His voice broke. “Tell me how I'm supposed to feel.”

“I don't know,” she said miserably. “Let's just go. There is no use discussing matters we don't understand. With the carriage, we can probably reach Reftshire in a few days if we push it.”

“Then let's push it.” Ansel's tone was kinder, but the shortness of his words made Della's eyes sting.

He gave her a boost onto the carriage without his touch lingering a second longer than strictly necessary before hoisting himself up beside her. The horses pranced a bit at the jostling behind them, causing the carriage to rock. Ansel swore under his breath, gripping the edge of the seat, and despite everything, a small part of Della liked that she got to be the fearless navigator this time.

With an experimental flick of the reins, the carriage began to move forward. As they clomped down the street in silence, Della bit her tongue before she could ask Ansel about “after.” After they found her mother. After they found answers. She couldn't bear it if his response was different now than it was in his letters, but how could it not be? How could he trust someone who couldn't trust her own memories?

By nightfall, Della's whole body ached from bouncing around on top of the carriage all day, and her heart ached from having to endure hours upon hours of Ansel's hip pressing against hers with every roll of the horse's gait. Ansel felt impossibly far away, even though he was right there with her. She missed him terribly. She swallowed a broken hiccup, turned her face away, and pressed her lips firmly together to keep from making a sound.

It snowed as they rode, covering the dreary landscape in a blanket of sparkling white. The world had an odd hush to it, the only sound the crunch of their horses' hooves and the creak of the carriage wheels through snow. The guilt in her belly soured further. The silence reminded her of all the times she'd displeased Ms. Loughty, when she'd spent hours or days bracing herself for whatever punishment was yet to come.

After a while, Ansel wordlessly handed her his gloves, seeming to notice her fingers growing blue around the reins. She fumbled with them, her fingers stiff. He shifted to face her, helping her tug one on, then the next. The way he treated her with tenderness made her more confused than ever.

She smelled his musky lilac soap and the familiar scent of the particular laundry detergent used on the Miss Demeanor that was beginning to smell like home. Heart-wrenching loneliness hit Della at once. Her thick throat stifled her every breath, and her eyes smarted fiercely. She'd hurt him too much to feel bad for herself, even if it was done inadvertently. And all because she couldn't simply grin and bear it, couldn't find contentment in her own story, couldn't just keep her chin down and her wits about her and stop dreaming of *more.*

Eventually, they stopped at a town and used Radcliff's money to purchase food for the horses, a couple of rooms for the night, and a change of clothes from the innkeeper to help them blend in. It was frankly unfair, the way Ansel looked in a waistcoat and cravat. While Della's dress was ill-fitting—too short and tight in the sleeves—Ansel's clothing fit like it was tailored to his body. It made the distance between them even more painful, made her fingers twitch to touch him all the more as they parted to their separate rooms.

Around noon the following day, as their horses plodded along a seemingly endless road splitting an empty snow-blanketed field in two, Ansel surprised her by remarking gruffly, "I once met a blob-like creature with pliable skin he had so much muscle control over, he could mold his face into any shape he desired."

"How extraordinary," said Della, bewildered.

"Maybe that's how you used to look different."

"You think I'm a blob creature?" She didn't know if she ought to laugh or be offended.

"The most adorable blob, darling," he said easily. His words were softer now than they had been before.

How dare the infernal man try to make her laugh, try to start a *conversation*? It was somehow cruel, the way he took care of her when he surely was still angry. It made Della nervous. Like her defenses were being softened so that when an attack came, it would hurt deeper. It brought to mind the occasions when Mrs. Loughty acted as though she viewed Della as part of the family—doting on her and giving her hand-me-downs from her daughters—right before she belittled her in front of guests to remind her of her place. *See how nicely I treat you when I have no reason to?* those instances seemed to say.

At last, the carriage rolled into the town where they would spend another night.

As they walked across the courtyard from the stable to the inn, Ansel took Della by the arm and turned her to face him.

Ice clung to his lashes, and the effect made his dark eyes even more startlingly stunning. "Talk to me."

"Are we to quarrel, then?" Della asked, bracing herself, knowing she couldn't avoid his anger forever.

"If . . . you want to?" he said, like it was a question.

"What do you mean, 'if I want to'?" Della blinked rapidly because of the frigid air biting at her eyes, the tears threatening to spill, and her utter and complete *bafflement*. "You're the one who's angry."

Ansel stuck his hands in his pockets and cocked his head. "You're the one who *deserves* to be angry."

"Whatever for?" she said, voice rising as though they really were arguing, which was ludicrous when they were only arguing about arguing.

"Della, I sent you away." Fog coiled from his lips, white against the dimming backdrop of cobblestone and flurrying snow. "And then the next time I saw you, I acted like what happened in the past was all your fault when you're as confused as I am. I'm not angry at anyone but myself at this point. I'm *mortified* about how I treated you, and I'm sorry."

Something thawed between them even while the world froze around them. This mess *was* her fault, even if she didn't remember what happened years ago, and he blamed himself for the rift between them.

"I deserved all of that," she protested.

He recoiled. "You did *not* deserve it. I was surprised and hurt, but so are you. We're in this together. I should be helping you through it, not blaming you. You fought for me, and now it's my turn."

"You have no reason to treat me so kindly, you great lump," she exclaimed, her raised voice strangely flat and muffled by the snow coating the abandoned courtyard.

"No reason?" he repeated, almost angrily. "I'll be damned if

I let the woman I vowed to love forever think that I don't care about her anymore."

"Oh, stop it. You know our promises weren't real." Della was chilled to the bone, emotionally exhausted, and irrationally annoyed by the relentless grace he'd shown her.

"They were real to me, once, and maybe I've decided they're real to me again." His jaw set at that stubborn angle she'd come to know so well.

Della's heart broke all over again. Here he was, even though he should have washed his hands of her. Here he was, even when all she'd brought into his life was difficulties and sorrow. Here he was, thanks to his sense of duty, even though—

"You should hate me," Della whispered into the darkness.

"Please, do continue telling me what I should and should not feel," Ansel said, echoing words she had said to him once.

With the addition of her past, she was no longer the person he thought. He would soon realize fighting for her was as futile as trying to bring back the dead.

"I don't want you to love me out of some kind of obligation. I want you to love me because you do."

Ansel shook his head. "Of course I do. Nothing that happened is your fault, Della. You are not irredeemable. Stars know I've done worse. I never should have sent you away. I was harsh and impulsive, and I needed a second to breathe, but I don't hate you, nor do I have plans to hate you in the future. Well, actually I did pencil it in for next Friday, but Xaks wants to go out for drinks, which frankly sounds more fun than hating you, so I'll have to cancel this time. I'll let you know if I decide to reschedule."

How could he be making *jokes* at a time like this? "You don't know who I am. *I* don't even know who I am."

"I don't need to know your past to know who you are now." He stepped forward, curved a hand around her hip, and tugged her against him. "You are the woman who dares to keep dreaming while everyone else begs to wake up. You're the woman who tamed the monster outside her bedroom window. You're the woman who ruthlessly teases me when most people fear me. You are funny and kind, and you are brave, Della. Incredibly, beautifully, *stunningly* brave. I can't stop loving you, so don't bother trying to make me."

A rush of warmth flowed through Della's ribs. She'd misjudged him. This thing between them was not fragile, though it was new. She knew him, too—knew all his focused intensity and single-minded determination. She should have known that as soon as he decided he was hers, his devotion would not be so fickle. Despite the mystery of their past and the uncertainty of their future, he was hers. She was foolish to think his kindness was a trap.

For so long, she'd had to protect herself from the cruelty of others, but he was comfort, love, and understanding. Peace. They would face their troubles as something to overcome together, rather than something to tear them apart.

Ansel's mouth curved. "Although, if you're determined you deserve some sort of punishment, I can certainly oblige." His frigid fingers found her neck, dropping a chunk of ice down the back of her dress.

"You awful man!" Della squirmed as the snow slid a wet, frigid path down her back.

She packed a snowball and flung it at him. He caught it easily, tossing it loosely back her way. It crumpled apart against her skirts. She scooped up another fistful of snow, but Ansel stepped forward and caught her arm. He slipped another clump of snow down her bodice, and she felt the wet coldness slide between her breasts.

She kicked up a flurry of snow in her attempt to escape, spraying slush up her legs, and Ansel laughed, a low, heart-stopping sound. She couldn't escape his hold. Not that she wanted to, for her pulse pounded, and a wild thrill of happiness soared through her.

Della reversed tactics, hurling herself against him instead of away, catching him off balance. The two of them tumbled into the snow. She straddled him, digging up handfuls of snow and piling them on top of him.

"Beg for mercy," she demanded, which only made him laugh harder. She supposed snow was an amusing torture technique for a man who'd endured far worse.

Della had once wondered what it would take to snap Ansel's smooth, arrogant control. She'd supposed it would happen in a flash of anger. She never thought it would happen like this, with joy and snowflakes sparkling under streetlamps. But it had. His laugh was free of irony, his eyes clear and bright with mirth. His mouth was far better suited for smiling than it was for frowning, even though it practiced the latter far more often.

Like this, he very much resembled the boy in the memory the dust had shown her. His hair was growing out, blond roots glinting against the rest of his darkly dyed locks. She'd quite literally wrestled a piece of the boy he used to be out of him, the boy who loved to love. An overwhelming sensation of affection swelled in her heart for this man, this secretly sweet man who always tried his best when the world had tried its best to make him his worst. The boy who'd always loved her. Who'd *only* loved her.

At last, the misery of the past few days melted away. "I love you, you despicable knave," Della said, pelting him with more snow.

Ignoring the projectiles, Ansel sat up. He gripped the back of her neck with icy fingers and pulled her down, capturing her mouth in a cool, invigorating kiss. Handfuls of snow turned to water and dripped through her fingers, forgotten. She parted her lips for him, letting him explore her with gentle, roving strokes of his tongue that left her trembling, each caress hot and slick.

Her chest expanded as though he was helping her breathe all over again when she hadn't in so long. *At last, at last, at last,* her body sang. The universe felt right once more.

Pulling away slightly, he kissed her nose and said, "You're murder on my jacket collection," before shrugging off his coat and draping it over her shoulders.

The playfulness ebbed as he tucked the jacket around her and nuzzled her temple, brushing his lips across her skin. When he pulled back, the intensity in his gaze made her breath catch.

Ansel took her face firmly in his hands. "My wife," he said, somewhere between a gentle reminder, a stern order, a pleading request, and a confession of love.

"If you insist." Della smiled before lunging forward and tackling him back into the snow.

He laughed and began poking her in the sides to get her to release him. She attempted to pin his biceps to the ground, but her fingers caught in his shirt, pulling the collar down over his shoulder. The fabric snagged on the bandage around his left arm. Ansel flinched at the contact, and she jolted her hand back, afraid she'd hurt the still-healing wound.

He tried to slide the bandage back up his arm through his shirt, but the effort was clumsy and clearly uncomfortable.

"Stop, I can fix it for you," she insisted, leaning in to unbutton a few of his shirt's top buttons so she could access the bandage more easily and rewind it.

"It's fine," Ansel said quickly, but she'd already pushed his shirt aside and loosened the first loop of linen.

Her eyes caught on the letters carved into his skin, the scars still a tender pink. She'd known Balor had carved something into his bicep but hadn't felt right about asking about it. But now, now . . . Her breaths slowed as she read the first three letters.

R-I-K

Ansel caught her fingers and tried to shrug his shirt back

over his shoulder, but she fought back, holding fast to the end of the bandage. "Let me see."

After a moment, he sighed and released her fingers. With shaking hands, she peeled the binding the rest of the way off. The fabric fell away, revealing a name.

R-I-K-T-E-L

CHAPTER 33

"I didn't tell you because I don't see why it matters," Ansel said the next morning. They walked side-by-side, leading the horses after them as they picked their way through a section of path too overgrown to navigate on top of the carriage. "So you met Balor when he was a child? It doesn't mean anything."

"Of course it does!" Della exclaimed. "It changes everything. I taught Balor what friendship was. If I hadn't done that, he never would have befriended you, which means he never would have betrayed you, which means—" All of the pain in Ansel's life circled back to her. "How long have you known?"

He shrugged, shifting the reins to his other hand. "Since a few days ago, when we found out you met me before."

"But I thought of Riktel before then. I remembered the dream I thought I'd had of him the night I went to you in prison. Did my book not record that?"

"I never went back to read that part of your book. That was the same night as your dinner with the Duke, which you begged me not to read about, so I didn't ever flip back to that chapter. That must be why I never read about you remembering Riktel before a few days ago." Ansel sighed deeply. "And I didn't tell you about Riktel being Balor because I knew you'd blame yourself for the choices he made. We can't change the past. There's no point in regretting what happened."

Della shook her head. "We were so young. He was lonely,

and I only wanted to fix it. No one had taught him what friendship was."

Ansel held a limb out of her way, letting her pass under his arm. He let his fingertips trail across her lower back as she passed, and she flushed, thinking of the night before. How he'd gotten her into the inn and tossed her onto the bed before either of them even bothered to undress. How the cool hardware of his dangling suspenders had pressed against her thighs as he buried his face against her neck and whispered obscene praise into her ear in a nearly unintelligible murmur. She never thought she would enjoy such vulgar words directed her way, but she did. Oh, she did.

"No one on Lumeria comprehends the concept of emotional connection," Ansel was saying, and she forced herself back to the present. "Aside from Balor, of course. I always wondered how he came up with an idea like that. Now I guess I know."

Della shivered, her shoes soaked through from the snow. The forest darkened with every step. "If it weren't for me, you wouldn't have been there to take the fall for his crime. You'd be home right now, and you never would have—" Della drew up short, something ahead catching her attention.

"If it weren't for you," Ansel said, catching up behind her, still unaware of what lay before them, "I wouldn't have the Miss Demeanor or the crew, and most of all, I wouldn't have you."

"Ansel," Della whispered, unable to make sense of what her eyes showed her. "What's that?"

She pointed to an eerie blackness oozing around the trees ahead of them. At first, she'd thought she was seeing shadows, but the blackness was complete and consuming, forming a gelatinous wall. Della hurried forward to get a better view. The trees thinned, and she looked up. Bubbling darkness stretched all the way to the heavens, blotting out the sky ahead as though the earth had simply come to an end.

"What the fuck?" Ansel breathed, which was a less eloquent

way to phrase the very questions running through Della's mind. "Be careful," he warned as Della inched closer, weaving around a few more trees until she stood several yards away from the chilling void.

It was a churning liquid thing. Some of it dribbled out into the snow, staining it black. It dripped off the branches overhead and trickled around tree trunks as though trying to swallow them whole. Where the ground met the darkness, it was jagged like the edge of a cliff. A glance both ways told Della the void stretched left and right as far as she could see.

A slick drop splattered onto her wrist. Ansel let out a yell of warning and yanked her back. With trembling fingers, she touched the spot on her skin, her fingertips coming away coated in the substance.

"It's all right," she told Ansel even though the unnatural sight felt anything but all right. "It hasn't harmed me."

"What the blazes *is* it?" he asked.

Della rubbed the black liquid between her fingers, the answer just beyond reach. She gave it a hesitant sniff, and, with a jolt, realized what it was. "Ink." Chills prickled along her skin. "It's a wall of ink."

She barely heard Ansel's increasingly agitated questions trailing behind her as she began looking for a way around the liquid barrier. Yet no matter how far she walked, expecting to see a glimpse of sky ahead that told her the end was near, it never came, as though the wall stretched to infinity.

Della lifted her skirts, her walk turning into a haphazard sprint. Her heart pounded along with her feet, filling her ears with blood. This wasn't possible. She must be dreaming, for worlds did not simply end a two-day journey from the town where one had spent the majority of one's life—even if she *had* spent a fair amount of time wondering if anything existed past the walls of Poling. Yet here it was, this jagged void, as though someone hadn't bothered to finish creating the rest of her planet.

Snow slipped under Della's heel, and her feet flew out from under her. She landed hard, catching herself on her wrist, which gave a painful twinge of protest. Racing footsteps crunched up behind her, and seconds later, Ansel skidded to a stop beside her, dropping to his knees.

"This isn't possible," she babbled. "I grew up in Reftshire, which everyone knows is three days west of Poling. It must be behind the wall somewhere." Her mother. Oh god, her mother. She was on the other side. If there *was* another side. She rocked onto her knees, clutching her stomach.

"Do you remember the journey from Reftshire to Poling?" Ansel asked her, somehow managing to remain calm even though tiny specks of ink flecked over his cheeks from the gurgling wall beside them. "Maybe we took a wrong turn."

"I was sixteen. Of course I remember . . ." But Della trailed off, because she realized she didn't remember. Not at all. She had never specifically thought about how she got to Poling; she'd only assumed somewhat subconsciously that she'd made the journey, perhaps in the back of a mail coach. Only now, when she actually searched her memories, she came up blank.

It was as though she had just woken up in Poling one day, and there her life had begun.

Uncontrollable tremors shuddered through her limbs. She couldn't breathe. God, she couldn't breathe. A hysterical laugh bubbled from her lips. "I don't know why I think I grew up in Reftshire. What is Reftshire? Does it exist, or is it some backstory my mind made up to make my life feel true? Am I even real, or nothing more than a character in a book?"

Ansel took her hands in his and positioned himself between her and the wall, forcing her to stop looking at it. "Della, sweetheart, listen to me. We're going to find out what's going on."

She touched his cheek, expecting him to dissolve into ink. "Are you real? Perhaps I'm daydreaming again, and you're another figment of my imagination I made up to make my existence bearable."

"I'm real, Della. You're real. This is real."

Della blinked hard, opening her eyes as wide as she could, the way she did when she forced herself awake from a nightmare. Perhaps she would snap upright and find herself in Mrs. Loughty's kitchen, or maybe she'd be seven years old again, in her mother's apartment, and that was why she had no recollection of large chunks of her past. Everyone always said she dreamed too much. Perhaps she was layers deep in a reality of her own making, forever lost to whichever plane of existence was the real world.

She needed out.

Della staggered to her feet and stepped up to the boiling wall of ink. Gritting her teeth, she plunged her hand inside, searching for anything past the ebony veil that might indicate something lurked beyond. Ink lapped at her elbow.

"Della!" Ansel's strong arm wrapped around her waist, yanking her away from the wall even as she flailed against him.

"It's fine!" she shouted. "It's not real. I just need to wake up. I need to wake up. I need to—" She was crying, she realized, as Ansel wrestled her to the ground, snow melting through her clothing and dusting her cheeks with cold, biting kisses.

"Fucking listen to me." The hard edge of fear in Ansel's voice sliced through her panic, and she stopped struggling. He had her wrists pinned to the frozen ground as he straddled her hips. "You know what's real and what isn't. Don't lose yourself."

Della took a few steadying breaths, realizing he was right. She knew she was real, even if parts of her life eluded her.

She'd always assumed her blurry past was thanks to her fever. But with this new development and with the lost memories the cosmic dust showed her, a horrifying suspicion struck her that perhaps something more sinister had happened to her.

She'd traveled into books before, but it was as if someone had surgically removed all the magical bits of her life, her *story*, leaving her with only the unfortunate half of a fairy tale.

"Do you think someone knew I could slip into books and wanted to put a stop to it?" she asked quietly.

Ansel's eyes widened. "Shit." He released her wrists, touching her chin with slick, ink-coated fingers. "You know what your world is, don't you?"

"A figment of my imagination?" she asked, for what else could it be? It was barely even a real place at all, more like a daydream—a fragment of a place detached from reality.

"No," Ansel said grimly. "Someone doesn't like that you were playing with magic." He looked up at the infinite wall of blackness. "I know a prison when I see one."

"If you're right, do you think my mother knows what happened to me?" Della knelt by the stream they'd found to wash the ink from their hands as best they could. She broke through the layer of ice covering the surface and plunged her hands into the achingly cold depths below.

"I don't know." Ansel knelt beside her, rinsing his hands in a similar manner, though it did little good. Their skin would be stained for days.

At first, Della hadn't wanted to consider Ansel's theory. It didn't make sense. This was the world where she'd grown up. But the more she considered it, the more she realized she couldn't remember anything of her childhood outside the walls of her mother's apartment or her classroom. Those places could have existed in any city on any world.

She'd only glimpsed the courtyard outside her childhood bedroom in one of the memories the cosmic dust had shown her—a glittering fountain and building spires in the distance.

Indeed, now that she thought about it, the architecture in her memories was nothing like the buildings found in Poling—as though the place where she grew up didn't belong in the same world as Poling at all.

"There is nothing left for us to do here," she said, standing and walking over to the horses. "We could follow the wall for as far as it takes us, but I think we both suspect it would only lead us in a circle back to where we are now, eventually. My mother is not here."

"What do you think we should do, then?" Ansel asked, walking up behind her.

Della flipped open the saddlebag and withdrew their books. "We must return to the Miss Demeanor and find the cosmic dust. If we cannot find *my* dust, we will find new dust, and I will feed it until it unravels my memories, until I discover the truth about my mother, and about myself."

CHAPTER 34

Della held onto Ansel's hand as she finished writing the sentence that would send them back to his ship. Her stomach dropped out from under her, and as she opened her eyes a smile split her face, for there she was, back on the bridge of the Miss Demeanor.

She'd barely had time to be relieved that the book didn't decide to spit them out into space before she realized that something wasn't right. Strange lights pulsed outside. Something impacted the ship, making the floor shudder beneath her.

"Nice of you to join us," Xaks called from the bridge.

Ansel rushed to look out the window, Della on his heels. She drew up short and gasped. In the distance loomed a much larger vessel than the Miss Demeanor, its violet lights flickering ominously. Its cannons were all swiveled to point directly at them. Every few seconds, they flashed, sending an eerily silent streak of energy across space that struck the Miss Demeanor's shields with a sudden tooth-rattling throb of energy and a low rumble so deep it made Della's stomach tremble. The blue dome surrounding the Miss Demeanor seemed to be holding for now, but here and there, Della could see fissures of darkness where it weakened.

Ansel swore beside her. "That's Balor's ship."

Dread struck Della like a viper. Ansel was already off, sprinting up to his place on the bridge beside Xaks. Della hiked up her skirts and climbed after him.

Ansel flipped a few dials and reached up to pull a headset down from a compartment over his head. "What happened?"

"He apparently made a rapid recovery and decided revenge was in order." Xaks's hands were a blur over the control panel as she brought the Miss Demeanor broadside to Balor's ship with a sickening lurch.

"How bad is it?" Ansel asked, and Della winced. She knew how much he was berating himself for not being here when he should have been. Instead, he'd been with her. She felt useless, standing behind him wringing her hands.

"We're holding him off for now," Xaks said. "He took us by surprise. We didn't even have a chance to use the SPM-500 again, and now running the shields at full power has us spread too thin to try."

Della shook her head. "Without the Megacannon, we don't stand a chance, do we?"

"We'll be okay," Ansel said. There was something behind his eyes she didn't like. A fracture. A sad sort of certainty. The look of a man who'd been disappointed enough times that he'd come to expect it. She had a matching scar on her own heart, but it was more painful to think of his wounds than hers.

To come all this way, only for it to end like this, was a tragedy. "We have the books," she murmured. "Perhaps it would be best if we gather the crew and use them to flee." They could even escape back into her world, as small and isolated as it might be. The thought of showing up at the Duke's next dinner party with Yaggrel at her side did have an amusing sort of appeal. And they could at least be together, safe. Her family, the only people in a million universes aside from her mother she could call *hers.*

Even as she thought it, though, she knew none of them would be happy. They all wanted more than the cowardly half-life she'd once lived. They'd been working for years for this moment, to face Balor. And daring to subject them to magic's whims might land them in an equally precarious situation anyway. The last time she went to Poling, she wound up pinned to an alleyway with a knife to her wrist.

Another flare of light in the corner of her eye caught her attention. She braced herself for the worst, only to realize the light wasn't laser fire. A familiar swirl of purple and gold had slipped through the cracks in the shields as easily as a hot knife through butter. Della descended the steps of the control platform and walked to the floor-to-ceiling glass, pressing her hands to the pane.

The cosmic dust outside reared up excitedly, tendrils of energy reaching out to tickle the other side of the glass under her palm. "Is it really you?" Della asked softly, hardly able to believe the dust, *her* dust, had traveled all this way and found her.

As if in response, the dust warmed the glass under her hand. She didn't know how it did so, considering it wasn't a living thing. It should be cold and dead, but it was pure power.

Della didn't know much about Ansel's *electricity*, but he'd said it was like lightning. Her dust was similar, an elemental force thrumming with energy.

An idea took hold of her. She crooked a finger, beckoning the dust to follow as she slipped off the bridge. Ansel was too busy to notice her disappearance.

The dust swirled alongside her outside the hall's windows as she walked. As she detoured to leave her and Ansel's books safely in her chambers, she lost sight of it for a time in the windowless sections of the ship. But when she climbed up the ladder to the tiny circular turret that housed the SPM-500, there the dust was. It churned overhead like her very own galaxy, as if it already knew what she wanted.

Della wrestled her skirts out of the way as she perched behind the gun. She wrapped her hands experimentally around the handles on each side of it. The turret followed her movements, swiveling this way and that. A cross in a circle provided an X-marks-the-spot over whatever she aimed at. Between the handles was a screen that flickered feebly. Two words flashed over and over: *low power.*

"Shall we remedy that?" Della asked, glancing up.

In response the dust whooshed down, encircling the barrel of the gun that protruded into space. A whine filled the air. The screen flared bright, and the handles warmed in Della's hand.

"What was that?" Della heard a distant voice, and she looked over to find another headset in a compartment beside her. She looped it over her ear the way she'd seen Ansel do many times.

"Some kind of power surge," Eryl was saying. "I don't know where it came from."

"Ansel, darling," Della said, forcing the tremble from her voice. "If you don't mind pointing the southernmost turret toward Balor's ship, I think you'll find the SPM-500 is quite operational."

"Della, no!" Ansel's voice came through the device on her ear in a panic. "Don't tell me you're in the turret. The moment the shields collapse, the cannons are the first things Balor will target."

"Then you'd best turn the ship posthaste so that I may fire upon him before he saps our power again, Captain."

If there was one thing Ansel couldn't argue with, though he often tried, bless him, it was logic. And very soon Della felt another dizzying force as the ship swiveled so that the towering hull of Balor's vessel loomed before her. It was closer now, its mass as all-consuming as that inky wall in her world.

Sweat coated her palms, making the turret handles hard to grip. She wiped them on her skirts and took hold once more. Unlike the inky nothingness in her world, in her *head*, she could do something about this.

She pointed the barrel in the direction of Balor's ship—really, it was hard to miss—and squeezed both triggers.

CHAPTER 35

It was bizarre, seeing such a large thing brought low by just a few shots, like seeing a bear downed by a handful of bee stingers. But the SPM-500 did its job, puncturing through Balor's shields like arrows through paper. A few shots to the thrusters had the ship incapacitated. A few more had Balor's cannons bursting apart, debris flying into space. Della stopped before the ship was too destroyed to allow them to board, lest Balor and the precious Stone be lost forever.

Yaggrel fired a grappling hook through one of the gaps in the shield and began reeling the ships together until their sides scraped with a horrible screech that left Della's teeth on edge.

As they came to a stop, the cosmic dust lifted off the ship. It glowed duller now, moved slower, as though it had completely exhausted itself. Della pressed her fingers to her lips, then to the glass, mouthing a silent *thank you.* The dust blinked a few times, as if it understood.

Della left her perch in the turret and made her way back to the bridge, where she discovered the rest of the crew had gathered, armed to the teeth in preparation to board.

Before she could say anything, someone helped her into a space suit while someone else shoved a blaster into her hand. There was something gratifying about the fact that no one suggested she stay behind.

"How'd you boost the power?" Xaks asked, eyeing Della

suspiciously as Ansel aligned the ships' airlocks to allow them passage.

"I had a little help." Della nodded to where the dust wearily flickered outside the window.

Ansel hopped from the control panel and caught Della's chin in his hand before she could slide her helmet on. "The books?"

"Safe in my room."

Nodding, he gave her a quick, firm kiss. He didn't say anything more, but she saw at least a half dozen fumbling confessions of love, worry, and gratitude behind his eyes. She knew he wished she'd stay behind but was grateful he didn't try to change her mind.

"Shall we?" he asked the crew.

Everyone agreed that yes, they should.

The next several moments passed in a haze.

The doors separating the ships slid open.

Yaggrel threw a grenade into the smoke on the other side of the door. Yells of alarm issued from beyond. A tremendous *boom* rattled down the hallway, followed by guttural screams that had Della's stomach churning.

Yaggrel's wicked teeth flashed, then he lowered his visor and leaped into the chaos.

Ansel gave her hand a quick squeeze. "Just stay behind me."

She nodded, her helmet feeling heavy and ridiculous. As they stumbled through the pandemonium of Balor's ship, her vision swam from one place to the next. Xaks was locked in combat with two of Balor's men. Over by the wall, a few more struggled to carry an injured comrade away from the fighting. Yaggrel's high-pitched, battle-crazed laughter echoed off the steel walls, explosions and oozing corrosive poisons sizzling in his wake.

"We have to make it to the bridge!" Ansel yelled over his shoulder. "That's where Balor will be."

Della nodded stupidly and trailed after him, nearly tripping over a prone figure on the ground. She kept her focus fixed on Ansel's back, on placing one foot in front of the other as he fired this way and that, clearing a path for them.

It seemed almost too easy, the way they carved a path from the brunt of the firefight to quieter, abandoned passageways. Balor's ship was nothing like the Miss Demeanor—polished panels instead of rust, lights bright and operational instead of half burnt out and flickering, stoic where the Miss Demeanor was full of good-natured ribbing and laughter. There was a quiet danger in the air, as if the ship were a beast licking its wounds, ready to lash out at the first thing that crossed its path.

"We're here." Neither had spoken in so long that Ansel's voice startled her. He nodded at the door before him. "Brace yourself. I'm sure he's waiting with guards."

Della nodded and raised her pistol, arms shaking.

Ansel elbowed the switch next to the door. Della didn't really expect it to slide open without a fuss, but it did. Cautiously, they stepped through and entered the bridge.

The space was vast, with multiple control boards positioned around the perimeter and a main central station in the middle. And it was abandoned. Warnings scrolled over screens with no eyes to read them. Gauges flickered, lights flashed, and the room was silent save for the distant wail of the ship's alarm.

Until the whine of a blaster filled the dim room.

Della whirled to find a shadowed form sitting behind the center control panel, his feet kicked up on its surface. "You made it," a silky voice purred, and Della wondered if they'd gotten here so easily by design.

"Balor." Ansel shoved Della behind him, drew his blaster, and fired.

Balor ducked with a speed his relaxed posture had fooled

Della into thinking wasn't possible. Ansel's shot melted into the wall behind where Balor had sat.

Balor stood and began walking toward them, unconcerned.

Ansel fired again, three blasts in quick succession. This time, Balor was not able to duck. In fact, he didn't even try. But instead of dropping to the ground with blood sizzling in his open chest as Della expected, he simply stood there. The shots dissolved into his chest, a strange blue halo surrounding his skin and absorbing the energy.

Ansel looked down at his blaster as though it had betrayed him.

"You cannot kill me, Ansel, though I admire the effort," said Balor. "Did you really think you could, when I have in my possession a superconductor powerful enough to protect a nation?" Balor's boots clicked across the floor as he walked closer. He was a lithe man and might not have looked intimidating except for the lazy way he held himself, which spoke to the power he held. In his icy blue eyes, Della caught only the barest of hints of the tiny boy she once knew, the boy who wrote poetry and crafted himself a flute because a world without art was one he didn't want to live in.

Balor patted his chest, where Della imagined the Shield Stone must rest against some inside pocket. "You may have broken into my ship, but nothing can break its power when it's condensed around my person."

Della's heart sank. He was virtually invincible.

Balor let out a sharp whistle. Doors whisked open around the bridge, and four guards stepped through, surrounding them.

Ansel's next shots went wide as two of Balor's men seized him, wrenching his hands behind his back. Della fumbled to raise her own weapon, but Balor walked up to her and swatted it out of her hands as though she were a misbehaving toddler.

"Delilah." He smiled. "Naughty, naughty. We're friends, remember? I remembered *you* as soon as I saw you on the prison security footage. I didn't recognize your face, of course, but I'd recognize that sickening optimism anywhere. The girl who dream-walks into worlds where she doesn't belong. Do you remember when we'd play hide-and-seek? I always find you in the end, don't I?" Balor nodded at a guard, who stepped forward and handed him—

Della's throat went dry as the guard handed Balor the books.

No. If they'd found the books, that meant the guards had made it past the crew to the Miss Demeanor. Della removed her helmet and sought Ansel's gaze. The guards had already ripped his own helmet off, so she could see the heartbreak in his eyes that meant he'd realized the same thing she had. She refused to believe the crew wasn't still alive.

Balor dangled Della's book between his fingers. "I knew there was something special about these books when I saw your little prison rescue mission. Is *this* how you come and go? Some kind of teleportation device?"

"Don't do this," Della pleaded. She didn't even know what his plan was yet, only that it wouldn't be good. "Why do you hold such animosity toward Ansel and me? All we've ever done is try to help you."

Balor's nostrils flared, and she saw him then, the angry little boy no one noticed. "You both abandoned me."

"I didn't mean to," Della said at the same time Ansel snarled, "Only when you planned to endanger an entire city for personal gain, mate," which earned him an elbow to the gut from one of the guards.

Balor stiffened. "Was it really so bad that I was willing to do anything for you? We could have been rich, escaped, and found our place among the stars. You were going to help me, before *she* turned you against me."

Della's lips parted. "You knew I came back?"

"Of course I knew. I grew curious about where Ansel was

going every day and saw the two of you." Balor made a face. "You convinced him I was evil. You *took* him from me."

Della flinched, thinking of Riktel, the little boy. How desperate he was for connection. And now Balor, the man, slicing his name into Ansel's flesh because it was the only way he could carve himself into someone else's life. He loved Ansel, Della realized, in his own twisted way. It hurt that Ansel refused to help him, and so he lashed out, turned on him. Yet he still couldn't let Ansel go, not fully. He needed to be a part of his life, even if it was as his enemy.

Tears bit at Della's eyes, and a lump lodged in her throat. She tried to remember exactly what she'd told Balor, how the definition of friendship from a seven-year-old could be interpreted in such a skewed way that it became the manipulative thing Balor turned it into.

Was it her fault he'd turned into this, or was Balor simply a monster? A monster who now had the books at his fingertips.

"Seize her." With another gesture, Balor had one of the guards step forward to detain Della too.

Before she could consider what she was doing, Della whirled, scooped up her pistol, and fired it into the man's knee. Balor might be invincible, but his guards were not. Her second shot landed in the arm of the guard to her right. She spun and pointed her blaster at the two holding Ansel, but she didn't trust her aim enough to risk it.

She needn't have worried. Ansel used the distraction to elbow one guard in the groin, then kick the second in the shin hard enough she heard bone break.

"Enough!" Balor roared, whipping his own blaster from its holster and leveling it at Ansel's chest.

"No!" Della shouted as laser fire blinded her.

Ansel twisted the guard he was grappling around so he took the shot in the shoulder, acting as a human shield.

Balor cursed and fired again. Ansel ducked, the shot soaring over his head. This one buried itself in the bridge's windshield. Cracks spiderwebbed over the glass. There was a collective inhale of breath as all waited to see if it would hold. The Shield Stone might protect Balor from blasters, but Della doubted even he would survive the grip of space.

A hiss met Della's ears. A few chips of glass flew from the center of the pit into space as air leaked past. Not enough to depressurize the chamber, but enough to let some air out—and something *in.*

Purple and gold dust rushed through the tiny pinprick. The guards screamed but needn't have bothered. Their screams were soon cut short as the dust sapped enough of their life forces to silence them for a good, long while.

Then the dust coiled to the center of the room. It was still dimmer than usual, even after feeding on the guards. It was more void than light now, with a few flickers here and there, like lightning behind a thunderhead.

Without warning, it surged toward Balor. Della watched, sickened as it coated him head to toe until he was more shadow than man. Still, he showed no signs of alarm, merely stood there and allowed the dust to feed.

Except it wasn't feeding. It churned over his flesh, trying to find purchase, but the blue of the Shield Stone's power shone through, forbidding the dust access.

"As I said," Balor said, the last of the dust giving up and alighting from his limbs as he strode toward Della. "Nothing you can do can hurt me."

Faster than Della thought possible, Balor lunged forward and caught her around the wrist, pinning her back against the control panel.

Ansel growled and bolted forward, but Balor carelessly aimed his blaster behind him and fired.

A flash of red light.

Della heard Ansel hit the bridge's floor. The smell of cauterized flesh filled the air anew.

"Ansel!" His name left Della's throat as a raw scream. She struggled to see past Balor, even though she dreaded what she might find.

"I'm fine, Della," Ansel rasped, though he was on his knees, clutching his stomach, and horrified tears filled Della's eyes, which she then fixed on Balor.

"Don't look at me like that, Delilah," Balor tsked.

"My name is Della," she gritted out.

"Is it? I guess we'll find out." He drew a knife from a sheath on his thigh and slid it neatly across from her palm, down her wrist, and jaggedly across her forearm.

Della's spine prickled at the cold feeling of the knife sliding deep into her skin. Distantly, she heard Ansel cursing Balor in vicious, cruel language, but she could not process what he was saying as crimson blood trickled down her wrist, slicking between Balor's vice-like grip and her arm.

The dust wavered closer. Cautiously. Almost shyly. For the first time since she'd encountered it, Della felt afraid of it. She'd asked too much of it today. It was weak. Starving. And what wild creature could resist fresh blood?

It descended onto her arm, congregating on the growing pool of red, like ants to a dew drop. When it did not feed on anything more of her than what she'd already lost, she breathed a small sigh of relief.

Across the room, Ansel began to crawl to her, desperation in his gaze. His face was marred with sweat, grime, and blood. He looked like something feral, a dark fairy-tale creature pushed to the brink of madness.

Balor didn't turn to look, but he could likely hear the slide of cloth over steel, the labored breathing. He lodged his blaster under Della's chin. "I wouldn't come any closer, if I were you."

Ansel stopped, his gaze so apologetic it broke Della's heart. She yearned to go back to the beginning and do it all over, differently. She wished she were back on the Miss Demeanor, where everyone was safe and happy. She even missed her wretched time bot. They should have simply run away, maybe forever, and never let their pasts track them down.

As always, she wished too much. Shapes began to move overhead as the cosmic dust brought her dreams to life. She looked up to see the dust reflecting a vision of herself finding a book in a puddle.

Before she could stop her *stupid*, dreaming heart, her and Ansel's story spilled out before Balor in beautiful, radiant color.

CHAPTER 36

Della's skin crawled as Balor drank in their story: their meeting, their adventures through the stars, their falling in love. Their story was too tender, too intimate, and Della felt raw, flayed open.

Ansel knelt several paces away, murder in his expression, helpless to do anything but watch. On and on and on it went, scene after scene, until Della was dizzy and her vision began to swim. She just had to hold on until they reached the end of their tale and Balor would let her staunch the bleeding, surely. But even as the story overhead drew to a close, Balor did not release her.

"What do you want from me?" Della's voice rose along with her panic as her limbs grew weaker from blood loss and Ansel braced a hand against the floor for support, his eyes growing dimmer and dimmer.

"I want you to find my book, of course," Balor said, scanning the scenes overhead. "One of your lost memories might tell us where it is. Where it *really* is. Because you obviously didn't find it in a house your mother used to clean, considering that town your mother lived in doesn't actually exist."

Della's heart dropped as she realized what Balor meant to do—to use the dust to dissect what she was. She wanted to figure out more about her past, but not when Balor would use it for evil. "What are you going to do with your book?"

"What anyone who could control their fate would do, I imagine. We've always wanted the same thing, Delilah. Answers. Power. Control over our lives."

So that's what this was about? Power and wealth? She supposed it made sense, why a boy who had nothing but the scorn of others would want to prove everyone who'd called him useless wrong. He'd already hurt, *killed* so many with the power of the Shield Stone. Who knew how many would suffer if he had his book too.

"Having the books doesn't give you the power you think it does," she said, voice wavering more than she'd like. "The more you try to change your life, the more things go wrong. You can't rewrite your past or change your future. Only your actions can write your story."

He chuckled. "A pretty thought. Now stop thinking of the present and start thinking of the past so the dust will show me something more useful. Your *real* past."

"I'll let you bleed me dry before I give you what you want."

"Delilah, Delilah, Delilah," Balor tsked, his voice a mocking singsong, and Della grieved for the boy who once sang out of joy, not derision. "I think you'll reconsider." Balor let her go with a rough shove that sent her sliding to the floor.

Clumsily, she fought to stand, but her knees buckled, and she slumped against the leg of the control panel.

Ansel's eyes caught hers as if to say *I'm with you.* She didn't like the broken way he bent over his side. She'd thought she'd seen him wounded badly in prison, but there was something far more grave to the sallowness of his skin now, as though he were already half-corpse. She feared the wound Balor had carved into Ansel's flesh this time was too deep to heal.

Balor paced between her and Ansel, holding their books in his bloodied hands. "The dust shows fears, not just fantasies. It will show you your past because your past terrifies you." Balor flipped through the pages of one of the books, stopping somewhere toward the beginning. Ansel's name glinted on the spine. "I think you'll find it's time to let go of those dreams of yours." Balor smiled then, a horrible, corrupted version of the smile she'd brought to his lips so long ago. "And face reality." Without warning, he tore out a page from Ansel's book.

Della cried out and tried to lunge, but she was too weak, and she fell to her knees.

Balor regarded the torn paper with disinterest. "Look at that. Your first conversation. Gone. What do you think happens now that it doesn't exist in Ansel's story? I'd wager it no longer exists in his brain either. I cannot undo the past, but I can erase you from *his* reality. You will cooperate, or you will lose him."

"No." Della gasped, inching over to Ansel, thinking of the first time they spoke—the shared daydream, the imaginary carriage, the borrowed jacket. Her time with Ansel once felt vast, epic, written in starlight and destined for greatness. Now it suddenly felt fragile and short, condensed to a handful of precious pages Balor could rip out on a whim.

Balor didn't bother stopping her, and Della half-sobbed as she reached Ansel, falling against his chest. He swayed. She reached up to touch his cheek with a wildly trembling hand. "Ansel," she breathed. She was cold all over and couldn't stop shaking. "You know me still, right? You remember?"

He stroked her hair with tragically weak fingers. "Of course I do."

Della searched Ansel's expression. Perhaps Balor was wrong, and removing pages wouldn't cause him to forget. "The first time we talked, what did we speak of?"

Ansel only shook his head, eyes oddly hazy. "I—I told you what electricity was, then you wrote in my book and asked me to write in yours."

"No, we'd spoken the night before of many things," Della said, her teeth chattering uncontrollably. "We imagined what would happen if you had met me on that muddy road instead of the Duke. Don't you remember?"

His eyes went distant, his expression falling. And Della's ribs pinched unbearably, her lungs too tight around her shattering heart.

"Focus, Delilah," Balor called. "Or I will tear out his memories of you piece by piece."

"It's fine, Della," Ansel whispered. "You can't help him find his book. Don't give him that power. It would be my pleasure to get to fall in love with you for the first time, for a third time." The fact that he was still trying to make her smile only made Della's sorrow deepen.

Balor walked closer until he stood over them. "As touching as this is, if you still decide not to cooperate after I remove you from Ansel's brain, I will kill his crew, one by one. I'm sure my men have them detained by now."

Murder clouded Della's vision.

"Ah, there's your weakness." Balor smiled. "Friends are so useful. I believe you taught me that." He kicked Ansel away from her, his boot striking still-unhealed ribs.

Pain lanced through Ansel's expression as he sprawled roughly to the floor, pinching his eyes shut. He'd toppled too easily, like a limp rag doll, and Della let out a cry. She tried to go to him, but Balor stepped between them.

Her blood boiled with rage. She wanted to make him pay for everything he'd done. Overhead, the cosmic dust flared brightly before displaying an image of Balor pinned to the floor, her hands around his neck.

Balor clucked his tongue. "Such violent desires." Without looking, he tore another page out of Ansel's book. "Show me what I want or there will be nothing left of you inside Ansel's head by morning."

Della squeezed her eyes closed and willed herself to overpower the sickening fury festering in her gut. She heard Ansel's shallow, rasping breaths from where he lay.

Crawling forward, she took his hand, gently running a thumb over his battered, bleeding knuckles. His eyes fluttered open. "Stay with me, Della dear," he mumbled thickly.

He needed her. The crew needed her. There was no choice, save for compliance. So she released her arm from her side, letting her blood flow. She thought of her mother's voice, humming a song. She needed her the way everyone needed their mother when their life was at its lowest. She yearned for home, to be seven years old again, safe in bed—to blink and discover this was all just a nightmare. Tears oozed out from beneath her eyelids but never fell. If only she were in a book where the ending was always happy and the villains received justice.

"I knew you'd see reason," Balor said, and Della opened her eyes to find the image in the dust had changed to that of a library, the shelves extending so far into the heavens that clouds veiled the ceiling. One scene blurred into the next. Della was no longer a brown-eyed woman but a blond-haired girl. Delilah. The dust showed her everyday life—the isolation and ridicule she faced at school, cozy evenings spent reading books, curling up on the couch with her mother. And then the visions deepened and lengthened until the truth was revealed.

CHAPTER 37

An apartment. Cherry blossom wallpaper.

"Why do you write fake books when you can read a real one anytime you want?" the voice of Delilah as a child asked. "Everyone at school says it's pointless to read about people and worlds that aren't real."

Her mother looked up from her writing. "Real books are destined to end in tragedy, when there's no one left to tell a story about. Fictional ones can end while everyone is still happy. Don't you enjoy my stories?"

Of course she did. The bedtime stories her mother made up were far more delightful than any real book found in the library. Yet she couldn't block out her schoolmates' teasing—that her mother was odd, authoring stories that could never be real. Everyone knew librarians could never belong in a book of their own; they belonged outside of them, guarding the tales of others.

A schoolroom, empty save for a teacher, who knelt beside a young girl's desk, listening to her cry.

"They called me a mistake and my mother a whore." Delilah's youthful voice sniffled as the teacher listened. "I will never belong here. I shouldn't have been born, and half of me will never be a librarian."

"Your mother fell in love," the teacher said gently, pushing his glasses up his nose and adjusting his long robes. "She is a great librarian who made a mistake."

"The greatest mistake," Delilah said miserably. "Librarians must never tamper with the books they keep."

"Her heart was much too soft for the tragedy department," said the teacher. "She always did enjoy romance. We should have known it was only a matter of time before she wrote her own."

Picking a lock in a forbidden room of the library. Finding a book and meeting Riktel, and then—

Her eyes flew open, beholding her mother's panic-stricken face inches from her own.

"Delilah?" her mother asked, voice trembling. "Where were you?"

Groggily, Delilah sat up, her bed quilt sliding off her shoulders. "I was dreaming."

Her mother looked greatly troubled. "You weren't, darling." She held up a book. Something odd happened. Before her eyes, the title on the spine shifted from Riktel, Vol. 1 *to* Delilah Farley, Vol. 1.

"You mustn't tell anyone what happened, or they won't let you near a real book again," her mother said in a rush. "The other librarians already think you don't belong here, and if they find out you took a story, they'll send you away." She tucked the book under her arm. "I will make a duplicate and hide this copy. They will never know. Never let yourself slip into another book ever again."

Her mother, a librarian, a watcher of books like the ones Della and Ansel had found? It seemed preposterous. Della's mother was a simple housekeeper. And yet the dust showed her otherwise. He mother had once leaped into a book, just as Della had, and met . . . Della's father. Was it possible Della had a father somewhere still, lost in an unknown book?

"Do not stop," Balor snarled. "Show me more. Where is this library? If your mother is a librarian, why are you here and not there? How did you smuggle these books out?"

Wrestling her emotions into submission, Della focused her thoughts on her missing past.

Delilah didn't disagree with her mother's warnings, but she had no way of controlling when she slipped into a book. Other librarians needed pens to transport themselves into books—which of course was generally prohibited regardless, but Della was powerless to resist their call. And it wasn't as though she could simply avoid books altogether, considering she lived in a library.

And anyway, was visiting a few stories really so bad? Of course she knew librarians were forbidden from tampering with stories, but she was only half librarian, so she figured she only had to halfway keep the rule. And she wasn't tampering, not really. She wasn't hurting anyone, and her visits were always quick—not that she could control them, but they never lasted longer than a handful of hours.

The only troublesome thing was that every time she exited a book, her name appeared on the spine, replacing the previous title. Luckily, the librarians couldn't keep an eye on every single one of the trillions of books in the library, so if one or two tomes found themselves shoved under a bookcase, none would be the wiser.

Until one day Delilah slipped into a story in the middle of class. One moment, she was listening to an instructor droning on, the next she'd awoken in the book he'd been using as a demon-

stration, meeting the boy within, and fake marrying him under an oak tree.

She awoke heartbroken, yearning to return but knowing she never could, for her mother was there when Delilah opened her eyes. And standing behind her were two library elders.

The stacks of books that had previously cluttered every corner of Delilah's room were gone. Having been surrounded by books since the moment she was born into the great library, Delilah immediately noticed their ominous absence.

"You told me you hadn't visited any books since the first one," Delilah's mother said, brow knit with worry.

"I—" Delilah tried to say she hadn't, but she couldn't bring herself to outright lie. "Only a few times."

"Eighty-two, to be exact," said the sterner of the two elders, stepping forward, her mouth set in a thin line. "We've had apprentices scouring the library these past two weeks to find them." She reached into her robe and pulled out a book, a copy with a purple cover that Delilah remembered visiting last year.

Her own name was printed on the spine: Delilah Farley, Vol. 75.

"You do know books are to be kept on the shelves, not under them?" the second, kinder-looking elder asked, her lips curving into a smile, as though she were trying to lighten the mood.

"Don't worry about the titles," Delilah managed, sitting up in bed, the covers pooling into her lap. "I watched to make sure, and the sequels all come in with the proper names again."

The number of volumes containing a person's life depended on how eventful their life was, but in general, one volume held about five years. After the old volume filled up, new ones would appear in the library's drop box, their covers soft and shiny, their pages empty and ready to be filled. The librarians would then take them to their respective places on the shelf, where they would be guarded as they filled with adventures. If a person happened to change their name during their series, their new books' spines would reflect the alteration. If Delilah's name took up one book in a whole series, she didn't see the harm.

"Books don't take kindly to being tampered with." The stern elder drew herself up. "No matter if the new books come in bearing the correct names, you still rewrote people's backstories. Their pasts. They deserve to be the authors of their own lives. And every plot twist caused by outsiders always comes with a terrible surprise. Why do you think we're forbidden from writing in the books?"

Guilt poked at Delilah's stomach. Did she really hurt everyone she met? How could she have ruined her electrician's life when every moment spent together felt so good and right? "You're wrong. You have to let me go back," she pleaded. "My electrician . . . He'll worry when I don't meet him this evening."

The kinder-faced elder walked to her bedside and rested a hand on Delilah's shoulder. "We've written a hologram into that young man's story of you bidding him farewell. Hopefully, closure will direct his life back on track. Though it is doubtful his life will turn out how it should have."

"No." Delilah fought back tears. "He can't think I left him. He'll think I didn't care for him, but I do, I—"

Delilah's mother reached for her hand, her eyes shimmering. "Oh, darling. I know. I know."

"It is as we always feared," the stern elder went on coldly, and Delilah noticed her mother flinch. "Your existence poses a risk to the library."

Delilah turned to her mother. "You said that when I was born, no book with my name on it appeared in the drop box. You said that was proof I'm librarian enough that I belong here."

"Clearly she was mistaken." The stern elder tucked the purple book back into her robes. "Only half of you belongs here. Your soul cannot be content without its own book, as ours are. Half of you craves a story of its own and won't rest until it finds one. You will continue slipping into books, trying to make them

your own as your restless spirit seeks to find its place in the universe."

"We are tasked with guarding stories," said the other elder. "You've derailed the lives of eighty-two wards. Rectifying your influence is going to take a lot of tedious work, if it's even possible. We can't—"

"Change the past," Delilah finished automatically. Librarians must only guard, never tamper. And now everyone knew Delilah was fundamentally incapable of honoring the library's purpose to protect the books.

Delilah was lucky the elders even let her live once they found out about her birth. Now they'd just seen confirmation that her very existence put the entire library in danger.

Della grew weaker and weaker, fading in and out of consciousness, and still, Balor would not allow her to staunch the bleeding. She lay in a pool of her blood, rendered purple and gold by the cosmic dust feasting upon it. So this was why she'd never felt as though she belonged, as though she was constantly chasing adventures she could never have. Only half of her belonged in a story of her own.

It even explained why she was able to communicate with Ansel and the crew, though they all spoke different languages. She was born into a world of words, destined to be the keeper of a trillion stories. It was no wonder she could understand any language.

And yet this still didn't explain what had happened to her memories, or how she'd ended up in Poling.

"I'm waiting, Delilah," Balor called, and she heard the nightmarish noise of ripping paper.

"What will happen to me now?" Delilah asked quietly. She and her mother sat in the kitchen of their apartment. The elders stood a few paces away, giving them the illusion of privacy as they allowed Delilah's mother to explain what came next.

"They want to put you in your own story," Delilah's mother said.

For a moment, Delilah's spirits lifted. Having her own story might not be so bad. "May I go to Lumeria?"

Her mother shook her head sadly. "You can't go to a real dimension. You don't belong in any of them and will corrupt too many timelines. They're going to put you in a story of your own. A fake one." She nodded to the stack of fairy tales sitting on the table before them.

The thickness in Delilah's throat choked her hopes. "You will put me in a world where I am alone."

"Not alone. There will be other people there." Her mother smiled sadly. "We will turn fiction into your reality."

"But they'll just be characters brought to life. They won't be real, not really." Delilah shook her head, slowly at first, then fast. Frantically. "And then what is the point? What is the point of me?"

Tears shimmered in her mother's eyes.

The kinder elder stepped forward. "We will write you into whatever book you choose, as whatever character you like. You can be whoever you want, Delilah. You will change in looks as well as mind until you no longer know your past self. Your new identity will be your new reality. We will write that you had a fever that made your childhood memories fuzzy. You will forget enough to believe your life is real. It will mean something to you."

Delilah didn't want her life to mean something to her. She wanted to mean something to other people, the way she was a friend to Riktel and the first love of a golden-haired boy. She felt like a little girl again playing hide-and-seek, stuffed behind a cabinet, listening to the other children laugh in the next room—separated from a world she desperately wanted to be a part of but that didn't even know she existed.

"I don't want to forget you," Della said to her mother, throat growing thick.

"We will not make you forget your mother, not entirely," the kind elder said. "We're not cruel; we only want peace. You may write letters to her, though you may never see her."

"You'll finally have a book of your own," her mother said encouragingly.

The severe elder slid the stack of bedtime stories closer to Delilah. "Pick one."

"You have the power to choose your own story," her mother whispered. "Make it a good one."

Delilah didn't move. It didn't matter. Nothing mattered. She didn't matter.

"Here." Her mother nudged a story toward her. "A fairy tale." Her mother mustered up a smile that was supposed to look encouraging but mostly looked like she was going to be sick. "You always did like Della's story. You'll have a tough road ahead, but you'll meet a handsome duke and live happily ever after."

Delilah slammed the book onto the table. "I don't want to live happily ever after. I want to live*."*

But then she noticed something in her mother's gaze, urging her to take the book. Her mother had written this book. She might have found time to write a way out of it.

"I love you, Delilah," her mother whispered.

Delilah couldn't speak. She only nodded once and handed the elder the fairy tale that would be her prison. The last thing she saw was the elder raising a gilded pen over the page before her life as she knew it was gone forever.

Balor opened Della's book as the image dissolved into sparks. Her mind reeled. Her past still did not feel like her own. She couldn't remember any of it, even after she'd been shown every piece. And yet it had to be true.

Della had escaped the prison the librarians had placed her in. Ansel's book, however it had found her, had been her salvation, and she'd damned him. Corrupted every thread of his life until it was no longer his own. Was it her fault they were all here now, in this miserable place? She felt hollow, as though her emotions seeped from her veins along with her blood.

As she watched, Balor withdrew a pen from an inner pocket of his coat.

Della licked her dry, cracked lips. Fatigue weighed down every cell in her body. "What are you doing?" she choked out, even though she wanted to close her eyes and never wake up.

Balor bent over the book. "Writing that I find the library and my book, of course."

Maybe she should let him. She'd like to see magic squash every horrid dream he had, the way it had done to her.

But if he survived magic's whims and found the library and all the innocent lives within, he'd be even more invincible than he was now. Would the librarians even be able to stop him? Her memories had shown no weapons they could use to defend themselves if a man with a pistol appeared in their midst.

Ansel struggled to his knees beside her. "No," he croaked, but Balor ignored him. He was barely able to keep from toppling back over, and his chest rose and fell too shallowly.

Della silently begged the cosmic dust to help them, but it was too starved, too single-mindedly consumed with lapping up her blood to come to her aid. It was up to her to figure out a way to save them.

She looked at Balor and thought of a lonely little boy she'd met long ago, of children's laughter bouncing between trees, of teaching him the song her mother hummed to her at night in the hope it might comfort him the same way it did her. "You can still stop," Della said. "You may think you are too far to turn back, but you are not yet lost to me. You don't need a book to have some say in your destiny. Being good and kind was always within your power."

Balor scoffed, and she couldn't help but think that his mockery was similar to the kind he'd received as a child. People liked to stifle those who shone brightly, too short-sighted to see that, without light, the entire world would wither away in the darkness they found so glamorous.

"You don't need power to make your life into some grand thing." Della swallowed, her bravery weakening with every passing second. "You want everyone to know your name and remember you as the boy they once called useless, but historically, it's always the bad that's remembered—the evilest of men, the most catastrophic disasters. Perhaps it is better to be forgotten. Let your legacy live on silently in the smiles of those you have touched. Fill the universe with beauty and plant seeds of joy that will grow to outlive everyone who has wronged you. Let happiness be your revenge against their misery and spare them not a thought more."

For a moment, she thought he would agree. A tremor fluttered at his temple.

Then Balor's jaw tightened, fury slamming down over his expression. He marched across the room, plucking Ansel's book off the control panel. "Do not speak to me as though you understand me," he snarled. "You took *everything* from me. We are not friends." Balor grabbed a fistful of pages.

"No!" The scream tore from Della's throat while Ansel lurched forward, agony coating his expression, but it was too late.

Balor ripped the pages from Ansel's book, and Della felt her heart tear right along with them. He flipped forward and tore out second handful, and then another. It seemed not all monsters could be tamed. “How does it feel, having him *ripped from you*?” Balor tossed Ansel’s book indifferently to the side. It splayed upon the floor, tattered and flimsy.

The precious time Della and Ansel had spent together, gone. The secrets and confessions, smiles and tender moments, severed as if they’d never shared them at all. Della’s vision darkened around the edges, and her ears felt stuffed with cotton.

Ansel paused. He blinked, then looked down at himself, as though he couldn’t quite remember why he was in such a desperate position, on his hands and knees, reaching toward a book on the floor. Lines appeared between his brows. He grimaced and clutched his side, then looked about, eyes widening when he saw Balor.

“Ansel?” she whispered.

He slowly turned to face her. When he blinked, it was sluggish, his eyes rolling back until he forced them to focus. “Has death sent you for me at last, then?”

No. *No, no, no.* He was back to thinking she was some kind of spirit of the afterlife, the exact way he had when he first laid eyes upon her. “It’s me, Della,” she whispered. “Don’t you know me?”

The tiny shake of his head was like a knife to the gut.

The only person who truly understood her looked at her as though she were a stranger. She’d been carved out of the only story where she felt like she belonged. She was alone. Oh, she was so alone.

An agonized sob wracked through her. She’d always known a great romance might end in heartbreak, but this was a different type of pain entirely, for their romance had been erased as though it had never happened at all. It was not something profound they could look back on with bittersweet fondness. Balor had rendered their time together meaningless—a daydream that existed only in Della’s mind.

Maybe, if he survived this, Ansel could read about their love in her book if she ever got it back, or see his lost memories in a swirl of cosmic dust, but it was no replacement for living it. He'd only feel the detached happiness anyone might experience from reading a tale of romance that was not their own.

And then Ansel half-fell back onto his elbow, and she realized she had greater things to worry about than the past. She helped him ease back onto the floor, blinking back tears. If he'd have only this one moment of her, she ought to make it a good one.

She cradled his head in her lap and gently pushed his hair aside, her bloody fingers leaving trails across his skin. His confused gaze began to grow cloudy as he looked up at her.

Her heart broke for him too, for all that he'd lost, though he didn't know it. When they first met, he was alone with his true thoughts, cold, suspicious of anyone who offered him kindness. He might never remember just how precious the life he'd stolen for himself was. He might die thinking he'd failed. That he'd never found a home.

"You are loved more profoundly than you know," she murmured, tasting salt on her lips.

In the corner of her eye, she saw Balor turn to the control panel and pick up his pen once more. Then she simply held Ansel's gaze until his eyes drifted shut.

CHAPTER 38

Tink tink tink.

The sound of metal skittering over metal snapped Della to attention. A small round object rolled into the dining room. A tiny red light blinked on its surface, slow at first, then faster. Della's eyes widened as she recognized it. She'd cataloged the item into its section on Ansel's ship with Yaggrel. *Minor explosive, flashbang.*

Della squeezed her eyes shut as the room imploded. Her eardrums closed over with a dull whine of protest, and white light strobed behind her eyelids. Everything shook around her, and smoke coated her tongue and nostrils.

Her pulse raced. The crew. They must have escaped Balor's men.

At the same time, doors whisked open on the other side of the bridge, and another squadron of guards rushed through, joining the fray. Then gloved hands were yanking at Della's wrists, urging her up. Someone was shouting at her, but the voice was too distant to make out.

Something pinched in her arm, and a rush of adrenaline flooded her veins. Della's vision cleared, and she blinked to find Xaks's masked face inches from her own as she shook her. "Della?" Her mouth formed her name. "Are you okay?" Xaks yanked a syringe out of Della's arm.

Dizzily, Della nodded. Whatever Xaks had given her seemed

to have bolstered her strength, at least temporarily. "Ansel," she managed, her own voice sounding like it was coming from underwater in her ringing ears.

Eryl was already at Ansel's side, injecting an identical syringe into his bicep.

Ansel sat up with a tremendous inhale. His hand shot out and gripped Eryl's shoulder, his eyes wild. Della's breath caught, her chest soaring with the fierce hope that he would live.

"Balor," Ansel snarled like a curse, yanking another syringe off Eryl's chest plate, where they were hooked in a neat row. He stabbed the needle into his own thigh before tossing it aside and struggling to his feet. He spared Della one more slightly confused look, like he couldn't figure out why a spirit of the afterlife was still there when he was no longer dying. Then he spotted Yaggrel fighting off three guards at once, and he barreled into the chaos, his face set in determination.

As Xaks, too, launched herself back into battle, Della searched the hazy room and hoped beyond hope that Balor had not already written himself away. The cosmic dust was drifting around, the fighting having disrupted its dinner, and its glow bounced off the smoke, casting the scene in even more confusion.

Della's gaze caught on Ansel's book where it still lay crumpled and bent several yards away, in danger of being trampled. Tucking her arm against her side, she staggered forward as quickly as she could. She darted this way and that, keeping low. Scooping up the book, she scampered toward the control panel in search of her own book, and Balor.

Muffled shouts rang out, but Della's hearing was too compromised to understand the words. Blaster fire zipped through the smoke like red lightning behind gray clouds. They were so horribly outnumbered. Unless she did something and put an end to this awful mess, everyone would suffer for it.

Della didn't see Balor, but hopefully that was because he'd taken cover when the explosion went off, not because he was gone. And then she saw it . . . there. Her book, sitting abandoned on the edge of the control panel. Shaking with panic, she grabbed the book, hugging it along with Ansel's to her chest.

Balor's pen rolled off the panel and landed at her feet. The fact that it was still here meant Balor hadn't used it yet, for it would have vanished along with him if he'd written himself away.

Della looked at that pen by her toes, then up at the impossible battle around her. The mayhem her meddling had caused. The elders had been right to send her away. All they'd wanted to do was keep people like Ansel safe. Safe from her.

The books needed to be placed back in the protection of the elders. They would know how to fix everything. Maybe she'd be returned to Poling or a less comfortable type of prison. It didn't matter. They would only do what was best for the books they cared for. She didn't belong anywhere, and it was better if she stopped trying to find her place in the world.

Della picked up the pen. She needed to do this now and be done with it. She spread her book open on the control panel. She raised her pen—

A bloody hand clawed its way out from the other side of the panel, fingers digging into the metal inches from Della's nose. Before she could react, the dark barrel of a blaster appeared between her eyes. Della stumbled back. Balor grinned as he staggered to his feet on the other side of the panel, his mouth forming words she couldn't hear. Blood speckled his face and coated his teeth. Whether it was his or not, she couldn't tell.

"Drop the book," Balor said, Della's fractured hearing barely picking up the words.

In response, Della opened her book and pressed the pen to the page.

A tremendous force crashed into her as Balor dived over the panel. The wind slammed out of her as she hit the floor. She managed to keep hold of the books, but the pen skittered under the control panel. Balor pinned her under his weight, trying to pry her fingers off the covers of the books. She clung to them, feeling her nails rip as he clawed at her fingertips. A necklace slipped free of his collar as he fought her, a flawlessly cut gemstone catching the feeble light.

The Shield Stone. It had to be. If she could grab it, he'd be defenseless, but she couldn't release her hands from the books.

Balor gave up on her hands and went for her throat. Della squirmed as his fingers wrapped around her neck. His grip was vicious, unrelenting, tighter than she thought possible.

Her vision dimmed.

And then a hand appeared, snatching that dangling gemstone into a fist and yanking.

The necklace tore free. Ansel stood over them, holding the Stone up to the light. Balor's gaze turned desperate. He looked from the books in Della's arms to the necklace in Ansel's hand. Then he released Della and dove for Ansel. The two of them rolled a few yards away, exchanging punches.

Della coughed, rising to her knees and opening her book. She crawled forward and retrieved the pen from under the control panel. As she held the pen, the temptation to try to write something, anything, that might allow her to save everyone without giving everything up herself tugged at her.

But those thoughts were dashed when she looked up to see Balor standing over Ansel, who was on his knees, the necklace still dangling from his fist. She had to stop trying to escape the inevitable once and for all, or others would continue to pay for it.

"You don't know how to activate the shield," Balor was sneering.

"Then fucking shoot me," Ansel snapped, his voice impatient with years of weariness. "Just do it so we can be through."

The blaster whined as Balor looked down its sights.

"No!" Della stood, the books in one hand, the pen in her other.

For one moment, the battlefield froze, and Ansel turned to look at Della, and she knew that this was the only goodbye she would get.

Back when she lived in Poling, Della often thought she needed to be more like the heroines in the stories her mother read to her if she ever wanted to have her own adventures. She needed to be wittier or braver or funnier. In actuality, none of those attributes would help her save the day now. The type of strength she needed was the type she'd always had. The quiet type that turned the other cheek and smiled even when tears throbbed behind her eyes.

"I love you," she whispered.

Ansel reached for her, and for one wild, ridiculous moment, the part of her that still believed in fairy tales and happily ever afters thought a simple declaration of love had made him achieve the impossible and remember everything. But of course not.

He was only shouting a warning as Balor turned the blaster from him to her, the same way Ansel would defend anyone Balor set his sights on.

It took physical effort to reluctantly press the pen to the page of her book. Her lungs shuddered as she suppressed a sob. Great sadness gripped her insides, begging her not to do what needed to be done. For once she left this adventure, she would never allow herself to have another. Not when it hurt so many.

She thought of Ansel and the crew and the ship, all the love and laughter and *belonging.* She'd lived a dream, a beautiful, perfect dream. But now it was time to wake up.

With wobbling penmanship, Della wrote: *Della returned the books to the library outside of time and space.* As she dotted the last period, Balor fired, a flash of red consuming her vision before blackness took her.

CHAPTER 39

The smell of parchment and ink woke Della. It was the smell of her childhood, the smell of forgotten memories. A familiar melody reached her ears—humming, soft and gentle. The same song Della hummed in the kitchen aboard the Miss Demeanor. The same tune Ansel had recognized because she'd taught it to Riktel all those years ago.

Della's eyes flew open. Cherry blossom wallpaper filled her vision. Her quilt smelled of lavender. She sat up, finding herself in her childhood bedroom. Sunshine poured through her window, and the distant sound of a gurgling fountain from the garden outside met her ears.

Beside her sat a woman with periwinkle eyes and hair the color of corn tassels.

"Mother?" Della breathed.

Her mother stopped humming. "You're awake." She looked at Della with fragile restraint. Her chin wobbled.

"Mother," Della said again, and her mother's expression crumbled.

She rushed onto the bed beside Della and scooped her into her arms as though she were a child again with scraped knees. Her mother's existence outside of Della's thoughts felt too sharp, too bright, and she could hardly bear it. Her heart finally broke. For no matter how commendably a heart might try to hold itself together, one sympathetic look from a mother could tear down the whole facade.

"How am I here?" Della asked as warm tears flowed over her cheeks.

"I begged them to let me see you one more time before they return you to Poling."

So she'd be going back, then. Della clung to her mother's shoulder, a sob wracking her body. Cool fingers stroked through her hair, and Della wept. It was the deep, soul-purifying cry one could only manage when in a mother's arms—the type of cry that broke all the poorly patched, mangled pieces of yourself apart so that you could be put back together properly this time. She cried until her mother's shoulder was wet with her tears, until her sobs faded to shuddering hiccups, leaving her insides feeling the way the aftermath of a fresh rain smelled: cleansed, renewed.

"I don't understand." Della pulled away and scrubbed at her raw, gritty eyes. "Are you even sick? The medicine, and your heart, and—"

"I don't need medicine," her mother said gently. "Oh, my love. The heart that was broken was your own."

Confusion buzzed in Della's skull as she tried to work out what was real and what wasn't.

Her mother let out a long breath, puffing stray strands of hair from her face. "Brains have a funny way of lying to themselves to make themselves comfortable. They prefer false realities over painful truths." Regret filled her mother's expression. "When the elders pulled you from Lumeria, you were heartbroken. I can only assume your brain failed to rationalize a broken heart in your new reality, where you had no cause for such great sorrow. So your brain decided I was the one with the faulty organ. In the end, some part of you knew returning to Lumeria, to Ansel, was the key to fixing a fractured heart. You just didn't realize it was always *your* heart that was broken." Then her mother leaned in and said in a whisper, "We must talk quickly, while we're alone.

The elders keep me under arrest in my home, but I will find a way to save you again, I swear it."

"Again?" Della asked. "Was it you who brought Ansel's book to me?"

Her mother nodded. "It was easy enough to write that your electrician's next volume would appear inside your fairy tale rather than in the library drop box. After all, I'm the author of your book. I simply penciled it in before I handed over the book to the elders.

"Getting your story to him was more difficult. Luckily, I still had Riktel's story from so long ago—the one I replaced with a decoy. After the elders placed you in that fairy tale, I wrote it into Ansel's knapsack. I didn't think it would take him so long to find it."

That must have been the rucksack Ansel lost in prison for four years and didn't bother to open for four more once he was out.

Della shook her head in wonder. "And the elders never found out what you did when my fairy tale just vanished one day?"

A mischievous smile spread across her mother's face. "Of course they knew I did something, though without the books, they didn't know where it ended up, until today."

Della blinked with bewilderment. Had her mother always been like this? Reckless and a little odd? Della wondered if as all children grew up, they woke one day to find their parent was a real person with their own thoughts and feelings and wants—a creature somehow simultaneously less and more than the invincible beacon of benevolence the children had always seen them to be.

Then, her mother's smile faded. "It will be harder this time. I'm not allowed near the books anymore. They keep me locked in here, and—"

Della was already shaking her head. "Enough scheming and saving. The elders are right. I should not be allowed in stories."

Her mother started to argue, but Della cut her off, rising from the bed. "Tell me I'm wrong." Desperation clawed at Della's throat, but she knew she was right. Some things couldn't be fixed, not even by mothers. "Tell me your involvement in my father's life didn't hurt him."

Darkness entered her mother's eyes, and instant regret burrowed into Della's belly over causing her such pain. She didn't know who her father was or what had become of him after the elders found out what her mother had done, but she doubted the words *happily ever after* were involved.

Her mother's cool fingers slipped from Della's hands. "I can't." Utter defeat and indescribable grief laced her voice.

"Please, if you care for me, don't try to save me again," Della said. "And what of you? You don't deserve to live like this as punishment for trying to help me, especially when it's a futile cause."

"I don't mind, Della," her mother whispered. "For you, I'd give the world."

"You already gave me a world once," said Della. "And it was really quite miserable."

There was a pause, then her mother began to laugh, and the tension dissolved between them. "Oh, you didn't enjoy Poling? In my defense, the Della I wrote originally did not fall in a mud puddle. She met the Duke and they had a lovely afternoon stroll. That was your own doing, my dear."

"A lovely afternoon stroll?" Della exclaimed. "And the wretched Mrs. Loughty didn't send the constable out looking for her? And what of that horrible Radcliff fellow?"

"Every story has a villain," her mother said defensively.

"I thought you said you wrote happy stories," Della grumbled.

The two of them dissolved into giggles, because if they did not laugh, then they'd cry.

"I must accept my fate," Della said after a moment, sobering.

"Do not try to talk me out of it. Let us simply enjoy the time we have."

So they talked about nothing of importance, for if Della thought too much about her fate, she would lose her resolve. She would be filled with wanting again, to seize hold of a life of her own. She'd let mother fill her head with more impossible fairy tales. Tales that love could prevail and evil could be vanquished with a few clever words and a touch of magic.

Too soon, a knock came at the door, and she knew their time was up.

She faced her mother and let out a ragged breath. "I'm ready."

Her mother embraced her, long and hard. "I'm not." And then her voice lowered even further. "I know you likely won't remember this, but if you happen to run into a farmer with a fondness for poetry, would you mind telling him hello for me?"

Della pulled back in shock. "Are you saying . . . ?"

Her mother pressed a finger to her lips and eyed the door, then winked. "You were never as alone as you thought you were."

PART 5

OUTSIDE OF TIME AND SPACE, a group of elders and librarians looked over two tattered, bloodied books and wondered how they were supposed to make sense of them. The girl had to be sent back to the book she'd escaped from; that much was certain. But what of the others? The men she'd visited as children. She'd thrown their whole lives off course, and despite the elders' best efforts, the situation hadn't righted itself. If allowed to survive, the men would continue altering the timelines of everyone around them. Their existences could derail the lives of everyone in their reality.

Just then, a disgraced librarian burst in, shaking off the elders who chased after her. "I'd like to propose a plan."

"And why should we listen to you, after all you've done?" scoffed a librarian.

"My daughter begged me not to interfere. You ought to know me well enough by now to know I'd never defy her wishes. And my plan is a merciful one."

One of the elders waved for her to continue.

"An explosion on the ship. Fast and quick. The respective crews will mourn Della, Ansel, and Balor for a while, but then their lives may go on and, with any luck, course-correct with the captains no longer present to continue the corruption. It's the least disruptive course of action."

"It is a tragedy," said the elder.

"Perhaps," the librarian said, then smiled, thinking of the twist she was about to reveal. "Perhaps not. Ansel, Balor, and Della don't have to die. Everyone in their world simply has to think they did."

Not that the elders would ever know, but it wouldn't be the first time she'd smuggled a character out of a tragedy and into a fairy tale.

CHAPTER 40

Della Farley's life resembled the unfortunate half of a fairy tale—at least, to a certain extent. For while it was true she was a penniless maid condemned to a life of servitude, that was where her similarities to heroines found in fairy tales ended; she could not find it within herself to dream of adventure or love. Such hopes were futile. A happily ever after would never be hers.

Her shoes squelched over slush-covered cobblestones as she made her way through the city of Poling. Mrs. Loughty would be expecting her home to serve tea soon, and Della had dawdled too long at the market.

She kept her head down as she walked. It wasn't as though she was missing anything. Poling was a dreary mismatch of monotones, one swatch of gray piled atop a thousand more.

She therefore didn't notice the carriage whooshing toward her until it was too late. Though she attempted to dodge out of its path, one of its wheels bounced into a melting puddle, sloshing a cascade of grime across her skirts.

Della closed her eyes. Icy mud slid off her in great globs to plop in the muck at her feet. She couldn't even find it in her heart to be dismayed. Misery in its various forms was just so *typical.*

"Apologies, my lady," a smooth male voice said behind her. "My driver wasn't watching where he was going."

Heat rose in Della's cheeks as she turned to face the speaker.

As soon as she caught sight of him, she fumbled her way into a curtsy, her feet making an awful sucking noise in the mud as her weight shifted. "Your Grace."

For he was Ansel Tulzok, the Duke of Eshford, unmistakable and utterly rakish with his sardonic smile and unkempt hair. She'd heard he was staying in Poling to visit family but never expected to lay eyes on him herself. His tailcoat was unbuttoned, his cravat half-loose as though he'd been dragged from the throes of passion, which was improbable, considering he'd just stepped out of a respectable-looking carriage in the middle of a Tuesday afternoon.

"Do you purposefully make yourself look disheveled to maintain your scandalous reputation?" The question popped out of Della's mouth before she could stop it, startling her as much as the Duke. Generally speaking, she wasn't one for spouting impertinent observations, yet something about the Duke's daring smirk invited her to be just as improper as he.

"He does, and it's insufferable," said another voice from the carriage. A slender man poked his head out of the window, a piece of his slicked-back dark hair falling over his brow.

"You know, I find your contributions rarely add anything of value to conversations, Balor," the Duke observed.

The other man, Balor, laughed before retreating into the carriage.

"I don't suppose you'd accept a ride from a disheveled gentleman and his buffoon of a friend?" the Duke asked her. "We must return you home swiftly before you catch cold."

Della's teeth chattered. "I ought not. It wouldn't be proper."

"Ah yes, propriety." He paused then, halting mid-eye-roll to give her a once-over. He frowned. "Sorry, have we met before?"

He had to be referring to that overly familiar way in which she'd addressed him. Heat flooded her cheeks. "No, Your Grace. I'm sorry for my forwardness, Your Grace."

He waved her off. "Don't be sorry for it. In fact, I wish you'd be *more* forward."

"You cannot simply tell young ladies you wish they'd be more forward," Balor called wearily from the carriage without bothering to stick his head out this time.

"If you will not accept a ride, you must agree to join us for dinner at my estate this evening," the Duke continued as though his friend had not spoken. "It's the least I can do since my *utter nincompoop of a driver*"—these words were shouted pointedly in the direction of the carriage—"can't watch where he's going."

"I couldn't." Della gasped.

"Do you not want to?"

"Of course I *want* to," she said hurriedly. She'd be a fool not to want to dine with a charming duke who made her skin tingle under his gaze. "But I—"

"Then you shall, and anyone who tries to keep you away will hang."

"You have no authority to have people hanged." Balor's bored voice issued from the carriage once more.

"If ever I do, you will be the first to find out," Ansel called back with false cheer before turning back to Della. He took her hand in his gloved one, and she swore she could feel the warmth of his touch even through the leather. "Until tonight, then?" She nodded, and when his lips brushed her knuckles, she dared to hope that maybe, just maybe, a happily ever after rested in her future after all. "In the meantime, you're cold." The Duke shrugged out of his coat. "You ought to borrow my jacket."

EPILOGUE

Della slipped out of the ballroom onto the veranda. The cool night air soothed her flushed skin. Happily ever afters required a great deal of socializing, and she needed a moment to catch her breath.

She gazed up at the stars. Moonlight reflected off the white satin of her dress and off the facets of her wedding ring. She twisted it around her finger, smiling as she remembered the story Ansel told her—how he'd found the gemstone in his pocket the day he met her, and knew that one day he'd place it on her finger. She'd of course teased him about being so immune to his own wealth that he apparently forgot leaving priceless diamonds in his coat pockets.

Suddenly, the ring heated around her finger, barely noticeable at first, then scalding.

Crying out, she twisted the band off her finger as quickly as she could and placed it on the veranda railing. It began to glow, and she scrambled back in fright, wondering what was the matter with the thing.

As she watched, gold and purple sparks began swirling from the Stone. She bit back a scream and started to turn to fetch help, but the sparks wavered, forming an image.

Then a powerful gemstone, made a little extra powerful thanks to a cosmic hitchhiker, painted a story across the starry sky.

Outside of time and space, there existed an infinite library . . .

The stardust showed one scene after another. A woman who wished for adventure. A man who longed for a home. A librarian outside of time and space, and the son of a poet, for DNA does not contain only a person's memories, but traces of their ancestor's memories.

Della watched in wonder as the impossible tale played out before her. She gasped as she realized she'd fallen in love with Ansel before, and not just once, twice. She watched their adventure through the stars before its eventual end aboard Balor's ship. She learned her wedding ring was no simple diamond, but a crystal capable of storing incomprehensible amounts of energy. The dust showed her how, unbeknownst to the elders, it slipped into the Stone in Ansel's pocket moments before he, Balor, and herself were dragged out of one story and into another.

Here she stood, at her happily ever after, while the very heavens showed her another possibility. She could simply turn her back on the truth and enjoy her current reality. But already, she felt her heart yearning to chase another dream, for life wasn't about the endings, but about the how-did-they-get-theres. And she'd very much like to get back to *there*, aboard a dilapidated spaceship that looked like home.

She'd always wanted to live vibrantly and fully, and denying the past meant she'd only be living a half-life. She deserved more. *Ansel* deserved more. Despite her mother's promises not to interfere, Della suspected she'd left another loophole to escape somewhere. It likely involved a farmer with a fondness for poetry.

Della vowed that somehow, they'd find their way back into Ansel's story, return the Shield Stone to Lumeria, and take their rightful place among the stars. Her wedding ring was not just a symbol of love. It was a piece of something left unfinished, a promise that their adventures would continue long after their happily ever after.

Della always did like endings that left a little something up to the imagination.

She wondered how her new husband would feel about spending their wedding night planning adventure, espionage, and escape.

As she lifted her skirts and raced back into the ballroom to find Ansel, she heard her mother's voice whispering across the cosmos: *You have the power to choose your own story. Make it a good one.*

ACKNOWLEDGMENTS

A huge thank you to you, reader, for taking a chance on this book. It's my hope that something in my words made you feel seen. Or, at least, like Della, you were able to find an enjoyable escape from reality for a little while to experience the adventure between these pages.

Thank you to my agent extraordinaire, Lucienne Diver, who believed in this weird genre-bendy book from the beginning, and to my wonderful editor Elizabeth Hitti Musicant, for your lovely words of encouragement and brilliant advice. All your notes really helped bring out the heart of the story, and I'm forever grateful we get to work together! To Emma Gillette for the dreamy cover, and to the rest of the team at Atria for all your hard work to bring this story into reality.

My never-ending gratitude to my critique partners and writing friends for all your amazing feedback and unhinged comments during the writing process of this book, especially Beka, Jenny, Heather, Leslie, and Mae. This book would not exist without you. A special shout out to the SP group chat for your support and friendship.

Always, thank you to my husband Shawn, for being my irl comfort character, for always being available to provide snacks or help me through whatever plot dilemma I'm stuck on (and for challenging me to level up space mermaids to the much-cooler stardust monster). I love you bigger than the whole sky.

And finally, a small thank-you is also warranted, I think, to my younger self, who was just a little bit too good at hide-and-seek. You always were more comfortable in imagination than reality, and thanks to the fact that you never stopped dreaming, we now get to share our stories with the world.

ABOUT THE AUTHOR

Sloane Brooks loves writing stories filled with romance, humor, and magic. She lives in the Midwest with her husband, two cats, and too many houseplants. She is the author of *The Underachiever's Guide to Love and Saving the World* and, under the pen name Shannon Bright, her debut paranormal rom-com, *Every Wish Way*.

Atria Books, an imprint of Simon & Schuster, fosters an open environment where ideas flourish, bestselling authors soar to new heights, and tomorrow's finest voices are discovered and nurtured. Since its launch in 2002, Atria has published hundreds of bestsellers and extraordinary books, which would not have been possible without the invaluable support and expertise of its team and publishing partners. Thank you to the Atria Books colleagues who collaborated on *Written in Starlight* as well as to the hundreds of professionals in the Simon & Schuster advertising, audio, communications, design, eBook, finance, human resources, legal, marketing, operations, production, sales, supply chain, subsidiary rights, and warehouse departments who help Atria bring great books to light.

EDITORIAL
Elizabeth Hitti

JACKET DESIGN
Emma Gillette

MARKETING
Aleaha Reneé

MANAGING EDITORIAL
Paige Lytle
Shelby Pumphrey
Sofia Echeverry
Abigail Borchers

PRODUCTION
Emma Navarro
Barbara Rivera Nieves
Lisa Wolff
Davina Mock-Maniscalco

PUBLICITY
Holly Rice

PUBLISHING OFFICE
Dana Trocker
Abby Velasco

SUBSIDIARY RIGHTS
Nicole Bond
Sara Bowne
Rebecca Justiniano